The Summer King Bundle

Also from Jennifer L. Armentrout

Fall With Me
Dream of You (a 1001 Dark Nights Novel)
Forever With You
Fire In You

By J. Lynn
Wait for You
Be With Me
Stay With Me

A Blood and Ash Novel
From Blood and Ash

The Covenant Series
Half-Blood
Pure
Deity
Elixer
Apollyon
Sentinel

The Lux Series
Shadows
Obsidian
Onyx
Opal
Origin
Opposition
Oblivion

The Origin Series
The Darkest Star
The Burning Shadow

The Dark Elements
Bitter Sweet Love
White Hot Kiss

Stone Cold Touch
Every Last Breath

The Harbinger Series
Storm and Fury
Rage and Ruin

A Titan Novel
The Return
The Power
The Struggle
The Prophecy

A Wicked Novel
Wicked
Torn
Brave
The Prince (a 1001 Dark Nights Novella)
The King (a 1001 Dark Nights Novella)
The Queen (a 1001 Dark Nights Novella)

Gamble Brothers Series
Tempting The Best Man
Tempting The Player
Tempting The Bodyguard

A de Vincent Novel Series
Moonlight Sins
Moonlight Seduction
Moonlight Scandals

Standalone Novels
Obsession
Frigid
Scorched
Cursed
Don't Look Back
The Dead List
Till Death

The Problem With Forever
If There's No Tomorrow

Anthologies
Meet Cute
Life Inside My Mind
Fifty First Times

The Summer King Bundle

By Jennifer L. Armentrout

The Prince
The King
The Queen

1001 DARK NIGHTS
PRESS

The Summer King Bundle
By Jennifer L. Armentrout

1001 Dark Nights

ISBN: 978-1-951812-25-6

Published by 1001 Dark Nights Press, an imprint of Evil Eye Concepts, Incorporated

Table of Contents

One Thousand and One Dark Nights

Once upon a time, in the future…

I was a student fascinated with stories and learning. I studied philosophy, poetry, history, the occult, and the art and science of love and magic. I had a vast library at my father's home and collected thousands of volumes of fantastic tales.

I learned all about ancient races and bygone times. About myths and legends and dreams of all people through the millennium. And the more I read the stronger my imagination grew until I discovered that I was able to travel into the stories... to actually become part of them.

I wish I could say that I listened to my teacher and respected my gift, as I ought to have. If I had, I would not be telling you this tale now.
But I was foolhardy and confused, showing off with bravery.

One afternoon, curious about the myth of the Arabian Nights, I traveled back to ancient Persia to see for myself if it was true that every day Shahryar (Persian: شهريار, "king") married a new virgin, and then sent yesterday's wife to be beheaded. It was written and I had read, that by the time he met Scheherazade, the vizier's daughter, he'd killed one thousand women.

Something went wrong with my efforts. I arrived in the midst of the story and somehow exchanged places with Scheherazade – a phenomena that had never occurred before and that still to this day, I cannot explain.

Now I am trapped in that ancient past. I have taken on Scheherazade's life and the only way I can protect myself and stay alive is to do what she did to protect herself and stay alive.

Every night the King calls for me and listens as I spin tales. And when the evening ends and dawn breaks, I stop at a point that leaves him breathless and yearning for more. And so the King spares my life for one more day, so that he might hear the rest of my dark tale.

As soon as I finish a story... I begin a new one... like the one that you, dear reader, have before you now.

The Prince

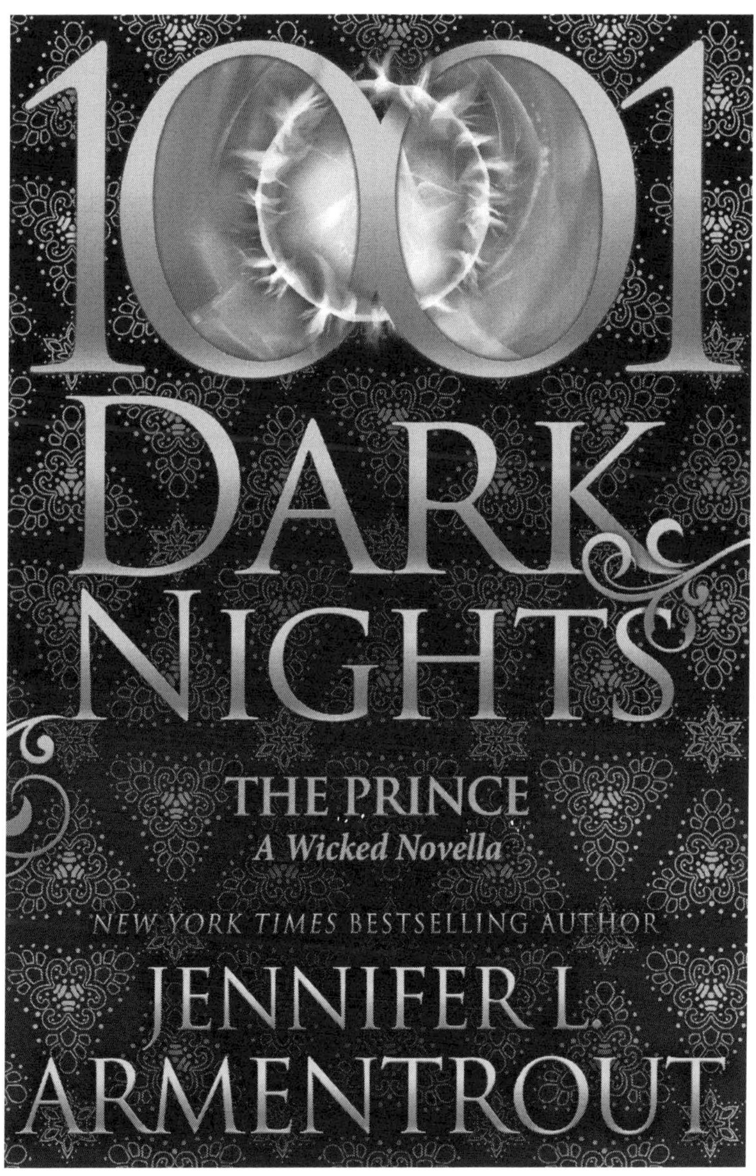
1001
DARK
NIGHTS
THE PRINCE
A Wicked Novella
NEW YORK TIMES BESTSELLING AUTHOR
JENNIFER L.
ARMENTROUT

Acknowledgments from the Author

Thank you to the team at 1001 Dark Nights, especially Liz Berry for inviting me to be a part of this amazing family of authors and Jillian Stein, for the beautiful friendship that has come with it and for making sure that I'll always be able to see the stars.

Chapter 1

Did it make you a bad friend if you were completely, a hundred percent envious of that friend? Yes? No? Kind of?

I figured it was somewhere in between.

That's what I was mulling over as I watched Ivy Morgan brush thick, red curls over her shoulder, laughing at something her boyfriend Ren Owens had said to her.

At least I wasn't envious of that—their love. Okay, well, that wasn't entirely true. Pretty sure anyone who was as single as me would be envious of all that warm and fuzzy that was passed back and forth with each long look or casual brush of skin. The two could barely tear their gazes away from one another to eat the dinner we'd grabbed at the cute little diner inside the shopping center on Prytania Street.

I honest to God couldn't be happier for them. They'd been through so much—way more than two people should ever have to go through to be together, and here they were, stronger and more in love than ever, and they deserved that happiness.

But their epic love story wasn't the source of a current case of the green-eye monster that was sitting on my shoulder.

Ivy was just such a… badass.

Even right now, relaxed in the chair, surrounded by twinkling Christmas lights with her hand in Ren's and her belly full of a cheeseburger deluxe and crinkle fries and half of my tater tots, she could kick ass and take names along with addresses, telephone numbers, and social security numbers.

If the proverbial poo hit the fan, you called Ivy or Ren.

If you needed to know what streets Royal intersected with, you called… me. Or if you needed coffee or fresh beignets but were currently busy, you know, saving the world, you'd call me.

The three of us were all members of the Order, a widespread organization that was literally the only thing that stood between mankind and complete, utter enslavement and destruction by the fae.

And not the super cute fae found in Disney movies or some crap like that. Humans thought they were on top of the food chain. They were wrong. The fae were.

The only thing pop culture got right about the fae was their slightly pointy ears. That was it. The fae were more than just beings from another world—the Otherworld—they were capable of glamouring their appearance to blend in with humans. But all Order members, even me, were warded at birth against the glamour. We saw through the human façade to the creature that lurked beneath.

No amount of imagination could capture their allure in their true form or how luminous their silvery skin was or how they were beautiful in the way a leopard stalking its prey was.

The fae preyed on humans—on the very life force that kept our hearts beating and brains working. Much like the mythical vampire feeding on blood or a succubus feasting on energy, the life force that they stole from humans fueled their abilities, which truly ran the gamut. They were faster and stronger than us, and nothing on Earth rivaled their predatory skills. Feeding off humans was also the way the fae slowed their aging process down to a lifespan that rivaled immortality. Without feeding, they aged and died like humans.

There were some of them who didn't feed on humans, something we'd only discovered recently. The fae from the Summer Court chose not to. They lived and died like us, wanting nothing more than to be left alone and out of the crosshairs of their enemies, the Winter fae.

My fingers drifted to my wrist, where I wore a bracelet that, combined with the words spoken at our births, held the charm that blocked the fae's ability. I never took the thing off. Ever.

Four leaf clovers.

Who ever would've thought a tiny plant would negate something as powerful as a fae?

But a week ago tonight the Order, along with the Summer fae, had done the impossible. The psychotic and wholly creepy fae Queen who went by the name Morgana had been sent back to the Otherworld. She could come back, but no one was expecting her to. Not for a long time. Maybe not even in our lifetime, but the Order would be ready when she did. So would the Summer fae.

That's why the three of us were having dinner—a little celebratory dinner. We'd survived the battle with the Queen and those who supported her had crawled back into whatever cesspools they were hiding in. We all could take a deep breath now and chill out, knowing that while there was still a metric crap ton of Winter fae out there who needed to be hunted down and stopped, we'd leveled out the playing field with the Queen's defeat.

Things were as normal as they'd ever be for an Order member. Hell, Ren and Ivy were even planning to take a vacation after Christmas. How crazy was that? Super crazy!

I wasn't planning a vacation, because I hadn't really taken part in the battle. If I had, I wouldn't be sitting here. I'd be dead. Like clinically, irreversibly dead.

I'd only received minimal combat training before that had come to a grinding halt when I was twelve. And while I still took the Order-mandated training classes along with Ivy, I've never seen any real action. Working through take-down maneuvers or knowing how to avoid a punch or a deliver a bone-snapping kick was completely different than actually taking that knowledge and using it against someone who was actively trying to straight-up murder you.

If my life hadn't veered off track at twelve, I would've been just like Ivy and Ren—a walking weapon on two legs–but everything had changed when my mother had been captured by the fae she'd been hunting.

My mother was a fighter, much like my father, who'd died when I was too young to remember him beyond the photographs that hung in the hallway. She had been one of the greatest, most skilled fighters in the Order - dare I say, even more badass than Ivy. She'd raised me while still pulling all nighters, patrolling the streets of New Orleans for fae, hunting them before they could hunt humans. When I was younger, I swore I was going to be just like her—like every child raised in the Order planned. We were indoctrinated at birth and our duty to protect mankind was what all of us prepared for. Training started young, at the age of eight. Mornings were dedicated to schooling and afternoons were part learning about the habits of the fae and part training.

But then came the morning, when I was a few days shy of my twelfth birthday, that Mom… she hadn't come home. Those days that had followed, those days that felt like an eternity, were some of the worst memories I will ever have.

Mom had been found on day four, in one of the bayous several miles out from the city, left for dead. Even as skilled as she was, she had fallen to the fae. They'd tortured her. Worse yet, they had fed on her, and while they hadn't enslaved her, all those feedings had done something to her. To her mind. Thank God, my mom had come home to me.

But she hadn't come home the same.

There'd been days and weeks where it was like nothing had happened to her, and then things weren't okay. She'd just up and disappear one day or would refuse to come out of her room. She'd rant and rage and then break into fits of laughter that would last hours. Things got easier in the months and years following her attack, but taking care of her had replaced training, and when I came of age, I was given an administrator-type job with the Order, something reserved for the lucky few that made it to retirement. I accepted it even though the money the Order had paid out to my mother for her 'injured in the line of duty' situation was substantial.

But I was hoping that could change now. Things were going to simmer down, and I was hoping with a little more training, I could start patrolling. The Order needed me—needed all the help they could get since so many had been lost in the battle with the Queen. I could become just as badass as Ivy and Ren and then I'd finally be able to fulfill my duty.

I'd finally be… useful. Worthy of those I called my friends and, most importantly, worthy of the legacy of my family. I could—

Fingers appeared directly in my line of vision. They snapped, causing me to jerk back in my seat. The fingers lowered to reveal Ivy staring at me.

My cheeks heated as I laughed softly. "Sorry. I spaced out. Were you saying something?"

"I was saying that I was about to strip naked and run outside."

Ren's green eyes practically twinkled. "I am so down for that."

"Of course you are." Grinning, she gestured at the menu. "Did you want dessert, Bri?"

Only Ivy called me Bri. Everyone else called me Brighton or Ms. Jussier. I hated the latter. It made me feel like I was three decades older and should be living in a home full of stray, un-neutered cats. And I was already twenty-eight and living with my mother. I didn't need to feel worse than I already did.

"No, I'm good." I'd already peeked at the menu. If they had cheesecake, I would've made room.

Ren glanced over the menu and then shook his head as he handed it back to Ivy. "So, you going to let Tink move in with you?"

I nearly choked on the sip of diet Coke. "What?"

Dropping the menu on the table, Ivy smiled as she clasped her hands together. "If Ren and I go on vacation, Tink's going to need an adult in his life."

I opened my mouth, but I had no words. I could not have heard them right. No way could I move Tink into my house—my mother's house—because not only would Tink most likely destroy it, he was….

Well, Tink was Tink.

"And he really likes you," Ren added. "He actually listens to you."

My brows lowered. "That's not true. Tink listens to no one. Not even his boyfriend. And why wouldn't he stay with him?"

"Well, I made that suggestion, and according to Tink, he's not ready for that kind of commitment," Ren replied dryly.

"What? That's not a commitment," I reasoned. "It would only be temporary, right?"

"We tried explaining that to Tink." Ivy rolled her eyes. "But you know how he is."

I didn't. I really didn't. I lowered my voice so we weren't overheard. "Why can't he stay at Hotel Good Fae?" That was what Ivy called the compound the Summer fae lived in. "They *love* him. Like near worship levels."

"We suggested that, but he said, and I quote, he can't 'be himself' around them. That their admiration is too much pressure on him."

I stared at Ren. "You're joking."

"I wish." He leaned back. "You know we can't leave him alone. He'd burn down Ivy's apartment."

"He'll spend all my money on shit from Amazon," Ivy added as her phone rang. She picked up her bag. "Anyway, we'll talk out the details later."

We were so not talking out the details later. "But—"

"What's up, Miles?" Ivy held her hand up, and I snapped my mouth shut. "What?" She glanced at Ren, who was alert and all eyes on Ivy. "Yeah, we're nearby. We can check it out." There was a pause. "I'll update you in a few."

Disconnecting the call, she pulled out her wallet and said, "Miles said Gerry didn't show up for his shift and no one can get ahold of him," she explained, and that wasn't normal at all. Gerry was habitually on time. "He asked if we could swing by his place and check things out."

"Can do," Ren answered as Ivy dropped several bills on the table. "By the way, I'm pretty sure Tink is at your place now with Merle."

"Wait. What?" I immediately forgot about Gerry not showing up for patrol.

"Yeah, he said something about wanting gardening tips or something bizarre." Ivy shoved her wallet into her bag. "Honestly, I wasn't really listening."

"Oh God." I fumbled for my wallet as visions of my mom impaling Tink with steak knives danced in my head. "He cannot be there alone with my mom."

"I think Merle likes Tink," Ivy said.

"Really?" I dropped cash on the table—more than enough cover my food and a tip. "Depends on if he's Tink-size or people-size."

"I feel the same way," Ren muttered, and then he slid a sly glance in my direction. "By the way, I'm pretty sure your mom has the hots for Tanner."

I was frozen, halfway standing. Tanner ran Hotel Good Fae. In other words, he was a fae and my mom—well, Mom did seem to like visiting him, but she also talked quite frequently about killing fae, all kinds of fae. Shaking my head, I decided I really didn't have the brain space to process any of that. "I better get going. God only knows what my mom and Tink could get into."

"I figure it'll either be epic or epically disastrous." Ivy grinned at me as she and Ren stood.

"Agreed." Wishing they had mentioned all of this at the beginning of dinner, I slung my purse over my shoulder and said my goodbyes.

Hurrying through the small diner and skirting the oversized Christmas tree, I made my way outside. Cool wind caught the fine strands of hair around my face, blowing my ponytail over my shoulder. I lived a handful of blocks from the shopping center, and it was quicker just to walk instead of trying to order an Uber.

Shoving my hands into the front pocket of my oversized hoodie, I jogged across the street. The Garden District was beautiful any time of year, but it really amped up its curb appeal during the Christmas season. Lights of all different colors decorated porches and balconies, twisted around wrought iron fences, and twinkled from the massive oaks that lined many of the streets.

I could not believe Tink was at my place. What in the world were Ivy and Ren thinking? Mom didn't hate Tink, but Mom had also, at one time, suggested to Ivy's face that Ivy should be put down.

All because Ivy wasn't exactly a hundred percent human. She was a halfling and there had been this whole prophecy that involved her permanently opening the gates to the Otherworld, allowing the armies of the Winter Court to enter our world, but all of that was over. Thank God.

And Tink was definitely not even one percent human.

Cutting down a side street, I tried not to let my imagination run wild with what could be happening at home. They could be sitting together and watching Harry Potter. Or Tink could've brought his boyfriend, who just happened to be Prince Fabian—one of the two Princes of the Summer Court—to the house. I doubted Tink would've brought Prince Fabian's brother with him. At least there was that.

A shudder racked my shoulders as an image of *the* Prince formed in my head. I'd never seen him when he was under the Queen's enchantment, masquerading as the Winter Prince. He'd terrorized the city, becoming a living and breathing nightmare who had kidnapped Ivy to fulfill said prophecy.

I'd only seen him after the enchantment was broken, and even then he'd been the most intimidating creature I'd ever laid eyes on. And when he looked at me, I couldn't help but feel—

"Mom." My steps drew up short as I spotted her coming down the wide sidewalk, her thin housecoat flapping behind her like wings. "What are you doing out here?"

She stepped under the street lamp, her short blond hair messy from the wind. "Oh, I was just getting… antsy and decided I wanted to go for a walk."

I hurried to where she stood, taking her hands in mine. Her skin was cold. "Mom, why didn't you put on your jacket?"

"Honey, it's not that cold outside." She laughed, squeezing my hands.

"It's cold enough for something heavier than this robe you've got going on. Let's head back home." My stomach twisted with nerves as I looped my arm through hers and turned her back around.

Anxiety and the inability to stay still was usually a sign that we were about to hit a rough couple of days. It came out of nowhere and nothing and everything could trigger it. She would go from being clear minded and sharp as a tack for weeks, months even, and then wham! She would start roaming off and then the nightmares would start. She wouldn't be able to sleep and things would…they would just spiral.

Worry was like a virus. By the time you felt it, you were already drowning in it. "How long have you been outside?"

"Long enough to walk from the house to here," she replied, and I resisted the urge to roll my eyes. "And what's wrong with my robe?"

There were several things wrong with her roaming around the Garden District in a robin's egg blue robe.

I slowed my pace to match hers as I guided her across the street. "Did you have company while I was gone?"

"Company?"

Maybe Ren and Ivy were wrong about Tink being there. "Did Tink come by?" I asked, starting to get nervous.

She was quiet for a moment and then she chuckled. "Actually, come to think of it, he was watching a movie and then he stepped outside to make a phone call."

"So, he was still there when you—" The street lamp above us flickered once and then faded out.

All the way down the block, as far as I could see, the lights flickered and then disappeared.

"That's odd," Mom commented, a shiver working its way through her. "Brighton?"

"It's okay," I said, swallowing hard. "Everything is okay."

A blast of what felt like arctic air swept down the block, lifting the edges of Mom's housecoat and stopping both of us in our tracks. The tiny hairs all along the nape of my neck rose as I scanned the empty street, only lit by the faint, twinkling Christmas lights. I recognized the for sale sign in front of the empty antebellum home. We had another two blocks to go.

"Mom," I whispered, heart pounding in my chest as I started walking again, dragging her along with me. "We need to—"

They seemed to come out of nowhere, moving so fast they were nothing more than shadows at first, surrounding us.

A scream built in my throat as I saw them. Silvery skin. Eyes filled with hate. Four of them, and they were on us before the scream could even part my lips.

Chapter 2

Sunlight.

That's what I felt on my skin and tasted on my lips. *Sunlight.* Its warmth seeped through my skin, buzzed through my veins, and settled into my muscles and bones.

Was I lying outside? That wouldn't make sense, though. It was December, and not nearly warm enough to sunbathe, but I knew I had to be lying close to the sun. I could feel its touch on my cheek and my lips still tingled from the closeness.

I opened my eyes, but I didn't see the sun. I saw a form… a shape of a man. The features blurred, but I knew the man. It was him.

The Prince….

But that also didn't make sense. None of this made sense. Confusion crept into the fuzz crowding my thoughts. Something was off. I tried to lift my hand, but my arm felt like it was weighted down. Something was wrong, very badly wrong, and I needed to remember—

Sleep.

The desire to slip away hit me hard and fast, obliterating the confusion and consciousness, and I slept. I slept for what felt like years and then I heard a steady beeping. It intruded on wherever I was, becoming so loud, so obnoxious to me, that I had to pay attention to it. A part of my consciousness zeroed in on the sound, clung to it, and I followed it back, tethering myself to the rhythm. With each passing second, my surroundings became clearer. Footsteps. I heard footsteps. Whispers. There was the sound of hushed voices. I dragged in a deep breath, and a shock hit my system. The breath *hurt.* Like my chest and ribs were too tight and a simple deep breath was too much to take—

Mom.

I saw her in my mind, as clear as day.

I saw her lying on her back in the darkness, her eyes wide and fixed on mine. There was nothing behind those eyes. No life. Nothing.

The beeping sound sped up.

The horrifying image of my mom faded like smoke, replaced by luminous skin and bloody smiles and taunts and…

Pools of blood. Actual pools of it. The ruby-red liquid spilled across stone, forming rivulets that ran between the spacing in the pavers. Why had there been so much blood? A vague feeling of wet warmth bubbling up my throat and choking me swept through me.

"Bri? Are you awake? Brighton?"

I recognized that voice. Ivy. She was speaking to me, and I took another breath, relieved to discover it didn't hurt as bad as the first. But my… my body felt weird. My face felt weird. Like it was swollen and stretched too tight. It was the same with every inch of my skin.

My eyes felt like they were glued shut, and it took forever for them to open. Hours maybe. But when they did, I found myself staring at a drop ceiling and florescent lights.

"Bri." Ivy spoke again, and her fingers lightly brushed my left hand.

Slowly, I turned my head toward the sound of her voice, to my left, and I saw her pale, drawn face. All that bright hair was pulled back in a bun. Her eyes were red and swollen and full of sympathy.

And I knew.

I *remembered.*

The fae had come out of nowhere, surrounding Mom and me. They'd dragged us into the courtyard of the empty house. There hadn't been four of them. I'd been wrong. There'd been five and one of them had been an Ancient.

I swallowed, or tried to, but the motion hurt my throat. *Everything* hurt. My legs and face, but especially my stomach. That felt like someone had dug around inside and pulled everything out.

Ivy's fingers curled around mine. She squeezed gently. "Are you in pain? I can get the doc."

I squeezed my eyes shut, and I saw flashes of teeth and razor-sharp claws. The fae didn't need to use their teeth to feed, but they liked to use them to cause pain.

"Mom," I croaked out, and Ivy's hand spasmed around mine. When she didn't answer, I forced my eyes open again. "She's… she's gone?"

Ivy pressed her lips together as she nodded jerkily. "I'm sorry. I'm so sorry, Bri."

My gaze dropped to where Ivy held my hand. Instead of seeing her hand, I saw my mother's blood-soaked one squeezing mine. I saw it slip from my grasp as I felt the strength seep out of her.

"They made several hits, all across the city," Ivy was saying, curling her other hand around mine, clasping it between her two palms. "That's why Gerry didn't show up for his shift. Ren and I found him. That's when we knew." Her voice turned hoarse as she started naming names—names of those killed and there were so many, an endless stream. "They must've been watching us. They knew where to go. So much violence, all in one night."

Ivy dropped her forehead to her hands. I didn't see her, though. I saw the five faces. I remembered their faces. I would always remember their faces.

"You're going to be okay. The doc says it's a freaking miracle, but you're going to be okay," she said. "They'll probably keep you for a couple more days, but then you can come home with me, if you want. Tink said you can take his bedroom—"

"I… I couldn't stop them."

"What?" Ivy lifted her head. Her eyes were glassy.

"I… I couldn't fight them off."

She slowly shook her head. "Bri, you were hunted down and—"

"I couldn't stop them!" The shout tore at my raw throat, but I didn't care. "They killed my mother and I couldn't stop them!"

"No." Ivy rose, leaning over the head of the bed so her face was right in mine. "I know what you're thinking. Trust me, I *know*. This is not your fault. I would've been screwed if I was caught off guard and surrounded like that."

I didn't think that was the case. Ivy would've fought tooth and nail. She wouldn't have panicked and flailed. She wouldn't have let them get her on her back, the number one thing they taught you to never let happen in training. Ivy might've struggled, but she would've prevailed.

"What they did to your mom and you is on them." Ivy placed the tips of her fingers against my cheek. The touch was light, as if she knew if she pressed too hard, it would hurt. "There was nothing you could've done, Bri. Nothing. You survived. That's all that matters. And it's going to be okay. Everything is going to be okay."

As I stared at her, remembering what I'd said to Mom, and knowing that it had been a lie, I knew that this also wasn't true. That wasn't all that mattered and it wasn't going to be okay.

Things were never going to be okay.

Chapter 3

Two years later….

The heavy, rhythmic beat thumped from the speakers above and flowed over the packed floor. Gleaming bodies twisted and churned under the flashing overhead lights, lost to the music and the press of flesh against flesh. The scent of perfume, cologne, and sweat turned my stomach as I lifted my hands, scooping the long strands of hair off my damp neck.

Tonight I was a wild redhead with bright, red lips.

Last night I'd been a raven-haired seductress with smokey eyes.

The past weekend I was a naïve blonde in pigtails with flushed, peachy cheeks.

Each time I was someone different, but I was always the perfect victim, and every night ended the same.

I swayed my hips to the beat, to the hard, warm body behind me as I scanned the dance floor, searching.

Hands moved over the silvery sequins of my dress, slipping over my stomach. He hauled me against him, pressing his front to my back.

He was *really* into this.

A lot.

Those questing hands dragged down my hips, inching closer to my outer thighs. Letting go of the hair, I caught his wrists and tossed a reckless grin over my shoulder. "Behave."

The nameless man gave me a toothy smile. He was cute, definitely younger than me by a good decade and some change. Probably in college at Loyola or Tulane, which meant two things. He'd choke if he knew I was pushing thirty-one and this was the last place he should be. A tiny part of me wanted to warn him, to tell him to find his fun and pleasure anyplace but the club Flux.

But I wasn't here for him.

Holding onto his wrists, I let my head fall back against his chest as my gaze flickered over the dance floor and the horseshoe-shaped bar at the front. I couldn't see into the shadowy alcoves surrounding the floor or upstairs, on the second floor VIP area.

That's where I needed to be, because I knew *he* was up there.

A squat, broad man blocked the staircase. Behind him was a red rope. Entry to the second floor was by invite only, and those up there didn't come down here. They sent scouts instead, scouts that were trained to find a certain type of human.

And I was the living embodiment of that type and tonight was the night.

"Hey," the man said into my ear.

I kept searching. "Yeah?"

"What's your name? I'm Dale." He tried to move his hands again, but I kept them on my hips.

"Sally," I lied as a tall, slender woman at the bar pushed away and turned to the dance floor, a vibrant, too-bright purple drink in her hand. Nightshade. She lifted the drink to her lips as she stared out over the floor.

I'd found who I was searching for, and I saw her for what she really looked like.

"You wanna get out of here, Sally?" Dale asked, his lips brushing the side of my neck. "I know a place we can go to."

"No, thank you." Letting go of his wrists, I pulled away from the man, walking off and slipping between the bodies before his shocked expletive could get under my skin.

Keeping an eye on the scout, I eased around a couple who were practically mating right there on the floor. I couldn't tell where one of them ended and the other began.

Goodness.

I passed a high, round top table, plucked up the forgotten, half empty pink drink, and made a beeline for the bar. As soon as I stepped out of the cluster of bodies, I slowed my step and fixed a lax smile on my face as I neared the female. She wasn't focused on me, instead eyeing two young college girls who were dancing and laughing, obviously buzzing. She started toward them.

Letting the borrowed glass dangle from my fingers, I tripped, bumping my shoulder against the female.

She turned to me in a slow, calculated snake-like movement. Her lips peeled back in a sneer as she lowered her glass of nightshade. To everyone else in this club, her smile appeared normal. To me? I saw the two wickedly sharp incisors on each side of her mouth. Not fangs. Just sharp as an obsidian blade teeth that could tear through flesh.

"I'm so sorry." I teetered on my high heels as I spoke over the music, placing my free hand on her arm. "Someone bumped me. Ugh. People are so rude."

She lifted a single dark eyebrow.

"What in the world are you drinking? It looks *sooo* amazing."

The female cocked her head to the side as her pale blue eyes drifted over every inch of my body, from the thick red hair and bright lips to the plunging neckline of my strappy silvery dress that showed off more than it hid. She must've approved of what she saw, because a tight-lipped smile replaced her sneer. "This drink is a little too hard for you."

"Oh?" I bit down on my lower lip. "I like… hard drinks, though."

"Do you?" When I nodded, the female stepped closer. She was my height, so her gaze lined up with mine. "How hard do you like it?"

"Very hard," I repeated, forcing myself to hold her gaze as I giggled.

She tilted her head slightly. "I might have something better for you. You here alone?"

"My friends already left. I was getting ready to go, but… I think I have another good hour or so left in me."

"Perfect." The moment her black pupils constricted was brief and not noticeable to anyone who didn't know better, but I did. I knew what she was doing, entrancing me. I forced my muscles to loosen, for the eager smile that said I was down for anything to slip off my face. I stood before the female, silent… and waiting as she leaned in, brushing her lips against mine as she whispered, "Come with me."

She plucked the borrowed drink out of my hand and placed it on the bar beside us, then she took my hand in her cool grasp. Her pace was fast and steps long as she led me around the bar to the staircase.

Jackpot.

The man standing at the foot of the stairs stepped aside, and one glance at his vacant expression told me he was a human that had been fed on until he was completely under the fae's control. And just as dangerous and unpredictable as the fae themselves.

She led me up the wide spiral staircase, her grip tight as she all but dragged me along, turning right at the top to a dimly lit balcony. Downing half of the nightshade, a drink toxic to humans but more like tequila to the fae, she led me to a set of occupied couches and chair. I registered several fae, all with a tranced human by their side or in their laps. It was likely none of these humans were going to make it out of this club alive tonight.

"Look what I found, Tobias." The female pulled me forward with a strength that didn't match her willowy frame, and I let myself be shoved, even allowed myself to stumble. The fae caught my arm, stopping me from toppling flat on my face.

My gaze darted around, and then I saw *him*.

He was sitting on a small, black couch, his arms and legs spread in an arrogant sprawl. I saw the human façade just for a brief second. Pale skin gave way to a silvery tone. Hair and features remained the same. Blond and handsome, he looked like a frat boy with silver skin and pointed ears. He was definitely one of *them*.

And now I had a name to match a face I'd never forget.

Tobias.

A rush of anticipation shot through my veins, spreading goosebumps all over my skin. It was him. There'd been five of them total and he was one of the three that remained.

"You always treat me well, Alyssa," he said, his pale blue gaze crawling over my length. "You know how I have a soft spot for redheads."

"A soft spot." The female fae called Alyssa let go of my arm. "More like a hard-on."

Oh dear.

I kept my face impressively blank as Tobias jerked his chin. Oscar worthy, really. Another fae came forward, out of the shadows. He was a tall one and it took everything in me not to flinch as he put his hands on me, skimming them down my front and back, checking for weapons. The fae had gotten smarter in the last two years.

So had we.

The fae's hands moved up my legs meticulously and then my hips. His fingers glanced over the wide cuffs at my wrists. "She's clear."

"Good." Tobias leaned forward. "Come here, Red."

I forced my steps to be slow and uneven, and when he lifted his hand to me, I placed mine in his even though it utterly sickened me.

Tobias didn't pull me into his lap like I expected. Instead, he rose from the couch. "What time will Aric be here?"

Aric? That name wasn't familiar to me; then again, it wasn't like I hung out with these murderous, psychotic Winter fae.

"You have an hour, tops." Alyssa tossed herself onto the couch. "Make good use of it."

"You bet." He circled his arm around my waist, drawing me to his front. He smelled good. Like winter mint. But they all smelled good. They all looked good, too. And this fae was obviously in the mood for more than just feeding, which was what I was betting on. "You want seconds?"

"Sure," the female fae purred. "If there's anything left."

Tobias lifted me up without warning, tossing me over his shoulder like a damn Neanderthal claiming his prize. To go limp scratched at my skin as he stalked across the short distance. A door opened and then we were inside a room that I imagined a lot of very bad things happened in. He kicked the door shut behind us and I heard the lock turn without him touching it.

His hand curved over my ass as he lowered me onto the floor. Strands of red hair had fallen in front of my face, and I stood there as he brushed them back behind my ears. "Do you know why I like redheads? No. Of course you don't."

I blinked slowly, taking in the room as he let go. There was a chair. A bed that looked… well used. My stomach churned with nausea. But he didn't go to the bed; he went to the throne-like chair with crushed velvet cushions. He sat and stared up at me.

"Come on. Don't be shy." Those pale eyes seemed to burn. "We're going to get to know each other, aren't we?"

"Yes?" I whispered.

A half smile spread across his lips as he hooked a finger in my direction. "Come on then."

I forced a small smile as I shuffled to him. The gasp was real when he grabbed my hips and tugged me down into his lap, causing the skirt to ride up my thighs. He toyed with the straps of my dress, tracing the low v-shaped neckline.

"You want me?" he asked.

That was an odd, unnecessary question. Guess someone had a low sense of self worth or something. "Yes."

"You'll let me do anything to you, won't you?"

I forced myself to nod. "*Yes*."

"Then touch me," he ordered softly.

My jaw clenched as I placed my hands on his shoulders, smoothing them over his chest.

"Honestly, I really don't like redheads." His hand moved fast, closing around my throat. "I hate them."

Oh, hell.

He squeezed not too gently, digging his fingers into my windpipe as he drew me forward. His icy breath danced over my lips as I winced at the spike of pain. "Why?" His other hand was on the move, sliding down my spine, going lower. "They remind me of the bitch halfling."

I knew exactly who he was talking about.

Ivy Morgan—wait, she was Ivy Owens now, having gotten married over Christmas to Ren.

Then, before I had a chance to process what he was doing, his cold mouth was on mine. Lips. Teeth. Tongue. It was harsh and brutal, and I wondered if he even knew how to kiss or if he cared. He let go of my throat, and I figured there'd be bruises there later.

I held still as he eased the straps of my dress down my arms, fueled by one of the most powerful emotions known to man.

Vengeance.

I was so close to retribution, I could taste the bitter sweetness of it on the tip of my tongue. It burned through the iciness his kiss left behind.

The top slipped, pooling low on my hips and exposing the black, seriously uncomfortable strapless bra. My gaze fixed on the ceiling as his cool lips skated down the column of my throat and then lower, over the swell of my breast. I forced my body to stay loose, accepting even as the tips of his fingers skated over my sides to where the material bunched. His fingers brushed the thin, silver chain that rode low around my hips.

Tobias drew back, and I could practically feel his gaze roam over my chest and then my stomach, and I knew what he saw. Not smooth, unmarred skin. Pale, shiny scars that covered the entirety of my stomach. Teeth marks. Multiple ones that had healed and faded to a shade or two lighter than my normal skin. Deep groves made by sharpened claws. All of them a permanent reminder of the night nearly two years ago when the fae who'd supported the defeated Winter Queen had sought bloody vengeance and commenced wholesale slaughter. They hadn't even fed on us. They'd just wanted us to hurt.

And we did.

The night my mother, who had already suffered so much at the hands of the fae, had died, nearly ripped apart by their teeth and claws.

The night I should've died.

His hands clenched my hips, digging into my skin. "What the hell?"

I lowered my chin as he tugged on the chain and the small, circle medallion pulled free from the dress. I knew the exact moment he recognized the encased four-leaf clover. Tobias knew what that meant.

I wasn't under his glamour.

Tobias's pale, furious gaze flew to mine. I smiled then. "Remember me?"

Powerful muscles coiled underneath me as recognition flared in those eyes, but I was faster than I had been that night, than I had been for my entire life, and the Order had gotten smarter at hiding our weapons. I twisted my right wrist and the wide cuff bracelet disengaged a collapsible iron stake. The deadly metal shot out over the palm of my hand. Clutching his shoulder, I jabbed my right arm out, slamming the iron stake deep into the fae's chest.

Surprise parted his lips as he gasped out, "Bitch."

"Yeah."

Then it happened.

As quick as a heartbeat, the sick bastard collapsed into himself as he was sucked back into the Otherworld, locked away and as good as dead to me. Falling forward, I caught myself on the back of the chair, my knees slipping across the cushion. I disengaged the stake, hearing the mechanical click as it folded back into the bracelet.

Dragging in a deep breath, I held it as I squeezed my eyes shut. There had been five of them that had found my mother and me. Five of them that had gone after an old woman and her daughter. Three were now as good as dead, and that left two more. A fae and a—

An odd thump hit the wall outside of the room, causing my eyes to snap open. Pushing off the back of the chair, I spun around and dragged the straps of my dress up my arms. There was a hoarse shout and then the sound of the door unlocking from the outside was like cannon fire in the room.

Damn it. I hadn't planned on anyone coming in this quickly. I needed time to—

The door swung open, and terror poured into my chest as I saw who filled the entirety of the doorway. It was….

It was *the* Prince.

Chapter 4

The fae didn't scare me anymore, not like they used to, but this one… this one terrified and enthralled me in ways I couldn't understand. Ways in which I really didn't even want to try to figure out.

Air lodged in my throat as his gaze immediately zeroed in on me, and I didn't need to pretend to be entranced. I was frozen, rooted to the chair by invisible vines.

I hadn't seen him in what felt like forever, and I wasn't even sure that I had seen him at the hospital after the attack or if that was some kind of bizarre hallucination. I'd been on a lot of powerful drugs. I didn't even know he was still in New Orleans. I'd figured he'd gone to Florida, to the community his brother oversaw.

The Prince was what was called an Ancient, fae that had lived for hundreds of years, if not more, and were not only capable of a hell of lot more than a normal fae was, but they were nearly impossible to kill. Stabbing them with iron did absolutely nothing beyond pissing them off. You couldn't send them back to the Otherworld. You had to kill them, and that was only accomplished by separating the head from the body.

And good luck with that.

Ancients were the most powerful of the fae and they could be Knights or Princesses or Princes or Queens.

Or a King.

They didn't look like a fae. Their skin wasn't silvery and the point to their ears was hardly noticeable, which enabled them to blend in with humans and escape the Order's detection until it was too late.

He was supposed to be good, so why in the hell was he here, at Flux, in a club frequented by the enemy—*his* enemy?

The Prince cocked his golden head to the side while my heart threw itself against my ribs. Did he recognize me? There was no way. I was well disguised, even beyond the wig. I'd discovered that I had a flair for makeup. I basically reshaped the features of my face with contouring and a keen eye and steady hand.

He couldn't know it was me, because it wasn't like he'd paid attention to me. It wasn't like *anyone* paid attention to me. I was a ghost in most rooms, unseen even when I wanted to be seen and heard. That was one thing that hadn't changed after the attack. And it was freaking ironic that the one thing I hated the most about myself, how easily I took to just blending in, had become my greatest asset.

I willed my heart to slow, but when he closed the door behind him, my heart launched into my throat. He was supposed to be good, but he was *here*, and if it came down to fighting, there was a slim chance I'd win.

Or land a single kick.

"You're alone." His voice… God, his voice was deep and melodious, an odd accent that reminded me of twinkling lights and lush flowers. "Are you alone?" he repeated.

I let the façade of being entranced slip over me and murmured, "Yes?"

"Is that so?" He strode forward, coming closer, into the dim light offered by the exposed lightbulb screwed into a ceiling fan. The Prince was…. God, he was strikingly beautiful.

Golden blond hair brushed broad shoulders and framed high, sharp as a blade cheekbones and a jaw that could've been carved out of marble. His brow was several shades darker than his hair and his nose straight, aristocratic. Full, expressive lips were currently pressed together in a hard line. There was no glamour to fade away. This was what he looked like, an example of inhuman perfection designed to lure the prey in.

My pulse pounded as I kept my gaze level.

"You were in here with someone."

Oh God, there was a good chance I was going to vomit. Just a little. In my mouth.

"Where did he go?" He was now in front of me, standing a few feet away.

"I… I don't know?" I said it like it was a question, like I knew humans under a trance would speak.

"Really?" His voice dripped with derision.

A fine sheen of sweat broke out along my skin. Not for one second did he sound like he believed me, so I didn't answer. I stared at his stomach and chest—his rather defined chest that stretched the black thermal he wore.

"Look at me." His voice was a crack of thunder, and I felt like I was tranced.

I lifted my gaze, and I immediately wished I hadn't. I was no short woman, but even if I wasn't sitting down, he would've towered over me. The Prince was around six and a half feet and every inch of him was intimidating. To meet his gaze, I had to tilt my head waaay back.

His eyes.... They were the palest blue color that was startling against the blackness of the pupil and the thick, heavy fringe of his lashes. Only a fae had eyes like that.

Something flickered over his face, gone too quickly for me to figure it out. "What is your name?"

"Sally," I rasped out, throat dry.

"Is it? That's... odd."

One of two things was going to happen at this point if he recognized me. Either he wasn't on Team Good Fae and he was most definitely going to kill me, because there was no way I was going to win a fight with a Prince. That would... suck. Or he was going to haul my ass out of here, report what I was doing to the Order, and then everything would be over. I couldn't allow that to happen either. Not when I was so close to finding the last two fae. So close to complete retribution.

His hand snaked out faster than my eyes could track. Warm fingers folded around my forearm, sending a jolt traveling up my arm, much like the static charge I got from dragging my feet over a carpet. He eyed the bracelets with a sardonic twist of his lips. Would the Prince recognize what they were? I wasn't sure.

Then his gaze lifted to mine as he folded two fingers under my chin, guiding my head farther back. A sound rumbled from him, reminding me of a very animalistic growl. My stomach hollowed. A long, tense moment passed and then he pulled his fingers away from my chin.

"So, Sally, I am confident that you entered a room with someone I am looking for." His thumb slipped over the skin just below the cuff I wore. "Those outside told me he was in here." He paused. "Then again, those outside this room are unable to tell me anything else."

What did that mean?

I thought about the odd thump against the wall. Had he done

something to the fae out there?

"He was in here and now he's not." The thumb moved in a slow circle along my skin, causing a tight, confusing shiver to hit me. "Now, what could've happened to this fae? There's only one small window behind you, but I doubt he'd be able to climb out of that. So, it appears as if he… disappeared into thin air."

Well, that did kind of happen.

"I'm rather disappointed, as there were things I needed to discuss with him."

I wanted so badly to ask why the *reformed* Summer Prince needed to talk to a Winter fae.

His hand slid up my hand, so now his thumb was tracing idle, slow circles on the inside of my elbow, just below another scarred bite mark. A mark Tobias could've noticed if he hadn't been so arrogant and stupid.

"Sally, Sally…. What am I going to do with you?" he mused as thick lashes lowered, shielding pale, wolf eyes.

That was… that was a really bad question. And why was he touching me like this, coming so close to the bracelet? And why was it making me shiver instead of making me want to scrape the skin off that he was touching?

I was going to blame his unexpected appearance for my reaction.

When I didn't answer, one side of his lips kicked up in a mockery of a smile. "Stand."

Having no idea if he really believed I was entranced, a tremble coursed through me as I stood on locked knees. The change in position was a blessing. I wasn't looking at his eyes anymore. My gaze was level with his chest.

"Where are you from, Sally?"

The question caught me off guard and it took a moment to answer. "Lafayette," I threw out, figuring my accent betrayed that I was from somewhere south.

"Lafayette?" His other hand landed softly on my waist, and my entire body jolted.

Damn it.

A human entranced would have no reaction. He had to know I was faking this, but that didn't mean that he knew who I was. I couldn't imagine that he did, not when he'd only seen me twice, and both times I hadn't looked like this.

Another tremble coursed through me, and I knew he could feel it, because his grip on my waist tightened, bunching the material of my dress.

"Well, Sally from Lafayette, there's something very interesting about you," he said, and a stuttered heartbeat later, the entire front of my body was pressed against his.

The contact was a shock to my system, and when I drew in a deep breath, he smelled like summer thunderstorms and reminded me of glistening beaches. My skin burned and tingled and the reaction was swift, potent. His hand slid to the center of my back, and the next breath I took caught in my throat.

What in the world was happening? Was he—?

"Your pulse...." His hand followed my spine, tangling in the strands of hair as it curled around the nape of my neck. His warm breath danced over my forehead as he tipped my head back, pressing his thumb right against my wildly beating pulse.

Without warning, he spun me around. My heart skipped a beat as he hauled me back against him. I drew in a ragged breath, fully aware of how my body fitted against the hard slabs of his muscles and the...*holy crap*, the other thing that seemed equally proportioned to his large body, and I desperately wanted to pretend I didn't feel that.

And I also desperately wanted to pretend I didn't feel how my stomach twisted in a pleasant, confusing way or how liquid heat pooled low. I wasn't attracted to him. No way. No way at all, because behind the raw heat building inside me was also fear.

The Prince brushed the heavy hair off the back of my neck and then his fingers were against the taut muscles, working to soothe the tightness there.

What in the hell was he up to?

I'd never had a neck massage before. Honestly, I kind of hated random people touching me, but this was... this was oh so nice. Against my will, my neck arched into his hand as the warming in my stomach spread low, really low. My body seemed to relax and tense all at the same time.

I needed to stop this. Right now.

My eyes drifted shut as his hand made its way from my neck, skimming down the side of my body, over my lax arm. The tips of his fingers coasted over mine, and then found their way to my hip. A pumping pulse picked up in several key points in my body, responding to the light, forbidden touch.

He didn't speak as his warm breath kissed the curve of my cheek and I didn't say or do anything. I could stop him. I knew I could. Or I could at least try.

I did nothing.

His hand slipped over my stomach, below my navel. I jerked, bringing us closer. Way too close once more, and I couldn't breathe as something bizarre happened inside me. It was like all my senses woke up at once, sparking with life and flaming heat through my veins.

His hand dropped to the front of my dress, right above where a deep, deep ache had started. He growled deep in his throat as he said against the flushed skin of my neck, "Your pulse is racing so fast—too fast for someone entranced."

Hell.

Oh hell.

The Prince might not recognize who I was, but he knew I wasn't entranced. Fight or flight response kicked in, overriding the confusing heat pumping through my body.

Two years ago, I would've chosen flight. That was all I'd been capable of. Not anymore. A whole different instinct took over, a newly developed one. I had no idea why the Prince was here, in the pit of his enemies, and I wasn't willing to risk finding out or being caught by him.

Spinning around, I gripped his forearm as I ducked and twisted, slipping free of his grip. I saw the flicker of surprise on his face and then I spun back toward him. Still holding onto his arm, I used his weight as an anchor as I leaned back. Planting my left leg back, I lifted my right and slammed my knee into his midsection.

The Prince grunted as he let go, but he did not move even an inch. That kind of kick would've brought a human down. Probably would've even knocked a normal fae back several steps, but not an Ancient. He lifted his chin, eyes narrowed with annoyance.

"That was unnecessarily violent," he said, straightening to his full height.

He hadn't seen unnecessarily violent yet.

I spun, picking up the chair. It was surprisingly heavy. Grunting, I swung it around, prepared to at least knock him once upside the head. Wouldn't kill him, but would definitely give me a chance to escape without having to answer questions.

The Prince's speed was mind-numbingly fast.

I didn't even see him lift a hand. He just suddenly had ahold of the leg of the chair. He wrenched it from my grip, tossing it aside. The chair hit the wall with a bang, shattering into three large pieces.

Damn.

He tilted his head, lips pressed into a hard, flat line. "I'm going to chalk that up to one bad life choice fueled by fear and a little bit of stupidity, and logically reason that you're—"

Spinning into him, I swung my arm out. He dipped to the left, causing my elbow to glance off his chest. Cursing under his breath, he shot toward me. Before I could even take a breath, he had both hands on my shoulders. My back hit the wall, and then he was there, his large body crowding mine in. Panic began to blossom, but I fought it down. I started to raise my leg, aiming for where it counted, but he pressed his hips in, trapping a large thigh between mine.

"Foolish. So very foolish," he said. "Also kind of hot."

Wait. What?

"But that's neither here nor there." He wrapped his hand around my chin, forcing my head back against the wall. His gaze snagged mine. "Are you out of your mind? Do you know how easy it would be for me to kill you? Do you?"

Heart thundering in my chest, I kept my mouth shut as I glared back at him.

"Do you?" he repeated, his eyes churning with anger and… and something… something else. "Answer me."

"Yes," I spat out.

"And you still tried to attack me?" His thumb sliced over my chin. "When I made no move to harm you."

I wouldn't exactly say he made no move. He had grabbed me. That I didn't appreciate.

"I think I can guess what happened to Tobias."

My jaw ached from how tight I was clamping it shut.

Fury poured off him, but when those heavy lashes lowered, I swore his gaze had zeroed in on my mouth. He cursed again, and then suddenly released me. I wasn't expecting him to do it. Off balance, I stumbled forward. He caught my arm, straightening me, and then dropped his hold as if my skin burned him.

"Go," he growled out. "Go before I do something we both will end up regretting."

I didn't need to be told twice.

Backing away from the Prince, I spun on the sharp heel of my boot and then I ran.

Chapter 5

The beautiful antebellum style home I grew up in sat nestled in the middle of the Garden District. With its wraparound porch, second-floor balcony, and the courtyard Mom and I had spent many sunny afternoons in, it was one of the houses that was an utter blast from the past—with the exception of the kitchen and bathrooms that had been renovated about five years ago.

There were days when I thought about selling it and moving on to anywhere but here even though I had been born in this home and New Orleans was a part of my blood just as much as the Order was. If I did decide to sell, I knew this home wouldn't last a second on the market, but I couldn't bring myself to let go of it. At least not yet, when I could still recall all those good memories.

But on nights like tonight, when I was rattled and exhausted as I unlocked the door my mom had decided to paint blue, I was swamped with the bad memories.

The attack had happened less than two blocks from here. We'd been so close to making it back, and I had to think that would've made a difference. Tink had been here.

Then again, if I hadn't panicked and had fought back instead of flailing like a pinned insect, that could've also made a difference.

Swallowing down the bitter ball of emotion, I opened the door and stepped inside, locking it behind me. A lamp on the entryway table was on, casting a soft glow to the formal sitting room to the right—a room that legit was never used, and a cherry oak library to the left. I could hear some sort of conversation coming from the living area at the back of the house, on the other side of the kitchen.

I dropped the keys on the table and strode past the staircase, the heels of what I liked to refer to as my stripper boots clacking off the wood floors as I entered the dining room, another place in the house that saw little use. The kitchen was quiet, the under cabinet lights on, shining down on the gray and white quartz countertops.

Stepping under a rounded archway, I took in the living area at the back of the house. One entire wall was nothing but windows that overlooked the porch and courtyard. The blinds were drawn and the heavy, ceramic lamp was lit. On the screen, my favorite *Stranger Things* kid Dustin was currently trying to lure a baby demogorgon into the basement. There was an enormous bowl of Lucky Charms on the round coffee table. I knew this because the empty box was sitting next to the bowl. No milk. And it looked like all the colorful marshmallows had been picked out of the cereal.

Again.

I sighed as I counted the cans of open soda. Four. How anything could consume that much sugar and not slip into a diabetic coma, I had no idea.

Twisting at the waist, I scanned the normal hiding places. Behind pillows. Under the coffee table. Waiting behind the end tables. The room was empty.

Picking up the remote, I turned the television off and then I grabbed the bowl of cereal. I brought it back to the kitchen and placed it on the counter before returning to grab the empty soda cans. I tossed them into the recycling bin, all the while not thinking about what I'd done tonight or the Prince or how sore my throat was. Once I was done cleaning up, I went through the narrow hall that was lined with framed photographs of Mom and me, and older ones of my father. Back to the foyer, I double-checked the locked door.

Couldn't be too safe.

As I wearily climbed the stairs, I spotted a tiny shoe no bigger than half my pinky sitting between two wooden spindles on the steps. Stopping, I looked for the other shoe, but didn't see it and decided to leave that shoe on the step, because I figured it was there for a reason.

The upstairs hallway light was already on, so I turned it off as I reached the end of the hall and then closed the bedroom door behind me.

Feeling several years older than my age, I crossed the quiet room and walked into what used to be a small nursery, but had been converted into a walk-in closet ages ago.

Then I started my routine of becoming me again—becoming Brighton Jussier.

I bent down and got to unzipping the boots. Kicking them off, I reached up and moved my fingers through the hair, finding the extra bobby pins I used as an extra precaution. I plucked them out, dropping them in a glass tray sitting on the waist-high table in the center. Slipping the wig off, I placed it on the plastic mannequin-head stand and then peeled off the cap that helped keep my hair flat. I had no idea how to braid, so I worked with a low bun. After another half a dozen pins joined the rest in the tray, my hair was free, falling past my shoulders. A rush of blood hit my scalp and I closed my eyes, enjoying the tingles.

Lifting my hands, I looked up as I pinched my fingers, removing the contacts that had changed my eyes to blue. I placed them in their container.

The dress came off next, going straight into the trash. I never wore them twice. I just couldn't bring myself to do it, because even though this one was sparkly and sexy, it would forever make me think of Tobias and his icy touch. It would always remind me of the first time I saw him and why I had hunted him down.

Undressed, I tugged on the fluffy robe and then padded barefoot back across the room to the bathroom.

I turned on the shower, letting the steam begin to fill the space. It took two towelettes to remove all the makeup on my face, but after a handful of moments, it was *my* face staring back at me in the mirror.

Blonde hair fell limply around cheeks that were pink from all the scrubbing. Faint shadows clung to the skin under eyes that reminded me of my mother. They were wide-set and brown. Someone once called them doe eyes, and I think they might've been suggesting that my eyes gave them the impression of a deer in headlights. Right now, that would be accurate. I stared at myself like I didn't recognize anything about my own face. My gaze lowered, to where my lips were slightly parted and then lower still.

Pale blue marks had formed on either side of my throat.

Without having to try, I heard the sound the Prince had made when he'd tipped my head back. Smoothing my fingers over the faint bruises, I wondered if the Prince had seen them. Was that why he'd… growled?

What in the hell was the Prince even doing at Flux?

And I couldn't help but wonder why he hadn't struck back at me. He could've. I'd kicked him. Swung a chair at him. Hit him, and all he did was restrain me and then told me to leave. He'd been pissed, that much I was sure of, but he didn't try to hurt me.

Steam crept across the mirror, blurring my reflection as I pulled my hand away from my throat. When I'd left the room, there hadn't been a single fae in the alcove on the second floor. The couches and chairs were empty. There wasn't even a human in sight. The Prince had done something to the fae.

I didn't think he'd warned them off.

He'd taken them out, and that made sense. The fae that frequented Flux were the Winter fae, the enemy of the Summer Court and humans, but what didn't make sense was why he was looking for Tobias.

I knew why I'd been there. Just like I knew I would go back to Flux, because eventually the remaining two fae would make an appearance. They always did, and I would do the same thing I'd done tonight. Watch them. Learn their habits. Strike fast and get out, hopefully without The Prince showing up. I would kill them or die trying, and there was a good chance that would happen, because one of the two remaining fae was an Ancient.

And he'd been the cruelest, the sickest.

I shuddered as I gripped the sink. Closing my eyes, I inhaled deeply and then held my breath a second before the all-too-familiar thought blasted forward, shoving everything else out of the way.

This isn't who you are.

Stalking the fae and putting myself in ridiculously dangerous positions wasn't who I used to be. That was who I'd wanted to be, but what I had become was some kind of twisted version of that.

Being consumed with vengeance was something I never thought I'd experience, but I was knee-deep in it and I wasn't coming out anytime soon.

Who I used to be was a woman I could barely remember. I'd once thought that my life had changed when I was twelve and that my life could never be that rattled again. I'd foolishly believed that every human had a cap to what kind of tragedy they'd experience, and I'd already had my fair share. My father had died in the line of duty, as many Order members did, before I could even form one memory of the man. My mom had been brutalized but survived to never be a hundred percent the same again. I'd watched friends die in the battle against the fae, and naïvely, stupidly thought that we were free and clear, because how could anything else happen to me or my mother? We'd experienced enough tragedy to last a lifetime. God couldn't be that cruel to deliver yet another soul-crushing blow.

I'd been so wrong.

Thinking back to the night of the attack, I wondered if I had misjudged the reason for Mom being antsy. Maybe it wasn't a sign that she was about to have another episode. Maybe it was some kind of primal instinct had told her what was coming that night. What if she had known that those were the last hours of her life?

Guilt churned, flooding the pit of my stomach with acid as I walked myself back through the night. Our shouts of surprise and screams of pain had been quickly silenced. They'd swarmed us within seconds, pulling us into the courtyard of the empty home.

They'd torn through clothing, skin, and muscle. The pain… God, it had been shattering and devastating. They hadn't even attempted to feed on us. I'd learned later from Ivy that Gerry and the others hadn't appeared to have been fed on either. The attack was all about pain and blood, and there'd been so much blood. It had coated my skin and soaked my hair.

I'd fought to stay conscious, but it was all too much. The pain. The blood. The *sounds*. The shock of it all. I wasn't able to hold on, and the last thing I'd felt was my mother's hand slipping from mine. The last thing I'd seen had been her. I'd seen what they had done to her. No human could survive that.

My chest and throat burned until the point I started to feel faint. Dragging in a deep breath of air, I opened my eyes and saw nothing but mist.

Leaning forward, I dragged my hand across the mirror, wiping away the steam until I could see myself staring back at me.

It was my face and my hair. No makeup or special contouring. Those were my lips and my eyes. I was staring at me, but I….

I didn't recognize who I'd become.

Chapter 6

I jolted awake, heart racing and my pulse throbbing in very interesting places as my eyes snapped open. My gaze fixed on the churning ceiling fan. Oh my God, I'd been dreaming.

Not the usual one, reliving the final moments of the fae I'd sent back to the Otherworld, like I normally dreamt after such an event. I'd been back at the club, in that dingy room, but Tobias was nowhere to be seen. I'd been in that same chair, though, and I hadn't been alone.

The Prince had been underneath me.

It had been his warm lips skating down my neck, his hot fingers skating along my sides, and I hadn't been sitting there, holding myself immobile. Oh no, I'd been rocking against him, head thrown back, panting as I moved over him, against him, feeling things I hadn't felt in… in what felt like forever, if *ever*.

I'd woken up right when his fingers had found the clasp of my bra, and there was a tiny, stupid and utterly insane part of me that was now staring at the ceiling fan, disappointed.

Good God, I needed help.

Lots of mental help.

A soft purring sound drew my attention as I willed my heart to slow down and my body to get back on the sane and safe path. I turned my head to the right and found myself eye to eye with two yellow eyes.

Meow.

I frowned as the all gray cat—except for its tail, which looked like it had been dipped in white paint—stretched out his little legs and yawned right in my face.

"How did you get in here, Dixon?" I asked the cat, which was named after a character on The Walking Dead. Dixon didn't belong to me, but he was kind of a package deal at the moment. Not that I minded. I liked the little guy.

Dixon flopped on his side and twisted his head so he was staring at me upside down. I raised a brow and then heard a soft creaking noise. I rose onto my elbows. The iPad slipped off my chest and fell to the floor, the soft thump drawing a sigh from me. I'd fallen asleep… putting a jigsaw puzzle together.

Again.

Kind of lame, but it always relaxed me, helping shut my brain down so I could sleep, but I really needed to stop falling asleep mid-puzzle like a narcoleptic.

I scanned the large dimly-lit bedroom, but the buttery glow from the bedside lamp only held the shadows back from the bed. The thin slice of slivery moonlight seeping through between the curtains did very little to cut through the darkness, but I was confident no one was—

A lump formed under the thin bedspread near the foot of the bed, about the size of a crab. A really *large* crab.

What in the holy hell?

I watched the lump work its way up the bed, stop every couple of inches, and then start moving again. I waited until it was near the top and then leaned over, gripping the bedspread and ripping it back.

The *crab* let out a surprised shriek as I revealed the actual owner of the cat. Tink was… well, he was not of this world. Obviously. He was a brownie, a creature that stood about twelve inches tall, had a major addiction to sugar, TV and film, and Amazon Prime. He'd gotten trapped in this world several years ago while trying to close one of the doorways to the Otherworld. Ivy had found him in St. Louis Cemetery with a broken leg and wing. Instead of putting him down, like all members of the Order were required to do at the time, she'd felt bad for the little guy and taken him home, helping him recover.

What Ivy hadn't known was how crazy powerful Tink was, and that his current state, when he was about the size of a Ken doll, was a size he *chose* to be. Tink was what I liked to call giant-sized when he wanted to be. Ever since he'd come to stay with me, he'd been this size. Why, I had no idea.

Tink used to freak me out. I like to think a flying brownie would freak any normal person out, especially because he was the only brownie ever to be seen in our world. But not only had he grown on me, he was the reason I hadn't bled out on the sidewalk alongside my mom the night I was attacked.

It had been Tink—full-sized Tink—who had found us.

And since then, since I returned home from the hospital, it was like I suddenly had joint custody of Tink. Not that Ivy or I really had custody of him, but he spent the same amount of time with me as he did with her nowadays.

"What are you doing, Tink?" I asked.

The brownie was still flat on his stomach, mid-military crawl. One gossamer wing twitched. Vibrant blue eyes were wide and blond hair a spiky mess. "Hi?"

I narrowed my eyes. "Tink."

He sighed heavily, as if I was the one who had disturbed him, and pushed up on his small arms. He rose onto his knees. "I woke up."

"Okay."

"And I was bored."

"All right."

"Then I went downstairs to finish watching Stranger Things, but someone turned the TV off. Not going to name names or anything—"

"You know it was me, and you could've turned the TV back on." I didn't even bother pointing out that I knew he'd watched both seasons at least eight times. If I did, it would've started a conversation about how he was comparing the upside down to the Otherworld, and I really wasn't in the mood for that conversation at the moment.

"I could've, but then I was like, that requires effort. You have no idea how long it takes these little legs to get down all those steps."

"Couldn't you just fly?"

"That's a lot of work."

"Couldn't you just become people-sized?"

He cocked his head to the side. "But I'm cuter like this."

All I could do was stare at him.

Tink stood and started stomping up the bed, toward Dixon. "So, anyway, then I was like, I wonder what Brighton is doing."

I didn't even want to know what time it was, but I figured it was either really late or really early. "Sleeping, Tink. That's what I was doing."

"But your light was on." He lifted his hand, and Dixon reached out with a paw the size of his head. "So, I thought you were up. Dixon and I decided to visit you, because we're good friends like that."

Sighing, I lay back down.

"Guess what?"

"What?" I asked, scrubbing my hands over my eyes.

"I rode Dixon in here, like I would ride a mighty steer charging into battle."

Lifting my hands, I looked over at him. I really had nothing to say to that.

Tink flashed straight, sharp teeth. "Ivy always gets mad at me when I do that, but Dixon likes it and I like it."

"The world is your oyster, Tink."

"Any-who-boo, we waited up for you." He caught Dixon's paw with both hands and shook it. "You were late. Super late. So, we went to bed."

"You don't have to wait up for me. I told you that." I rolled onto my side, facing him. Tink was still shaking Dixon's paw. For the hundredth time since he showed up at my doorstep a week ago with Dixon in tow, I wondered why he was still here and not in Florida. "Can I ask you something?"

"You can ask me anything, Light-Bright."

I grinned at the ridiculous name. "Why didn't you go to Florida with Ivy?"

"Because she was with Ren." He rolled his eyes.

"You like Ren. Don't play."

"He's *tolerable*."

I searched his face. "And Fabian went down to Florida. Wouldn't you want to be with him?"

"I went down to Florida with him last September, and I decided after thorough exploration that Florida is the Australia of the United States. The place scares me," he said, and I snorted at that, because it was sort of true. "He's not going to be down there forever. He's coming back."

I wondered if there was something wrong between him and Fabian. "Is everything okay with you guys?"

"Of course." Tink dropped Dixon's paw and pinned me with a look that said he couldn't believe I'd actually asked that question. "Fabian not only thinks that I'm the most amazing creature to walk this world and beyond, he's so in love with me, it's adorable."

My grin grew as I reached over and scratched Dixon behind the ear. "That's good."

"Speaking of love, how was your date?" He changed the subject as he plopped down on the pillow beside mine and crossed his legs, leaning back against Dixon's fluffy belly.

"Date?" I almost laughed right in Tink's face. As if I ever had a date. Kind of hard meeting people when you were a member of the

Order, knew that fae existed outside of Disney and fairytales, had a twelve-inch brownie who sometimes was people sized and often crawled into my bed when he was Tink sized—*wait.* His brows lifted. "Oh, it wasn't that good. Nothing to write home about."

Tink folded his arms. "You lied to me. You didn't have a date."

"I—"

"You went hunting instead, didn't you?" His little mouth pursed with irritation. "You went hunting for one of those fae who hurt you, but you didn't want me—the most awesome of awesome company to ever be blessed with—to tag along."

"Tink—"

"Not only am I freaking awesome, I am also pretty damn badass. If you go out there hunting those fae, you take me with you. I can help."

"Tink—" I tried again, no point in lying. He knew what I was doing. He was the only one to figure it out. "I know you're awesome company, but the moment they saw you, they'd know what you were. That would kind of throw a wrench into everything."

"Oh, yeah, and you ending up dead or worse would also throw a wrench into everything." Tink leaned away from Dixon. "What you're doing is dangerous. If Ivy knew—"

"Ivy's not going to know. Neither is Ren or anyone else," I told him. "Look, I get that you're concerned, but I don't want you out there, putting yourself at risk. You've already done so much," I told him, meaning it. "You saved my life."

Tink shook his little head as he stared at me, gaze somber. "I didn't save your life. I found you. That's all I did."

"You still saved me."

"No," he said, louder this time. "It wasn't me who saved you."

I opened my mouth, unsure of what to say. The way he said that struck me as odd, but before I could say anything, he spoke again.

"Did you find who you were looking for?"

"Yes."

"Did you take him out?" Tink asked, holding my gaze.

"Yes," I whispered.

Tink smiled then. "Good."

Chapter 7

Miles, the leader of the New Orleans branch of the Order, called first thing Monday morning with a request that both confused and interested me.

The Summer fae had requested a meeting with the Order, but Miles couldn't spare any of the *essential* members to go see what they wanted.

Since I was not considered an essential Order member, I'd been assigned the task to figure out what they could possibly want.

Tink was passed out in the living room next to Dixon, so I didn't bring him along with me. Granted, I could've woken him up, but the fae treated Tink like he was some kind of golden calf to be worshipped, and Tink's head was already overinflated, adorably so.

So, that's where I found myself Monday morning, staring at the beam of sunlight that shone through the large windows of the office inside Hotel Good Fae, keeping the room nice and toasty despite the chilly March temperatures outside.

That's what Ivy called this place, and it did remind me of a hotel—a really glitzy, mammoth hotel. To humans and even to the Winter fae, Hotel Good Fae appeared to be nothing more than an abandoned power plant on St. Peters Street.

Based on the old maps I'd found in my mother's past research clutter, I suspected all the strange markings of places that couldn't or shouldn't exist were more well-hidden communities.

This might not be the only one.

Hotel Good Fae was a massive structure set up a lot like a hotel. Several stories tall with hundreds of rooms on each floor and sprawling communal areas outfitted with multiple cafeterias, theaters, shopping, gyms, and even space for a school of sorts, the compound had the ability to house thousands of fae. The Order had no idea exactly how many fae lived in this place, something that I knew disturbed Miles and the other Order members.

The kind of power and magic the Summer fae used to glamour the building was astonishing.

It was a good thing they didn't want to feed off humans and seemed to like us, because if not, we'd be so screwed.

Then again, I knew that Prince Fabian fed, supposedly on willing humans who knew what he was, because he didn't age and was capable of extraordinary actions. I assumed that his brother, *the* Prince, fed too.

Tugging on the neck of my chunky cable-knit sweater, I was beginning to think I would melt in this office before anyone showed up. The sweater had been perfect for when I was outside and it covered the bruises on my neck, but now I was sweltering in it.

If Ivy hadn't been in Florida with her husband handling some kind of super-secret mission, she'd be here, sitting in the Hotel Good Fae, acting as the liaison between the Order and the fae. Not me. She was better at handling these types of meetings, and right now, the best needed to here, because things between the Summer fae and the Order were tense.

I found myself staring at the long, narrow desk in front of me as I waited, smoothing a blonde strand of hair back into the ponytail. The surface was free of clutter. Just a large desk calendar and computer monitor. An iMac. My desk at home looked like maps and books had thrown up all over it. I couldn't even see the top of my desk, let alone use the keyboard to what was definitely not an iMac.

I used one of the guest rooms upstairs for my office, which was perfect, because I could close the door on the room and pretend that a hoarder didn't live there.

Nervous energy filled me as I dropped my hand and ran my fingers along the neck of the sweater. My throat was still tender and I knew it probably would be for a couple of days. At least the weather was cool enough to wear a turtleneck.

Got to look on the bright side.

Pressing my lips together, I dragged my gaze from the empty desk just as I heard footsteps outside the room. I dropped my hand. Seconds later, the door opened.

The Summer fae known as Tanner strode into his office. His real name was totally unpronounceable, as were the names of most of the fae who lived here. Almost all of them, including the woman behind him, had adopted human sounding names. Even the Winter fae did that, because I doubted Tobias had been that bastard's real name.

Tanner drew up short when he spotted me sitting there, as did the female fae called Faye, who was carrying a file. Odd reaction considering when they saw me, I looked like I normally did, no wig or heavy makeup. No façade.

I was Brighton today even if I… I didn't feel like her.

I only saw the mask Faye and Tanner wore for a second before the humanity seeped away and I saw them in all their fae glory. The only thing that hadn't changed was their hair. Both were dark haired, but Tanner's was salt and peppered, proving that he was aging like a human while Faye was younger, her hair a deep flaxen color.

"Ms. Jussier." Surprise colored Tanner's tone as he crossed the room and stopped in front of me, offering his hand. "I am surprised to see you."

"Brighton," I corrected him as I glanced at his outstretched hand. The moment of hesitation didn't go unnoticed by Faye. The shrewd female cocked a dark eyebrow. I took Tanner's hand, shaking it as firmly as humanly possible. I didn't even know why I hesitated other than just being weird—and I was weird. A lot. "You know you can call me Brighton."

He squeezed my hand affectionately. "Goodness, Brighton, I haven't seen you in ages. I'm… I am so sorry to hear about your mother and for what happened to you."

I couldn't remember the last time I'd been in this office or to Hotel Good Fae, but it was before the attack.

"Merle was an amazing and unique woman," he continued, his tone and pale blue eyes full of genuine sorrow, and I wasn't surprised he said that. He and several of the Summer fae had attended her funeral. "She is greatly missed."

The next breath I took got stuck in my throat. I pulled my hand free, placing it on the velvety arm of the chair I sat in. I opened my mouth, but found that I couldn't speak as sorrow and anger threatened to rise up and smother me. I couldn't let that happen. Not here.

Clearing my throat, I pushed away the messy emotions and focused. "Thank you. My mother enjoyed knowing you."

"She did?" Tanner chuckled as he stepped back from me and turned to his desk. "Your mother was a hard woman to win over."

"She had… trust issues," I explained, shifting in the chair. "But she trusted you. Both of you."

As crazy as that sounded, it was true. Mom actually liked Tanner. I thought she might've been developing a crush on the fae, which sounded absurd considering what she had been through, but she really did like Tanner.

A faint smile crossed Faye's face. "And we consider that a great honor."

Nodding, I wished that the bitter, razor edged ball of emotion that now sat heavily on my chest would just go away. It was time to get this meeting underway. "I can tell you weren't expecting me. Ivy was unable to make it. She's with—"

"Prince Fabian in Florida," Faye finished, standing a few feet from me beside the end of the desk. "We are aware that Ivy isn't available, but we thought they'd send… someone else."

I wasn't sure how to respond to that. I kept my face blank as Tanner sat behind the desk. "I'm sorry, but Miles is busy with the new recruits."

"I imagine he does have a lot on his hands." Tanner smiled, and he was always smiling politely. It was like his face was permanently fixed that way. "But we expected someone… higher up."

Heat crept into my cheeks as my hand on the chair became rigid. *They knew.* I glanced between the two fae, feeling the warmth travel down my throat. They knew that Miles had sent me in for the meeting, because, in all honestly, he was too busy to deal with Tanner and, at the end of the day, didn't really care enough to pull any of the members off the street or out of training. That was why I'd been sent in, because in Miles's eyes, I had disposable time.

I wasn't remotely essential.

I lifted my chin. "I can assure you that I, like every other Order member, has been born and raised within the organization. In reality, I'm more knowledgeable about anything that has to do with the Order than Miles." I wasn't being a braggy-mc-bragster either. That was the damn truth. That was my job at the Order. The researcher. The reader. The studier. I was the *Willow* in an army of *Buffys* and *Angels*. "I can assist you with whatever it is that you need to speak with us about."

"I'm sorry," Tanner was quick to reply. "I didn't mean to insinuate that you couldn't handle this. It's just that…."

"What?" I lifted my brows, waiting.

"You're uncomfortable around us," Faye stated plainly. "Which I can completely understand with what happened to you—"

"What happened to me is irrelevant."

Faye's gaze softened just a little. "I can smell your anxiety. It reminds me of woodsmoke."

Now my face was on fire. Was it truly that obvious that I was anxious? "You can smell my anxiety?"

Faye nodded.

Well, that was something I never knew and that was somewhat creepy.

"And you're gripping the chair like it's some kind of lifeline," Faye pointed out. "It's like you've already forgotten that two years ago, we fought beside the Order and pushed the Queen back into the Otherworld."

Tanner tensed at the mention of the Queen. Couldn't blame him. I'd never seen the Queen, but from what I heard, she was a whole bucketful of nightmares.

"That we lost many good fae that night," Faye continued. "And it seems you've also forgotten that the biggest betrayal did not come from us, but came from within the Order."

"I haven't forgotten." How in the world could I? Betrayal had come from the top of the Order, starting with David Faustin. He was the head of the New Orleans Sect, keyword being *was*, and his betrayal had spread throughout the Order like a virus, infecting nearly everyone. Those within the Order who hadn't died at the hands of the not-so-friendly fae, the Winter fae, had done so at the hands of those they'd trusted.

I exhaled roughly as I eased my grip off the arm of the chair. "I…." I started to apologize but stopped and decided to be as bluntly honest as Faye. "I was raised to hunt fae and taught that there was no such thing as a good fae. And yes, there were some members of the Order who knew of your existence, but the majority of us didn't know that the Summer Court had escaped into our world after the war with the Winter Court, and were just trying to live their best lives as human. If anyone had suggested two years ago that there were good fae out there, fae who weren't feeding on humans, I would've laughed straight in their face."

Faye's jaw hardened, but I wasn't done. "And you know damn well the Winter fae, those still loyal to the Queen, far outnumber you all. Two years, Faye. That's all I've had, all many of us had to come to terms with the idea that not all fae are evil incarnate. So, yes, the fae make me uncomfortable. Just as I'm sure we make you uncomfortable."

"Of course some of you make us uncomfortable, considering there are still some Order members who want to kill us," Faye shot back.

"I think what Faye is trying to say this whole time, is that we have a fairly serious issue, and we're worried that your… uncomfortableness may get in the way of helping us resolve this issue." Tanner folded his hands on the desk. "That is all."

Okay. Wow. This was getting awkward. "May I be painfully honest?"

"Of course." Tanner sat back.

"Besides Ivy and Ren, there is not a single member of the Order who isn't uncomfortable around the fae or may be somewhat prejudiced by all their years fighting fae who want nothing more than to enslave mankind and destroy them. Even Ren isn't exactly going to be rolling out the red carpet, and his wife is half-fae," I said, holding their stares. "So, if you're worried that my *uncomfortableness* is going to be an issue, then you are going to have the same problem with any Order member besides Ivy. Either you tell me why you wanted a meeting with the Order or you wait until Ivy gets back. Your call."

"It's not just that we make you nervous." Faye tapped the file on her denim-covered thigh. "It's also that we scare you."

My head snapped in her direction. "You do not scare me."

"Is that so?" she murmured.

"That's so. And just to clarify, the anxiety you're sniffing isn't because of you two. I'm just an anxious person ninety percent of the time. You guys make me uncomfortable, but you do not make me anxious or scared. There's a Mississippi River's worth of difference between the two."

A measure of respect filled Faye's eyes. Not much, but I saw it.

"Well then, we will make do, won't we?" Tanner said.

Slowly, I turned back to him, thinking he sounded like he had as much faith as I did that Tink wouldn't create a mess by the time I got home. "I guess so."

"We needed to speak with the Order because we've been noticing a disturbing trend." Tanner took the file Faye handed to him. "Over the last month, several of our younglings have gone missing, and we fear the Order is involved."

Chapter 8

All right, I wasn't expecting that.

He opened the file, and I could see a glossy colored photograph of a young man—a young fae. "As you know, many members of the Summer Court do not venture outside these walls. It's not something that we prohibit, but many find everything they need provided for them here."

I nodded absently. The fact that most of the Summer fae remained within the hidden, sprawling compound worked perfectly for us. It often meant that the fae we encountered on the streets weren't the friendly neighborhood sort.

"Some of the younglings want to experience the… human world and all it has to offer. It has become a sort of rite of passage in a way." Faye propped a slim hip against the desk. "They always keep their loved ones in the loop and they're never gone too long."

"Four in the last month have not come back," Tanner said grimly. "Their parents and friends have not heard from them and the last we've seen them is when they left."

I took several moments to process this. "When you say younglings, are we talking about children size, teenagers or early twenties?"

"Children size?" murmured Faye, blinking rapidly.

"All four are in their late teens, early twenties," Tanner clarified. "These are their photographs and identification."

Watching Tanner display four photographs along his desk sort of stunned me. I started searching for the right thing to say and ended up giving up as my gaze glanced off what were similar to driver's license photos. "You're sure they're missing?"

"Unless they're here and currently invisible, yes," Faye replied dryly.

"That's not what I meant." I scooted forward, getting a better look at the four young fae. All male. Each one named underneath his smiling photo. They were young, probably early twenties, and handsome. I was willing to wager a bet they were even hotter with the glamour and probably were having the time of their lives in the Quarter. "This is New Orleans. There is a lot of stuff they can get into. Crazy stuff."

"We understand that. Many of our younglings do… have an enjoyable time, but they are always in contact with their loved ones," Tanner stated.

I lifted a brow. "A lot of younger people get caught up in the party scene here. They meet new people—" *And hopefully don't feed on them.* "—and they lose track of time. The city swallows people whole, and I don't mean that in a bad way—" *I sort of do.* "—It often spits them back out, exhausted and ready to make better life choices, like, for example, keeping your parents up to date on your whereabouts."

"Do human children not keep their parents informed of their whereabouts, for days if not weeks?" Tanner asked.

I pressed my lips together to stop myself from laughing, because I could tell that was a genuine question. "Some do, but not nearly enough."

"Human offspring may have a lack of respect and courtesy toward their elders, but our younglings do not." Hardness seeped into Tanner's tone. "Our offspring are not raised that way."

"Pretty sure eons of human parents have said those same exact words."

Faye cocked her head. "Be that as it may, that is not the case with our younglings."

Glancing between the two, I shook my head as I chose my words wisely. They thought… they thought the Order was going to be concerned about missing fae, even fae from the Summer Court? As terrible as it sounded, I knew that the Order could freaking care less. "I'm sorry, but I'm not sure what this has to do with the Order."

Tanner didn't respond immediately. "There is a burgeoning concern that they were… mistakenly targeted by the Order."

Tension crept into my muscles. "Are you suggesting that these young fae are not missing, but were killed by the Order?"

"As I said, it is a burgeoning concern and hopefully, a misguided one," Tanner said slowly. "But there have been incidents in the past two years where innocents were slaughtered."

He was right.

Before the war with the Queen and the reveal of the Summer fae, the Order had been 'kill first and most likely never ask questions'. There had been no such thing as good fae. Things were different now. Complicated. "There are new protocols in place, Tanner. The Order does not blindly dispense justice. Any fae targeted by the Order is monitored now and based on whatever evidence gathered—"

"You and I both know that most Order members operate on the basis that the Summer fae do not interact often, if ever, with the human populace." Faye's pale blue eyes glinted. "They assume that every fae they see on the street is the enemy."

I stiffened. "That is not the case."

"Really?" Faye challenged. "Solomon posed no harm to humans and he was slaughtered."

Solomon was a fae who'd been killed a year ago, having been wrongly identified by one of the newer Order members.

"That was a mistake, a terrible mistake, and I'm sorry that it happened." And I was. I wasn't remotely okay with *any* innocent being killed, fae or human. "But that doesn't mean that is the case with these guys."

"There hasn't been just one mistake," Faye pointed out.

"I know that." There'd been… several mistakes. "And I wish there was something I could say or do to change that, but—"

"But the Order is trying to adapt. We understand that and we also understand that this is a learning period for all of us," Tanner said, ever the diplomat. "We know that many Order members have died with the new protocols in place."

Many had.

Six times more than any Summer fae who had been injured by the Order.

Taking the time out to make sure you were killing the right fae proved to be a wee bit dangerous. We'd lost the upper hand and the element of surprise. By the time we'd figure out if a fae wasn't on Team Human, the fae realized who we were.

The Order had been nearly decimated two years ago, and we hadn't been able to rebuild our numbers.

Which was why Miles was always busy with new recruits.

"Is it possible that these fae chose to go off the grid?" I asked, toying with the neck of my sweater. "Perhaps they don't want to live here. There's a big world out there, and some of them that live here have to be interested in seeing it. Especially since they watch our TV shows and movies, read our books and magazines. As nice as this place is, maybe they wanted to experience the world beyond these walls, this city?"

Tanner stared at me like he hadn't considered that.

Silence crept into the room. Faye shattered it as she reached over, picking up a photo of a dark-haired fae. "This is my younger cousin. His chosen name is Benji. He's been missing for a week, and I can assure you that he would not do that to his mother. Not after his father died two years ago, fighting the Queen."

My stomach twisted as I focused on his picture.

"This is his friend Elliot, who went missing about two weeks ago. Benji had told his mother he was going to look for Elliot," Faye continued. "He disappeared since and we haven't heard from either Elliot or Benji."

"I'm… I'm sorry," I whispered, lifting my gaze to hers. "Truly, I am."

"Then help us," Faye said quietly. "You will help us find my cousin and these young fae if you feel sorry."

"All we want is to know if the Order has any idea what happened to them and if they could possibly keep an eye out for these younglings." Tanner spoke up as Faye looked away, her throat working. "Kalen has been out there, searching for them with no luck."

I jolted at the mention of the fae who'd worked closely with Ivy and Ren. I'd assumed he was with them and Prince Fabian.

"I can help," I said after a moment. "Can I have those photographs?"

Tanner nodded.

"I can check with the members to see if any of them look familiar." I wasn't sure if any of the Order members would fess up if they had anything to do with these fae. They were supposed to, but I was learning in the last two years there was very little consequence for these types of situations. "I can also make sure they keep an eye out for them."

Faye handed over the photo of her cousin to Tanner, and he closed the file. Rising from the desk, he walked it over to me. "We appreciate anything the Order can do."

Nodding, I took the file and stood, hoping that none of the Order members recognized these young men. If they did, it probably meant they'd met a tragic, unfair ending.

The meeting was officially over. Faye and Tanner were quiet as they led me out of the office and down an empty wide hall. Upon entering the building, I'd been escorted through the front and not the amazing courtyard, and it looked like they were leading me to the front once more.

As we neared the cafeteria area, I began to see more fae. Some lingered outside the wide archway, others walked to and fro, in small groups or alone. Most didn't pay any attention to me. Others looked on in curiosity while some stared with outright distrust as we made our way to the grand, brightly lit lobby that truly reminded me of an upscale hotel.

"Please contact me directly, whether or not you have any information," Faye said as we passed several occupied couches and chairs.

"I will." I reached into the pocket of my purse, searching for my phone. From here, I was going to have to Uber it back to headquarters over on St. Phillip Street. I glanced over at Faye, and could see the worry etched into her face. The concern tugged at my heart. Lord knew I had this same kind of wretched experience of living through the disappearance of someone you loved and not knowing what happened to them. The desperation was the worst, the need to do everything and anything to find them, but not knowing if what you were doing was right or would even help.

Faye was experiencing all of that.

Stopping, I reached over and placed a hand on her arm. The contact surprised her as she swung her head toward me. "I'm sure your cousin is fine."

Faye held my gaze. "I hope so. After losing his father…."

A slight frown pulled at my brow as Faye trailed off. She tilted her head slightly as a hush descended over the lobby and then she turned back to where we came from. Out of the corner of my eyes, I saw Tanner turn back as well.

"You should leave now, Brighton," she whispered.

An acute shiver danced over my shoulders and the tiny hairs along the nape of my neck rose as I stared down at her dark, bowed head. *Don't turn around. Keep walking.* That's what I kept telling myself. I was done here, and Faye was right, I should leave now.

But I turned around, because some primal instinct inside me already knew who had arrived. And some insane, disturbed part of me just had to see him.

The Prince had entered his lobby, dressed very much like he had been Saturday night. Dark pants. Dark thermal. He wasn't looking at Tanner or Faye or any of the other fae.

Pale, ancient eyes fixed on mine. *He didn't recognize you.* That's what I kept telling myself as a wave of goosebumps spread along my flesh.

I took a step back. Wrong move. Oh God, total wrong move.

The Prince's eyes narrowed.

Tanner murmured something in his native language, and the Prince spoke. I didn't understand a single word he said, but his voice was deep and booming and yet quiet somehow.

The fae turned to stare at me, because the Prince… the Prince hadn't taken his eyes off me.

My heart hammered in my chest as I opened my mouth to say what, I had no idea, because the words turned to ash on the tip of my tongue as the Prince strolled across the lobby, heading straight for me.

Chapter 9

My first reaction to seeing him was the realization that there was a good chance I was going to have a massive heart attack. Dead before thirty-one, right here in the grandiose lobby of Hotel Good Fae.

Which, I guessed, was only a little bit better than dying alone at home, suffocated by stacks of dusty books and piles of handwritten maps.

My second, and probably the most troubling of reactions, was that rollercoaster dip in my stomach in response to seeing him, followed by an acute wave of shivers that had nothing to do with who he was.

Goodness, he was just… I couldn't find the right words other than he did some really stupid things to my hormones.

Somehow I managed not to go into cardiac arrest or punch myself as he stalked toward me with the graceful prowl of a predator. I was a hundred percent human with absolutely no special abilities, but I could still feel the leashed power rolling off him, filling every nook and cranny of the lobby. It was base survival instinct, I figured, alerting the human mind that they were in the presence of a predator.

He didn't recognize you. I repeated that all the way up to the moment he stopped in front of me. *He doesn't know it was you he had his hands on—*

"What are you doing here?" he demanded.

Throat dry, I blinked once and then twice. "Excuse me?"

His pupils seemed to constrict in response to my voice. "I asked why you were here, Brighton."

Air caught in my throat at the sound of my name. "You know my name?"

The Prince tilted his head to the side and the look that crossed his face made me think he was questioning my intelligence.

Okay, that was a stupid question. But in my defense, other than Saturday night, when I was confident that he had no idea that was me, I'd only seen him twice before, both times brief. And we'd never been introduced. Ever. And I couldn't even be sure that I had seen him in the hospital. That could've been a hallucination. Or a weird dream. Like the dream I had Saturday night, when I'd been in his lap and he'd been—

Oh my God, my eyes widened as I felt heat blast my face. I was so not going to think about that when I was standing in front of him. Because it was weird. Totally weird and stupid, but I swore I could feel the warmth from his hands on my sides and his lips—

Good God, I really needed to stop thinking.

Those pupils seemed to constrict even further as he dipped his chin. I drew in a sharp breath. He was closer now and his scent.... Goodness, it reminded me of lazy summer afternoons. Being so close to him again was like standing next to a heater.

Tanner cleared his throat. "My liege, Ms. Jussier is here on behalf of the Order. She will be helping us with the missing younglings."

"Is that so?" he replied wryly.

My eyes narrowed. "Yes, that is so. Tanner contacted the Order and I was sent to handle the meeting and now since it's over, I'll be on my way." I turned from the Prince to Faye, who was currently staring at me like I'd lost my mind. "I'll be in touch, Faye."

I didn't make it very far.

Actually, I was only able to turn halfway by the time I felt the Prince's warm fingers curled around my left wrist. Like before, the contact of his skin against mine was a jolt to the system. It was almost like he was charged with electricity, but I didn't think that was possible.

"Do you understand how serious it is that these younglings are missing?" he asked, speaking low enough that I didn't think anyone else could hear him.

"Yes." My gaze skittered over his shoulder. We had an audience, a rather large, curious audience. Unnerved, I tried to pull my hand free and failed. "Of course I know it's important."

"But do you care?" Those odd, striking eyes latched onto mine.

A shiver danced over my shoulders. "Yes, I care." Offended that he would even ask that question, I tugged on my arm again, getting nowhere. "Can you let go of me?"

"Why would you care when the entirety of the Order does not?" He didn't let go.

"How do you know they don't?" I fired back even though he was mostly right.

"The fact that you'd have to ask that question makes me doubt your intelligence," he said. "Then again, I already have good enough reasons to doubt that."

My mouth dropped open. Literally. "Did you just say that to me?"

"I am confident that I spoke in your native language and quite clearly."

Anger flashed through my system. "You don't even know me."

"Oh, I know you." His voice dropped even further, eliciting an unwanted, confusing as hell shiver from me. "I know exactly what and who you are."

My fingers curled into a fist. "I don't even know what you're suggesting."

"You know just as well as I do that the Order doesn't give a damn what may or may not have happened to a few Summer fae." As he spoke, the space between us seemed to have evaporated. "And you stand before me, claiming that you do while you won't even admit that the people you work for couldn't care less."

I opened my mouth and then closed it. Damn, he had a point. A good point, but that didn't mean I was apathetic. "I do care. If I didn't, I wouldn't have taken this file. I wouldn't have told Tanner and Faye that I would see what I could find out. If you actually did know who and what I am, whatever the hell that means, you'd know that I wouldn't lie."

Faye's audible sharp inhale warned me that my voice had risen even though the Prince's hadn't, and at least she could hear me.

I didn't care. Frustration and irritation had long since replaced the healthy sense of fear. "And seriously, dude, can you let go of my arm?"

The Prince ignored my request yet again. "You are nothing but lies and façades."

My entire body jerked at that comment, striking too close to home for comfort. "Let go of me."

He held my gaze as he slowly lifted one finger after another, releasing my wrist. That bitter knot was back in my throat. The Prince had let go and his heavy lashes lowered, shielding his powerful gaze, but I swore I could still feel it. "My apologies," he murmured. "That was uncalled for."

A feather could've knocked me over right then. He was apologizing? The Prince? "Yeah, it was." I swallowed hard, taking a step back from him.

"Even if it is true," he added.

"Wow. Way to ruin an apology," I muttered. "Not that you probably even know why you just apologized."

"I do. It hurt you. Those words."

"What? You can smell that, too?"

Those heavy lashes lifted, and the intensity of his gaze pierced me. Suddenly I thought back to the day I woke up in the hospital, to those eyes. "I can sense many things."

Oh.

Oooh.

I had the distinct impression that he was talking about earlier, when I was thinking about the dream I had. And boy, didn't that make me want to crawl up in a hole somewhere. At that moment, I made a mental note to legit not feel anything when I was around him or any other fae.

One eyebrow, several shades darker than his golden hair, lifted.

"Wait. Can you guys read minds?" I asked, voice hushed and thinking I didn't know nearly as much about the fae as I thought I did.

"We don't need to."

Relief hit me, but it quickly faded when his words cycled back through my head. *We don't need to.* Meaning picking up on our emotions probably gave them enough insight on what our thoughts were.

Nice.

"Well…" I held the folder closer to my chest. "That's freaky."

His lips twitched.

"And I need to go." I started to turn once more, ordering myself not to run out of the lobby like it was on fire. But I stopped, facing him again. "I do care about these younglings. I will find them or I will find out what happened to them."

The Prince inclined his head. A moment passed and then he nodded. Thinking this super awkward face to face was now, thankfully, over, I started to turn away again.

"Brighton?"

Desperately ignoring how the way he said my name made me think of stormy summer nights, I faced him, even though common sense screamed that I shouldn't. I just couldn't help myself. It wasn't a compulsion. It was apparently really bad self-control. My wry gaze flickered over his face, and I bit back a sigh. He was the strongest, the deadliest of his kind, and that knowledge did nothing to dampen my appreciation of his masculine beauty.

"The red hair was a nice touch, but I prefer it this way."

And then with those parting words, he turned and stalked off, leaving me standing there knowing one thing only.

The Prince knew it was me Saturday night.

Chapter 10

Damn.

Damn it.

Damn it all to hell.

Faye followed me out into the thick, overcast skies. "That was weird."

"You think?" Shaken, I pulled out my phone and opened the car service app. Thank Mary Mother of God, Faye hadn't heard what the Prince had said before he walked off. "Yeah, that was super weird."

My heart was still pounding like I'd just done an hour on the treadmill. He knew. Damn it, he knew it had been me. He probably also knew why Tobias had disappeared.

I dragged my teeth along my bottom lip as I checked out what cars were nearby, resisting the urge to rip off the damn sweater. It was much cooler out here, but I still felt too hot.

"Brighton?"

Lifting my chin, I glanced at Faye. She stared at me with some sort of wonder in her eyes. "I don't think you understand how out of character that was for him."

"Oh, trust me, I was on the receiving end of all that weirdness. I understand."

She gave a slight shake of her head. "No, you don't. I've never seen him speak to anyone for that length of time."

"Really?" I choked out a laugh as I glanced over my shoulder at the door that now looked like a rusted-over scrap of metal. The glamour had settled into place. "He spoke to me for about a minute, two tops."

Faye nodded back at me.

"Seriously?" I lowered my phone. "That's not very long. Does he not talk?"

"Not really."

"To anyone?"

"No." She folded her arms as she stepped in closer to me. "Not even his brother. He's… well, you know what he's been through."

And I knew what he, under trance, had put others through. But I kept that to myself.

"He's not very communicative," she said.

He didn't seem like he *peopled* very well, but I also kept that to myself and instead let curiosity get the best of me. "Has he been here this whole time? In the city, since the fight with the Queen?"

"Yes." Her dark brows knitted together. "He actually hasn't left New Orleans at all, not even to travel to the other large community in Florida with his brother."

I thought that was odd, that I hadn't seen him, and none of the Order had ever mentioned seeing him while on patrol. But I had a feeling the Prince knew how to stay unseen until he wanted to be.

I wanted to ask her if she knew why he would've been at Flux looking for a Winter fae, but asking that question would expose that I had been there.

Brushing my ponytail over my shoulder, I returned to the app on the phone. I tapped on the nearest car. "I honestly don't know what to say. It was weird, but it's over. I need to get to the Order. They'll have their afternoon meeting soon and that's the perfect time to see if any of them recognize these guys."

"What was he saying to you?" she asked.

I held onto my phone and the file as I turned to the road, wishing the car would magically appear. "Nothing," I said. "Nothing that's important."

Faye didn't respond to that, and she didn't say anything while she stood out there with me until the car arrived and I climbed in. I doubted that she believed me. When I closed the door and looked out the window, she was already gone.

"St. Phillips Street?" the driver asked, checking my request in the app.

"Yes." My gaze was glued to the rundown brick building as the driver turned around and headed back toward the Canal. "Thank you."

Once I could no longer see the building, I fell back in the seat with a sigh. God, what had just happened? Usually no one paid any attention to me on any given day and the Prince, who apparently didn't speak to anyone, knew it had been me Saturday night and I had a sinking suspicion that he'd somehow known I'd been there and sought me out.

I ran my hand under my throat, wincing as I placed too much pressure on the skin. The Prince knew what I was up to, but he hadn't exposed me in front of Tanner and Faye. Did that mean he wouldn't go to the Order?

And what in the hell did he mean by the claim that he knew who and what I was? Those words haunted the short trip back to headquarters.

Thanking the driver, I climbed out and glanced at the first floor Order-owned shop. Mama Lousy sold all kinds of random stuff, featuring a lot of iron amidst an interesting amount of voodoo tools and authentic *N'awlins* spices. It was currently staffed by one of the grouchiest old men I'd ever met. Jerome had retired from the Order well over a decade ago and somehow ended up in the position that made least sense.

He was so not someone who should be in a customer service position.

Honestly, I was surprised Miles hadn't assigned me to the shop. I snorted and then sighed, because I figured that day was coming sooner rather than later.

One glance through the shop windows, I could see him sitting behind the counter, glaring at the tourists who were picking up various masks and trying them on. He didn't see me, and if he did, it wouldn't have helped with his attitude.

Grinning, I headed for the side entrance and threw open the door. I headed up the narrow, cramped hallway that smelled vaguely of sugar and gym sneakers. A small camera was positioned at the top of the stairs. Things had gotten more high tech in the last two years since the headquarters had been breached by the Prince when he was all 'kill, kill everyone'. A sensor was on the door, above the hand. Pressing my finger on it, I waited as the contraption read my fingerprint. The door unlocked in a jiffy, and as soon as I opened it, I saw that I'd made it back just in time.

The main room was full with at least a half dozen Order members. I immediately saw Jackie Jordan. The dark-skinned woman was sitting on a desk, one long, lean leg curled up as she watched something on her phone. Standing next to her was Dylan, decked out in black tactical pants and a fitted black T-shirt. Besides Miles and Ivy and Ren, they were the only original Order members left. The rest were gone, having perished in the battle or afterward, when the Winter fae unleashed their anger at being foiled. Those members were now replaced by various members from other cities or brand spanking new ones.

An unwanted but familiar heaviness settled in my chest. There had been so much loss and there were echoes of it everywhere. In Jackie and Dylan's weary eyes and in all the new faces crowding the main room.

What had happened to my mother and me hadn't been isolated. Dying in battle was a far better death than being hunted down, caught off guard and unprepared, slaughtered before you even knew what was happening.

I glanced down at the file. Were any of them really going to care about these missing younglings when so many of them had lost friends and family while fighting the fae? Would it matter to them that the Summer Court had come through for us and had fought side by side with us?

I had a terrible feeling I already knew the answer to my questions.

Holding the file close to my chest, I ducked my chin. Skirting around the group that was waiting on Miles, I passed several closed doors and then the surveillance room, where I could always find our leader. And there he was, standing before several rows of monitors hooked up to various cameras all across the city in the dimly lit room. He wasn't alone.

Rick Ortiz sat in one of the chairs, his finger clicking away on the mouse, changing the images on the top row of monitors. As I entered the room, he glanced over his shoulder and lifted a dark eyebrow. That was about the only reaction I got from the olive-skinned man that had transferred to NOLA from Houston. He returned to clicking through the video feed.

Drawing in a short, irritated breath, I started to speak.

"How'd the meeting go?" Miles asked.

Did the man have eyes in the back of his head, hidden by the brown hair cropped close to his skull? "It went okay, but rather unexpected."

"How so?"

Stepping forward, I cleared my throat. "Several of the younglings have gone missing. They're worried that they may have met an… untimely demise at the hands of the Order."

Rick snorted. "Untimely demise?"

"Well, yes." I shifted my weight from one foot to the other. "Untimely because the Summer fae—"

"Are not to be killed, I know." Rick sat back in his chair and spun it around, facing me. The man was handsome, with dark hair and a neat, trimmed beard, but I also liked to refer to him as Rick the Dick, because his handsomeness was outweighed by his douchieness. "But I just find it funny that they call it untimely."

Having no idea why that was funny and deciding I was not going down that rabbit hole with Rick the Dick, I shifted my attention to Miles, who still wasn't looking at me. He was focused on a camera that was across from the haunted LaLaurie House. The feed wasn't set up for that home. Nope. It was for the rather plain, squat two-story home next to it, the location of one of the doorways to the Otherworld. Why was he watching that so intently? Was there activity there? My stomach dropped all the way to my toes.

The Queen could come back. She had the means—a crystal that powered the doorways from the Otherworld. I started to ask, but I didn't get a chance.

Rick the Dick apparently wasn't done. "You know what else I find funny? That they think we care that some of their spawn are missing."

Miles sighed so heavily it could've rattled the monitors.

Taking a deep breath, I counted to ten. "They want to see if perhaps any of the Order members recognize them and to keep an eye out."

"You got photographs of them?" Miles asked.

"Of course—"

"Hang them up on the bulletin board, so everyone can see."

I started to frown. "I was planning to do that, but I thought I could check with them before the meeting gets started—"

"That won't be necessary." Miles faced me then. The man was in his late thirties, possibly early forties, and he'd seen a lot of messed-up stuff, especially after David's betrayal. He was the hardest man to read, and I couldn't remember ever seeing him smile. Not even once. "Hanging up the photographs should be enough."

That wasn't enough. I knew damn well no one ever looked at the bulletin board. There was still a picture of kittens Jackie had been trying to adopt out over a year ago. "Talking with them would only take a minute or so. One of these missing younglings is Faye's cousin," I added, thinking that would get him to agree, since Faye had helped the Order a million times over.

Miles strode over to where I stood and took the file out of my hands. He opened it and thumbed through the photos. "None of them look familiar." He turned to Rick. "What do you think?"

Glancing over them, Rick lifted a shoulder. "Not to me, but they all kind of look the same."

"Really?" I tensed. "Did you really just say that?"

He smirked. "It's the truth."

"No, it's not, and that sounds really—"

"Don't say racist," Rick cut me off. "The fae are not human. They are not people."

"Wow." I started toward where he sat and stopped myself. "They are kind of a race of beings, so the term racist would apply."

"That's not how that works," he replied, grinning that irritating shit-eating grin up at me.

Miles spoke before I could. "Hang up their photographs, Brighton. I'll tell those on patrol to keep an eye out for them." Closing the file, he handed it back to me. "But I'm telling you now, if one of them did come across one of those younglings and it ended badly, ain't none of them going to come forward with that info."

I figured that much, but hearing Miles say it like it was no big deal sent a wave of disappointment through me. "They should. They're not supposed to harm them. If you think they have, shouldn't there be consequences?"

Rick laughed—straight-up laughed.

"What?" I demanded, feeling my cheeks start to warm.

"You don't patrol, honey. You sit behind a desk and you read books and study maps, sometimes you help out in the infirmary and you handle shit that we don't need to know about. If you did patrol, then you'd know that shit happens out on the street and one second of hesitation can get yourself killed. We're not going to punish someone for doing their job."

Heat blasted my face, and I came so close knocking him out of the chair and explaining to him that I knew exactly what happened when you hesitated, but I managed to restrain myself. "First off, don't call me honey, and more importantly, don't sit there and talk to me about how dangerous these streets are. I know better than you do."

He opened his mouth, but I wasn't done. "We're not supposed to harm the Summer fae. End of story. That's not our job and the new protocols—"

Rick scoffed as he lifted his hands. "Fuck the new protocols."

"Do you hear him?" Exasperated, I turned to Miles. "I mean, you're standing right there."

"Thank you both for stating the obvious and speaking as if you are the leader around here," Miles replied dryly. "Hang the pictures, Brighton. And you?" He turned to Rick. "Shut the hell up, Rick, and get out there."

And with that, Miles stalked out of the office, whistling loudly to gain the attention of everyone who waited in the main hall.

I was dismissed without really even being dismissed. How freaking messed-up was that? Not that I should be surprised. Again, to Miles and to everyone here I wasn't *essential.*

Rick rose, brushing my shoulder as he walked past me. He stopped at the doorway and waited until I faced him. "What?"

He studied me a moment. "I don't get it."

"Get what?"

"Why you'd even care about those fucking fae, after what they did to your mother—did to you?"

Nausea twisted up my insides, but I pushed past it. "The Winter fae attacked my mother and me. Not the Summer fae. Not these boys."

"Does that really matter? What court they claim to belong to? Does that make a difference?" he challenged.

"Yes. It does." It *had* to.

Something akin to pity crossed his face. "Whatever. You do realize that hanging their photographs up is pretty pointless, right?"

"Why?" I lowered the file. "Because no one is going to care?"

"Well, yeah, that. But it's pointless because if they're legit missing and one of us does recognize them, they're probably no longer in this realm. They're dead for all intents and purposes."

Chapter 11

I'd copied the photographs and tacked them onto the bulletin board, over Jackie's year-old kittens' poster, even though Rick didn't think it would make a difference. I'd also managed to corner Jackie before she headed out for patrol. She hadn't recognized any of the younglings, and I believed her. Jackie might be old school and not exactly a fan of any fae, but she wasn't a liar.

When I got home, I'd made Tink and me pan-fried hamburgers for dinner, cleaned up and then went upstairs to change.

There was another spot in the city the fae frequented called, ironically, The Court on Canal. It was a little more laid back on the first level, featuring a bar that was surprisingly busy for fae on a Monday night. The second floor was not laid back. It was... well, I had seen some *things* up there. Things boric acid couldn't erase from my eyes or my brain.

The place was near the Quarter, a little hole in the wall that tourists and many of the locals overlooked. I'd spotted one of my targets there once before, but I'd lost sight of him once he left.

The Court on Canal couldn't be discovered on a Google search or on any must-see lists for when someone visited New Orleans.

The place was where nothing should be.

I'd found it on one of my mother's maps and one day I'd checked out the location and discovered that it was very much a real place—a place that not even the Order seemed to be aware of.

Once I was done finding the fae who'd attacked that night, I'd hand over the maps to Miles. I would tell him about The Court... and the other places. Just not yet.

I was hoping tonight would be as fruitful and not as eventful as Saturday night. I wasn't worried that I'd run into the Prince again, even though he so obviously knew it had been me Saturday night. I'd been to The Court numerous times and hadn't spotted him once.

Plus I was planning to keep an eye out for the missing younglings during my travels. I knew it was unlikely, at least I hoped, that I'd see one of them at The Court.

After a quick shower, I pinned my hair flat and got down to becoming someone else. Walking into the closet, I knew the perfect dress for tonight.

Black. Short. Simple.

Plucking it off the hanger, I wiggled into it, relieved to see that the material was some kind of stretchy knit as I tugged the hem down. It ended mid-thigh. I turned to the floor-length mirror and did the bend-over test.

Breasts pushed against the plummeting neckline, coming *this* close to falling out, and the cheeks of my butt peeked out under the stretchy material.

I straightened, smoothing my hands down the sides of the dress. Okay. Definitely not bending over in this in public.

Rolling my eyes, I grabbed my makeup case and went into the bathroom. The makeup took awhile, because I had to take my time to get it right, but when I was done, my face was virtually unrecognizable. Cheeks contoured until they were sharp and high. Lips outlined to be plumper and filled in with a color that was only a shade or two darker than my natural lips. I even filled in my eyebrows before tackling the eyes. I gave myself what I thought was a dark and smoky, mysterious look. Since I was leaving the contacts out, I put on some false eyelashes, and decided that if I didn't end up with a sty at some point during this, I was a mutant.

Back in the closet, I browsed the selection of wigs as I nibbled on my fingernail. Blonde. Red. Brown. Black. Purple. The vibrant wigs would draw too much attention at a place like The Court, so I picked the short, chin-length black wig and slipped it on, securing it in place and then combing it down so it was smooth and sleek.

The boots were… difficult. Made of some kind of stretchy material that covered the calves and knees with no zipper, I almost winged them across the bedroom trying to get them on. Sweat dotted my forehead by the time I was completely dressed.

And I was panting, a little out of breath as I slipped the iron cuff on my wrist.

Done, I turned to the mirror and grinned at my reflection. "I look like Aeon Flux," I said, cocking my head to the side. "A much sluttier version of Aeon Flux. Perfect."

* * * *

The Court on Canal looked like a, well, like a dump from the outside. The kind of place you'd expect to get a little food poisoning with your crawfish if you were brave enough to actually eat whatever they served, but the inside was all upscale.

Bar and booths made from wood refurbished from Katrina. Thick, leather-cushioned stools. Shiny, always clean high top round tables, and I'd never so much as seen a stray napkin in any of the private booths that sat back from the tables, lining the walls.

I carried only a black clutch as I strolled to the bar, wholly aware of the glances that lingered and followed while pretending that I wasn't.

It was weird to me. The knowledge that dressed like *this*, looking like *this,* I wasn't invisible. I was no longer a ghost, but I was….

What had the Prince said to me?

You are nothing but lies and façades.

Ugh.

He was right, and I really, seriously disliked him for that.

I wasn't this incarnation of myself. I could feel the warmth of embarrassment creeping up my throat in a prickly flush as I heard a low whistle from a man who was at one of the tables.

But I also wasn't the Brighton before the attack. She was gone, dying the night I should've died. Because while I was embarrassed by the attention, there was still a half grin that appeared on my lips.

Maybe the Prince was wrong.

Maybe I wasn't completely a façade.

I had no idea.

Climbing onto the stool as ladylike as humanly possible, I crossed one leg over the other and placed my clutch on the bar top.

A human bartender was behind the bar, but so was a fae. I wasn't quite sure if the female actually worked here, but she was the one I always saw when I came here, ferrying Nightshade back and forth to the non-human clientele.

Right now, she was carrying an entire tray of glasses to one of the booths along the wall. My gaze skipped away. There were a handful of fae among the humans chatting and drinking. None of them recognizable.

And definitely none of the younglings.

So far.

"What can I get you?"

I turned back to the bartender and smiled. He was young and his gaze was clear. Focused. Obviously not under any trance or control, but he had to know that not everyone who was served here was human. There was no way he couldn't, what with the Nightshade being served and what went on up on the second floor.

"A rum and Coke," I said.

"Coming right up." He picked up a glass and got to making the quick, easy drink. "Tab or pay now?"

"Cash." I opened my clutch and slid the money over to him. "Thank you."

The man smiled and then he was off, serving someone at the other end of the bar. Sipping my drink, I twisted around on the stool so I was facing the main bar floor, but was able to keep an eye on the back hallway, where the elevator serviced the second level. I pulled out my phone and pretended to be engrossed in it as I scanned the floor.

Within a few moments, two more fae entered the bar, their glamouring fading away to reveal their silvery, luminous skin. They made a beeline for the back hallway.

The second floor was a… different kind of service area, one that didn't just cater to fae looking for their dinner, but also sex.

Lots of sex.

Only once had I gone up to the second floor, and that had been pure luck, sneaking in behind a group of humans who were being led by two fae. Once was enough.

The humans I'd tagged along with had not been entranced. Based on their giggling and whispered dares to one another, they knew at least one of the things that went on upstairs.

"Excuse me."

Looking over my shoulder, I spied a man—a human man. He was older, maybe in his fifties? Tall with dark hair graying at the temples. Handsome, too, dressed in a very nice dark suit. A silver fox was what Ivy would've called him.

Pretty sure Tink would call him Daddy.

I immediately wanted to punch myself in the face after the image that conjured forth.

The man smiled, and wow he was handsome, and if I was anyone else, I would be extremely pleased with the attention. However, I wasn't here to meet silver foxes.

"I'm waiting for someone," I said apologetically.

Dipping his chin, he chuckled. "He said you might say something like that."

My brows lifted in surprise. "He?"

"I am not here to buy you a drink or to make an advance," he explained.

Oh.

Oh.

Well, this was awkward, and I sort of wanted to fling myself off the stool. "Sorry?"

He smiled tightly as his gaze drifted over my shoulder, to the bartender. He nodded. "My name is Everest. I am the owner of The Court and I'm here to escort you out."

Dumbfounded, all I could do was stare for a moment. "Excuse me?"

Everest moved closer, his brown eyes not nearly as warm as his smile. "You, my dear, are not welcome here."

A chill swept down my spine as I stared back at him. Only one possibility circled through my thoughts. Somehow, he knew I was a member of the Order and he facilitated what occurred here.

I played it cool, though, lifting my drink and taking a sip. "May I ask why?"

He didn't answer. Just smiled at me blandly. Out of the corner of my eyes, I saw a large man shift in our direction. Another human wearing another nice, expensive suit was moving our way. A bouncer.

And then it hit me. Everest had said…. My hand tightened on the damp glass as I leaned toward the owner. "He's here, isn't he?"

Everest continued to smile.

"The Prince," I said, and I said this loud enough to cause the woman at the table near us to turn and look.

The smile slipped from Everest's face and that was enough confirmation for me.

Son of a bitch.

I couldn't believe it. He'd been at Flux and now he was here? And not only was he here, but he was in a position to order the owner of this establishment to kick me out? An establishment, by the way, that was yet again frequented by the Winter fae?

At least I had a good reason to be here— a slightly psychotic reason but a reason, and the Prince was not going to get in my way.

Oh, hell to the no.

Anger flared to life like a solar storm. He was not going to interfere with me finding justice. No way in hell. "You can tell his royal Dickness that this is a public establishment and he does not get to dictate where I go and what I do."

The man's eyes widened slightly. "However, as the owner, I do get to dictate who stays here and who goes."

"True," I said, taking another long, healthy sip of my drink. I was raised to be a fine, upstanding Southern lady, but I was pissed. "Did he tell you what I am?"

Everest lifted a hand, stopping the bouncer from coming any closer.

"I don't know if he did, but I assure you that I can cause a lot of trouble for your *fine* establishment, and I mean a lot." I smiled now, all sugary sweet. "So unless you want that to happen, you can tell the Prince to go fuck himself."

Everest tilted his head slightly and a long heartbeat passed. Then he said, "You can tell him that yourself."

Chapter 12

The tiny hairs along the nape of my neck rose. I drew in a shallow breath as Everest stepped back, clasping his hands. Slowly, I lowered my drink and looked over my shoulder.

Standing not even a foot behind me was the Prince.

I couldn't help but notice immediately that he appeared different tonight. Hair pulled back from his face was a good look on him. A black silk shirt had replaced the thermal I'd seen him in, and that also was a good look.

But he was just about as angry as the last two times I'd seen him, so that hadn't changed.

Actually, he seemed angrier. "I can assure you, I have no attention of fucking myself tonight, *Sally*."

Steam practically shot from my ears at way he said my name—my fake name. "Good to know, but not my problem."

"Oh, but it is now your problem."

I drew back, eyes widening. "I have no idea how *that* is my problem."

Lifting blue eyes to Everest, he nodded. I didn't need to look to know the man had left.

Before I could say a word, he plucked the drink out of my hand and placed it on the bar. Then his hand wrapped around my empty one. I didn't dig my heels in like I wanted to, knowing that we already had several eyes on us.

My gaze dropped to where he held my hand as he guided me off the stool.

"You are becoming a pain in my ass," he said.

"I'm about to become a much bigger one. One you're going to need to see a doctor to treat. You try to make me leave," I said, lifting my gaze from his hand to his eyes, "I will make a scene in here so bad you'll spend the next year glamouring memories."

A muscle flexed along his jaw as his gaze searched my face. "You would, wouldn't you?"

"Yes. Now, if you'd unhand me, I think I might want another drink." In reality, my stakeout of The Court was ruined, but I would stay here half the night on principle alone. "And maybe some chicken wings." I had no idea if they served chicken wings here. "Then dessert. I'm definitely in the mood for dessert and none of those things include you."

The Prince threaded his fingers through mine, stopping me from yanking my arm free. "We need to have a chat."

"No, we don't."

"Oh, sunshine, we do."

Sunshine? My face puckered up. "There is nothing we need to talk about—" I gasped as he moved in so quick, so close, right there at the bar, in front of fae and human alike. Still holding my hand, he cupped my cheek with his other, splaying his fingers as he tilted my head back and lowered his.

Was he going… was he going to kiss me? That seemed like a bizarre response, but he lined his mouth right up with mine, and there were only inches between our lips. My heart rate shot into cardiac territory. "What are you doing?"

His warm breath danced over my lips as he spoke. "You should have left when you had a chance. Now, you and I are going to have a discussion that is way past due, and you're going to say yes and you're going to *behave*."

"Behave?" I sputtered.

He nodded as those thick lashes came down, shielding his eyes. "Don't test me."

My heart skipped a beat. "Is that a threat?"

"It's an advisory," he corrected.

"Same thing. Like totally the same thing."

His lips twitched as if he wanted to smile. "If you want a scene, I'll give you one. I'll throw you right over my shoulder, and with that dress?" Leaning back, I felt his gaze like a hot caress. "I don't think you'll want that."

I didn't.

I so didn't.

Seeming to sense that, he pulled me against the side of his body. The contact was jarring. Not because he did it roughly, because he didn't, but because feeling his body against mine stunned me.

Letting go of my hand, he then draped an arm over my shoulders like we were friends or even lovers as he steered me away from the bar. People were staring, human and fae alike, but the fae had more than just a reaction born of curiosity. As we walked near them, they backed away, giving us—giving the Prince—a wide berth. There was no mistaking the distrust and fear that pinched their striking features. They knew who the Prince was.

So, what was he doing here?

I held onto my clutch as we walked down the narrow hall, passing the restrooms and then the elevator. He walked me to a swinging door marked EMPLOYEES ONLY. With his free hand, he pushed open the door and we entered a small kitchen, staffed by cooks—human cooks. They only lifted their brows as he led me past them, narrowly dodging a waiter carrying a tray stacked with chicken wings.

So, they did have wings… and they looked yummy too.

My stomach grumbled, loud enough for the Prince to dip his head and look at me questioningly.

"Hungry?"

"No," I lied.

One side of his lips kicked up as we reached another door. That one opened to reveal another hallway and a narrow set of stairs.

"Should I be worried about where you're leading me?"

"You should always be worried." He dropped his arm. "Up the stairs."

"That's not reassuring," I told him, eyeing the dark staircase. "I'm getting stranger danger vibes right now."

"Is that all the vibes you're getting?" he asked.

I wrinkled my nose. "I don't know what you mean and I don't want to."

He smirked. "Up the stairs, Brighton."

The use of my real name startled me, even though we were alone. My gaze traveled from him to the staircase as I exhaled slowly. As crazy as it was, instinct told me that I was safe with the Prince. My instinct could be completely off base, but I also knew that if I made a run for it, I wasn't going to make it.

So I started up the stairs.

He said nothing as he walked behind me. We reached the next floor and entered a dark hallway where I could hear the steady thump of music coming from what sounded like the other side of the staircase.

The hall also smelled like… fresh beignets. Part of me wanted to question that, but then the Prince brushed past me, the warmth of his body causing me to bite down on my lip. As he opened a door, I peeked around him. The room was circular, featuring a long, cushioned bench against the wall and a set dining table in the middle. There was a short rack glass on the table. Bright purple liquid filled half the glass. Nightshade.

"What kind of room is this?" I asked, folding my arms across my midsection.

"A private dining or party area. There are five of them on this floor. Nice hair, by the way." He stalked past me.

"Shut up," I muttered.

Smirking, he picked up his glass of Nightshade. "Still prefer the blond."

"I still don't care." I watched him walk to the wide cushioned bench against the wall and sit. "What are you doing here?"

"I could ask you the same thing, but I already know."

I ignored that. "This place is frequented by Winter fae and you're the Summer Prince. I don't understand how you can be here, hanging out and drinking with them."

He eyed me as he sipped from his drink. "I help Everest out here. Make sure none of the fae get out of hand."

Interesting. "And the Winter fae have no problem with you being here?"

"They usually don't see me until it's too late. Tonight is different because someone decided to refuse to leave."

"Perhaps you should've just left me be," I shot back as I started to pace. "So, what is this place, really? A front for fae to hang out and feed?"

"Everest is a… unique businessman who caters to all." He lowered the glass to his knee. "And he does so with the utmost discretion while providing a… safe place for both species."

"Safe place?"

"The fae can come here and see to their needs without harming humans in the process."

My lips parted. "I've seen what goes on up here."

He tilted his head. "And how, pray tell, did you find yourself on this floor? Didn't know the… activities up here were your kind of thing."

"They're not," I snapped, flushing. I turned from him, pacing away.

"I got up here once, very carefully."

The Prince didn't respond to that immediately. "And when you got up that one time, did the humans look like they were here against their will?"

"Oh, so they're volunteers?" I faced him. "Want me to go grab you one of them?"

"I already had Everest do that for me."

My eyes narrowed on his faint smile.

"Sometimes, when Everest is expecting a certain… clientele, he will reach out to me to make sure there are additional resources here just in case."

I mulled that over. "How do the humans here keep this a secret if they aren't glamoured?"

"Who would believe them?"

"They could obtain evidence."

"They don't," he said, and then he took another drink. "You know, you won't be allowed back here now."

I smirked at that as I started pacing in front of him. "I'm not worried. I can get back in here if I want to."

"He'll be looking out for you."

"He won't recognize me."

"But I always will."

I shivered, unnerved by that. "Do you live here? Are you always here?"

The Prince didn't answer that.

"What do you think will happen if the Order ever discovers this place exists? They're not going to allow it to continue to operate."

"Who says those who need to know don't already?"

I stopped and stared at him. "Are you suggesting that Miles is aware of this place and hasn't shut it down?"

"I'm not suggesting anything. You filled in the blanks."

I snapped my mouth shut. My first reaction was not to believe him, but the Order had… It had lied about a lot of things and kept a lot of secrets. I knew that. So certain members knowing about this venue could be true.

"I knew it was you Saturday night, from the moment I saw you in that room."

"That much I figured," I said, but my stomach still dropped. "Why didn't you call me out, if you knew it was me?"

He was quiet for a moment. "I wanted to see how far you would let it go."

Heat blasted my cheeks. "Not very far."

The Prince lifted a brow. "My hand was right above your—"

"I know where your hand was," I snapped, cutting him off as that heat in my face hit my veins. "Trust me. It's something I won't forget."

"No doubt," he murmured, his lips curling into a faint smile.

My eyes narrowed. "As in not in a good way."

"I'm curious," he replied, watching me through hooded eyes. "If it wasn't in a good way, why did you allow it?"

I inhaled sharply. "I was pretending to be entranced."

"Hmm."

"I was!"

"If that's what you need to tell yourself."

I caught his meaning and I was this close to throwing my clutch at him. The dude was insufferable and mainly because he was so freaking right, and I sort of hated him for that. "I have no idea how you knew that was me."

"I… I just knew," he said like that was an acceptable answer.

Irritation flared to life and I decided right then and there I could also ask demanding, annoying questions as I dropped my clutch on the table. "So why were you at Flux? A club frequented by your enemy?"

He was dragging his thumb along the rim of his glass. "I was there looking for Tobias, but you already know that."

"Why were you looking for him?"

"Do you always ask so many questions?"

"You wanted to have this chat," I reminded him, crossing my arms again. "Why were you looking for him?"

"He knows how to find someone I need to speak with." His gaze dipped and there was a flash of straight, white teeth as he dragged them along his lower lip. I looked away as he said, "Alas, whatever information he had, he took that back to the Otherworld with him."

"Can't say I'm too torn about that."

"Of course not," he replied wryly.

"What information do you think he had?" I asked.

"He knows where a certain Ancient is that I would really love to murder."

My brows lifted at that. "Let me guess, an Ancient that sided with the Queen?"

The Prince nodded.

"Do you happen to know his name?"

A heartbeat passed. "Aric."

That name rang a bell. "Tobias did mention someone by the name of Aric."

Everything about The Prince became very still, so much so he could've stopped breathing. "Did he now?"

"Yes. Aric was coming to meet Tobias and the other fae. He would've been there within an hour."

"Are you serious?"

I nodded. "That was all they said about him."

The Prince cursed under his breath. "Perfect." Lifting the glass, he downed the rest of the Nightshade in one impressive swallow. "I know why you were at Flux and why you were here tonight. I know what Tobias did to you."

A ripple of shock rolled through me as I stared at him. "You don't know—"

"I know he was one of the five fae who attacked you and your mother." Leaning forward, he placed his empty glass on the table. He didn't settle back, and instead, placed his hands on his knees as he stared up at me. "I know that you're seeking revenge because of what they did. I know you're here tonight to see if you can find one of the other fae and I know you put yourself in ridiculously dangerous situations to get that revenge."

Arms falling to my sides, I took a step toward him and then stopped as my stomach twisted nauseously. "How do you…?" My throat thickened. "How do you know?"

He didn't answer for a long moment. "Because you are doing the same thing I am, but for different reasons."

I drew in a stuttering breath as a tremor rolled through my arms.

"I know what it's like to be consumed with revenge and the need to seek justice against those who have done you wrong so terribly. I understand that. It is why I am searching for Aric. He was once a trusted friend of mine, and I know he is the one who set me up to fall to the Queen's spell," he explained, and I felt pressure clamp down on my chest. "I know he's still alive and he's here. I will find him and I will kill him for what he has done to me. And if I ever get my hands on the Queen, I will rip her limb from limb."

That might sound shocking, but I couldn't fault him for wanting that. Not with what she had done to him—made him do.

"Well," I said hoarsely, hating the feel of the bitter knot creeping into my throat, "I guess we have that in common."

"I know what it is like to lie awake all night, consumed with what you could've done to change what happened and how you could've stopped it."

"How could you have stopped it though?" I asked, my question genuine. "You were injured in a battle, right? Weakened?"

"Not only do I believe he is spending every moment trying to aid the Queen's return, it was Aric who shoved a sword right through my chest."

My eyes widened. Swords? Man, the Otherworld always sounded archaic but swords? I shook my head. "The Queen placed you under an enchantment. You didn't have a choice."

"I know everything I did while under her spell. Every person I hurt or killed. Every horrific act I committed." Thick lashes lowered, shielding his gaze as my heart turned over in my chest. "I remember in vivid detail what I put Ivy through."

Pressing my lips together, I blinked back unexpected wetness. I couldn't imagine what he was going through. In a way, I knew it was worse than what happened to me and my mother. He'd been the bad guy. He'd done terrible things and now he lived with the guilt even though it hadn't been his fault.

So I told him that. "It wasn't your fault."

"Tell me," he said. "When you look at me, tell me you don't think about how I kidnapped Ivy? Tell me you don't think about all those Order members I killed with my own hands. Tell me—"

"I do," I admitted, flinching. "I do think of those things, but I also realize it wasn't your fault. You had no control. You didn't have a choice," I repeated, meaning it.

"And you were outnumbered by creatures a hundred times stronger and faster than you," he said, meeting my gaze. "What could you have done differently?"

"If I had been better trained, I could've fought back," I said without a second of hesitation.

He stared at me for a long moment. "Even better trained, you most likely would've died, sunshine. You have a soul of a warrior, but that is not enough."

A soul of a warrior?

That was… that was kind of a nice thing to say.

"You need to stop this, Brighton."

Biting down on the inside of my lip, I looked away as I shook my head. "Are you going to stop looking for Aric? Are you going to move and take the higher road and not seek revenge?"

"I'm different."

I rolled my eyes. "Why? Because you're the Prince?"

The faint smile didn't reach his eyes. "Yes."

Irritated that he understood why I needed to do what I had to, but was trying to stop me, I threw up my hands. "You can't stop me."

He arched a brow at that as he sat back. "I can stop you."

Caring and sharing time was so over. "You know what? I don't even get why you care. We barely know each other. You're the Prince, and I'm just… I'm just me. I'm a—" I almost blurted out ghost, but stopped myself.

"You're what?" Curiosity crept into his features.

I shook my head. "It doesn't matter. I appreciate your concern. I do. It's unexpected, but I appreciate it. It's not going to change—"

"You're what?" he repeated.

Pressing my lips together, I shook my head in frustration.

"What were you about to say?" he persisted.

"I'm just a ghost," I blurted out, surprised that I allowed the words to take flight, because once spoken, you couldn't take it back. "That's who I was before the attack and…"

He was watching me intently. "And you're not a ghost anymore?"

"I don't know what I am anymore," I admitted, blinking back the stupid burn of tears again. "And I don't even know why I'm telling you this. I don't even like you."

"You don't even know me."

"You know? You're right. And no matter what you say, you don't know me either." I started for the door. "I'm done with this conversation. I'm done with your interference. You do whatever you want to do and I'll do whatever I need to do. Goodbye, Prince."

"You're right." A muscle flexed a long his jaw. "You're just a human," he said, and the way he said that made the word human sound like a venereal disease. "In your own words, you're already half dead. I won't stop you from finishing that job."

Chapter 13

The Prince's parting words stung more than they should have as I stared at him. There was a part of me, a stupid, tiny part of me that was hurt by those words. The rational part of me knew that was stupid because I'd called myself a ghost.

But to hear him say it?

Brighton from two years ago would've never found herself in this situation in the first place, but if she did, she would've definitely run from the room to lick her wounds no matter how stupid those wounds were.

But I wasn't her.

And I might not know what the hell I was anymore, but in that moment, I wasn't a ghost. Not anymore.

I met his gaze and then smiled as I slowly lifted my hand and flipped him off.

His nostrils flared.

With that, I pivoted around and stalked out of the weird room with my head high. The moment I yanked open the stupid door, my mind immediately went berserko on me, replaying every word we exchanged.

My head was a freaking mess as I slammed the door shut behind me, mainly because I'd never shared with anyone else what I shared with him. I had no explanation for why, none that made sense at least. I couldn't even believe that I'd spoken those words to him. Embarrassment rose as I stalked down the dark hallway, toward where I remembered the stairway was, hearing the thump of music once again. As I opened the door, I briefly fantasized about racing back into that room and spin kicking him in the face.

That fantasy was probably why I didn't realize the stairwell wasn't empty until it was too late.

A shadow peeled off the wall and came at me fast and hard. I didn't even get the chance to engage the cuff and release the stake. My right arm was twisted behind my back as an icy hand curled around my neck.

A burst of panic punched through my chest as I was flipped around and my front pushed against the wall. The side of my face slammed into the cool brick. Stinging pain exploded from my nose and I tasted blood in the back of my throat.

"I recognized you," the voice said, and I couldn't place it. "You were in the club Saturday night. You went into the room with Tobias. Your hair was red then. Different eye color, too."

Hell.

Shock that my disguise had been seen through gave way to finely honed instinct. Going limp, my sudden weight caught the fae off guard. He stumbled back a step, giving me the room I needed. Bringing my legs up, I planted them in the wall and used it as a springboard. The fae slammed into the wall behind him, the impact jarring his hold loose enough for me to break it.

I fell forward, my knees cracking off the cement. Knowing I only had seconds, I shifted my weight to my palms as I looked over my shoulder, kicking my leg out. My booted heel connected with the fae's midsection, sending him back again to the wall with a grunt.

Popping to my feet, I engaged the cuff bracelet as I whirled around.

The door to the hallway suddenly swung open, blocking my view of the fae and then the door wasn't blocking my view.

It was the Prince.

He seemed to know what was happening, because he went straight for the fae. He was so fast that literally only seconds had passed between him stepping into the cramped stairwell and placing his hands on either side of the fae's neck, snapping it.

The fae slumped to the floor, twitching, and then tumbled down the narrow flight of steps, coming to stop in a twitchy heap on the landing.

My mouth was hanging open as the Prince casually pulled his phone out of his pocket, hit a few buttons and then said, "Everest, I have some trash that needs to be taken out. Back staircase."

Then, slowly, he turned toward me. "You're bleeding."

I touched my nose. It was sore, but nothing major. "I'm fine."

"You've had worse."

I had and I didn't need to confirm that. "How did you know what was happening?"

A moment passed. "Luck."

My eyes narrowed, and for some reason, I didn't believe him. He knew something was happening in this stairwell; how was left to be determined.

His head cocked to the side. "Why did he attack you?"

Glancing down at the spasming fae, I winced. "He recognized me from Flux. I don't know how, but I think he might've been with Tobias."

"I killed all those fae."

"He may have left before you got there." I lifted a shoulder. "You know I can take care of him."

"Everest will handle it."

I thought that was unnecessary, but whatever. I disengaged the iron cuff as I dragged my gaze from the fae, more annoyed than anything else. I hated to admit it to myself, but if that fae had seen through my disguises, there was a good chance that another fae could.

Wiping the blood off my nose with the back of my hand, I then bent and picked up my dropped clutch.

"A soul of a warrior," he murmured, repeating what he'd said earlier.

I didn't know how to respond to that as I looked at him, discovering that he was staring at me intently once more.

"But like I said before, it's not enough."

That I knew how to respond to. "I was doing just fine before you showed up, just so you know."

A tight smile formed, one I imagined a parent gave a child when they came in dead last during a race. "You hungry?"

I blinked. "What?"

"Are you hungry?" he repeated, angling his large body toward mine. "For food." Amusement was clear in his tone.

"I didn't need the second part clarified. Thanks," I muttered.

"I know this place down the street that has the most amazing crab cakes. Would you like to join me?" he asked, and in the dim light of the stairwell, those pale eyes were piercing.

I should say no.

I definitely should say no for a multitude reasons.

"Okay," I said instead, because I was an idiot and honestly, the offer knocked me off guard. "I guess."

One side of his lips kicked up. "Good, but I just have one request."

"You invited me to grab something to eat, but you have one

request?"

"I do," he said. "I want you."

My eyes widened as the heat from earlier returned in full force, and goodness, that was annoying… and a little frightening. "Excuse me?"

"I want you to be yourself. I don't want *this*." He gestured in the general direction of my head. "I want you to be… *you*."

* * * *

I'd used a restroom on the second floor to change… back into myself. Of course, I wasn't able to get rid of the makeup. That required near industrial strength makeup remover, but I took off the wig and unpinned my hair, shaking it out. That was the best I could do, and I wasn't even sure why I'd done it.

Maybe it was because no one… no one ever seemed interested in me before, the real me, that the request stunned me into complying. That was the best reasoning I could come up with as I found myself sitting across from the Prince in a brightly lit Creole House, toying with the paper wrapper from my straw as the amazing scent of spicy seafood had my stomach rumbling.

We were… we were getting a lot of looks. Strange ones. Long ones with raised eyebrows. I figured it was partly because the Prince was so big and so freaking nice to look at, that people were probably wondering if he was a celebrity they couldn't place. I also figured that some of the looks were due to the fact I looked like a hooker.

I like to think I at least looked like an expensive hooker.

"You're nervous," the Prince commented after we placed an order for crab cakes and, per the Prince's request, a crawfish platter.

I glanced up at him. Was I nervous? Uh, yes. I was currently sitting across from the Prince in a restaurant looking halfway like my normal self, and I really had no idea how I'd ended up here. "Do you smell it?"

A faint smile appeared. "Don't need to. You're building a compost pile over there."

Frowning, I glanced down and saw that I did have a significant pile of torn paper in front of me. I dropped my hands to my lap and drew in a shallow breath as I lifted my gaze. "I don't… I don't think this is a good idea."

His stare was unwavering. "It's probably not."

My heart skipped at the agreement. I don't know what I was expecting him to say, but I wasn't thinking he was going to agree. "You asked me to join you."

"I did."

I stared at him. "So why did you ask me to join you if you think it's a bad idea?"

He leaned against the booth, tossing his arm along the back. "Because good ideas are ideas rarely wanted… or needed."

Flattening my hands on my thighs, I wasn't sure how to respond that. "Okay."

"Why did you agree if you think it's a bad idea?"

I let out a dry laugh. "Honestly? I don't know."

The faint smile reappeared. "So, since you were recognized by the fae tonight, will that be enough for you to rethink what you're doing?"

"Is that why you asked me to come here?" I picked up my diet Coke and took a sip. "To involve yourself yet again in something that does not concern you?"

"It concerns me."

I put my glass down. "How is that?"

He dipped his chin and stared at me through lowered lashes. "That's not going to deter you, is it? The added risk."

Shaking my head, I lifted a shoulder. "Do you want me to tell you what you want to hear or the truth?"

There was a flicker of amusement that crossed his face. "You risk too much."

"I haven't risked nearly enough."

"How do you see that?"

I leaned forward, placing my hands on the table. "I've spent thirty years playing it safe."

His brows lifted. "That's your logical reasoning for putting your life on the line?"

Sounded pretty illogical, but whatever. "You know why I must do this, risk or not. Just like you would go after Aric or the Queen even if it meant your death."

A muscle ticked along his jaw. "As I said before, it's different." There was a pause. "I remember," he said. "I remember the first time I saw you."

A shiver danced across my shoulders as I lifted my gaze to his.

"You were scared of us—of me and my brother, but mostly me. You stood in the corner of Tanner's office, not daring to come close," he continued, and that was true. Both had scared me, but especially him. "And then I saw you the night we fought the Queen. You were still afraid, but you helped my brother. You helped my brother and me even knowing what I'd done while under the Queen's control."

The night resurfaced. Prince Fabian had been severely injured by the Queen and he'd needed to get back to Hotel Good Fae. I had offered to help. "I didn't do much. I just drove you guys back to the hotel."

He leaned forward, his gaze never leaving mine. "You were afraid of us. You were unsure of us, but you still helped us when it was needed. That is doing everything and that is why I owe you an apology."

"You do?"

"For what I said about you looking for the younglings and knowing how important it was," he explained. "I shouldn't have doubted you, not when I know you will come through when needed."

While his doubt had been frustrating, it was understandable. "It's… not a big deal."

"It is." The Prince sat back. "In my experience, it is."

I didn't know what to say, so I said nothing as I stared at my glass of soda, watching the little bubbles race to the surface.

"It would be such a shame for the world to lose someone… someone like you, especially after being given a second chance."

Air hitched in my throat. That was yet another word of kindness from him that I didn't know how to process. "That's nice of you to say, but you… you don't know me well enough to think that."

"I am hardly ever wrong about these kinds of things."

A laugh escaped me. "Okay. Even if that is the case, like I said before, I don't understand why you care this much to have this conversation again. Remember? I'm just a human woman and I'm already half dead."

His jaw worked as those lashes lowered again. "I should not have spoken those words."

"Why? Because they were ignorant?"

"Because what you said about yourself is a lie."

I stilled. "What do you mean?"

A long moment passed, so much so that I thought he wouldn't answer, but then those thick lashes lifted and those eyes seemed to see straight through me once more. "You're not a ghost. You never could be one, not when you burn as brilliant as the sun."

Chapter 14

It was Friday evening—pizza night in the Jussier household, a tradition carried on for many years and now continued with Tink and me. After eating, I'd gone upstairs and changed into warmer clothes because I planned on heading out tonight to see if I could do some recon on the other two fae I was still looking for and the missing younglings.

I'd checked in with Faye on Wednesday and there'd been no word from any of the missing fae. And with each passing day, I could tell she was losing hope and becoming more convinced that the Order had harmed them, rather intentionally or unintentionally.

Even the Prince hadn't said as much, but I knew he probably speculated the same.

Then again, the Prince was adept at giving vague answers.

Over the last couple of days, I did everything in my power not to think about what we'd said to each other. What we'd admitted. Or the dinner that had started out awkward and ended rather normally, with me somehow talking about all the TV shows Tink was addicted to. And I definitely wasn't thinking about how he said I could never be a ghost.

That I was as brilliant as the sun.

Nope. Wasn't thinking about that or how no one, utterly no one had ever said something like that to me. I also wasn't lying awake at night thinking about how he… he wanted to spend time with *me*. The real me. I wasn't thinking about that at all. Nope.

I hadn't seen the Prince since our dinner of very yummy crab cakes and crawfish. Half of me had expected to run into him when I was out Wednesday night, but he hadn't magically appeared out of thin air like he had before. And that was a good thing.

Wasn't like I was actually looking forward to seeing him.

So I decided to focus on the important stuff, like what I learned about this Ancient named Aric who might or might not be trying to make contact with the Queen.

And that was really bad news.

The problem was if I talked to Miles, he'd question how I came about the information. That put what I was trying to accomplish in jeopardy. If I had to confide in someone who just might understand where I was coming from it would be Ivy and she would be back in the city in about a week.

I had time.

Anyway, I'd only been gone twenty minutes tops, so I was rather shocked by the current condition of the kitchen when I returned.

Crossing my arms and then unfolding them before crossing them again, I looked around the room. I took a breath and then exhaled slowly. "Why does it look like the FBI raided my kitchen while I was upstairs?"

And that's what it seriously looked like.

All the cabinet doors were open. Glasses were pushed around. Plates askew. Tupperware on the verge of toppling onto the counters. Pots and pans in the lower cabinets turned so their handles were jutting out.

"Well, you see, it's kind of a long story." Tink sat on the edge of the island, his legs swinging and his wings twitching while the scent of fried meat mingled with the peach-scented candle that was burning behind him. Dixon was lying beside him, his long tail swishing idly.

I turned to him and opened my mouth, but I was at a loss.

"Dixon and I were playing hide and go seek."

That explanation didn't help either. "How do you play hide and go seek with a cat?"

Dixon's ears flattened as Tink gasped dramatically. "Are you suggesting that Dixon doesn't have the brain capacity to play hide and go seek?"

"Dixon is a cat—a very smart cat, but a cat." I shook my head as I walked over to the small kitchen table. "You are so cleaning this up."

"I was planning to." Tink took flight, following me over to the table. He landed on the back of the white chair. "What are you doing? And don't lie and say you have a date."

"I'm actually going to walk the Quarter," I said, deciding not to lie. "There's some younglings that have gone missing and I'm going to see if I can find any of them."

His brows knitted together. "Fabian mentioned something about that, but he didn't seem too concerned."

"Well, Tanner and Faye are. They contacted the Order."

"Oh, and I bet the Order cares sooo much about a few missing Summer fae." He walked along the narrow back of the chair like it was a balance beam. "They were basically 'not my problem'?"

"Pretty much. That's why I was going to head out. The chance that I see any of them is pretty nil, but it can't hurt to try." Glancing back to the island after I heard the soft thump of Dixon dropping to the floor, I made another quick decision. "Do you want to come with me?"

Tink halted, one little leg up in the air. His forehead wrinkled as he looked up at me and then glanced down to where Dixon was weaving himself around my ankles. "Nah, I need to clean up the kitchen."

"You sure?"

He nodded as he flew up so he was eye level with me. His wings moved quietly through the air. "Yeah, and I discovered this new show that I'm only a few episodes into."

Tink gave me a lot of crap about going out hunting without him, but Tink didn't go out often. Sometimes I wondered if he had some kind of phobia surrounding the outside human world and that was why he didn't travel to Florida with Fabian. Then again, he had traveled with Ivy and team to San Diego when they were searching down leads to stop the Queen.

"What show?" I asked.

"Santa Clarita Diet. It's about this woman who becomes a zombie, but she's not like a Walking Dead zombie. She's basically trying to live her best life with her husband and daughter as a flesh-eating zombie."

"Okay." I drew the word out. "Sounds like you have a fun evening planned."

"I do." Tink flew with me as I went into the small mudroom that exited onto the porch and picked up my Saints cap. "Will you keep in contact with me?"

Grinning, I pulled the cap on and shoved my ponytail up under it. "Of course." Watching Tink when he was this size use a cellphone was quite amusing. "I won't be out too late."

"Coolio," he murmured, zooming back into the kitchen. A second later, I heard him yell, "Giddy-up Dixon, we must conquer the kitchen and then it's Netflix time!"

Shaking my head, I picked up my keys and shoved them into the back pocket of my jeans. I pulled my peacoat from a hook and shoved my arms through it. The last thing I put on was the iron cuff. That was a just-in-case thing. I started for the door and then stopped, pulling out a gray basket. I snatched up an iron stake and placed it into the pocket of my jacket. That was another just in case.

I slipped out the side door and, after making sure it was locked behind me, I turned around and halted.

An odd feeling crept along the nape of my neck as I stared at the narrow pathway that connected the front yard to the courtyard out back. Tiny bumps rose all along my body as I shivered, not from the cold but from… from the feeling of being watched.

I walked to the end of the porch and saw no one in the courtyard or anywhere near the house. My gaze flicked to the house next door. All the curtains were in place. Coming back to the side door, I checked yet again that it was locked and then made my way to the front of the house.

As I stepped off the porch and walked toward the front yard, I told myself it was just my imagination, but I couldn't shake the eerie sensation.

Couldn't shake it at all.

* * * *

Emerald green beads whizzed through the air as the drunken college-aged guy in a one-piece hot pink bathing suit twirled in the middle of Bourbon Street, his white sneakers pounding off the pavement. The suit was cut high along the hips and the front was nothing more than two panels of cloth held together by a jeweled clasp. It was not the kind of bathing suit made to wear when someone actually planned on swimming.

Or made to wear on a chilly March evening.

The man spun, winging another strand of beads into the night as the crowd cheered him on. The back of the suit showed more of the man's ass than it covered, but I had to say, it was a nice ass.

Mardi Gras had ended over a month ago, so I really had no idea what this dude was doing with the beads and the bathing suit. But it was Friday night in the French Quarter, so I knew I was going to see far weirder crap before the night was over.

Leaning against the brick wall of The Swamp, I sipped my ginger ale as someone shrieked happily from the courtyard behind me. Raucous laughter followed, and I figured someone had gotten thrown from the mechanical bull.

One of these days I imagined that bull was going to snap and pitch a person head first through a window.

Grinning at that because I was a terrible person, I took another sip of the carbonated goodness as I scanned the packed streets, looking for people that weren't quite… people. I reached into the pocket of my lightly lined cotton peacoat, feeling a sharp trill curl down my spine as my fingers brushed over the warm, slim piece of metal.

There was an eight-inch iron stake in my pocket and I was so not afraid to use it.

I couldn't help but wonder what I would be thinking if I had been out here two years ago. I wanted to be doing this, but I didn't have the lady balls. Not only would the Order members have laughed like deranged hyenas, I would've laughed… and had a minor panic attack simultaneously, because I'm a good multitasker like that.

Now I was more than capable of patrolling for the Order, but they didn't know that and if they did, it wouldn't matter. Just look at how they'd treated me today. Even if they saw me in action, it wouldn't change their views.

In their eyes, I wasn't the same as them and I'd never be ready to take to the streets. Not at my age. It was so ridiculous, considering the Order had been nearly decimated.

I drew in a shaky breath and it got hung up on the knot that had formed in my throat as my gaze swiveled back to the mayhem in the middle of the street.

The guy in the hot pink bathing suit had no idea how close the world had come to chaos. None of the people partying in the streets, laughing, drinking, and shouting knew that so many people—people I missed with every breath I took—had their lives brutally ended in an unknown war with the fae.

Hell, they didn't even know that the fae were a real and almost always deadly thing that walked among them, blending in and hunting them. I never once wondered what it would be like to not know there were things out there that could end your life in a snap of their fingers, but I guess there was a blissfulness in that ignorance.

Across the street, a woman stepped out from the throng of people milling up and down the narrow sidewalk, dressed in black leather pants and a tight black thermal.

Crap.

Recognizing Jackie, I slinked back against the wall and reached up, tugging the bill of my Saints' ball cap lower. The dark-skinned Order member stood on the curb, arms crossed as she watched Hot Pink Bathing Suit Guy, out of beads now, bend over and twerk.

Jackie was grinning now, but if she saw me, she wouldn't be smiling anymore. She'd legit kick my butt and then drag said butt back home, because she'd know what I was doing out here.

Which was utter bullshit. Logic dictated that the Order needed all the help they could get.

But I wasn't out here to patrol. I really was keeping an eye out for the younglings. I'd saved their photos to my phone, and pretty much had their faces committed to memory at this point. I figured if they were anywhere down here getting into trouble, they would be near Bourbon or Royal.

Part of me didn't think it would be a big deal if Jackie saw me or not. Probably would never cross her mind that I'd be out patrolling or anything like that. She'd probably think I was out grabbing dinner or something.

I couldn't risk it though.

Because if she did figure out what I was doing, I risked her discovering my other extracurricular activities.

Pushing away from the wall, I shoved both hands into my pockets as I pivoted to the left and headed for St. Louis Street. Crossing the street, I kept an eye out as I made my way toward Royal. It was so easy spotting tourists in the winter months. Locals were bundled up even though it was in the low fifties. Visitors were in T-shirts and jeans and skirts, obviously hailing from much colder climates. The Summer fae were the same, all toasty in their heavy jackets and wool beanies. You'd think it was below freezing seeing them, but the Winter fae? This wasn't nearly cold enough for them.

And it didn't take me long to find one.

Nearing Royal, I spotted the first suspicious fae of the evening and it wasn't the fact the young man was wearing a thin shirt and worn jeans that gave him away as a not-so-friendly fae. At least this fae was a normal one.

A shudder worked its way through me as I picked up my pace. I knew that the fae in front of me was not of the Summer Court, and it had nothing to do with how he dressed. It was the fact he was stalking a young woman who appeared to have just gotten off work from one of the many restaurants, her all-black server clothing partially obscured by one of those fluffy down jackets.

I wasn't technically patrolling, but if I saw a fae going after someone, I wasn't just going to stand back and do nothing.

I was so not about that kind of life anymore.

My fingers curled around the thickest part of the stake as the distance between us evaporated. Fae hated all things iron. Just a mere touch would sting them, continuous contact would burn them.

And this fae was about to meet the business end of the stake. A direct hit to the chest wouldn't kill them, but it would send them back to the Otherworld. And with the doorways to the Otherworld currently sealed, that was as good as dead.

Well, until the Queen decided to make another run for taking over the world and blew the doors wide open, but totes as good as dead until—

The young male glanced over his shoulder, not paying a lick of attention to me, but I stumbled.

Holy crap, I recognized the fae.

It was Elliot—the missing cousin's friend. I was sure it was totally him, but that didn't make sense. He was of the Summer Court and lived at Hotel Good Fae. And he and his parents didn't feed or prey upon humans.

That didn't mean they couldn't. It was a choice they made, so that meant it was a choice they could change at any time. And who knew how many times that had happened in the past? It wasn't exactly something anyone in the Order tracked.

Elliot suddenly hung a sharp left, slipping between two buildings, into a narrow alley. The girl was almost upon the intersection of Royal now, no longer of interest to him. Maybe I was wrong about the whole stalking thing. That was good news, but what the hell was he doing and where had he been?

Irritation spiked. Everyone worried the Order had killed this boy or that some other horrific thing had happened to him, but here he was, partying it up in the Quarter? So freaking annoying.

I hesitated for a moment at the mouth of the alley, knowing that following a fae, even if they were friendly, into an alley wasn't exactly the brightest thing to do.

Jackie would follow him.

Ivy sure as hell would do it.

I could do it.

I *needed* to do it.

Squaring my shoulders, I drew in a shallow breath and followed him into the dimly lit passageway, prepared to let loose a lecture my mother would've been proud of—

Wait.

My steps slowed as a frown pulled at my mouth. The alley was a dead end, blocked by another brick building. Where in the hell did he go? I walked farther, past a large dumpster. Unless he was hiding in here, he'd….

Slowly, I lifted my gaze to the two- and three-story buildings crowding the alley that smelled like stale beer and poor life choices. A fae could easily climb or jump that height, but not a fae who wasn't feeding. A fae who didn't feed was stronger than a human, yes, but they didn't have super jumping—

Thump.

Tiny hairs along the nape of my neck rose as I heard something land softly behind me. Instinct roared to life as I clutched the iron stake and spun around.

Elliot stood in the center of the alley, in the spot that had been empty seconds ago. Startled, I took a step back. For him to have made that jump…

"You're following me," he stated.

Apparently I had not been as stealthy as I thought. "Well, yes—"

"I know you," he interrupted, arms loose at his sides as he drifted closer.

He did? I didn't recall meeting him, but there was a chance he'd seen me at Hotel Good Fae in the days and weeks leading up to the battle with the Queen. But that was two years ago.

"I'm not sure if we've met." My heart started hammering in my chest. "But I know your parents."

His head cocked to the side, and in the darkness, his eyes looked like black pits.

The hair along the back of my neck was still standing. "Your parents are worried about you, Elliot. Where have you been?"

"My parents?" He straightened his head and moved even closer. "Those stupid posers? Those weak wannabe humans? They're not my parents. Not anymore."

Uh oh.

"And I know you. You're with the Order." Elliot hissed like a cornered cat, a very large and very pissed-off cat, and even in the shadowy alley, I could see the sabertooth-like teeth descending from his gaping mouth.

Oh crap, Elliot was so not on Team Good Fae anymore. Not at all.

There was no chance to question why in the hell Elliot was suddenly all psychotic. Yanking at the stake, I realized too late I should've just engaged the cuff. Elliot launched into the air like a rocket. In one stuttered heartbeat, he was on me, his body crashing into mine. The impact knocked me off my feet and my baseball cap off my head, and I went down hard. Air punched out of my lungs.

Never let them get you on the ground.

Those words from the most basic of trainings roared through my head as my eyes opened wide.

I'd been on my back before. I knew how this ended.

Elliot crouched over me, gripping the collar of my jacket. Our gazes connected—

Something… something was wrong with his eyes. They weren't the pale blue of the fae. They *were* pitch black, so dark I couldn't even see the irises.

I'd never seen anything like that, not in person or in the many books I'd studied on the fae.

Panic sparked deep in my chest as I struggled to get my stupid hand out of my pocket. The wicked sharp edge caught on the interior of my coat, snagging and tearing the cloth. He lifted me upward as he swung a fist back. Elliot punched down, but I flung myself up and over. His fist slammed into the pavement as my forehead cracked off his.

He cursed as he jerked.

Rocking backward, I ignored the bitter taste of fear and swung my legs up, wrapping them around his narrow waist. Using my weight, I flipped Elliot off me as I rolled. On top of him, I reared back as I pulled the stake out, tearing the pocket in the process. I lifted it high, preparing to jam it straight through his chest.

Elliot's fist connected with my stomach. The burst of pain stole my breath, but I powered through it, swinging the dagger downward.

The fae was fast, slamming his hands into my chest. I flew backward, landing on my butt. Before I could recover, Elliot shot off the ground and was on me once more. I'd held onto the dagger, gritting my teeth as his hand came down on my throat, his fingers digging into my windpipe. I swung the stake around, thinking a head shot would do the trick.

His hand suddenly left my throat and then Elliot was flipping through the air as if invisible hands had snatched him up.

Gasping for breath, I rolled onto my side, my free hand splaying across the pavement. Several strands of blonde hair had slipped free from my ponytail, blocking one eye.

Elliot was rising to his feet. He spun and then his body jerked back a step. He was frozen for a moment and then his body just caved into itself, sucking itself back into the Otherworld with a faint pop and sizzle.

"Holy smokes…." Breathing heavy, I started to sit up. Gratefulness warred with dread. Obviously an Order member had intervened, which was great, but also meant I was busted, so freaking busted.

A tall, broad shadow strolled forward. The light of the lamp sliced over an iron dagger and black gloves. Gloves? It was cold, but not *that* cold.

Wait.

I started to rise as I lifted my gaze. Every muscle in my body locked up. I saw who'd come to my quite unnecessary rescue and anxiety exploded like a buckshot along with a hefty amount of WTF.

Now I understood the gloves.

It wasn't an Order member who'd intervened.

He now stood under the lamp, and I would swear the light intensified as it shone down on him, as if powered by his presence.

The Prince stood before me. "We meet yet again."

Chapter 15

My hand tightened on the iron stake as the buzz of anticipation swept through me. No way should I be excited to see him—and the mere thought of that was so utterly confusing—but I was.

So I ignored the feeling. "You totally just stabbed Elliot."

His brows lowered as he hooked the stake to what I assumed was some hidden sheath. "I did."

"You do realize he was one of the missing younglings, right?"

"You do realize you were trying to stab him in the head, which would have roughly the same result as what I did?"

Okay. He had a good point.

"And you do realize he was about to choke the life out of you?"

"I completely had that handled," I said. "Completely."

"Is that so?" He folded his arms across his chest as he stared down his nose at me. "You looked like you had everything under control with his hands around your throat. Just like you looked like you had everything under control Monday night, when—"

"I had that fae under control and I *was* about to stab him in the head," I reminded him. "Before I was rudely interrupted."

The Prince cocked his head to the side. "Saving your life is rudely interrupting you?"

"I didn't need my life saved, thank you very much." Pushing to my feet, I met his stare with a glare I was rather proud of.

"That's not the thank you I was expecting, but I'll take it." His lips curled into a smirk as my mouth clamped shut. "What were you doing out here, Brighton? I thought we had an understanding."

"We did? Because I'm pretty sure that I never gave you any indication that we had an understanding." I turned away from him and then gasped, stumbling a step back. He was in front of me. "Jesus."

"Not quite." His arms were at his sides.

"Ha. Ha." I rolled my eyes as I fought a grin.

"Why are you out here, Brighton?" He was not nearly as amused as I was. "You're not an Order member."

"I am an Order member." And whatever amusement I was feeling evaporated. My hand around the stake twitched and I resisted the urge to lob it at his smirking face—his very attractive, smirking face. "I was born into the Order and I am willing to give my life to fulfill my duty to the Order."

"I stand corrected," he demurred, dipping his chin. "However, you are not a hunter."

"Gee, thanks, Captain Obvious."

He stared down at me.

Exhaling roughly, I shook my head as anger and a good dose of embarrassment churned inside me. I was a real Order member. God. "Look, thanks for getting involved when you weren't needed, but I've got things to do that don't involve standing in an alley talking to you."

"Really? What are those things you have to do? Go to Flux? The Court? Risk being seen again?"

I ran my tongue along the roof of my mouth. "Actually, no. And you know what, why are you out here? How did you just happen to be in this alley? Not exactly a place on the must-see list of New Orleans. I'm beginning to think—" I sucked in an unsteady breath. I hadn't heard him move, but he'd shifted closer.

"Think what?" he asked.

I tossed the stake up and then caught it. "It's just weird."

"What?"

"How in the last week, you've nearly showed up everywhere I've been. It's almost like you're following me."

"What if I was?"

I almost dropped the stake as my gaze flew to his face. His expression was unreadable and I couldn't tell if he was being serious or not. "Really? That's not creepy or anything."

His sigh was so heavy I was surprised it didn't shake the buildings. "You shouldn't be out here."

"What do you want from me?" I challenged. "I mean, really? Are we going to have this conversation every five minutes?"

"What do I want from you?" An emotion flickered across his face, parting his lips. "That's a loaded question."

I started to frown as I tossed the stake up again. "Not really."

His hand shot out with a speed that was both unnerving and impressive, snatching the stake out of the air with gloved fingers.

"Hey!" I reached for it.

The Prince deftly avoided my grasp. "That is incredibly distracting—"

"It's not my fault you can't multitask," I muttered.

"And incredibly dangerous," he continued. "I really don't want to see it go through your hand."

I popped my hands onto my hips. "It wasn't going to go through my hand."

"Rather be safe than sorry." He smiled tightly at me, and that just annoyed me to no end.

I started to ask for my stake back, but he spoke again. "You're not a hunter," he repeated, changing the subject. "Why were you out here?"

Back to that again. I sighed. "I wasn't out here patrolling. I was seeing if I could find one of the missing younglings, which I did. However, that didn't end well."

"No, it did not."

Knocking a strand of hair back from my face, I glanced at the mouth of the alley. "I thought it was a Winter fae first because he was following a woman, so I kept an eye on him—and yes, I know, I'm not a hunter, but I'm not going to walk away and leave someone to fend for themselves."

"You should have."

My head swung back to his. "I didn't ask for your opinion."

His eyebrow rose.

"Anyway, I saw his face and realized it was one of the missing younglings. I thought maybe I misjudged what he was doing since he broke away from the woman and walked into this alley, but he knew I was following him," I explained, troubled by what had occurred. "It was a trap in a way. He came at me."

"That makes no sense," he said, head tilting slightly. "The Summer fae do not attack humans."

"Yeah, well, he attacked me and I did nothing to instigate it either." There was something pecking away at the fringes of my thoughts. "Wait a second. Elliot said some weird stuff. He said his parents weren't his parents any longer and he also called them wannabe humans."

"Did he say anything else?" he demanded.

I shook my head as I saw Elliot's face in my mind. "But his eyes were messed up."

"What do you mean?"

"They were pitch black, like I couldn't even see the irises…." I trailed off as I thought about his eyes. "I've never seen anything like that, but…."

He stepped toward me, voice low. "Are you positive that is what you saw?"

"Yes. He was this close to my face." I put my hand within kissing distance of my face to show him. "His eyes were all black."

The Prince's jaw hardened as he looked away.

There was a sudden feeling where I felt like I'd seen something or a reference to eyes like that before, but I couldn't place it. Like a word that rose to the tip of your tongue, but you couldn't quite grasp it. "Do you… do you know what could cause that?"

"I don't—" The Prince's head swung sharply to the left and then a curse exploded out from him. He moved toward me just as a shot rang out, echoing through the alley.

Chapter 16

The Prince crashed into me, taking me to the ground before I had a chance to see who was shooting at us. I had only a moment to prepare myself for the bone-shaking impact with the ground, but that never came.

Somehow, he shifted at the final second, taking the brunt of the fall. He hit the ground hard, my front plastered to his long length for about a heartbeat and then he rolled suddenly, shoving me under his body as the cracks of a gun firing went off again—and again. My entire body jerked in surprise as a bullet hit the ground right beside our heads, sending tiny pieces of gravel into the air.

The Prince lifted his head and those near transparent eyes locked onto mine. "Stay down," he ordered.

"W-What?"

Launching to his feet, he spun around and then he was no longer there, moving so fast I couldn't track him in the shadowy alley.

I flipped onto my belly, lifting my head as I kept low to the ground. I was going to stay down, because I really didn't want to get hit. Another shot rang out and then I heard a grunt as my gaze swung to the back of the alley.

Two large forms collided. There was a flash of reddish-yellow glow coming from the hands of the Prince, a circular flash of light that reminded me of a fire ball. And then the smell of burnt metal filled the air a second before one of the bodies flew back several feet, slamming into the building opposite me.

The body fell forward into the dim light. My eyes widened as I saw that it was a fae. That… that was uncommon.

They rarely used guns, but unless a human had doused themselves in silver paint and had their ears shaved into points, that was definitely a fae.

The Prince tossed the ruined gun aside, and I knew he'd been the source of the burnt scent of metal. He'd done something to that gun.

Dear God, that kind of power….

He prowled forward like a caged animal finally unleashed, his chin dipped low, and I swore those pale eyes were glowing. "Who sent you?" he demanded, his voice a deadly growl that sent a wave of shivers through me. "Was it Aric?"

Struggling to his feet, the fae swayed as he reached into his boot. I tensed, expecting him to whip out another gun.

I was wrong.

It was an iron stake.

The fae grabbed it with his bare hand. He hissed in pain, lips peeling back in a snarl as he straightened.

The Prince shot forward. "Don't—"

Too late.

Slamming the business end of the stake into the center of his chest, the fae ended it right then and there. Within a few short seconds the fae who'd shot at us was gone.

"Holy shit," I whispered, raising unsteadily to my feet. "Did that just happen?"

"Yes." The Prince was suddenly in front of me, causing me to jerk back a step. His expression was drawn and tight. "Are you okay?"

"Yes. I think so." I felt myself up, searching for holes that shouldn't be there. "What the hell just happened?"

"I do believe we were being shot at."

Hands stilling, I lifted my gaze back to his. "Gee. Really? Let me clarify my question. Why do you think a fae shot at us and then sent his sniper ass back to the Otherworld? That doesn't happen every day."

"It doesn't?"

"No. Not in my world. It happens in yours?"

"I've made a lot of enemies, sunshine. A lot who'd rather see me return to who I was," he said, and my chest squeezed at the mere mention of him returning to the Prince who was an absolute nightmare. "Or see me dead."

"That's kind of scary—" Gasping, I jerked my hand away from my stomach. It was wet, and even in the poor lighting, I could see the dark smudges. "There's blood on my hand."

"You said you were okay." One hand was suddenly wrapped around my wrist while the other was on my stomach, pressing.

"Hey!" I smacked at his hand, but he studiously ignored me. "I don't think I'm bleeding." When he still felt along my midsection, I caught his hand and squeezed hard. "I think it's your blood."

"I'm fine," he gruffed out. "Are you sure you haven't been hit?"

"Pretty sure I'd know if I'd been shot," I said, squinting at him. He was wearing a dark thermal and pants, like he had the first time I'd seen him. I placed my hand on his right shoulder and felt nothing. I slid my hand down his chest, and he sucked in a sharp breath.

"What are you doing?" he asked, voice deeper, thicker.

My gaze lifted to his, and I thought I probably should pull my hand away, but I didn't. I moved to the other pec, and it was me who sucked in air this time. Wet warmth hit my palm. "You've been shot."

"It's nothing."

"Nothing?" I exclaimed. He let go of my wrist, so I got both hands involved. "You've been shot in the shoulder, too!"

The Prince said nothing.

I didn't know the biology of Ancients, but I figured, like the fae, they could survive mortal wounds. But a chest and shoulder wound? I stepped back, lowering my hands and wiping them over my jeans. Did the pant leg of his right thigh look darker? Shot three times? That… that was a lot.

My stomach pitched with concern I probably shouldn't feel, but he *had* covered my body with his when shots rung out and he *had* paid for the crab cakes and crawfish.

"We need to get out of here," I said, looking over my shoulder, to the entrance of the alley. "With that many gunshots, police will be on their way. Can you heal yourself?"

"Normally." His voice was off. Not like it had been when I'd been feeling him up or Monday night, but there was something strained about it. "You should get out of here before the police arrive."

Or more gun toting fae showed up since this was apparently an everyday occurrence to him. "What do you mean by normally?"

"Do you always ask this many questions?" he demanded.

"Yes. Is it annoying?"

"Yes," he growled.

"Sorry, but you're going to have to deal with it," I shot back.

He'd moved back into the shadows, but I could practically feel his glare. "You know that the fae can heal from virtually any wound if they feed," he said.

And rather quickly too. That's what made fighting them so

dangerous. You didn't have a lot of time for what they'd consider flesh wounds.

"I know that, so you should…." Understanding dawned. "You… you need to feed?"

He let out a dry, racking laugh. "Something like that."

"When was the last time you… you fed?" Those words sickened me, and a part of me didn't want to know the answer.

"A while."

I stared at him for what felt like a whole minute. "What exactly does 'a while' mean? A couple of days? A week?"

"Try longer than that."

A frown pulled at my lips. "Longer than a couple of weeks?"

That didn't make sense to me, especially with him being at a place like The Court where humans were happily on the menu.

He said nothing.

"A month? A couple of months?" I whispered. Knowing what I did about the fae, they had to feed on a regular basis to slow down the aging process and give them their preternatural abilities. The Prince might look like he was in his mid to late twenties, but he had to be hundreds of years old, if not older. The fae metabolism was much like ours. They might not need three square human meals a day, but from the Order's research, they had to feed at least once every other day.

"You need to go," he said as the faint sound of sirens could be heard.

"And leave you here to bleed all over yourself, the alley, and perhaps even on police officers?"

"Do you really care what happens to me?"

My fingers twitched. "No."

"Then *go*." He started to back up.

I should go. I should leave his ass here to bleed out like a stuck pig. He was an Ancient, and even if he hadn't fed in a few months….

Holy crap.

It struck me then. "You haven't fed this whole time, have you? Not since the spell was broken."

He tossed a glare at me over his shoulder through thin slits. "Aren't you leaving?"

"What does that mean then if you haven't fed in like two years? Can these wounds—"

"Kill me unless it's treated or I feed? Probably not, but it'll take a while to heal." Grunting, he pushed against the hole in his shoulder. "I just need to get out of this alley."

"You can't go to the hospital." Having a very human doctor discover that fae were a real thing was not exactly on the to-do list for tonight.

"No shit," he grumbled.

I ignored that. "I can—I can get you back to Hotel Good—"

"No," he interrupted, and I thought that he might've swayed a little. "You will not contact them."

Confusion filled me. "What? Why?"

"Can you just accept an answer without following up with another damn question?" He let out another curse. "God, you're infuriating."

I lifted an eyebrow at that. "You know, if I am so infuriating, then you probably shouldn't have stalked me into the alley."

"I wasn't stalking you," he grumbled. "And if I hadn't been then you'd have ended up dead."

I threw up my hands. "First off, you just admitted to stalking me after saying you didn't, and we'll address that, but most importantly? I'm not the one bleeding all over myself, now am I?"

He didn't respond to that, at least not vocally, but I had a feeling he was mentally cursing me out.

"I'm fine. I just… I just need to get to my place," he said, and he sounded like those words pained him.

The sirens were getting closer, and I needed to make up my mind. He needed help, whether he wanted it or not.

Taking a deep breath, I walked over to where he stood and decided. "Like it or not, I'm going to help you."

* * * *

There weren't a lot of moments in my life where I had to stop and ask myself what in the fuck I was doing.

For the most part, I lived a practical, boring existence—well, outside of my plan to hunt down the fae who'd attacked my mother and me. Other than that, I was like a bowl of white rice without any soy sauce.

But here I was, waiting for the Prince—*the* Prince—to unlock the door to what appeared to be one of the many old warehouses that had been converted into upscale condos.

Luckily he hadn't argued with me when I'd led him out of the alley, and I was leading him. By the time we reached Royal Street, in the opposite direction of the sirens, his steps had slowed to a near crawl. I was able to flag down a cab and thank God, as far as I knew, he didn't bleed all over the backseat.

The Prince didn't speak beyond giving the cabbie his address. Not again after the ride. Not as I helped him get to the elevator and we went to the tenth floor, the top floor, and not as I stood beside him, shouldering what felt like the weight of a Volkswagen Bug.

The door finally opened and warm air rushed out as the Prince stumbled inside. A light came on, revealing a massive open floor design that… that didn't even look lived in.

The walls were exposed brick and the living area faced floor to ceiling windows. There were two doors. One near the entrance that I figured was some kind of closet and the other on the other side of the living room. There was a TV and a large black, sectional couch, but beyond that, there was nothing else. At all.

"You can leave now." He walked forward, stopping to place his hand on the white marble countertops that edged out the gourmet level kitchen that looked like it never once saw a meal cooked in it.

Because I was apparently making a series of bad life choices tonight, I followed him inside, closing the door behind me.

"Are you going to be okay?" I toyed with the button on my peacoat.

Lowering his head, he let out a long, shuddering breath. "Yes."

"That doesn't sound very convincing." I inched closer to him, and I could smell it now. It mingled with that summer scent of his. I saw it on his hand, the bluish-red tint of fae blood. "Is there someone I can call? Your brother—"

"Do not call my brother," he bit out, his fingers curling into a fist on the marble. "Do not call anyone."

Exasperated, I looked around the condo before my eyes settled on him. "Obviously you're not okay. You haven't fed and you're bleeding all over your nice wood floors. And I have no idea why you haven't fed in two years—not that I don't think that's great and all, but your brother says he uses human *volunteers*—"

"You say that like you don't believe it, but yes, my brother does not take from those who are not willing."

"And you couldn't find any volunteers?"

"There you go again, with the questions." He shook his head slowly. "You need to leave."

"But—"

"I do not think you understand." He lifted his head again, and yep, those eyes were definitely starting to glow. He stared at me like… like he was *hungry*. Starved, really. "You need to leave now."

A wave of shivers rolled over my skin as an innate sense forced me to take a step back from him. The atmosphere around us seemed to thin and charge with static.

The Prince turned, tracking my movements with a near predatory glint to those glowing faint blue eyes. "I won't tell you again. If you don't leave, you won't have the choice to."

Chapter 17

He didn't have to tell me again.

I got out of that condo as fast as my two legs would carry me and I made it down the long hall, to the steel elevator doors before I stopped and looked behind me.

"What are you doing?" I whispered, knowing I should just hit the elevator button and go. He wasn't my responsibility and just because I could appreciate his hotness didn't mean I liked him.

Because I didn't.

I stared at the elevator button.

Plus I had to figure out what the hell I was going to tell Tanner and Faye about Elliot and his weird as hell eyes. It would take Faye no leap of logic to jump to the conclusion that if Elliot had gone all evil fae, there was a good chance her cousin had too.

Turning from the elevator, I pulled my phone out of my back pocket. "Damn it," I muttered, folding one arm across my stomach as I called Tink.

He answered on the second ring. "Hey, Lite Bright, I was getting worried."

"I'm okay, but there is a problem." I glanced up the hall. "I'm with the Prince."

There was a pause and then, "Like *the* Prince?"

"Yes."

"As in Fabian's brother?"

"Yes, Tink, unless there are other Princes I'm unaware of."

"Why are you with him?" Tink demanded. "Oh my God, did you really have a date tonight and then lied about looking for younglings? Oh, my God, you *hussy*."

"Tink—"

"Hussy Brighton got good taste, though. Hold on, I need popcorn for this conversation."

"Tink," I snapped. "Come on, I'm not on a date with him and you don't need popcorn for this conversation. I was out looking for the youngling and I ran into the Prince." I figured I'd leave the whole Elliot part out at the moment. "He was shot multiple times."

"Oh, dear."

"Yeah, and he's in pretty bad shape. He didn't want me to call his brother or anyone from Hotel Good Fae."

"You just called me," he pointed out.

"I know that." Exasperated, I closed my eyes and kept my voice low. "I called because he's in bad shape and he hasn't fed."

"He should still be okay. Probably needs to sleep it off—"

"He hasn't fed in two years," I cut him off.

"What?" Tink shrieked. "Are you serious right now? I need to call Fabian—"

"Don't call him. He asked me not to." I had no idea why I was following his orders. "Look, is he going to be okay or not?"

"No, Lite Bright, he is not going to be okay!" Tink yelled, and my stomach sunk. "If he hasn't fed in two years, he's basically mortal except it's just going to take him longer to die!"

"Crap," I muttered, turning back toward the Prince's door. "Well, this sucks, because he's alone at his place, and I'm not sure I can lure a human back for him to snack on."

"You can feed him."

"What?" I almost dropped the phone. "Are you out of your mind?"

"It's not a big deal. Trust me. You'll probably like it."

My mouth dropped open.

"Brighton, he can't die. Do you understand me? If he doesn't feed, he will die and if he dies…."

"He'll be dead?" Screw this. "Go ahead and call his brother. I don't care if he gets pissed at me. I'm—"

"There's no time to call Fabian. He'll be dead by the time Fabian can get to him. You either need to offer yourself up as an all you can eat buffet of Brighton or you need to go kidnap some person and serve him up a dish of unwilling human."

I had no words.

"And considering his background and all the terrible shit he knows he's done while under the Queen's spell, I'm sure he'll be down for that," Tink continued on.

There was another pitch to my stomach. "That sucks, but this isn't my problem."

"You called me, so obviously you think it's your problem."

He had me there.

"He can't die," Tink said into the phone, his voice more serious than I'd ever heard him before. "If he dies, then the entire Summer Court will be weakened."

I started to say that also wasn't my problem, but it kind of was. When the Queen came back, because she would, the Order and the world would need the Summer Court at full power.

"And if he dies, then Fabian becomes King and he… he can't be King, Brighton." Tink's voice had dropped to a whisper. "If you can't help him, then I will."

"You helping him means you're going to kidnap someone." I turned, dragging my hand over my head. Crap! I hated my life. "I'll take care of it."

"Will you?" Tink asked. "Because like the entire Court and the world rests on you taking care of this."

I rolled my eyes. "Are you not at all worried he's going to suck me dry?"

"No." He was so quick to answer that I frowned so hard it was no wonder it didn't break my face. "He would never hurt you, Brighton. Never."

My face smoothed out as surprise rippled through me. It took me a second to even formulate a decent response. "Why would you even say that? You don't know that."

"I do know, because it's true." Tink took a big enough breath that I could hear it through the phone. "The Prince wouldn't hurt you. Not when he already saved your life once before."

"What?" I laughed. "What are you even talking about, Tink?"

"You said I saved your life the night you were attacked, but I didn't save your life, Brighton. I just found you," he said. "But it was the Prince who saved your life in the hospital."

The memory of seeing the Prince suddenly resurfaced as I clutched the phone. I saw him there, but I thought… I thought it had just been some weird trauma or drug induced hallucination.

"You were going to die, Brighton. Too much damage had been done, but he did something. Do you understand?" Tink asked. "He saved your life and now you must save his."

Chapter 18

How does one come to grips with the unexpected knowledge that someone they barely knew, someone who wasn't even human and just happened to be *the* Prince, had not only saved their life but did God knows what to do it?

Part of me couldn't even believe it because as far as I knew, the fae couldn't heal humans. Unless it was something only Ancients could do. But if so, that was yet another thing I was unaware of, and I was *supposed* to be the leading authority on all things fae.

Apparently I didn't know jack.

After promising Tink we were so going to have a conversation about all of this when I got home—*if* I got home—I found myself back at the Prince's front door.

I couldn't even let myself think about what I was doing as I reached out and turned the knob. It was still unlocked.

Saying a quick prayer that, all things considered, would probably go unanswered, I walked back into the quiet condo, closing the door behind me while hoping I was going to walk back out of there.

He saved your life and now you must save his.

This was insane.

What Tink had said was just unbelievable, but I kept walking.

The kitchen was empty and I stopped by the counter, spying a reddish-blue blotch of blood. That was probably going to stain the marble.

I don't know what I was thinking when I walked around to the kitchen sink, picked up a towel and wiped up the blood. Probably because I wasn't thinking at all.

There was no sight or sound of the Prince.

What if he was already dead?

He saved your life….

"Uh… hello?" I called out, tossing the towel into the sink. I eyed the door I figured led to a bedroom. "Uh, Prince? It's me, Brighton?"

Silence.

Concern wiggled around in the pit of my stomach like a nest of vipers. I started toward the bedroom, seeing that the door was ajar. Lifting a trembling hand, I pushed it open. I'd been correct. It was a bedroom and it was as personable as the living room. In other words, it didn't look remotely lived in. Just a super large bed in the middle of the room with deep blue sheets and comforter. There was a nightstand and a dresser. That was all.

Now you must save his….

Light spilled out from a room off from the bedroom and tiny tremors rattled my legs as I stepped farther inside. "Are you in here? Like alive?"

Several beats of silence passed and then, "I told you to leave."

The guttural voice caused my breath to catch in my throat, and I froze.

"And you left." There was another pause. "You should not have come back."

The entire world with the exception of Tink would agree with that statement.

But I was here.

"I know… I know you're not okay." I forced my legs to move, and it was like walking in quicksand. I neared the swath of light. "I know that you're going to be really not okay because you haven't fed."

There was no response.

Wanting to turn and run in the other direction, I did the opposite and stepped into the light.

And I saw him.

"Holy…."

The Prince was… he was shirtless, and while I'd seen a decent number of shirtless men in my life, I'd never seen one like him.

And that had nothing to do with the trails of blood running down his back and stomach, as terrible as that was to admit. My priorities were so, so wrong, because I wasn't checking out the ragged holes in his shoulder or chest. He was….

He was beautiful, even covered in blood.

All that golden, hard skin. Defined pecs. Abs tightly coiled and a dusting of golden hair that traveled below his navel to the band—

Oh, sweet Jesus, his pants were undone and hanging low enough that I could tell the man went commando underneath.

I should look away.

I couldn't look away.

Not when my gaze got hung on those interesting indentions on either side of his hips. How in the world did someone get muscles there? I'd never seen that on someone in real life. Only in photographs or on TV. I was beginning to think those kind of muscles were fake news, but he had them and then some. Actually, his body was absolutely freaking glorious, and it was clear that I needed to obtain sexual gratification from anything other than my trusty vibrator, because I was staring at him like I'd never seen a man before and—

"Do you like what you see?" he asked.

Jerking my gaze to his, I felt heat blast my face as I blurted out the stupidest thing possible. "You're bleeding."

The Prince tilted his head to the side as he held a bloodied towel in his hand. "I was completely… unaware of this."

A thousand smartass responses traveled to the tip of my tongue and died there, because he turned to the gray and black tiled shower stall. Muscles flexed and contracted as he tossed the towel into the stall.

"You have to know why I told you… to leave," he was saying, twisting at the waist and gripping the basin of the sink so tightly his knuckles bleached white. "I will be fine."

He saved my life? How?

He had to have, because why would Tink lie? And I knew I should've died that night. The pain and all that blood and the scars… the scars no one but those doctors have seen.

The Prince saved my life.

And not only that, he understood why I had to do what I had to do. He didn't like it. He made it more than clear he didn't want me to do it and now a lot of what he'd said made sense, but he still understood.

No one understood.

I'd never let anyone in the last two years get a chance to understand. Not even Ivy, but I let… I let the Prince in and I was now just realizing that. I'd let him in and even though I knew of him for two years, I'd only *really* known him for a week. And he already knew more about me than most.

What did that mean?

Something warm and confusing and consuming filled up my chest as I stared at this beautiful, complicated *man*. And that's what I saw when I stared at him. Not a fae. Not an Ancient. Not a Prince. Just a man.

A man who was dying.

And I could save him.

"No, you won't be okay." I found my voice and actually said something useful. "I know if you… if you don't feed, you will die."

His gaze swung to mine and his features were sharper, more stark. He took a deep breath and it lifted his chest. "Are you… offering yourself up?"

My heart stuttered in my chest as he pushed away from the sink and faced me. "I'm here and I really can't believe I'm here, but it's either me or I go out and kidnap a human, and the latter isn't going to happen."

His bloodied hands opened and closed at his sides. "I am not going to feed from you, Brighton."

"Then you're going to die."

A muscle flexed in his jaw and a moment passed. "You do not want me to feed from you."

"Not particularly," I admitted. I'd never been fed on before. Not even when I'd been attacked, but I knew what feedings could do. I could walk out of here like nothing happened or he could take too much.

He took a step toward me, and I tensed. His nostrils flared. "Then why are you here, offering yourself to me?"

I could lie, claim that I was an altruistic soul, but I had feeling he'd know that was utter crap.

"Because I… I know." I swallowed hard, meeting his gaze. Those eyes burned straight into me. "I don't understand how and I don't understand why, but I know you saved my life."

The Prince became very still, so much so that I feared for a moment he'd died right there and was about to topple over, but when he didn't, I continued.

"I thought I saw you in the hospital, but I wasn't sure. You were there and you did something to make sure I pulled through." Now my heart was pounding fast, too fast. "That's why the doctors said I was a miracle. Because I was."

The Prince closed his eyes.

I wanted to ask him why, but we'd already wasted too much time. Hopefully there'd be a chance to find out later.

"You saved my life, so I'm going to return the favor," I said, stepping back.

His eyes snapped open. "That's not why I did it. So you could return the favor."

"Well, I would hope not." I kept walking backward, relieved when he followed me like an animal stalking its prey. Probably not the best comparison to make at the moment.

The back of my legs hit the bed at the same moment I figured it out. "You saved me because I helped your brother the night everyone fought the Queen."

His head tilted to the side and he didn't answer. He didn't need to.

I knew.

Reaching into the pocket of my peacoat, I pulled the stake out and placed it on the dresser. "So, I, um, don't accidentally stab myself or you."

His chest was rising and falling rapidly as he watched me.

Nervousness nearly made my knees shake as I fiddled with my jacket. Then I undid the button, thinking it was too hot in this room. I shrugged off the ruined peacoat, letting it fall to the floor.

The jeans and the light, loose sweater still felt like too much, but I wasn't going to strip. "I'm not going to leave, Mr. Prince, and I'm not going to let you die."

In a blink of an eye, he was right in front of me. Caught off guard, I lost my balance and sat down on the edge of the bed.

"Do you know what will happen when I feed?" His voice was barely above a growl.

Staring up at him, I swallowed. "I know… I know some people like it… or so I've heard, but I guess…no, I really have no idea."

"You're going to like it."

A wholly unexpected thing happened. Heat boiled my blood. "I wouldn't go that far."

He stared at me for a long moment. "You have no idea what you're getting yourself into."

"I know what I'm getting myself into."

The Prince's hands moved faster than my eyes could track. His fingertips touched my cheeks. "You can leave."

"If I do then you die."

"Maybe that's for the best."

Stunned and more than a little disturbed, I lifted my hands and wrapped them around his wrists. "Why would you say that?"

He was getting paler by the second. Soon he'd be as white as a ghost. "You know what I've done."

"It wasn't your fault."

"There is no coming back from that."

"Stop," I said, my voice cracking. "You have come back from that, because you're standing here and you're going to feed so you don't die. That's it. This has been decided. Get with it."

He went still, but I saw the moment resignation settled into his features. Relief mingled with a little bit of fear. He was going to live, and I just hoped I didn't die in the process.

"I won't hurt you," he whispered. "And I won't let this go too far. I promise you this."

Before I could ask what too far meant, the tips of his fingers glided down my cheeks, along the sides of my throat. He tilted my head back and a heartbeat passed.

"I didn't save you because of what you did for my brother," he said, and then he brought his lips down.

Chapter 19

The Prince didn't kiss me. He didn't move his lips against mine. It was the lightest touch, and I still felt the contact in every cell, in every part of my body.

And then he exhaled against my lips.

It was like warm silk slipped down my throat and it tasted like sun-baked coconut. How strange was that? The warmth hooked itself into the very center of my being and then *pulled.*

My entire body jerked as if I too was being lifted, but I wasn't sure if I actually moved or not or if the Prince was holding me in place when his hands glided down to my shoulders.

It didn't… it didn't hurt.

Not at all. Instead, I felt… lighter. Like I was floating in warm water. The warmth from his body blanketed my skin, and I was only vaguely aware of my hands slipping off his wrists, to fall to my sides. But when he tilted his head to the side, the deep, deep tugging intensified and then—oh, God—then it turned into something else.

Everything inside me tightened all of a sudden. My heart raced as my senses overloaded. A rush of acute pleasure came out of nowhere, slamming into me with a force that turned my blood to nothing more than liquid heat as a coiling sensation began deep inside me. There was no stopping the sound that came out of me as my entire body arched—a sound that I knew I would be mortified about later.

The Prince shuddered as his hands curled under my arms. He lifted me up and then laid me down and then his weight came down on me.

I stopped thinking.

I stopped being me, whoever me was, and I just let what I was feeling happen, and what I was feeling was something so beautiful it was almost painful.

My hands slid to the bare skin of his chest and my legs spread as his thigh eased between them. My body wasn't my own, and I didn't care. I began to move, twisting and churning against his thigh, the friction so good it made me pant. One of his hands curved around my hip as he braced his weight on his other.

And then it happened.

The whirling force inside me whipped out of control as the first wave of pure, full-bodied bliss crashed over me. I cried out against his mouth as spasms racked my body, and it went on and on, a wave I rode for what felt like an eternity. When it was over, every muscle in my body was limp.

I only became aware as the soft tugging motion slowed, eased and then faded off. He wasn't feeding anymore, but his mouth was still close to mine and the pounding in my chest had turned to a throbbing in several pulse points throughout my body. That delicious ache was still there, pulsing, pounding, waiting for *more*, because while the experience had been amazing, there was this hollowness about what I'd just felt. And I knew it was from him feeding and I knew it was… it was simply because it was *him*.

The Prince lifted his head.

I opened my eyes and saw that his were closed. His head was thrown back, neck muscles taut and corded. He was striking like this, awe-inspiring. I lowered my gaze to his shoulder. The wound was healed, as was the one in his chest. Nothing but faint streaks of dried blood remained. I figured the one in his thigh was also healed, but he looked like he was… he was in pain.

I lifted my hand, placing just the tips of my fingers onto his cheek. "Are you… you okay?" When he didn't answer, I guided his chin down. "Prince?"

His chest rose with a sharp, unsteady breath and when he opened his eyes, I gasped. Their color had changed.

"Your eyes," I whispered. No longer were they the pale wolf's blue. Instead, they were a stunning shade of amber, rich and intense.

"It's all right," he said, voice thick. "It was… it was bound to happen."

My brows knitted. "What… what does that mean?"

He gave a little shake of his head. "Nothing. Are you okay?"

I managed a nod.

Those eyes drifted shut again. "Can you do me a favor?" He turned to my hand, startling me when he kissed the center of my palm. "Call me Caden."

"Caden?"

"That is my name." His lips brushed my palm again. "My name is Caden."

A swelling sensation rose in my chest. "Okay. Caden. I can do that." I lowered my hand to his bare shoulder and he flinched. I jerked my hand away. "Are you sure you're okay? Did you take enough?"

"Did I take enough?" He let out a dry laugh as he dropped his chin to the chest. "I took enough."

"Then what's…?" Air caught in my throat as the Prince—no, as *Caden* shifted just an inch, pressing against me, and I felt him then, hard and heavy against my hip.

He was aroused.

Seriously so.

Those odd eyes were closed again and those features were just as stark as they had been before he fed. He was hungry… he was hungry for *me*.

I don't know what it was. If it was what we just shared that gave me the courage or if it was something deeper than that, but whatever it was, I welcomed it.

Grazing his cheek with my fingertips, I dragged my thumb over his full bottom lip, reveling in the way he inhaled sharply, as if my touch had some heavy impact on him. My thumb followed the line of his jaw and his eyes drifted shut as the muscle along his jaw flexed against my palm.

"What are you doing?" he asked.

"I don't know." That wasn't completely true. I knew what I was doing as I threaded my fingers through the silky soft strands of hair and curled my hand around the nape of his neck, tugging his head down as I lifted mine.

I knew exactly what I was doing when I brushed my lips over his parted ones, touching the tip of his tongue with mine.

Caden locked up. He didn't move. He didn't kiss me back. He just froze above me, and when I opened my eyes, his were wide and dilated.

Oh no….

Had I done it… wrong? It had been forever since I'd been kissed and even longer since I kissed someone, so I had no idea if I was doing this right or if there really was a wrong way of doing this.

I started to pull my hand away. "I'm—"

His hand left my hip and shot to my neck just as his mouth came down, stopping a hairsbreadth from touching mine. "We can't." His thumb smoothed over my wildly beating pulse. "We can't do this."

Confusion filled me. "We can't?"

Caden shuddered as he dropped his forehead to mine, his hips moving in a slow roll.

"No."

"No?" I whispered.

"I promised you that I would not let this go too far."

"I want this." To prove my point, I ran my hands down the tense muscles of his back and then lower, slipping my fingers under his loose pants. "Don't… don't you want this? It seems like you do."

"God," he groaned, moving his mouth to my neck. "I've never wanted anyone as much as I want you." He kissed the spot just below my ear, causing my back to arch. "But you can't say what you want is all yours. Not after me feeding."

"It feels like it's all me," I said, and I thought I felt him smile against my neck.

"I'm trying to be… better than who I was," he explained after a long moment. He lifted his head and that striking gaze latched onto mine. "I don't know if that will make a difference or mean anything, but I'm trying to be better and it's never been harder than this moment."

My breath caught as I slid my hand back along his jaw and I remembered what he'd said before he fed. That there were some things you couldn't come back from. I searched his gaze as a knot of emotion formed in my throat. I could understand that feeling—that there were some things in life, even if you weren't responsible, you just couldn't get past.

But I didn't… I didn't want that for him. "You aren't guilty for those things you did when you were under the Queen's spell." I caught his gaze when he started to look away. "You're already better. You didn't hurt me. You don't want to take advantage of me. You've saved my life, more than once. You're not him."

He was quiet for a long moment. "Knowing I didn't have control doesn't erase the memories. I was aware of everything, but I couldn't… I couldn't stop myself. I couldn't stop any of it."

My heart squeezed with sympathy. "I'm sorry, Caden. I really am."

His eyes flared wide and then he rolled off me, onto his back beside me. "You're really making this hard."

I bit down on my lip as I stared up at the vaulted ceiling of his bedroom. "Sorry?"

He didn't respond.

It took a surprising amount of energy for me to roll onto my side, but I managed to do it.

"Does your brother know you hadn't fed?"

"I think he's had his suspicions, but he's left it alone."

"Why haven't you fed? Are you wanting to live your life like Tanner?"

"We don't have that choice. If an Ancient doesn't feed, we just weaken and we age, but it's still at a substantially slower rate than humans. Wounds can become mortal and we lose our strength," he explained.

"So, why?"

His hands came to rest on his chest. "When I was under the Queen's control, my feeding was… gluttonous. Several times a day. Some I killed," he said quietly, and I flinched. "Some I enslaved. Others I have no idea what happened to them, and I didn't care. That wasn't the only aspect of my life that became… excessive."

"Sex?" I asked.

"I haven't fed and I haven't been with anyone since Fabian broke the spell. I just…."

I reached over, placing my hand on his arm. "It's okay. I understand."

He turned his head toward me. "You do, don't you, sunshine?"

"Yeah." At least I did on some level. I lowered my gaze to where my hand rested on his arm. "Why do you call me that? Sunshine?"

"Because I saw you smile once and it was like the sun finally rising."

That was… that was *wow*.

"And your hair is like golden rays of sun," he finished.

I laughed. I couldn't help it or stop it. The laugh just came right out of me.

He lifted a brow as a small grin played at the corners of his lips. "I just complimented you and you laughed at me."

"I did. I'm sorry. It's just… it's just coming from anyone but you that would sound ridiculous."

"And it doesn't sound ridiculous coming from me?"

"No," I admitted, lifting my gaze to his. "It doesn't."

That small grin appeared once more. It wasn't a lot, but it was a big deal, I realized.

"I… I have another question."

"Of course you do," he replied wryly.

I grinned at that. "How… how did you heal me? I didn't know that anything like that was possible."

"It's something only I can do."

"Why?"

The Prince sighed heavily, but there was a fondness to the sound, like my one hundred and one questions amused him more than they irritated him. "As the eldest of my Court, I can… how do I explain this? Reverse feed."

"Reverse feed? That sounds… weird."

"Instead of taking from a human, I can give. And if there is still life left in the human, there's a chance what I can do can save them."

I considered that. "So, you basically made out with me while I was unconscious in a hospital bed?"

He snorted. "Not quite. I would not do that. Who I was, though?"

"I know. I was teasing." I squeezed his arm and then started to pull my hand away, but the strangest thing happened.

Caden caught my hand and threaded his fingers through mine. "I did it once before," he said. "When I was under the spell of the Queen and I'd just come through the gateway." Pausing, he exhaled heavily as he turned his gaze back to the ceiling. "Ivy had followed me and we fought. She didn't… fare too well."

I remembered this. That was the night he got his hands on the blood crystal—the crystal that could open the gateway and was now in the hands of the Queen. I'd seen Ivy briefly after the fight and there didn't seem to be an inch of her that hadn't been bruised.

"She was pretty bad off," he said, and he started to loosen his grip, but I held on. His gaze found mine. "I healed her."

"Does she know?"

"Yeah, she does." There was a pause as his lashes lowered. "I think she thought it worked because she was a halfling. I never corrected that assumption."

"Well, thank you… for saving my life."

Those lashes rose. "You don't need to thank me."

"I do. If you hadn't done what you did, I wouldn't be here. I would be—" Unable to stop it, I yawned loudly, flushing at how obnoxious it was. "I'm sorry."

"It's okay." A faint smile reappeared, tugging at his full lips. "It's the feeding. You're going to be really tired for a couple of hours and you'll have the deepest sleep you've probably ever experienced. But when you wake up, it will be like any other time you wake up."

I looked around the room as I started to pull my hand free. It was getting late and the last thing I should do is pass out in his bed. "I should—"

"You should stay."

My gaze swung back to his. "Come again?"

"You can stay."

"I… I don't know." That seemed like a big step toward… toward I didn't know what and I wasn't sure he wanted me here. Yes, he'd saved my life. Yes, he called me sunshine and hadn't taken advantage of me. But he said he wanted me… more than anyone he ever wanted, and that was, well, that couldn't be true.

I didn't think that because I had low self-esteem or anything. I was just realistic. I knew what I was—what I looked like. I also now knew that he hadn't been with anyone in two years. He probably wanted *anything* more than *anyone* at this point.

And that shouldn't matter. It really shouldn't.

But it did nonetheless.

So that meant I really, really should go before I got in over my head when it already felt like I was there.

Tugging my hand free, I went to sit up and it took a moment, but I did it. "I do need to go. Tink will worry."

"Tink." Caden murmured the brownie's name as he sat up much faster and more gracefully than I did. "He's staying with you?"

I nodded as my gaze fell to my ruined jacket. Probably best it stayed here, which meant I wasn't able to take the stake with me. "I guess until Ivy gets back and so does Fabian."

"Do you wonder why he didn't go with my brother?" he asked.

"I have. I asked him why and he said he didn't like Florida. I think he called it the Australia of the United States or something." I reached up and could tell that my ponytail was half undone. I tried to tighten it, but gave up and just pulled the rubber band out.

"I like that."

I glanced over my shoulder at him, and almost wished I hadn't. The golden hue of his skin had returned and as he rose, his muscles did a whole lot of interesting things. "The whole Florida being Australia thing?"

"No. I have no idea if that is true, but I'll take Tink's word on it." He faced me. "I meant your hair. I like it down."

"Oh." My hand floated to the ends of my hair as I shifted my gaze away from his, landed on his chest and decided that was worse, and then I ended up staring at my sneakers. "It's a mess."

"Sunshine," he said, and then his hand was pulling mine away from my hair. He tugged me to my feet. "Still looks like sunshine."

I didn't know what to say to that. "I really need to go."

I thought he'd let go, but when he didn't, I looked up just as he pulled me to his warm chest. His arms went around me, holding me tight, and I… God, I liked that. I can't say I didn't know why I did what I did next. I know why I did, because I wanted to.

Drawing in a shallow breath, I closed my eyes and leaned in, resting my cheek against his chest. When was the last time I was hugged like this? I felt the next breath he took. When was the last time he'd hugged someone like this?

"Thank you," he said, voice rough as he rubbed my back, following the line of my spine. "Thank you for what you did tonight."

"It's no big deal."

He chuckled, the sound untried but nice. "You know that's not true." Pulling back, he dragged those hands up to my cheeks. "Thank you, Brighton."

"You're welcome."

He held me a moment longer as he glided his thumbs over my cheeks, and I thought he might not let go. He might insist that I stay, and if he did, I… would, no matter how much of a bad idea it would be.

But he let go.

Chapter 20

Tink was hanging upside down from my headboard, his wings spread out on either side of him and his little face inches from mine when I woke up.

That summed up how my Saturday morning was going.

"Were you watching me sleep?" I groaned, tugging the comforter up over my head. "Again?"

"I was making sure you were breathing," he answered. "Your chest was barely moving. I was kind of worried."

I rolled onto my side, keeping the comforter over my face. "You didn't seem worried last night when you told me to feed Caden and you weren't even waiting up for me."

"I did wait up for you!" There was a thump near my head that alerted me to Tink dropping down on the pillow. "And I wasn't worried about the—wait, what? Did you just call him Caden?"

Crap. I squeezed my eyes shut. *Caden*. That was his name and there was a flutter deep in my chest that made me want to smile and scream at the same time. "I meant the Prince."

"No, you didn't." A small hand pushed at the back of my head. "What did you do? Did you do more than feed him? Did you feed him with your vag—"

"Oh, my God, Tink, no." Not that I hadn't tried, but I kept that to myself. "And if you weren't worried about me then why did you think I wasn't breathing?"

"You're old. You could've had a heart attack for all I know."

"I'm not old." I ripped the comforter off my head and glared at the little brownie. He was wearing a pair of leather pants, and I had no idea how he got a pair of leather pants in his size nor why he was wearing them. "Jesus, Tink."

"Look, heart disease is the leading cause of death among women--"

"It's not heart disease. I was sleeping. Normally. But then you woke me up."

"Sorry?" He plopped down in front of my face. "So, I'm assuming *Caden* is okay?"

"He is." I wiggled a hand free and scrubbed it down my face. "He's okay. He's going to be okay."

"Good."

Rubbing my eyes, I shifted onto my back. "So, how did you know that he… that he healed me?"

"Fabian told me, and I don't know how Fabian knew. Guessing he told him."

"And you never thought to mention this to me once?"

"How was I supposed to bring that up? Oh, by the way, the Prince saved your life, pass the salt?"

"Actually, yes, you could've brought it up that way."

"It wasn't my secret to tell."

I turned my head toward him. "You did tell the secret."

"Yeah, but I had to. Anyway." Tink leaned forward, cupping his chin in his hands. "So, what happened between you two?"

"Nothing," I sighed.

"Something happened because you're calling him Caden," he pointed out. "And the only person who calls him that is his brother… and now you."

Head still clouded with sleep, I rolled onto my other side, away from Tink. "I need coffee," I told him, throwing the comforter off. "But I need a shower first."

"To wash away the aroma of a really, really good night?"

"Shut up." I tossed my legs off the bed and stood. The room immediately went tipsy turvy and I sat back down. "Whoa."

"You okay?" Tink was in flight, his eyes wide with actual real concern.

"Yeah." I pressed my fingers to my temples. "I just stood up too fast. That's all."

"You should be careful." He placed his hand on my arm. "Take it easy today."

I smiled at him. "I plan to."

His gaze searched my face and then he buzzed off toward the door. "I'll go turn the coffee on."

"Okay. Thank you."

Tink made it to the door and then stopped, facing me. "You do realize how much of a big deal it is that he told you his name?"

Pushing the mess of hair out of my face, I bit down on my lip. The fae were very peculiar when it came to their real names, as were most Otherworld creatures. Obviously, Tink wasn't Tink's real name, just one that Ivy had given him. "Is Caden his real name?"

His wings moved silently as he nodded. "I believe it is an abbreviation of his name, but yes, it is his name. He shared that with you. That means something, Lite Bright."

I opened my mouth, but I didn't know what to say. It didn't matter though. Tink flew out of the room. Did it mean something? I didn't have the answers, and honest to God, my brain was so not ready for a bout of over analyzation.

So, I got up a lot slower and got my butt in the shower. It was somewhere between shampooing and conditioning that I remembered where I'd seen something about black fae eyes.

It was in one of the old books about the history of the fae in New Orleans that Mom had curated over the years, collecting them from retired and deceased Order members. I'd skimmed through them as I shelved them, so I had no idea if it had any useful information, but as soon as I finished showering and towel drying my hair, I changed into a pair of black leggings and a lightweight black tunic-style sweater and decided to find out.

After making a pit stop in the kitchen to grab a cup of coffee, I went back upstairs to the office. The air was stale in the room and particles of dust floated in the beams of sunlight streaming in through the windows, so I flipped on the ceiling fan.

Ignoring the clutter on the desk, I walked to the bookshelves that lined the wall as I sipped my coffee.

There were *a lot* of books and journals, along with personal diaries. Hundreds of them. And I'd almost finished my drink before I found what I was looking for, a worn, forest green leather bound journal marked Roman St. Pierre.

Taking the journal to the chair that sat near the window, I placed my mug on the old chest and tucked my legs under me. I knew who Roman was. He used to be one of the doctors within the Order and I was pretty sure he'd passed away well over a decade ago. Thumbing past accounts of patrols and random passages about research, I found the section I was looking for.

Dated June 1983 was an entry about a fae who'd been cornered outside an establishment on Decater oddly named… Vanilla. My brows rose at that, but I kept reading and found what I was looking for.

Two male fae were viewed leaving Vanilla and captured a block west. Both appeared to be Changed.

Changed? What the…? I reread that line to make sure I'd read that correctly, and I had.

Their eyes were pitch black, opaque in nature, like the fae that had wounded Torres, confirming Torres' account of the previous attack. Once held in captivity, they experienced rapid degeneration, the likes of which we have not witnessed. Within four hours, there was nothing left of them but dust. Harris believes it was due to their inability to feed, however our previous research suggests that fae can continue living without feeding…

Harris was one of the docs who worked for the Order. Unfortunately he'd died since, so I couldn't call him and ask why in the world a fae would die in that short of a timespan. Or a better question would be what did they mean by infected? I kept reading, turning pages until I reached another entry dated a month later regarding the 'Changed fae'.

"Oh my God," I whispered, nearly dropping the book when I saw her name.

Based on the samples Merle brought back to headquarters, our suspicions concerning the Changed fae were correct. The drink the fae favored had been altered. Trace amounts of an unknown powdery substance similar to Devil's Breath was found in the nightshade. We believe that this substance, which has originated from the Otherworld, is responsible for the Changed fae's increased violent aggression and rapid degeneration. The effects of this substance may be similar to that of Devil's Breath.

Seeing my mom's name caused my chest to compress. It took several moments before I could continue, but when I did I discovered something quite disturbing.

Several pages had been torn out of the journal in many different places, and there was no other mention of Changed fae or Devil's Breath.

Closing the book, I sat there for a moment. Was that place still there? Vanilla? I didn't think so since I'd never heard of it. Rising from the chair, I hurried over to where the desktop computer sat. It took a Godawful amount of time for me to get to Google since there were about a million update alerts. After an eternity of false leads, I found the location of where I thought Vanilla used to be. Near the Candymaker store, there was now a bar called Thieves. I hadn't heard of the place, but that didn't mean much, because there were a metric crap ton of bars and clubs in and around the Quarter.

Pushing back from the desk, I went to the coffee table, where the stack of maps Mom had of all the secret fae hidey holes were. I spread the maps out, dragging my finger along the old parchment until I found where I was pretty confident Decatur was….

And yep, there was a mark above the location where Thieves was.

"Hell." I straightened, popping my hands on my hips. I probably would've eventually checked out the place, but I hadn't made it that far on Mom's maps.

Wondering what the hell Devil's Breath was, I went back to the computer and typed it in… aaand immediately wished I hadn't.

Devil's Breath was a very real thing, one of the most powerful drugs in the world derived from a *borrachero* tree. It was called scopolamine, South America's zombie drug. When used illegally, it could strip a person's free will, erase their memories, paralyze, and even kill them. Apparently, some doctors prescribed some form of it, for what, I didn't even want to know. But if there was an Otherworld plant similar to this, God only knew what it meant if it could strip the will of a fae—

Well, we already knew what that meant, didn't we? Caden was proof of what could happen when a fae—a very powerful fae—had their free will stripped.

Unsettled by the implications, I started Googling the bar known as Thieves and then moved onto public records such as tax and owner information. Hitting the motherload of information, the unease grew when I saw one of the names.

Marlon St. Cyers.

He was one of the Ancients who'd sided with the Queen and had been a powerful real estate developer. He was deader than dead now, but there was another name listed as the owner.

Rica Car I

That was a strange name. Like so strange the longer I stared at the name on the screen the more I began to think it wasn't an actually name at all but an anagram. An anagram for what?

Grabbing a pen and a notepad, I got down to writing out different variations and it didn't take long for me to come up with a name—a name that was the same for both words.

Aric.

Chapter 21

If Miles was to ever discover what I was about to do, the least of the things that would happen would be me being removed from the Order. The worst? They would treat me as if I'd committed treason, and there'd be no lawyers or a court to hand down punishment. The Order acted as judge and jury, and the penalty for betraying the Order was death.

And I was definitely walking a fine line when it came to acts of treason as I crossed the lobby of the building Caden lived in and hit the button for his floor Saturday afternoon.

I could've gone to Miles with the information I'd discovered, but I wasn't sure he would do anything since it involved missing younglings. If there was something crazy going on with the fae, with them Changing, it wouldn't be a problem the Order needed to deal with.

Yet.

But it could be a huge problem. Because if there was something out there that could strip a fae of their free will, and if that was what had happened to Elliot and the other missing younglings, that meant it could happen to *any* of the Summer fae. Hell, all of them.

And that would be bad. Very bad.

So I was going to Caden, because this concerned him and his court *now*.

As I rode the elevator up, I had no idea if Caden was home or not, but I had no way of getting in contact with him. If he wasn't home then I could either camp out here or go to Tanner or Faye to see if they had a way to contact him.

I wasn't acknowledging that I could've had Tink contact Fabian to get that information. I wasn't acknowledging that, because if I did, then I'd also have to acknowledge that I'd chosen to come to Caden's place, because… because I wanted to see him. And acknowledging that meant also acknowledging that I had taken the time to get changed before I came here. I also brushed my hair and left it down, which was more than I did on most Saturday afternoons, and I was wearing a sweater dress with sensible boots. Obviously, the stretchy royal blue dress was not nearly the sexiest thing I owned, but I always felt good in it.

And I also, *also* wasn't acknowledging why I needed to feel good going to Caden's place.

Heart thumping like I'd run up the stairs instead of taking the elevator, I walked down the hall toward his place, my hand twitching around the strap of my purse. Hand trembling a little, I knocked on his door and then took a step back.

He shared that with you. That means something.

I shoved Tink's words out of my head, and God, this was stupid. I should've just tried to get the number from Fabian. There was no reason for me to come here, especially after what had happened last night. He'd fed and I'd had a full body orgasm, which was freaking lovely, but things would be awkward now. And that was something I should've thought of before I came—

The door opened and there he was, standing before me, looking utterly surprised to see me, but looking really good while being surprised.

Caden was wearing a gray Henley that showed off his well-defined shoulders and chest, and he was actually wearing dark jeans and barefoot.

The man had sexy feet and that was something I never thought I'd think.

I'd never seen him so… normal.

Well, not that he could ever truly look normal, not when his features were so unbelievably pieced together perfectly.

"What are you doing here?" he asked, his voice low.

"Hi." My heart flopped around in my chest. "Sorry to, um, just stop by unannounced, but I've discovered something that…" I trailed off as Caden started to step out in the hallway, about to close the door behind him.

"Who's at the door?" came a voice—a vaguely familiar female voice.

My gaze shifted beyond Caden as I thought I heard him curse. His doorway opened right up into the kitchen and living room, so I saw her immediately.

At first, I didn't recognize her, because I'd only seen her briefly, and I wasn't expecting to see her again.

Because I was pretty confident that she was dead.

It was the female fae from Flux—the one who had led me to Tobias.

Alyssa.

She was wearing some sort of black sheath dress, one that clung to her lean, graceful figure and showed off the luminous silvery skin and cleavage and legs for days.

Her head tilted to the side as her brows rose. She looked just as surprised to see me as Caden had.

My gaze dropped to her hand. She was holding… a glass of nightshade and she was also barefoot.

Stomach twisting, I took a step back as my gaze swung back to Caden's. He said… he had said that he'd killed the fae who'd been outside the room I'd been in with Tobias, and Alyssa most definitely had been outside.

And now she was here with Caden, dressed in a sexy sheath of a dress, drinking nightshade with an equally barefoot Caden.

The intimacy of what I was so obviously interrupting was just as shocking as seeing Alyssa alive—a Winter fae with the Summer Prince, in his apartment, drinking nightshade.

Shock thundered through me as the pieces were trying to fit themselves together and the stupidest thing entered my head at that moment. *I've never wanted anyone as much as I want you.*

God.

I was so dumb it should be illegal.

"Who is this?" Alyssa asked, drawing closer, her red lips curling up in a curious smile.

Caden's gaze flickered over my face as he arched a brow. "No one."

My entire body jolted as my eyes locked with his. He stared at me like… like he honestly couldn't believe I was standing in front of him.

"That's disappointing." Alyssa was standing behind Caden now, and he tensed when she placed a hand on his upper arm and rubbed. "I thought it was delivery."

Delivery.

As in I was delivering myself as food to them. Dear God. My mind raced through the possibilities. Either everything Caden had told me from the get-go was a lie, including who he'd killed outside Tobias' room and the whole not feeding thing, or I was missing something very important here.

But at the moment, none of that mattered. I needed to get out of here. "I'm sorry," I said, my voice hoarse. "I have the wrong place."

"Obviously." Alyssa smirked as she curled her hand around his arm. "I don't do plain and old."

"Neither do I," Caden added.

I flinched. Wow. That was… that was freaking harsh. I started to turn, because I was this close to attempting to stab both of them.

"Wait." Alyssa stepped around Caden. "Wait a second. Do I know you?"

Shit.

"You look familiar," she said.

Caden turned into the female fae, circling his arm around her slender waist as he laughed. "You don't know her. Come on, there are things we need to get back to."

She was still staring at me. "But—"

Then Caden's mouth was on her neck, and he was saying something too low for me to hear as he guided her back into the apartment. A soft series of giggles erupted from her as he kicked the door closed in my face, without even looking back at me.

* * * *

I stood inside Thieves, nursing a rum and Coke as I scanned the crowded floor. I had no idea what I was looking for, but I was hanging out near the bar, hoping I would see something suspicious. So far, I hadn't even seen a single fae. However, I'd gotten two guys' phone numbers. Two guys who didn't think I was plain and old.

I took another drink, but it did nothing to ease the burn in my chest. Hours later, I still had no idea what I had really been seeing at Caden's place, but whatever it was, it wasn't good.

And that had nothing to do with the stupid, stupid ache in the center of my chest.

He'd lied about who he'd killed at Flux, but there was a tiny logical part of my brain that told me he could be using Alyssa to get to Aric. It was a tiny part, though, because at this point, I could be wrong about that.

Caden obviously lied about killing Alyssa and she would've had to have seen him that night. He could've lied about a lot of things. Like what he was doing looking for Aric. The whole not feeding thing… or having sex, because it sure looked like something was going on there between them.

I flinched. Again. I took another drink. Again.

Scanning the bar, I brushed a strand of long, dark hair over my shoulder. I'd gone home before I came here. Slipping on a long, brown wig, and a sexier, tighter black dress that was shoulder-less.

Ren and Ivy would be back in the next day or so, and I was going to tell them everything—well, I was going to leave out the whole me feeding Caden thing and the full-bodied orgasm, but I had to tell someone about the Prince, because if he was somehow playing for the other team while playing me for shits and giggles, we were screwed.

But that didn't make sense either, whispered that logical voice in my head. He'd killed fae. He'd saved my life. He couldn't be working with the Winter—

A steely, warm arm circled around my waist from behind, drawing me back against a hard chest and stomach. I tensed, preparing to slam my elbow into the stomach of a very inappropriately forward dude.

"What are you doing here?"

Recognizing Caden's voice, I froze sans shoving my elbow into his midsection even though I really wanted to even more now. "Let me go."

His arm tightened. "You didn't answer my question, sunshine."

"Don't call me that," I snapped as I tried to pull free and failed. "And you really need to let me go."

His sigh shuddered through me as he reached around me with his other hand and plucked the drink out of my fingers.

"Hey!"

He placed that on a table beside us and then his hand landed on my sternum, just below my breasts, stopping me before I twisted around to him. "You don't understand what you saw at my place."

"Gee. Really?" I looked around the packed floor, quickly realizing that no one was going to come to my aid. To the casual observer, it looked like he was embracing me. "And how did you find me here?"

The hand below my breasts flattened.

"What in the hell does that mean?" I demanded.

"A byproduct of saving your life. I can easily find you anywhere."

My mouth dropped open. "Are you freaking serious?"

Caden didn't respond, and he didn't need to, because it made sense, how he popped up where I was and how he said he'd know if I went back to The Court.

"Jesus," I muttered. "That's creepy."

He chuckled, and that annoyed me even more.

"It's not funny. And it's something you should've probably given me a heads up on."

"I didn't because I figured you'd have this response."

I placed my hand on the arm that circled my waist. "You need to let go of me."

"And you need to explain to me why you're here."

"Yeah, like that's going to happen now."

"You need to understand what you saw at my place. I wasn't expecting you."

"That much was obvious."

He made a noise that sounded an awful lot like a growl. "I was using her for information on Aric."

"Really? Because I'm pretty sure she's supposed to be dead."

"What?" He pressed his head to the side of mine, and his warm breath danced along my cheek, sending a shiver down my spine. "You need to elaborate on that statement."

"Do I really need to?"

"Yes." His thumb moved along my ribs and then the underswell of my breast. "You do."

My throat dried as my idiotic, lonely body reacted to the slight touch. A different kind of ache settled in my chest. "She was at Flux. She was Tobias's scout."

"I didn't see her when I showed up," he was quick to say. "She didn't even know I was there, but she was seconds from recognizing you, and that would have been bad, sunshine."

"Don't change the subject." My breath hitched as I felt my nipples harden.

"She wasn't there, but I knew she had ties to Aric."

"Am I supposed to believe you?" I demanded. "Really?"

The arm around my waist flexed as his head shifted ever so slightly. His mouth was against my ear. "Have I ever given you reason to not believe me?"

I opened my mouth, but snapped it shut. He hadn't given me reason to think he'd lie. At least as far as I knew.

"I was using her to find out where Aric is laying low at," he continued, and with each word he spoke, his lips brushed the shell of my ear. "She was about as useful as the bullet holes drilled into me yesterday."

"Oh, I don't know about that. Seems like she was pretty useful to you."

"No." His lips touched the spot below my ear. "She was not. Not a damn thing happened between us."

I stared straight ahead, finding myself watching a young man kiss a girl standing next to him.

"Our bodies are closer right now than she and I were," he went on as the couple clutched at one another. "I'm not going to lie to you. She wanted this." The arm at my waist jerked tighter. "She didn't get it."

Closing my eyes, I drew in a shallow breath. "It doesn't matter if she did."

"Yes, it does."

"I don't care."

"That's a lie."

"No, it's not." I turned my head toward his. The edges of his hair tickled my cheek. "I don't care if you did whatever with her. I just care that you're not working with her—working with them."

"If I was working with them then I'm doing a really bad job at it."

"Or a really good job."

He tilted his head down and those damn lips grazed my cheek. "The one person I am working with, or at least trying to, is you."

"The old and plain one?" I shot back before I could stop myself.

"You are neither of those two things." He rested his forehead against my cheek. "And you know that."

My heart launched itself into my throat. "I'm not old."

"No, you're not." It felt like he smiled against my cheek. "And you're not plain. You're the furthest from that."

I didn't respond as I closed my eyes. I could admit to myself in that moment that perhaps I had jumped to some pretty wild conclusions when it came to him working with the Winter fae or doing something shady in that aspect and my… personal issues needed to stay personal.

"I remembered something this morning. I'd seen a reference to those type of eyes before—the all-black eyes that Elliot had." The grip around my waist loosened enough that I was able to pull free and put much-needed space between us. I faced him and saw that he was dressed the way he was when I'd been to his place. "It was referenced in one of the Order journals."

Everything about his expression was alert and focused. "What did you find out?"

He listened intently as I quickly gave him the breakdown, everything from a substance similar to Devil's Breath to who I suspected might own this place.

When I was finished, the line of his jaw had hardened. "I don't know what substance could be used, but that doesn't mean it doesn't exist and I know who owns this place. It's not—" His gaze flicked over my shoulder and a sudden glint filled his eyes. "We've got company."

Caden gripped my hand, hauling me against him. I opened my mouth, but he all but shoved my face in his chest.

"Hi there." Caden's deep voice rumbled through me. "Is this a welcoming party?"

I placed my hands on his waist, listening.

"We want no trouble," someone said.

Caden's large hand dug into my hair, holding my head in place. "I would assume not."

"Neal wants to speak with you."

"Is that so?" There wasn't a response, but Caden then said, "She stays with me."

"He just wants to speak with you."

"And I don't care what he wants," Caden replied. "She stays with me."

There was a pause and then, "Follow us."

Caden shifted so his arm was around my shoulder, but his hand was still at the back of my head, keeping my face hidden. I caught a glimpse of two big males wearing dark shirts. I couldn't see enough of them to figure out if they were fae or not.

We were led to the back of the bar, through a narrow hall and then a door was opened.

"He'll be with you momentarily," one of the males said and then the door closed behind us.

Caden's hand slipped off the back of my head, and I got my first good look at the room. There was a booth and several unopened boxes along the other side of the wall.

"Should we be worried?" I asked, running my hand along the iron cuff.

He turned, eyeing the booth. "Not we. You."

"What?"

"The owner? He's not exactly a friend of mine nor is he a fan of your kind." He knocked back a strand of hair that had fallen forward, grazing his cheek. "And I'm not talking about you being with the Order.

He's not a huge fan of humans."

"That's kind of offensive." I glanced at the door.

"Yeah, well, it's too late to get you out of here. If he gets a real good look at you, he'll know you're with the Order."

I started to frown. "How will he know?"

"He just will."

Who was the guy that was coming?

"You're going to have to pretend like you like me."

"I don't know if I can do that." I turned to him.

"Do you think all the fae are as stupid as the three you managed to kill?" He glared at me, and surprised flickered through me. "They will figure it out. This one will definitely figure it out."

I waved him off and started to turn, but the sound of voices on the other side of the door grew close.

"Damn it," he muttered, and then his arm snaked out. Without warning, he slid into the booth, hauling me into his lap. Like legit into his lap, one leg tossed over his, the other curled against the cushion of the chair. The skirt of my dress rucked up, exposing most of my thighs. One wrong move, and my behind would definitely be on display.

Gasping, I immediately planted my hands on his chest and pushed back as I tried to scramble off his lap. We'd been closer than this last night, but this was different, because for some inane, annoying reason, I kept seeing her—Alyssa—with her hand on his arm and his face buried in her neck.

"Stop," he seethed. His arm was like steel around my waist as he tugged me back so I was flush with his chest. His eyes burned with irritation. "You better be really good at acting."

My fingers dug into his shirt. We were way too close. My senses were firing off in every direction, causing my head to spin. His hand slid up my back, sending a wave of acute shivers down my spine.

"Because when the door opens, and he figures out who and what you are, I'm going to have to kill him and then I'm going to be really, irrevocably pissed, because apparently there may be some shit going down here," he continued, curling his hand around the nape of my neck and holding my head in place. "So, sunshine, you better fake it till you make it."

Chapter 22

My face was currently shoved against the Prince's throat. Not that I had much of a choice. His grip was like a vise along the back of my neck, keeping my face hidden.

His thumb smoothed over the tense muscles of my neck, reminding me at that very moment that while he held me in place, his grip was gentle.

Later, I was going to have to examine all my life choices that had led me right to this very moment.

"Keep your face hidden, sunshine." Caden's voice was soft as his other hand landed on my thigh. "No matter what."

The door opened before I had a chance to respond and I heard an unfamiliar voice say, "I was surprised when they said…"

He trailed off, and I imagined it was because he wasn't expecting to see a woman in Caden's lap.

Luckily my face was buried in his neck, because I was sure even with all the makeup on, my face was as red as an overripe tomato.

A throat cleared and then the male said, "This is unexpected."

"Isn't it?" Caden squeezed my thigh as I let out a low growl. "Hope you don't mind. I don't want her getting into trouble."

"I can see where she would get in… a lot of trouble."

I was going to kill the Prince, straight up stab him in the chest with an iron stake. Better yet, I should've just let him die.

A door closed. "So, am I interrupting?"

"Not at all," Caden replied. "Just enjoying an evening snack when you interrupted me."

What in the hell? That comment was so not necessary.

Who I was guessing was Neal let out a low laugh, adding to my irritation. Sliding my hands up and around his shoulders, I dug my fingers into his hair and pulled hard enough that he had to fight the motion of his head jerking back.

Caden's other hand came down on my ass. Hard.

I yelped.

Both males chuckled.

I was going to kill him, so help me God, I was going to—

His hand smoothed over the stinging area and he squeezed. I bit down on my lip as I eased up on his hair. The sting… it burned. Muscles in my thighs tensed as a rush of heat flooded me.

Oh God…. I thought I… I thought I liked that, and that was bad, very bad considering my ass had just been slapped in front of someone.

"Not sure I'd want this one as a snack," Neal replied, and I rolled my eyes.

Caden continued kneading the area with his large hand, and if he thought that was going to make the burn go away, he was wrong. The burn was spreading. "Oh, I plan to keep snacking on this one."

I planned on kneeing him in the junk.

"You wanted to speak with me?" the Prince asked.

"I do." The voice was closer, and then I sensed that he sat at the booth. "I was surprised when I saw you on the security camera. You've been… *back* for two years now and not once have you come here."

"So, is this how you greet all newcomers?" Caden's hand drifted off my rear. That was a good thing—a great thing. At first. Because now his hand was on my bare thigh and his long fingers had slipped under the hem of my dress. My eyes widened. What was he doing?

"Only newcomers like you."

"I feel special," Caden replied.

"You should." There was a pause and then Neal asked, "So, what brought you here after all this time?"

Wanting to see who Caden was talking to, I managed to move an inch, and it was the wrong move because it put me more solidly in his lap. The Prince's hand stilled and tensed, holding me still.

Was he…?

Holy smokes, there was no mistaking the thick, hard ridge straining against my inner thigh.

I did not know what to think about that, but my body… Oh God, *my* body was way on board with what *his* body was doing, and that was wrong, just as wrong as me liking it when he smacked my ass.

"Did you know there were some missing younglings from the Summer Court?" The Prince's thumb began to move again, in a slow, idle slide across my inner thigh.

"I did not, but that is unfortunate to hear," Neal replied. "Do you think they have been here?"

"Possibly. I ran into one of the missing younglings last night. There was something odd about him."

"How so?" Neal sounded bored.

"His eyes were… wrong. So black I couldn't even see a pupil."

"Well, that does sound bizarre."

"Does it?" Caden asked carefully. "You know what's even more bizarre is that there's apparently a substance that can rob a fae of their free will and the substance apparently has a neat little side effect."

"Changes their eye color, I assume?"

I felt Caden nod.

"That is interesting, but I don't see how it has anything to do with my place."

"Do you know what that substance could be?"

There was a pause and then Neal said, "I have never heard of any substance that could have that kind of impact on a fae."

Now that was definitely a lie.

"I have a question for you," Neal said. "Heard through the grapevine that several of my… associates ran into an issue at Flux last weekend."

"They did," he answered, and I tensed. "And you should have better associates."

Wait. If Neal was somehow connected to Tobias, then wouldn't he be connected to Alyssa? I curled my fingers around the neckline of Caden's shirt.

"So, you're the reason why Tobias is no longer among us?" Neal asked, and I was a little surprised that this fae would speak so freely in front of me. He had no idea who I was.

Then again, based on my current position, he probably wasn't worried about what I'd say or do. He probably thought I was glamoured.

"I am," the Prince replied.

He'd just lied.

Holy crap, Caden had just lied for me, and he could've said anything, but he took responsibility for what I'd done. I didn't know how to process that.

Neal snorted. "Tobias was an idiot."

"True." His hand was moving again, and every fiber of my being zeroed in on its travels. "Why would Tobias be meeting with Aric?"

"He was?"

"And you don't know why he was at Flux?"

"I figured he was there to fuck and feed as most do."

I wrinkled my nose.

"And they can't do that here?" Caden asked.

"My establishment is a bit more… high class than that." Neal sighed. "You know, I have heard something else through the grapevine. From what I hear, Aric is wanting to test the loyalty of the fae here."

"Loyalty to the Queen?" he asked, and I sucked in a sharp breath.

Neal didn't answer vocally, but I was assuming he must've nodded, because the Prince asked, "Is Aric planning to find a way to contact the Queen?"

"That is something you'd have to ask him, but if I was a betting man, I would say yes," Neal responded. "Aric wants to be more than a Knight. He wants to be a King."

What the….?

The Prince scoffed at that as his hand crept farther under the dress, those fingers reaching the crease between my thigh and pelvis, causing me to gasp. His other hand squeezed the base of my neck, the touching oddly reassuring.

And that made no sense. So it had to be him. His scent was… it was doing strange things to my common sense, but he smelled amazing. A wicked spice and fresh scent that permeated. The skin of his throat was right there, scant inches from my lips. If I opened my mouth, I could taste him.

I shouldn't be thinking about that. I should be paying attention to this conversation, priorities and all, but he was messing with me, and after what I saw at his place and what I'd done for him, that really ticked me off.

Fake it 'til you make it? Isn't that what he said? Screw that. More like make this just as uncomfortable for him as it was for me. He thought he had the upper hand? He was about to learn that wasn't the case.

"Do you know where Aric—" The Prince's voice cut off abruptly as I flicked my tongue over his skin. The grip on my neck tightened, and I grinned. He cleared his throat. "Do you know where Aric is staying?"

"I don't." Amusement clouded Neal's voice. "You know that he knows how to stay hidden."

"Unfortunately." The Prince's voice was deeper, rougher. Then I did something I would've never thought I'd ever do. I dragged the tip of my tongue up the side of his neck, and when I felt his chest rise sharply against me, I nipped at his ear. His chest then rubbed against mine, and

I wanted to laugh. "There's something I want to know," he said, slipping his hand between my thighs, and the laugh died in my throat. I lost the upper hand that quickly. "Are you still loyal to the Queen?"

The question should've set off a million warning flags, especially since I was still convinced that the name Rica was just an anagram for Aric, but I couldn't think beyond where his hand was, how close his fingers were to *touching* me.

"I was never loyal to the Queen in the first place," Neal answered. "I am not loyal to Aric… or to you."

"I never asked for your loyalty." A moment passed and then he touched me with one finger, dragging it down the silk center of my panties.

I stopped breathing.

"You may not have asked, but don't tell me you don't want it. You're the Summer Court's—"

"I know what I am." His finger toyed with the edges of the panty, grazing sensitive skin. Hazy heat swamped me. I couldn't… I couldn't remember the last time I'd been touched like this. "That does not change that I have never asked for your loyalty nor do I expect it."

"Interesting," Neal murmured. "Can that lovely little morsel in your lap handle both of us?"

Hold up.

Every muscle in my body locked up as I held my breath. I had no idea how the Prince would respond. What if he said yes? If so, things were about to get messy.

"I don't share," the Prince growled.

"Well," Neal drawled. "That's a shame."

Part of me relaxed, but only an infinitely small part that wasn't humming from the swipe of the Prince's fingers. I was breathing heavy, my hands clenching at his shoulders at that sweeping heat. Two years ago I would have never imagined allowing something like this to occur, enjoying something like this.

But I was.

I couldn't lie to myself.

"I'm finding this conversation fairly hard to follow," Neal added, his voice thicker. "And the woman, although disappointingly human, to be rather distracting."

"You and me both," the Prince replied wryly while I wondered if he could feel how damp the thin piece of material was. He had to. So that meant I really would have to murder him. "There's something else I need to ask you."

"Make it quick."

I bit down on my lip as his finger traveled down the center of my panties again, but this time with more pressure. It was no slight butterfly touch. Oh no, this one had purpose. The other hand left my neck and curled around my ass.

"Is Aric partners with you?" the Prince said, and I couldn't stop my reaction as his thumb grazed over the bundle of nerves.

My hips twitched into his hand.

"If he was, wouldn't I know where he is? I just told you that I didn't nor was I loyal to him."

"You did." The Prince turned his head, pressing his hot mouth against my shoulder. The kiss… I don't know. It did everything to me. Startled and confused me. Stirred up the heat and newly discovered lust.

"Are you suggesting what I think you are?" There was a pause. "That I'm lying to you?"

"I'm suggesting that Aric is involved in the missing younglings, because I know the missing males wouldn't have willingly disappeared." His finger moved as he spoke, lingering at the most sensitive spot before traveling along the center. It was driving me crazy. He put the slightest pressure against the crotch of my panties, and I bit down on my lip until I tasted blood to muffle the moan. The Prince still heard it. I knew he did, because he rewarded me with a hard squeeze with his other hand. "Not after so many of them lost family members during the battle with the Queen."

"How many are missing?"

"Four so far." His mouth grazed my shoulder again as the hand on my ass pulled me down and against him—against his erection.

None of this was real. It was all an act. So I gave up and the twitch of my hips turned into a slow, grinding roll. I expected to feel shame and embarrassment, but I only felt desire and need and want.

My hands were moving of their own accord, exploring the dips and planes of his chest and stomach. Blood pounded through my veins as the conversation around me faded out. I was moving now, little rocks and twists, and he was pushing his fingers against me, making me wish there was nothing between his flesh and mine.

And that was *insane*.

I couldn't let myself think about what I was doing—riding his hand as he talked to the fae, flushed and hot and aching. Hell, I couldn't think even if I tried. There was a deep, sharp curl in my core, causing my breath to hitch, and it was different than what I'd felt last night. This was real, but….

It's just an act….

And I needed Neal to leave so we wouldn't have to keep up this act, but I didn't want him to leave, because I was so, so close to release, and I thought… I thought I heard a knock on the door.

"I'll let you know if I hear anything about the younglings." Neal's voice was fading away as I tuned back in.

"I'm counting on that." He swirled his thumb and there was no stopping the moan that slipped up my throat or the way his hips punched up in response. "Neal?"

"Yes."

"If I find out that you have anything to do with the missing Summer younglings or if you've been working with Aric, I will fucking destroy you."

"Understood." There was a pause and then, "Use the room however long you need it."

The door closed, and I was holding my breath again, trembling all over. Caden's fingers stilled against me, but he didn't pull his hand away and I didn't lift my head or jump off him like my legs were made of springs. We both were… waiting, and my heart was thundering, my pulse pounding.

"Do you want me to finish?" he asked, voice coarse and hushed.

Yes.

I wanted him to finish me.

But… what was I doing? Neal was gone and there was no reason for this to continue. No good excuse other than seeking a release from him—from the Prince.

No, not from the Prince. From *Caden*.

He folded his arm around my shoulders as he drew back. His lips moved against my cheek as my chin lowered. "You don't have to say anything, sunshine. You understand?"

I tensed so badly I wondered how I didn't break a bone. Trembling all over, I nodded.

Caden made this sound that should've been frightening, but all it did was set my blood on fire and then his finger was under the thin material, skimming through the dampness and heat. I jerked against his hand. No one—no one had touched me in so long. Years, actually, and I knew then that this was no act.

I shifted, spreading my legs and giving him more access and he took it, smoothing his fingers over me and then inside me. I cried out, letting my head fall back as I lost myself to his touch—to him. My hips began moving again, rocking against his hand. A fierce heat surfaced, overshadowing anything I had ever felt before. Building and building till I feared it would consume me.

And then he did something with his finger, hooking it and finding *that* spot. The tension coiled and then erupted. I came hard, hips bucking against his hand as my forehead dropped against his.

I don't know how long it took for everything that shattered to come back together and the room to come back into focus. When it did, I could feel him hard and throbbing under me.

Maybe it was the pleasant haze of post orgasmic bliss that gave me the courage. I lifted up ever so slightly and reached for the button on his jeans.

"Hey." His voice was soft and thick as he caught my wrist, stilling my hand. "You don't need to do that. What I just did, I did without expecting anything in return."

"I know." My forehead was still resting against his. "But I want to."

He groaned deeply. "I wouldn't be satisfied with your hand or your mouth. I'd want to get inside you and not only is this not the place for that, I sure as hell don't want to be inside you when you look like this. I would want it to be *you*."

I sucked in air, shuddering at his words. No one wanted me for who I was but Caden.

"We need to get out of here." He cradled the back of my neck. "Okay?"

Unsure of how to really process him pumping the brakes on this, whatever this was, I nodded. "Okay."

He drew my head back and then I felt his lips press to my temple. He kissed me there, and I don't know why, but that act squeezed at my chest like my heart was in a juice grinder. It was sweet and intimate and… It was everything.

Caden helped me to my feet, where I swayed a little as I made sure my wig was in place. He stood and extended his hand. I took it, threading my fingers through his. We both turned—

The door swung open without warning. Standing in the center was the damn female fae. Alyssa. And she wasn't alone. Behind her were two Ancients, and behind them was another.

"That's her," she said, lip curling. "I knew I recognized her. That's the bitch from Flux. The one who went into the room with Tobias."

Chapter 23

"Crap," I muttered.

"You have got to be kidding me." Alyssa sneered as one of the Ancients shoved another dark-haired Ancient forward, into the room. "Are you working with them too, Neal?"

It was that moment when I realized that Neal was an Ancient. He didn't look all that concerned as he faced Alyssa and the other two Ancients, but I was.

There were two bald-headed Ancients eyeing Caden and me like they wanted to rip us limb from limb, and as I eyed Neal, I really didn't trust the Ancient, because I kept seeing the name listed as co-owner.

"I really have no idea what you're talking about and I really don't appreciate being shoved around." Neal lifted a brow. "In my own bar, no less."

Alyssa, wearing the same black sheath, crossed her slender arms. "Do I look like I care?"

"You should," Neal replied, straightening the cuffs of his suit jacket.

The female fae smirked as her gaze flickered from Neal to Caden and then finally to me. "Do you think I didn't know why you were asking about Aric?" she said, speaking to Caden. "You're the Summer Prince. Wasn't like I was going to trust you."

"But you trust Aric?" Caden still held my hand. "You do realize he was one of my Knights before betraying me. Not exactly someone you should trust."

"*Was* being the key word," came a new voice from outside of the hall.

"Hell," Neal muttered.

Caden let go of my hand.

The two Ancients stepped aside as they were joined by another. He came to stand behind Alyssa and….

And my heart—God, it felt like it stopped, because I *recognized* him. I would never forget those high, angular cheeks or close cropped light brown hair. I'd never forget that mouth and the scar that cut through the right side of his upper lip.

"It's him," I whispered, my stomach twisting. I couldn't believe it. The Ancient Caden was looking for was the one who murdered my mother and nearly killed me. I could feel Caden's gaze on me. "It's *him*."

The Ancient's pale-eyed gaze flicked to me as he placed his hands on Alyssa's shoulders. His head cocked to the side. "I remember you." He laughed. "But you looked a hell of a lot different the last time I saw you. Not just the hair and the dress. Less blood."

I reacted without thought. Engaging the iron cuff, I shot forward with a scream of rage.

Caden snagged me around the waist, hauling me back. "That wouldn't be wise."

"Let me go!" I shouted, digging my fingers in his arm. "He killed my mother. He—"

"I get it." Caden's voice was quiet. "I do, but Aric's not yours."

I didn't care what Caden said or how he felt. Aric was mine.

"He knows." Neal crossed his arms. "About the *mortuus* and the younglings."

Alyssa frowned as my stomach sank.

"You son of a bitch," Caden growled, his arm sealing me to him. "You just lied to my face."

Neal lifted a shoulder. "Like I said, I wasn't loyal to you."

"And you said you weren't loyal to him," I spat back.

"You were listening?" Neal chuckled as he looked me up and down. "And here I thought you were… distracted by his hand up your skirt."

"Shut up," I seethed.

"Interesting." Aric glanced between us. "Very interesting, indeed, seeing you with her. A member of the Order. Can't say I'm that surprised. Do you know I've tasted her blood? Just for the fun of it? Kind of like history repeating itself, don't you think? Makes me think of that little bird of yours."

Little bird?

A roar erupted from Caden. He whipped me to the side and then behind him as he charged forward.

"Don't kill her. Not yet. She's very useable." Aric shoved Alyssa forward, and then drifted back as the two bald Ancients went at Caden.

He caught the first by the throat and lifted him several feet off the floor before slamming him down. The impact rattled the boxes as Caden lifted his head, his glare trained on Aric.

Alyssa slinked forward as the other Ancient caught Caden at the waist. Both flew backward, into the booth. Their weight crashed through the table, shattering it.

"He says I can't kill you," Alyssa said, and my gaze flew back to her. "But he didn't say I couldn't hurt you."

She swung on me, but I was ready. There was nothing stopping me from getting to Aric. If I could just take him out, I wouldn't even need to find the last one. *He* would be enough.

Alyssa cursed. "Oh, you're faster than you look."

"Yeah." I popped up behind her. "I am."

She whipped around, throwing out her arm. She caught me across the cheek, spinning me out. Pain burst across my jaw, but I spun back just as she launched herself at me. I threw out my right hand, catching her in the center of her *throat* with the iron stake. Bluish-red spit into the air.

Shock rippled across her face as I smiled. "Good thing no one told me not to kill you."

I yanked my arm to the side, breaking free of bone and tissue. Her head went to one side and her body went to the other.

The Ancient that had tackled Caden went flying across the room and hit the stack of boxes. They toppled to the floor. Bottles clinking off one another and cracking. Liquid poured out as the Ancient dropped to his knees in a mess of broken glass and whiskey.

Neal sighed. "Do you know how much that liquor costs?"

Beside him, Aric smirked at me as he lifted his hand and wiggled his fingers.

A hand clapped down on my shoulder. I swung out, but hit nothing but air as Caden whirled me back behind him. He started forward once more.

Damn it.

My hand closed into a fist, but before I could do anything, I saw movement out of the corner of my eye. The other Ancient was on his feet and in a blink of an eye, he was right in front of me.

I jumped back, but with him, I wasn't quick enough. Gripping the front of my dress, he lifted me up as I shoved my right hand out. He caught my arm as my feet left the floor.

"Crap," I whispered.

Then I was flying.

This was going to hurt.

But I didn't hit the wall. Caden was suddenly there, between me and what most likely would be a whole lot of broken bones. The impact with him knocked the air out of my lungs. Pain burst along my side as he brought me to the floor. Our gazes locked.

"I'm sorry," he whispered, and then pulled back before I had a chance to figure out what he was apologizing for.

Caden spun and spread his arms to the sides. Both Ancients were on their feet, coming between him and Neal and Aric. What the hell was he doing? I started to sit up, inhaling deeply and catching the scent of… the scent of fire and smoke. An orange-yellow aura appeared around Caden, outlining his entire body.

An enormous amount of heat blew backward, lifting the strands of hair from around my face. "What the…?"

The glow intensified until my eyes watered, but I couldn't look away from what I was seeing. A flame licked out from Caden's hand, rippling into the air and spitting sparks as the fire took the shape of a…

A sword.

A freaking *flaming* sword.

With the grace of a dancer, he spun with the sword, and a flash of bright light rippled out as the sword arced high. I caught a glimpse of Neal. His eyes widened as he stumbled a step, backing into the wall. He said something in their native language.

"Well, hell," Aric drawled. "That changes things."

And then the light and heat were too much. Throwing my arm up to shield my eyes, I scooted back against the broken booth. Only when the heat pulled back did I lower my arm and open my eyes.

The two Ancients were dead, heads separated from their bodies, and Caden and I were alone. Aric and Neal were gone.

There was also no sword.

Slowly, Caden turned to me and those eyes of his—the same amber color of the fire—glowed. And as I stared up at him, I had no idea what I'd just seen, but I knew it was something big.

"You okay?" he asked.

"Yeah." I was still sitting on the floor, arm frozen in the air. "Are you?"

Caden nodded, but as his gaze shifted away from mine and the muscle along his jaw ticked, I didn't think he was telling the truth.

At all.

Chapter 24

"I didn't trust Neal, but I didn't think he would be stupid enough to work with Aric."

I somehow resisted the urge to point out that I had thought the name Rica was suspicious as hell from the moment I saw it as we hurried down Decatur Street.

Caden's hand was wrapped firmly around mine as we cut around groups of people strolling on the street. When we'd left Thieves, I expected everyone to be running screaming from the building since the fight had not been quiet, but when we slipped out the back door, I could hear the conversation from the bar area. Those people had no idea that a fight to the death had just taken place with a freaking flaming sword.

Caden stopped suddenly, beside a sleek black SUV parked a block from Thieves, and opened the passenger door. "Get in."

I looked at the SUV and then at him. "You have a car."

One eyebrow rose. "Is that so surprising?"

"Not as surprising as the flaming sword," I muttered.

He shot me a bland look, and I climbed in and buckled up. I watched him jog around the front of the SUV. He was behind the wheel in seconds, glancing over at me as he hit the ignition button. The moment our gazes connected, they held and I let myself just for a couple of seconds really think about what had just happened.

Who I'd just seen.

"It's him," I whispered as the engine rumbled. "Aric was the Ancient who attacked me and my mother."

Caden reached over and cupped my cheek. He didn't say anything as he drew his thumb along my jaw.

"I can't believe it." A messy, raw knot of emotion formed in my chest. "It was him."

"I'm sorry. I really am," he said quietly. "And I know how badly you want to hunt him down, but you need to stay away from him. I don't say that because I doubt your skill or determination, but he is deadly and he is dangerous. He is as old as me, Brighton, and I'm positive he hasn't spent a day fasting."

A horrible thought occurred to me as his words sunk in. I pulled back. "Did you… did you know it was him?"

"No." He looked away, his gaze flicking to the rear view mirror as he pushed the SUV into reverse. "I'm not surprised. The bastard is sick and cruel, but I did not know."

I wasn't sure if I believed him and I didn't know how to process that right then. I didn't even know how to deal with coming face to face with the Ancient who'd ripped into my mother's throat and torn through my skin while *laughing*.

"We're going to have to involve the Order in this." He eased away from the curb. "With Aric behind the missing younglings and using whatever the hell *mortuus* is, we're going to need all hands on deck."

Hell. I knew what that meant as I shifted my gaze to the window. "I can't promise you that Miles will listen to me. They don't think I'm very… useful."

Caden was quiet for a moment. "What if the information came from Ivy?"

"They would listen. I can call her. Tonight."

"We also need to go to Tanner."

"Now?"

Caden clutched the steering wheel as he focused on the narrow street congested with cars and people. "Now. Call Tink. We'll pick him up."

I glanced down at myself as I pulled my cellphone out of my clutch. "Do we have, um, time for me to get changed?"

"Yeah, we've got time for that."

Calling Tink and getting off the phone quickly wasn't exactly an easy endeavor since he had a million and one questions, but I managed to get off and then I called Ivy.

She answered on the second ring. "Hey, Bri, what's up?"

"Um, a lot. Like a lot." I started quickly telling her about what had just gone down. "We're heading over to Hotel Good Fae now to talk to Tanner and Faye."

"We're actually a couple of miles outside the city now," Ivy replied. "We'll be there shortly after you." There was a pause. "And I hope we find some time to talk later."

"About…?"

"You're going to play coy with me, Bri?" Ivy snorted. "You and I need to talk about how you've been working with the Prince."

"Uh." I looked over at Caden. He didn't seem to be paying attention. "Okay?"

"Yeah. Okay. See you in a bit."

I slipped my phone back into the clutch, unsure of what I was going to tell Ivy when I wasn't even sure I knew what I was doing—what we were doing.

"Is everything all right?"

I nodded. "Yeah, Ivy and Ren are almost back in the city. They'll be there. I guess your brother is with them."

"Perfect."

And after that, Caden didn't really speak and even though there was a ton of stuff I wanted to talk about, like *everything*, right now didn't seem like the… appropriate time. The curious thing about this trip was the fact that Caden didn't need to ask directions to my house.

"Do I want to know how you know where I live?" I asked as we pulled up to the curb outside my house.

He slid me a long look as he turned off the ignition.

"All right," I sighed, opening the door. "Probably don't want to know."

Stepping out of the SUV, I crossed the sidewalk and opened the gate. I took one step and Caden was suddenly in front of me. Cursing under my breath, I shook my head. "You're going to give me a heart attack if you keep doing that."

Caden didn't respond to that as he took my face in his hands, cupping my cheeks. He stepped into me as he tilted my head back. My gaze flew to his. "Is… is everything okay?"

Instead of answering, he lowered his mouth to mine, stopping a fraction of an inch from making contact. Was he going to kiss me? My breath caught. His forehead brushed mine and then his lips touched mine.

The kiss….

There was nothing sweet or soft about it, not like most first kisses were. Oh no, this was fierce and powerful, consuming in the intensity. My lips parted as the tip of his tongue touched mine, and the entire world seemed to slip away. When he finally lifted his mouth from mine, there was a swelling motion in my chest, like I had just taken my first real breath of air.

Caden had kissed me like it was our first and our last.

His fingertips slipped off my cheeks as he stepped back and to the side, and as my gaze focused, I saw that my front door was open. Tink stood there—full-sized Tink. It was always jarring to see him at his full height and wing-less, which was almost the size of Caden.

"Let's head inside." Caden touched the small of my back.

More than just a little out of it, I nodded and walked forward. The closer I got, I could see how wide Tink's blue eyes were. I expected him to say something funny. Call me a hussy or point out that I was just making out with Caden in the front yard, but he didn't say anything. He was staring at Caden like he'd never seen him before.

Tink stepped back into the foyer as we climbed the steps and he didn't speak until we were inside my house, the door closed behind us.

Tink looked like he was about to faint as he stared at Caden. "Should I… should I bow?"

I frowned at him.

Caden shook his head. "No."

I had no idea what any of that was about. "I'm just going to get changed real quick. Make yourself comfortable."

Caden nodded as I hurried to the stairs and when Tink started to follow, he stopped him. "Can we talk for a moment?"

Figuring it was about what happened, I raced up the steps, nearly tripping to my death over Dixon, who sprawled out on the top step. "God," I gasped. "Really?"

Dixon lifted his furry head and meowed loudly as he stretched out his legs lazily. Rolling my eyes, I stepped over the cat and hurried to my bedroom, prepared to strip and scrub my face so fast I'd break records, but as I soon as I stepped into my bedroom, I came to a complete stop. Raising my hand, I pressed my fingers to lips that felt swollen.

I… I was feeling some pretty silly stuff. Perhaps it was everything that had happened in the last week causing me to think and feel like I…. Goodness, I didn't even know.

But instead of obsessing over Aric, over what he'd taken part in, I was wondering if… you could fall in love with just one kiss?

Chapter 25

When I came back downstairs, dressed in the leggings and tunic I'd had on earlier and face scrubbed free of makeup, it was only Tink waiting for me, and it was jarring to see him full size. When Tink was what he liked to call "fun sized," he was just adorable, but fully grown? There was no way you could help acknowledging how attractive he was, and that just made me feel weird.

Frowning, I looked around the foyer. "Where's Caden?"

"He went ahead and is going to meet you in Tanner's office," he said in a voice so much deeper than what I was used to. "He left his car here for you to drive us."

"Oh." That was weird. "Did he fill you in on everything?"

"Most of it." Tink stepped toward me. "He… he kissed you."

Heat immediately smacked into my cheeks. "Yeah, he kind of did."

"He didn't kind of kiss you, Lite Bright. He looked like he was devouring your mouth."

It had kind of felt like that.

"Brighton, I…." Tink trailed off as he slowly shook his head.

A kernel of dread took root in my stomach. "What?"

"Nothing. We should go."

We really did need to get going, so when Tink handed me the keys that would allow me to drive Caden's SUV, I took them. That kernel of dread grew though when Tink was unnaturally quiet as he sat in the passenger seat. And Tink, even when he was full sized, was never quiet.

And he was almost never full-sized around me, not since, well, two years ago.

When we arrived at Hotel Good Fae, Tink headed off to the cafeteria while I went to Tanner's office and waited for Caden. I had no idea how Tink stayed as fit as he did when I swore if he wasn't talking, he was eating something.

Must be brownie metabolism.

Taking a shallow breath, I roamed around Tanner's office, too antsy to sit down. Okay, I wasn't antsy. I was….

I was feeling a thousand different things. Disbelief. Anger. Shock, and then under that, under all of that, there was also anticipation.

Anticipation that had everything to do with Caden.

I rolled my eyes as I walked over to the window, ignoring the dull twinge in my side. There was a bubbling giddiness that made me feel *at least* a decade younger. Was that what love—

"Stop," I told myself and then I laughed, because telling myself to stop thinking what I'd already thought was kind of pointless.

I smoothed my hands over my hair, which felt weird against my neck. I was so used to wearing it up, but Caden had said….

He'd said he liked my hair down.

Actually, he'd used far more eloquent words than that. What had he said? My hair was like—

The door opened in that moment and I spun toward it.

Caden walked in, closing the door behind him, and as he looked over at me, seeming to know exactly where I stood, I got a little lost in… well, in staring at him.

Shamefully lost.

He'd changed, too. Wearing a white dress shirt tucked into a pair of tailored black slacks, he actually looked like a prince—a mouthwatering prince.

And he'd kissed me—really kissed me.

How crazy was that?

Totally insane.

Biting down on my lower lip, I tried to stop the grin from racing across my face so I didn't look crazy. I lost that battle as I started toward him, wanting to hug him—okay, I actually wanted to kiss him again. And I could do that, right? He'd kissed me and, well, he'd done more than that earlier, and—

"Do we have a moment?" he asked, and my smile slowly slipped from my face as I stopped. There was something… off about his tone. Empty. Cold? And his expression was utterly blank.

The sense of dread from the car ride rose as I swallowed. "Yeah, we have a couple of minutes."

His gaze flickered over my face before settling on the window. "I just wanted… to make sure we have an understanding between us."

"An understanding about what?" The dread gave way to a strange buzzing in my ears, adding a surreal element to all of this.

"About us."

I started to sit down, but found I couldn't move. "About us?" I repeated dumbly.

Still not looking at me, he nodded. "I know we have shared… intimacies, mostly under extreme circumstances, and we share this attraction."

Incapable of moving, all I could do was stand there as what felt like a fist reached into my chest and squeezed. That was how I knew what he was about to say. My heart already knew.

"I think you're incredibly brave, foolishly so at times," he continued, and a rush of prickly heat crept up the back of my neck. "You're intelligent and kind, and your beauty rivals that of the sun."

I sucked in a shaky breath. All of that sounded… sounded wonderful and beautiful and something I felt like I'd been waiting my whole life to hear, but…

I knew where this was going.

"Stop," I whispered, voice embarrassingly hoarse. "You don't have to do this."

"I do," he said, and I closed my eyes against the sudden, unwanted burn. "You are a treasure, Brighton."

"Okay," I laughed, the sound coarse to my own ears. "I'm a treasure?"

"You are." His voice softened.

I opened my eyes and I hated that. Hated how his expression wasn't void of emotion anymore. It was strained and tense and his gaze was conflicted.

Pressing my lips together, I dragged my hand through my hair as the wind seemed to whoosh out of my lungs.

"I don't want things to be awkward between us," he said, and another laugh crawled up my throat.

I turned back to him. "Why would it be awkward, *Caden?*"

He flinched at the sound of his name. "Because what we had, whatever that was, it wasn't real. It was an act that… that got out of hand."

There it was.

He wasn't beating around the bush anymore, but I didn't understand. I knew what he was saying, but it didn't make sense.

"You told me it was real." I managed to keep my voice steady.

"You even called me out when I lied about how I felt. You said you wanted me. You just kissed me. You said you—"

"The physical part was real. How could it not be? You're beautiful and I'm—"

"And you're a man, and that's just how it goes? Really?" My eyes widened. "That's how you're going to play this? There was just a physical attraction and that's all?"

"I'm not playing anything. It's just the way it is." Caden turned from me, shoving a hand over his head, through his hair. "It's the way it needs to be. You're human and I'm—"

"I know what you are." My heart pounded in my chest as I folded my arms across my stomach. "I've always known what you are."

"Then you should know," he said.

"No, I don't. You just kissed—"

"I know I kissed you and that was—that was a stupid *mistake*."

"A mistake?" I whispered.

"Things have changed." His voice hardened now. "I don't want things to be uncomfortable between us. We need to work together. You need to put this behind us. I already have."

The hole in my chest cracked my heart as I stumbled back from him. I knew it shouldn't matter. I was just acknowledging that I had feelings for him—how deep those feelings ran, I didn't know—but there was a hole opening up in my chest.

There was no denying he meant what he said. I heard it in his voice. I saw it in his face, and I had no idea how I'd misread things with him so badly. How I could've been so damn foolish to think there was more to what was between us.

Humiliation festered to life, settling into my bones and spreading like a fever, flushing my skin.

Caden—no, he wasn't Caden to me anymore. He was just the Prince, and he must've sensed the sharp, bitter swirl of emotions churning through me, because he stepped toward me.

"Brighton—"

"I get it." I cut him off as I stepped to the side. "Message received."

"I'm—"

"Don't apologize. God, please don't apologize. That's…." When his face began to blur I knew I needed to get out of this room. I would not lose it in front of him. I would not cry over what could have been when there was apparently nothing in the first place. "You said… you said you wouldn't hurt me. You lied."

He drew back as if I'd hit him.

"I need to go," I said.

And I did.

Ivy and Ren would've been here by now, waiting for us in the main common area, and I just… I just needed to get the hell out of this room.

Giving him a wide berth, I skirted around the chairs and made a beeline for the door. I made it and I made it out into the empty hallway knowing that the Prince could've stopped me at any moment.

But he hadn't.

He'd chosen not to.

Acknowledging that hollowed out my chest, and I walked to the common area in a daze, focused only on breathing around the burn in my throat.

Hands shaking, I kept them fisted tight as I picked up my pace, reaching the main hall. There were fae everywhere. They spilled out from the common area, their eyes wide and the hum of excitement charged the room.

I had no idea what was going on as I scanned the unfamiliar faces. There was a shock of red hair toward the back. *Ivy*. She and Ren were here, which meant that was probably where Tink was. Concentrating only on getting to them, I didn't notice the first fae to drop to their knee before me.

But then they went down in a wave, one after the other, dropping to their knees and bowing deeply, placing their right hands on the floor. All of them went down until I could see Ivy standing near the entrance to the common room and beside her was Ren. Both looked surprised as I felt.

Neither of them looked as shocked as Prince Fabian, though, which was saying something because both Ren and Ivy looked about as confused as I felt.

Prince Fabian's long blond hair was pulled back, revealing just how pale his face was as his lips moved wordlessly.

Then he dropped to his right knee and placed his right hand onto the floor.

"What the hell?" I whispered, turning around slowly, knowing they weren't bowing for me, because duh.

Things are different now.

I saw him in the hall I'd just hurried out of, the edges of his blond hair brushing those wide shoulders and those odd amber eyes were not on the fae who were bowing to him but on me.

"Oh my God," I whispered as Tink's words from the night the Prince was wounded came back to me in a rush. *If he dies, then Fabian becomes King and he… he can't be King.*

Did that mean…?

He closed his eyes and a reddish-yellow glow appeared, just like it had before, as if there was a halo of light behind him. There was no flaming sword this time when the glow receded.

Instead there was a burnt gold crown atop his head.

Caden was no longer the Prince.

He was the King.

The King

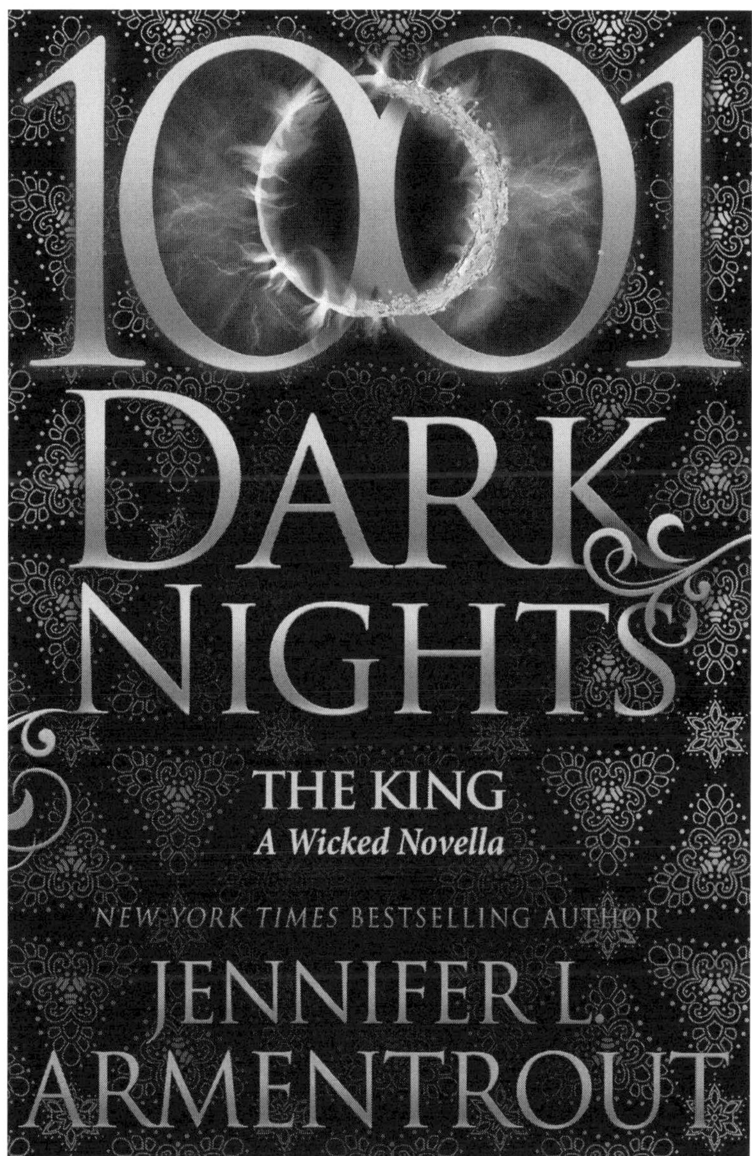

1001
DARK
NIGHTS
THE KING
A Wicked Novella
NEW YORK TIMES BESTSELLING AUTHOR
JENNIFER L.
ARMENTROUT

Acknowledgments from the Author

Thank you to Liz Berry, Jillian Stein, MJ Rose, Kim Guidroz, Chelle Olson, and the wonderful powerhouse team behind 1001 Dark Nights. Thank you for allowing me to continue to be a part of the family.

And thank you, the reader, always and forever.

Chapter 1

"I don't think this is wise," Tink said for what had to be the hundredth time since he realized I was getting ready for a night out. "Like I think this is very poorly thought-out, if you ask me, Lite Bright."

"I didn't ask you, Tink."

My uninvited roommate of sorts hovered outside my bathroom. Tink wasn't human, but right now, he looked like any normal twenty-something guy. Well, if normal, twenty-something guys had natural, shockingly white hair and were beautiful in a way that almost seemed fragile.

This was his full-grown Tink size, something I was still—even after all this time—getting used to. I was more accustomed to pint-sized Tink with the translucent wings. After all, he was a brownie.

After the attack that had taken my mother's life and should've ended mine, he'd basically moved in with me. He'd been here for the last two years, something Ivy's husband pretended to be grateful for, but in reality, I knew he secretly missed the dude.

"You should ask me," he replied. When I glanced over at him, I got a little distracted by the dazzle…emanating from the sequin tank top he wore. It was so shimmery that I wondered if he was using some of his magic.

Tink may be a goofball, but he was also one of the most powerful creatures in our realm.

Thank God there was only one of him.

"I am a wealth of amazing advice," he continued. Dixon, the cat he'd named after a *Walking Dead* character that Tink called "the hottest redneck eva" slinked around Tink's ankles. The cat was all gray except for his tail, which looked like it had been dipped in white paint.

I snorted. "When have you ever given me good advice?"

"When I told you two weeks ago not to eat the whole carton of beignets because you'd get sick and you did," he shot back.

I winced, picking up my mascara. I had gotten sick, but I deserved that carton of sugary, fried goodness. That day…

I didn't want to think about that day.

"And what about when you ordered that supreme pizza and ate almost all of it?" he said. "I told you that it would probably make you feel bad later."

Nose wrinkling, I tried to remember what night he was talking about. There were a lot of Friday nights—pizza night in my household—that I ate an entire pie and felt terrible afterward.

"Or how about that time I told you that the seared ahi tuna looked a little gray for my liking? But, oh no, Brighton knows better." He reached down, scratching Dixon between the ears. "You ate it all, and then I spent the night cleaning up your puke."

Ew.

I hadn't eaten seared ahi tuna since then.

"And let us never forget when you ate the whole bag of—"

"Why do all your examples involve me pigging out?"

Tink raised his brows.

I rolled my eyes. "Whatever. You know, you used to totally support me going out there and finding the fae responsible for killing my mother." I twisted toward him just as Dixon scampered across my bedroom, launching himself onto my bed. "I have a name now. The Ancient who was with the fae that night. The one who ripped my mother's throat out and tried to gut me."

"I know, and that's all the more reason you shouldn't go out there looking for him."

"I don't understand your logic." I pointed the tube of mascara at him. "I've been searching for him, and now he's here, somewhere in this city. I'm going to find him."

"Aric's an Ancient, Brighton," Tink argued. "They are not easy to kill, and they're incredibly dangerous. Way more powerful than an ordinary fae."

"I know that. Look, after I saw him at that bar Thieves, no one else has seen him. But Neal has been sighted at Flux. Neal is working with Aric." I turned back to the mirror, and heavily lined eyes stared back at me. "If anyone knows where to find Aric, Neal will."

"And you think you can make him tell you?"

"You don't need to sound so shocked by the idea," I muttered, opening the mascara.

"Neal is an Ancient, too. He's been alive for hundreds—"

"I know what an Ancient is, Tink. Look, they're doing something to the Summer fae younglings, turning them evil. This isn't just about me." And that was true. I suspected that I knew what *was* responsible, a substance called Devil's Breath. It was similar to one of the world's most powerful drugs derived from a *borrachero* tree—scopolamine, South America's zombie drug. Harris, who had since passed, wrote about it in one of his journals, saying that a white, powdery substance had been found in nightshade, a drink the fae favored. The only way to be sure that it was responsible for what had caused the youngling to turn as he had was to catch one who was infected or get my hands on the drink.

"We need to stop them," I said.

"Ivy and Ren will stop them." Tink leaned against the doorframe. "That's their job."

An uncomfortable rush of heat rose to my skin as I looked back at Tink. "It's my job, too. I am a member of the Order, despite the fact that everyone keeps forgetting about that."

Tink's pale blue eyes widened. "I know you are. I didn't mean it wasn't your duty. You're—"

"It's okay," I cut him off, knowing that whatever compliments he gave me about my battle prowess wouldn't be words he believed. Over Tink's shoulder, I saw Dixon stick his furry ass in the air, shaking it for a second before attacking my pillow, sinking his claws and teeth deep as he rolled.

I'd gone through so many pillows because of that cat.

I sighed, turning back to the mirror to get back to work finishing the rest of my makeup. In other words, I made myself look like a walking and breathing Snapchat filter.

It wasn't *just* makeup I was putting on. I was reshaping the angles of my cheeks and brow with shading and highlighting, skills I had picked up from a YouTuber who was probably all of thirteen years old. I was drawing in fuller, pouty lips with a liner, and creating the illusion of wider eyes by using thick eyeliner and deepening the lower eyelid with foundation and shadow. Combined with my newly contoured face and the long, curly, black hair courtesy of a wig, no one would recognize me as Brighton Jussier.

Except *him*.

He would know it was me.

I closed my eyes as a pang lit up my chest. Damn it. I was not going to think of Ca—of the King. Nope. Not at all.

After swiping on a layer of mascara, I shoved the wand back into the tube. Finished, I stepped back and got a full look at myself.

The thigh-length, super-tight, black dress and red lips combo could be summed up in one word. Vampy.

Dressing this way wasn't exactly normal for me. I was a sweats and a T-shirt type of girl, but no one in this world or the Otherworld was more distracted by tits and ass than the fae, male or female.

Brushing past Tink, I went back into my closet that used to be a small nursery.

Tink followed. "The black knee-highs would complete your I-charge-a-lot-for-sex look."

"Perfect." I snatched them up.

He watched me shove my feet into the footwear. "Why don't we have an *Avengers* marathon tonight?"

Right boot halfway zipped up, I stopped and looked up at him. "We have watched every one of those movies five times, even *Captain America*. I don't think I can sit through another *Captain America*."

"The movie is a little boring, but Chris Evans' fine ass makes up for it."

I tugged up the zipper and moved to the other side. "True, but not today. It's Saturday. Fabian is back. Aren't you going to spend time with him?"

"He can come over," Tink suggested, clapping his hands excitedly. "You know I'm leaving soon. I'm going to be out of town for, like, forever. We should spend time together."

Tink was finally going with Fabian to Florida, where a large populace of Summer fae lived. For the last two years, the Prince had been trying to get Tink to visit, but he wouldn't. The brownie claimed it was because he wasn't ready to make that kind of commitment, but I thought it had more to do with the fact that Tink didn't go out much. He'd gone with Ivy to California once, but other than a trip to Hotel Good Fae—the compound where the Summer fae lived—he stayed home. I imagined the human world was a bit overwhelming to him.

"You're not going to be gone forever," I pointed out, admitting to myself that I was going to miss him and Dixon since he was taking the cat with him. "You're only going down there for a few months."

"That is forever. Come on, it will be the best threesome ever."

Straightening, I arched a brow.

"Chris Evans. Popcorn. Face masks. That kind of threesome."

"Uh-huh." I reached into the cubby hole, grabbing what looked like simple bracelet cuffs. In reality, they hid iron blades sharp enough to pierce fae skin and cut an Ancient's head off. "You can still have that threesome without me." I snapped the cuffs into place. "I'll be home late."

Tink turned. "The King doesn't want you out there."

I stopped, and it took me a moment to face him. "That's why you've gone from wanting me to take you with me, to asking that I don't go out."

He lifted a shoulder.

Taking a step toward him, I reminded myself that I liked Tink and stabbing him wouldn't be cool. "Have you been telling *him* I've been hunting?"

The brownie's face went impressively blank. "I have no idea what you're talking about."

"Tink." I met his stare and held it.

He threw up his hands, startling Dixon enough that the cat released my pillow. "I didn't tell him anything, but just so you know, if he demands it, I have to. He's my King."

"Really?" I replied dryly.

"Yeah. Sort of. But, seriously, he hasn't asked me if you've gone out, but he has told me that he doesn't want you out there. It's not safe. He thinks—"

"I know what he thinks." I'd seen the King since he told me that there was nothing between us, which had come right after I admitted to myself that I was developing serious feelings for him—had already fallen for him, actually. Things weren't exactly amicable between us. I was confident that if Tanner, the fae who oversaw Hotel Good Fae, heard me call his King an asshole one more time, he was going to ban me from the hotel. My jaw tightened. "He's told me every time he's seen me that I have no business hunting fae. That it's the Order's job. I guess, like everyone else, he's forgotten that I work for them, too."

Which was why I kept calling him an asshole to his face. It wasn't because he didn't want me, even though he'd led me to believe that he did. It wasn't because he made me think I was special and beautiful and interesting without the makeup, the fake hair, and the skimpy clothes. He was a different kind of asshole for those reasons. In a way, his dickish attempts to control me—which had failed—made it easier to deal with what had happened. The deep hurt had quickly given way to anger. And cursing someone out was far better than lying awake at night, crying as I ate yet another cupcake.

"He hasn't forgotten." Tink's voice was soft. "I don't think you understand why he's done what he's done."

Oh, I thought I understood perfectly. I was nothing to him, and whatever we did have had just been a mistake in his eyes. After all, he was not only a fae, he was the King, and I was just…Brighton, a thirty-year-old who had helped his brother once when injured. The King claimed that wasn't the reason he'd healed me after the attack, but I believed differently. He felt like he owed me.

"I don't care enough to understand his motivations," I said. "I know why he doesn't want me out there."

The King didn't want me to stand down just because it wasn't safe. And while I at least hoped he didn't want to see me dead, I didn't think he was losing any sleep over the possibility.

No, the real reason was that the King was also looking for Aric. Back in the Otherworld, the Ancient had been one of his Knights. Aric had betrayed him to Queen Morgana, stabbing him through the chest and weakening him so that he was susceptible to the batshit crazy Queen and her magic. So, yeah, he had valid reasons for going after him.

But so did I.

If the King found Aric first, he'd kill him, and I would never get the chance to carry out my vengeance against the creature responsible for killing my mom. And, well, that was…that was all I had.

* * * *

The rapid thump of music from the overhead speakers matched my mood as I swayed in the shadows of Flux's dance floor, a club that catered to the fae. This was where I'd found and killed Tobias, one of the fae who'd joined Aric in the attack against my mother and me.

I wasn't worried about being recognized in the mass of twisting human flesh that churned alongside and against the fae in the place. Most of those that frequented Flux were of the Winter Court—the *bad* Court that actively hunted humans to feed on so the fae did not age. The very same Court that belonged to Queen Morgana. Every so often a Summer fae was spotted, but those sightings were few and far between.

I saw no fae at all tonight.

Questing hands slipped from my waist and slid down to my hips again. Frustration made me grab What's His Name's wrists harder than I intended. I'd honestly rather be scrubbing my lady bits with a brillo pad than dancing with an obvious first-timer to New Orleans, one who wore so much cologne, he could star in an Axe body spray commercial. However, lurking alone in a club like this was suspicious. Not when everyone came here to hook up.

"Damn, girl, you got a hell of a grip on you," he murmured into my ear. "That's hot."

I rolled my eyes as I placed his hands back on my waist.

"So, you come here a lot?" He squeezed my hipbones.

"No," I said, focusing on the dance floor near the stairs that led to the private second level, where the fae normally chilled in-between glamouring humans and feeding on them.

"Then I guess it's my lucky night, isn't it?"

I opened my mouth to tell him to not only talk less but also wear less cologne, when I felt a tight shiver of awareness. The kind of feeling you got when it felt as if someone were—

The man behind me shouted in surprise. His hands left my hips as I spun around. The dark-haired tourist stumbled, catching his balance on a nearby table. He shoved off it, puffing out his chest, but drew up short a second before broad shoulders and a tapered waist clad in a black shirt blocked my view. The guy's blond hair was secured in a short ponytail, and the scent of summer rain replaced the overpowering musk of cologne.

I sucked in a sharp breath of disbelief as I saw What's His Name dart to my left, intelligently wanting nothing to do with what stood in front of me.

I could not believe it.

Crossing my arms over my chest, I waited. I didn't have to wait long. He decided to grace me with a full-frontal of what had to be—unfortunately—the most beautiful male face I'd ever seen.

The King was here.

Chapter 2

The sense of deja vu was too strong to ignore. It felt like an eternity ago that I'd come face to face with him inside this very club, and the last time we'd met in here, I'd tried to spin-kick him.

I had a feeling that history might repeat itself.

Cad—*the King*, I corrected myself. The King was stunning. Cheekbones as sharp as a blade, nose straight and aristocratic, and a jaw that could've been carved out of marble. He had the kind of face you found yourself staring at and wondering how it could be real. And now, those full, expressive lips were tilted in a smirk.

Seeing him so unexpectedly seemed to short-circuit my brain because I wasn't thinking about how he'd hurt me. All I could think about was how good he'd made me feel. Not in the physical sense, though that had been amazing too, even though we hadn't had sex. But it was the important stuff. I…I missed that.

"You can do better than that, sunshine," the King of the Summer Court drawled.

My stupid, stupid heart skipped a beat at the nickname. He'd told me that he called me that because I reminded him of the sun.

Such BS.

Pulling the anger around me like a favorite sweater, I walled up my heart, protecting it from its own stupidity. I lifted my gaze, ignoring how the amber color of the King's eyes both frightened and tantalized me. "Don't call me that."

"Whatever you wish." He stepped forward, and my eyes narrowed. "I'm sure you can imagine my utter lack of surprise at discovering you here."

"And I'm sure you can imagine my utter lack of surprise realizing that you're stalking me again."

He arched a brow. "Well, who else is there to keep you from getting yourself killed?"

My jaw ached from how hard I clenched it. "I don't need anyone to do that other than myself. And I especially do not need you."

"That's your opinion," he stated as if it were the stupidest belief in history. "I know why you're here. You've learned that Neal was seen."

No point in lying. "And if you're here now, there's no way he's going to show up."

The King's smile was real, stealing a little of my next breath. "Exactly."

My hands curled into fists as the realization that tonight had been an utter waste slammed into me. The only thing I got out of it was being groped. If the King was here, Neal would be nowhere near.

"You're a jerk," I spat, spinning around and stalking off.

I didn't look back to see if he followed as I cut around the dance floor and made my way toward the exit.

I hadn't seen the King the entire week and a half I'd been out here looking for Neal or Aric—or any fae who may know where they were. A few times, I'd felt the creepy sensation of being watched, but if that had been him, he'd never revealed himself. Until now.

Shaking my head, I slammed my hands on the door and stepped out into the cool evening air, letting it wash over my sticky skin. Goosebumps rose, but I didn't care. In a few weeks, it would be as humid and horrible as Satan's balls.

Part of me wasn't surprised that the King had found me so easily in the club. Like I'd admitted while I was getting ready, he always knew it was me, no matter how drastically I altered my appearance.

How bizarre was that?

And I also wasn't surprised when I heard his voice behind me. "You should be home."

"You should mind your own business." A horn blew from somewhere along the packed Warehouse District streets. Ever since developers had decided to reclaim a lot of the empty industrial buildings and turn them into expensive apartment complexes, clubs, and bars, the traffic was getting as bad as it was over in the Quarter. I shot him a glare over my shoulder. "And you better not be talking to Tink about me. That's not cool."

"I'm not," he answered, and then his brow creased. "But he did tell me about something to do with tuna and a possible food illness."

My mouth gaped. "Tink told you about that?"

The King nodded.

I was going to kill that damn brownie with my bare hands. I picked up my pace.

The King easily caught up to me, walking on the side of the traffic. "What you're doing is my business. *You're* my business."

I shot him a look. "Yeah, no, I'm not."

"You're out here hunting a fae—"

"That you want to kill yourself. Cool story." I stopped at the street sign, tugging down the hem of my skirt. Power walking in spandex was not advised.

"That's not why. It's not safe."

"I can defend myself." The moment the little green man appeared on the light, I hurried across the street, toes cramped in the narrow boots.

The King was right beside me, his long-legged pace easily matching mine. "I do not doubt that."

"You don't?" I forced out another laugh.

"No, I don't, but this is different. You're looking for a Knight. A skilled warrior who has killed indiscriminately in the past. If you thought the Order had a right to fear me when I was under the control of the Queen, they should be even more worried about him."

That made me stumble. When the King had been under the spell of Queen Morgana, he'd been a psychotic killing machine. But I already knew that Aric was just as bad. I had the scars all over me to prove it.

But in reality, I knew very little about the Ancient. There was nothing in my mother's journals or on file with the Order. I'd checked. And it wasn't like the King and I had been on speaking terms beyond trading death glares.

I stopped, ignoring the muttered curses of the guy behind me. "Tell me about him. I want to know everything."

The King looked away, jaw tight. "He was my Knight, and he betrayed me, stabbing me through the chest while I fought."

"I know that. Tell me what he's like. What makes him tick. What—?"

"Why? Why do you think this information is important? So you can build a profile on him?" Fiery amber eyes met mine. "Nothing I tell you will help you fight him and survive. You," he said, stepping into me, "you are just…"

"What?" I challenged. "I'm just a human?"

"You're just Brighton," he said. "You cannot defeat him."

Just Brighton? What the hell was that supposed to mean? I didn't think I wanted to know. "Look, I don't care what you think. I'm going to find Aric, one way or another. You can't stop me, and frankly, I'm done talking to you. Goodnight."

I started walking again, getting halfway down the street before I realized that I was going in the wrong direction.

Damn it.

Not like I was going to turn around now. No way. Nothing screamed "*skilled badass*" like going in the wrong direction in the damn city you had grown up in.

"What's your plan, sunshine? Find Neal? Then what?" He caught my arm, stopping me at the mouth of a dimly lit alley. "How do you plan to make him talk? To bring you to Aric? You plan to use your feminine wiles?"

"Feminine wiles? Buddy, it's not the fifteenth century any longer." I tugged on my arm, but he held on. "And I plan to use an iron blade in his throat. That's how."

"Really?" The King's grip was hard, but his palm felt like fire on my skin. "Neal may not be much of a fighter, but he is still an Ancient, capable of throwing you across the street without even touching you."

"I will have the element of surprise."

"That's a godforsaken terrible plan."

My face flushed under the layers of foundation. "I didn't ask for your opinion."

"You should ask someone." His eyes widened with surprise. "Anyone. They'd tell you the same thing."

"I have a plan," I seethed, pulling on my arm. And I did. Kind of. Not that I was going to share it with him. "Why do you even care?"

His eyes flashed a stunning tawny color, and somehow, he was even closer, and we were no longer on the sidewalk but in the alley. Each breath I took was filled with his fresh scent. "Because if you do happen to find Neal and force him to bring you to Aric, he will kill you, and it will be slow and painful."

The image of Aric formed in my mind. Short, with light brown hair and a scar that cut through his upper lip. Coldly, cruelly handsome. He had the most…malicious laugh I'd ever heard.

"I already lost someone—" He cut himself off, and I frowned. "You have no idea what you're up against and the type of cruelty he is capable of. He already knows we're connected. You do not need to be on his radar any more than you already are. You're…" He trailed off, but my mind decided to fill in the blank with something he'd once said to me.

You are a treasure, Brighton.

Yeah, what he'd told me before had obviously been a lie. What had he said about us? Not like I'd forget that anytime soon. He'd said it was a mistake—a stupid mistake.

It hadn't been for me. God, it had been the opposite. I had opened myself up for the first time since the attack, feeling comfortable enough to talk about how I needed retribution and about that night. Because I had believed…I believed that he understood. I'd let him in.

I pushed all of that aside. "Let go of me. There's nothing I want to talk to you about."

He cocked his head to the side. "Agree to let this need for revenge go, and I will."

"How about you agree to do the same thing? Oh, wait, we've had this conversation. You think it's different because it's you."

The King's eyes swept over my face. "You want to know about Aric. I think you're being this way because of us."

"There's no us," I shot back.

"You're right."

The sharp slice of pain returned, cutting through me as if he'd jammed a knife into my chest.

His nostrils flared, and he took a step toward me. "Shit."

Damn it, he was sensing what I was feeling. There were a lot of things that annoyed me when it came to Caden, but this was probably in the top three.

The King looked away, jaw hard. "I'm—"

"Don't."

He ignored me. "I'm sorry."

"I don't care."

"But you do."

"And that's the problem, right? You know, I do have something to say to you. You led me on. But for what reason? That's what I don't get. What did you have to gain by pretending you…wanted me? Were you just bored and decided to mess with my head?"

His gaze snapped back to mine. "That was not it."

"Then, what? You felt like you owed me because I let you feed on me when you were dying?" I demanded. "Or were you just slumming it with the thirty-year-old human?"

The King's eyes widened, and when he spoke, his voice was so low that I almost didn't hear him. "Why do you view yourself so poorly?"

"What?" I gasped, skin flashing hot and then cold.

He shook his head. "You have to. It's the only reason you'd believe that was my motivation."

His words stunned me, and the little voice in the back of my head that whispered that there was some truth to what he stated propelled me into action. I yanked on my arm and, this time, he let me go. Unprepared for the shift, I stumbled backward, and my damn boots were no help.

The King sprang forward, catching me. A startled heartbeat later, I was in his arms, and my hands were on his chest.

Holy crap.

This was as close as we'd been since he kissed me, and I seemed to have forgotten how incredibly warm he was. His body heat chased the chill from the air. Standing this close to him was like sunbathing. My skin turned shivery as a deep, aching pulse took root.

Space. I needed space. Like a different time zone's worth of space.

But I didn't move.

Slowly, I lifted my head. Our gazes connected.

There was hotness to his stare. A thick, predatory gleam to his eyes, and a challenge to the way his lips parted. A wild thought occurred to me. He wanted me to push him away, and he wanted to chase.

A deep, hidden part of me wanted to be hunted by him.

And that was so wrong.

The King's gaze drifted over my face once, then moved lower. I felt my chest swell against his.

"I hate when you look like this," he said, his voice thick. "Not the dress. I love the dress. And the shoes. But the hair? Makeup? I hate it."

It took nothing for me to remember him telling me that before. The fact that he preferred me, the *real* me, was one of the reasons I…

Why I had started to fall for him.

His chin lowered. "You should burn all these wigs and throw away the makeup."

My heart pounded. "Not going to happen." I sounded way too breathless. Way too affected.

"That's a shame." His head tilted, and then his lips were inches from mine. When he spoke, I felt his breath. "I would pay any amount of money for that."

I considered that. "How much? Tink is an expensive roommate."

"I can imagine." His eyes took on a heavy-lidded quality, and I felt the softest, barely-there brush of his mouth.

I gasped.

The King jerked away. This time, he didn't spring forward when I stumbled. I caught myself as he moved back several steps until he wasn't even within arm's reach of me. Breathing heavily, I didn't know if I should feel relieved or disappointed that he hadn't kissed me. Well, the problem was, I knew I should feel relieved. And I didn't. Disappointment crashed through me as we stared at each other in the soft glow of the street lamps.

"Go home," he said after a few moments. "There's nothing here for you."

I flinched at the double meaning. His words stung, but a wave of prickly heat soothed the hurt. I latched on to it. "Don't tell me what to do."

"I'm not." He folded his arms. "I'm giving you a choice."

"Really?" I laughed as I mimicked his stance, crossing my arms. "Sure doesn't sound like it."

"Oh, but it is. I'm telling you to go home, and I'm giving you the choice to do so all by yourself. Or, I could pick you up, put you in my car, and drive you there."

My mouth dropped open. "I would love to see you try to do that. Seriously."

His head cocked to the side, and then he unfolded his arms, taking a step forward.

I threw out my hand. "If you so much as touch me, I will cut off your nuts and stab you in the face."

"Damn." He chuckled, sending a fine shiver down my spine. The sound was as deep and as nice as I remembered. "That's aggressive."

"I'm feeling really, really aggressive."

"Hmm." He tipped up his chin. "Normally when I touch you, you want to do other things to my balls."

My lips parted on a sharp inhale. A dozen different things I could do to his balls danced like really weird sugarplums in my head, and none of them included kicking him.

Then I saw the way his jaw had softened and noticed the curve to his lips. He was…*amused.*

Fuck that.

I stiffened my spine. I'd be damned if he found me amusing. "You know what? You're right. There was a whole lot of things I wanted to do to them. Kiss them. Lick them. Suck them."

His humor vanished as his gaze sharpened on me. An almost predatory glint filled his eyes, making them luminous.

"I wanted to get so familiar with them that we were on a first-name basis," I continued, keeping my hand up. "But that was before. Not anymore. Now, I'd rather cut them off."

"You sure about that, sunshine?"

"Don't call me that. And, yes, I'm a hundred percent positive. A hundred and twenty-five percent, to be exact."

"A hundred and twenty-five percent?" he murmured. "Interesting. Then why haven't you engaged your blade with me?"

With a frown, I glanced down at my wrist. He was right. I hadn't triggered the blade from the cuff.

Damn it.

Damn it all to hell.

Chapter 3

Why do you view yourself so poorly?

The King's words haunted me throughout the evening and all night long. Was that what he thought? That I had no self-esteem or sense of self-worth? Just because I couldn't understand why he'd pursued me and then wanted nothing to do with me.

Stewing over what he'd said, what it could have possibly meant, had kept me up for hours. But what woke me a few hours before dawn on Sunday morning, was the little voice that kept whispering that there might be some truth to his question.

After all, why *did* I think that he'd said all those wonderful things about me? Why had he kissed me and brought me such mind-numbing pleasure? Was it because he felt that he owed me for getting his brother back to Hotel Good Fae when he'd been hurt? Or because I had allowed him to feed on me when he was gravely injured with wounds that wouldn't have been so serious if he'd been feeding in the first place? He'd been shot the night I'd found Elliot, one of the missing fae younglings that had turned evil, presumably due to the tainted nightshade.

Not once did I think to myself that he'd simply been attracted to me, despite the fact that I was human, and he was surrounded by stunning, ethereal fae.

And there was a good chance that he was *still* attracted to me despite cutting things off. It seemed like he'd been about to kiss me on Saturday night. Hell, his lips had touched mine. Barely, but still. And what if he had kissed me? Would I have allowed that? I couldn't seriously be questioning that. I knew that I would've, and likely would have been pissed off at myself afterward.

I needed to get my life right.

Starting with finding and killing Aric and not allowing myself to be wooed by the King. Both, at this point, seemed of equal importance. None of this stuff with the King mattered, and neither did my possible lack of self-esteem. If I survived my showdown with Aric, I'd work on that with self-help books or something.

Sighing, I watched the early morning sunlight creep across the floor toward the edge of the bed where Dixon lay curled in a tight ball. He hadn't been there when I fell asleep.

The sudden creak of a footstep landing on the loose board I kept planning to fix stirred the cat awake. Dixon's furry head lifted toward the door I knew he'd managed to nudge open at some point during the night.

He started purring, sounding like a mini-engine.

Figuring it was Tink, who was probably about five seconds from dive-bombing the bed, I rolled onto my back and looked toward the door—

My heart stopped in my chest.

That was how it felt, like it came to an unexpected, jarring halt. My lips parted as my brain tried to process who I saw standing there. It wasn't Tink.

It was him.

The King.

He stood in the doorway of *my* bedroom like he belonged there, as if he'd been invited. And he most definitely had not been invited, nor did he belong in my house.

At all.

But it was him, his golden hair free and brushing the full breadth of his shoulders, his plain black shirt following the lines and curves of his muscles.

All I could do was stare at him.

One side of his lips curved upward. "Good morning."

I sat up so fast I startled Dixon. The cat stood, shooting me a baleful glare before hopping off the bed. "What are you doing in here?"

"Tink let me in." He glanced down as Dixon brushed against his leg, the cat's tail high. "You know, most people usually respond with 'good morning' when they are given that greeting."

"I don't care what most people do," I exclaimed, promising myself that I would straight-up murder Tink. Which was a promise that I made a lot. "Why are you up here? In *my* bedroom?"

Reaching down, the King scratched the cat's head, earning himself a rather loud purr from the feline. "I wanted to see you." It took me a moment to get my tongue to work. "I think I made it pretty clear the other night that I have no interest in seeing you." "I know." The King gave Dixon one more pat, and the cat scampered off down the hall. The fae rose to his full height, those tawny eyes meeting mine. "But we both know that's not true." "I-I—" I sputtered in disbelief. "You're out of your mind. Seriously."

"I was never in it." His gaze flickered over my face and then moved lower, lingering. "Definitely not now."

My brows puckered as my gaze followed his to the deep vee in my sleep shirt. The pale pink top had slipped off my shoulder, and the material was thin enough to reveal that there was a chill in the room. That was the reason my nipples were hard. It had absolutely nothing to do with the King's presence or the way he was staring at me.

Nope. Not at all.

I clenched the edges of the blanket. "You could've just waited until I got up."

"I'm not very patient." He strode forward, and I tensed, my eyes glued to him as he sat on the bed—*my* bed.

"I didn't say you could sit down."

"I know."

I stared at him.

The King stared back, his infuriatingly sexy half-grin appearing. "I wanted to talk."

"About?"

His gaze flicked from me to the wall. "About Aric."

Every muscle locked up. That was unexpected. "And this couldn't wait until later? Like when I'm not in bed?"

"No."

"No?"

"I've found catching you off guard makes conversation with you easier."

My brows slammed down. "I don't think that was a compliment."

"It actually was," he replied, his gaze tracking over my bedroom, lingering on the stacks of books and framed pictures of my parents and me. "He's truly evil."

I blinked, not following him.

"Aric. You wanted to know more about him. That's what you need to know. He's pure, unadulterated evil, and I do not make that statement lightly. Nor do I believe most have ever come across someone who is actually evil," he said, and I could not stop the shiver of dread from curling down my spine. "He cut straight through me in battle, weakening me so I was susceptible to the Queen's spell. But he wasn't always my enemy. At least I had not known him to be. But you knew that already."

I did.

"He wasn't just one of my Knights, assigned to protect me. We grew up together, his family closely linked with mine. He was one of my closest confidants. My friend. And the whole time, he was plotting to betray my family and our Court." The King looked away. "How does one look another in the eye, day after day, have supper with their families, and be privy to their secrets and desires, all the while hating them enough to destroy those closest to them?"

"I…" I swallowed. "I don't know."

"Neither do I." He cleared his throat. "He drew our Court into war by killing many of our younglings before taking someone who meant a lot to my family…to me. He did not just kill his captive. No, that would've been too easy. He did things that no creature—human or fae or animal—should ever suffer through. And he did this, all the while pretending to help us find our loved one, eventually leading us right to the body of…" He shook his head. "It's something I will never forget seeing. Even under the Queen's spell, the images… They remained."

"I'm sorry," I whispered, reaching out without thinking and placing my hand on his arm. His skin was warm under my palm as I squeezed gently. "I really am."

He looked down at where my hand touched him and, after a moment, he continued. "It wasn't until we were in the middle of the battle that he revealed that he'd been behind it all. And he *reveled* in my shock, my despair. He got off knowing how deeply that cut because I looked upon him as a brother—not of my blood, but of my heart."

Sickened, I had no idea what to say.

"And he made damn sure I knew what had been done to the one he took. To all of them. I saw the proof his words carried on the bodies of his victims," he said. "I saw what he was capable of. I *felt* what he's capable of. Some kill because they have to. Some because they enjoy it. He's the latter."

I believed that beyond a doubt.

"Do you understand why Aric is so dangerous? He is capable of anything." The King lifted his gaze from where my hand still rested on his arm. "Not just because he's loyal to the Queen, but because he is truly evil. A real monster who enjoys inflicting pain and terror. He's not like others you've faced. He's not…he's not even like me when I was under the Queen's spell."

"I do understand. He's done terrible things to you. To me. He's dangerous, and he's evil," I told him, swallowing the thick lump of emotion that had taken root in my throat. "But I've always known that about him. I know that I—"

"That you will most likely die seeking vengeance?" he cut me off. "A slow, most definitely agonizing death? Is revenge truly worth that?"

I pulled my hand back. "I think you of all people know the answer to that."

A muscle flexed along his jaw. "Brighton, please—"

"There's nothing you can say. Nothing you can do—" My words ended on a sharp inhale as he moved too fast for me to track. He was suddenly over me, his arms caging me in against the headboard. I inhaled, drowning in his citrusy scent. My heart thumped against my ribs as his warm breath coasted over my lips.

"I won't do it," he growled.

"Do what?" I whispered, shivering as he lifted a hand, placing his palm against my cheek.

"I won't do it," he repeated, sliding his thumb over my lower lip. I gasped. His head tilted as his hand slipped down my throat and over the bare skin of my shoulder.

My eyes drifted shut as heat filled my blood. Part of me hated how my body responded to him, how my heart swelled and raced whenever he was near. All of me wanted him, though, and I loathed that most of all.

"I too am capable of just about anything," he said, voice thick and low. "And I will not let you get yourself killed."

My eyes flew open, but the King was already gone.

* * * *

"Bri?" Ivy waved a hand in my face.

I blinked, focusing on her. "What?"

Her pretty visage broke into a smile. "You haven't been listening at all, have you?"

Glancing around one of the meeting rooms tucked away on the first floor of Hotel Good Fae, I saw that Ren was still poking around the box of doughnuts. The impromptu late Monday morning meeting hadn't kicked off yet.

"Sorry." I looked over to where she and Faye, one of the Summer Court who'd helped Ivy escape captivity a few years back, sat across from me. "What were you all saying?"

"Nothing of importance," Ivy replied, grinning. Her mass of red curls was down today, framing her face. There was a sort of elfin quality about her, but there was nothing delicate about her strength. "You just looked like you wanted to punch someone over there."

"My resting bitch face is strong today." I picked at the hem of my pale pink skirt. I was dressed as if I worked in an office, while Ivy wore the more standard Order attire of cargo pants, a cotton T-shirt, and the kind of boots you could kick ass with. Miles, the head of the Order, had me on the bench. Well, I'd always been benched, regulated to research, which wasn't bad. I mean, I loved learning things and tracking down info, either from scouring the internet or flipping through pages of books that smelled old. At least, I'd loved it up until recently.

Until I had to hide the fact that I was hunting, even from Ivy and Ren. All they knew was that I had been working with the King to find the younglings. They didn't know I was patrolling, just like they were.

And when the shit hit the fan, no one called me...unless they needed to know a location or needed someone to pick them up.

Now, I was feeling, well, not all that useful.

"No one's RBF is as good as Faye's." Ivy leaned back, hooking one leg over the other.

The dark-haired fae slid Ivy a long look, and...yeah, that was a really strong RBF. "Pot, meet kettle."

Ivy grinned. "Tink's leaving today, right?"

"This evening. I'm going to miss him," I admitted. "Don't tell him that, though. He probably won't go if you do."

"I'm glad he's going. It's about time he gets out there and sees something that doesn't involve the Amazon website."

I laughed.

"The community in Florida is excited to meet Tink," Faye commented. "None of them have ever seen a brownie. It's a big deal to them."

"They can keep him," Ren chimed in from sifting through the doughnuts.

"Whatever." Ivy rolled her eyes. "You'd be sad if he didn't come back."

Ren didn't respond to that, and I thought about how quiet my house was going to be tomorrow. No Tink. No Dixon.

"So, what's going on?" Ren returned, half a powdered doughnut consumed. How his shirt didn't end up looking as if he'd shoved his face in a pile of cocaine was beyond me. "Why the meeting?"

"I honestly don't know." Faye twisted the long strands of her hair. "Kalen texted this morning saying we needed to meet."

No sooner had she finished that sentence than the door opened. Tanner, who was like the head honcho of the day-to-day goings on at Hotel Good Fae entered first. I saw the way he presented himself to humans for only a few seconds before the glamour faded away. The only thing that didn't change was his hair. It was salt and pepper, proving that he was aging like a normal person would. There seemed to be more white each time I saw him. He hadn't fed in a very long time.

He wasn't alone. Kalen followed him, dressed very similarly to Ivy and Ren in dark cargo pants and a plain shirt. Fair-haired, he looked to be around Faye's age—in his mid-twenties, maybe a little older. Both he and Faye were fighters, warriors, and I was pretty confident that neither fed. Besides being highly allergic to iron, they could be taken out in just about any way a human could, even though they were faster and far stronger than we were.

Tanner smiled as his gaze moved over us, stopping on me. His grin faded a little. I sighed. He was still irritated with me. I started to look away, but then a third individual entered the room, and the air seemed to be sucked right out.

It was the King.

I wasn't surprised to see him here. He was always at these meetings, impromptu or otherwise, but no matter how many times I saw him, it was still a shock to the system.

Especially when he wore what he did now. There was just something about a loose, white dress shirt rolled up to the elbows that got me hot and all kinds of bothered. I had no idea why.

My gaze flicked up, and I saw that, like the last few times I had seen him, he wore no crown. I'd only seen it once, when he revealed it. How he made it appear and then disappear, I had no idea.

I looked away, exhaling long and hard. Today, I would just pretend that he didn't exist. I wouldn't interact with him, and I wouldn't rise to the bait. He could say whatever he wanted, tell me as many terrible stories as possible. It wouldn't change anything.

Faye rose, bowing elegantly in the King's direction.

"There's no need for that," he advised her. "I keep telling you that.

All of you."

"Habit," Faye murmured.

Despite what he had just said, all but Kalen waited until the King sat in one of the upholstered, gray chairs before they took seats themselves. Kalen remained standing just to the left of the King.

Because I apparently had no self-control, I glanced over to where the King sat. Our gazes immediately connected. *Crap.* I refocused on Tanner, my heart thrumming.

"Thank you all for coming." Tanner leaned back, clasping his hands together. "Unfortunately, Kalen has some distressing news that we felt we needed to share."

"Why don't you guys ever want to meet with us when you have good news?" Ren asked, having finished his sugary treat. I had to wonder the same thing.

Kalen gave a faint half-grin. "For a while, we had no bad news."

"And you never really called," Ren replied, sitting on the arm of the couch that Ivy sat on. "I'm beginning to think you all don't like us that much."

"Well..." The King drew out the word.

Ren's eyes narrowed, and considering that neither Ren nor Ivy had really gotten over the whole being kidnapped by him when he'd been possessed thing, I really couldn't blame the King for not wanting to be around a pissed-off, constant reminder.

"You know all of you are always welcome here," Tanner cut in smoothly, although I doubted he was talking about me. "No matter what is going on."

"Anyway," Kalen said. "Back to why we're all here. It has to do with Elliot."

Oh, no.

I looked over at the King, who had been the one to stab the young fae. I knew that he'd shared the news with Tanner and crew at some point. He was still looking at me, and I had to wonder if he was aware of how noticeable—and creepy—that was.

Faye shifted across from me, tensing. Her cousin Benji was also missing, and considering what had happened to Elliot, I knew she feared the worst. "What about him? Something happened to him that made him evil, but he's gone. Right?"

The King nodded. "He's been sent back to our world, but when I spoke to his family, his older brother didn't want to believe what'd happened."

"Which is understandable," Tanner said. "Everyone responds to grief differently, and denial is so much easier than anger."

"I've kept an eye on Avel, but apparently, not a close enough eye." Kalen folded his arms over his chest. "His parents just told us last night that he left here on Friday and has not returned since."

"We're concerned that whatever happened to Elliot has befallen his older brother," Tanner explained.

I pressed my lips together as the worst-case scenario formed. Damn it. Those poor parents.

"That's only a couple of days," Ivy pointed out. "Are we sure that's the logical conclusion? Is it possible that he just needed to get away?"

"It is totally possible, but the entire Court is aware that something happened to change Elliot," Faye said. "Of course, those of us who have missing family members are…assuming the worst. Even if Avel didn't want to believe what the King shared with him, he would've come to understand it. He is a reasonable man."

"If he understood it, then why would he have left?" I asked. "I'm guessing if you all told the Court, it was probably advised that they not leave the hotel."

"We haven't advised that. Not yet," the King answered.

Surprised, my brows lifted as my stare met Ivy's. She wore the same WTF expression as I did. "Something out there is capable of turning happy-go-lucky fae into murderers, and we're just going to let the younglings go out there?"

Tanner stiffened.

The King, however, smiled at me. It wasn't exactly a warm expression, and nothing about him was like the man who sat in my bedroom a little over twenty-four hours ago, telling me about Aric and coming…so close to kissing me. "Taking away the freedom of others because one has been changed does not seem like an appropriate measure to take at this time."

"Except we now have parents who lost one child and are now missing the other," I challenged.

"And we have hundreds of fae that come and go here every day without incident," the King continued. "We advise them to use caution. All of them are aware of the concern, and therefore, would not disappear without telling their family." That was said to Ivy. "Avel would know that his parents would assume the worst."

Their assumptions were probably true.

I got why the King didn't want to force all the fae to stay within

Hotel Good Fae, but it seemed like a pretty successful preventative measure to me.

"I know that you two are patrolling, so we wanted to let you know to keep an eye out for Avel," Kalen said. "I'll text you guys the most recent photo that his parents provided to us."

Ren nodded. "We'll keep an eye out for him. But, man, the other two haven't surfaced. Sorry," he said to Faye. She nodded, her shoulders tensing. "There've been Winter fae out there, and none of them are talking about the missing younglings. I fear we'll hit the same roadblock with Avel."

"It doesn't hurt to be aware, though." Ivy tipped forward, resting her elbows on her knees. "I'll talk to Miles, too. Let him know."

I snorted, earning strange looks from everyone but the King. "I'm sorry, but good luck with that. I already tried, and the Order are… Well, you can guess."

"That's bullshit," Faye snapped, rising to her feet. "Sorry for cursing," she added when Tanner frowned at her. "Bullshit was the least offensive word I could think of. We helped them defeat the Queen. We saved Order members' lives."

But the Order didn't see it that way.

I didn't say that, because I doubted anyone in the room needed to hear it.

"I will try to talk some sense into Miles. It's just that right now, we have a lot of new recruits still learning the ropes," Ivy advised. "Things are a bit chaotic on that front."

"But he could learn to multi-task," the King countered. "If not, I believe the Order needs a new leader."

Ivy looked at him dead-on. "I'll let Miles know you said that."

"Please do." His tight smile returned. "Perhaps it will motivate him."

Ren coughed out a laugh. "Hopefully, it motivates him to do what you intend."

The King lifted a shoulder that said he wasn't worried. Not even remotely.

Kalen turned to me. "The King told us you found something in your mother's research about Devil's Breath. Some kind of substance mixed with nightshade that changes those who drank it, correct?"

I nodded. "Actually, I found it in Harris's old journals. He said my mother had discovered it, but it sounded an awful lot like what happened with Elliot. I didn't see any rapid degeneration with his body that was mentioned in the text, but Harris wrote that it caused violent aggression."

"Degeneration? Like falling apart?" Ren asked.

"Yes."

"Like a zombie degenerates?" he added.

"Well," I said, my brow pinching. "I don't know if there's that much degeneration."

"I hope not." Ivy shuddered. "I really do not want to face down zombie fae."

Those were two words I'd never thought to hear combined.

"I was hoping that you could check to see if there was anything else written about it," Kalen asked. "How it's made or being used. Anything."

"I've looked through all of Harris's journals. There were a few pages torn out, which yes, is suspicious, but there's a lot of my mom's stuff. I haven't gone through all of it yet, and it's possible there could be something there. I will check." With all eyes on me, I felt a little nervous flutter in the pit of my stomach. "But I'm glad you brought that up because I've been thinking about it. The best thing I think we can do is somehow get a sample of Devil's Breath so we can test it. Even if my mother or Harris wrote more about it and I can find those notes, we still need it to see what it truly is."

"And how do you suggest doing that?" the King asked.

I remained focused on Kalen. "We know that what is being done to the younglings is related to Neal, who owns Thieves. And Aric. Now, we know that bars like Thieves cater to the fae. They have a ton of nightshade on hand. It's possible that this Devil's Breath could be there, too. We just need to get inside."

"*We* have thought of that," the King replied. "And we've been inside."

Surprise whirled through me as I twisted toward him. "You have?"

He nodded. "Over a week ago. We raided the place and took possession of the nightshade. The drinks were tested, and they came back clean. As did the entire bar."

"Well, first off, knowing that would've been helpful," I said, piqued. "And that's why Neal has disappeared. People tend to do that after they get raided."

"It was necessary."

"Was it? Really?" I shook my head. "For a several-hundred-year-old King, I'm surprised by your lack of stealth."

"Brighton," Tanner said under his breath.

"What would you have done?" the King asked.

"Glad you asked *now*," I said. "I would've snuck in and obtained samples of the nightshade while searching for what probably resembles bags of coke."

"Sounds like that would've been a good plan," Ren commented.

"And how would you have snuck in?" The King hadn't taken his eyes off me for one second. "I'm curious."

I doubted he was all that curious, but I'd tell him just to prove how dumb raiding the place was. "I would've—"

"Wait. Let me guess. Dressed up in a costume? Slipped past them and gotten behind the bar?"

Stiffening, my gaze met his. No one in this room other than he knew that I did that.

"Do you think that no one would notice that?" he continued.

"Not if I hid really well. I know how to blend in and not draw attention until I need a distraction." My fingers curled in my lap. "But that isn't a job I would do alone. I'd go with someone that could make enough of a scene so I could get behind the bar undetected."

"I doubt one could make that large of a scene."

"Okay, then the place could've been searched when it was closed."

The King smirked. "You think they don't have security?"

"Actually, we do need to search the place when it's closed," Kalen said.

"Security shouldn't be an issue." I smiled tightly at the King, aware that everyone was watching our exchange like a tennis match. "And it sounds like it wasn't to you."

"No, it wasn't, because we're *trained* fighters." The King's gaze flickered over me, and I sucked in a sharp breath. "By the way, you look much better than the last time I saw you out."

I looked better than the last time he saw me? The last time he saw me, I was in my pajamas in bed. The time before that, I'd looked like a vampy hooker. He'd said "out." My lips thinned. He wouldn't. Oh my God, he wouldn't.

"What?" Ren glanced between us. "How so? She looks the same to—" His words ended in a cough, and I suspected that Ivy's elbow had something to do with it. "I don't know what I'm saying. Ignore me while I get another doughnut." He rose.

"I saw Brighton at Flux," the King announced, and my mouth dropped open. "This past Saturday night."

"What?" Ivy exclaimed.

Ren stopped halfway to the doughnuts and faced us.

"That isn't the first time I've found her there," the King continued. "She's been hunting."

I couldn't believe it.

The asshole had just outed me.

Chapter 4

I shot out of the chair like a rocket had been attached to my ass. Suddenly, his words from Sunday morning came back to me. He'd said that he'd do anything to stop me. He hadn't been lying. "You son of a—"

"Ms. Jussier," warned Tanner. "He may not be your King, but you will respect him while you're here."

Respect him? I'd respect him when I had a reason to, which was not right now. "And when I'm not here? Can I disrespect him then?"

Kalen covered his mouth with his hand as he looked at the floor, seeming to find the hardwood fascinating as Tanner sputtered.

"Hunting what?" Ivy demanded, coming to her feet.

My head whipped to her in stunned disbelief. Did she really have to ask that? "Hunting rabbits?"

Apparently, Ren didn't even find that funny. His bright green eyes narrowed. "That's what you'd better be doing. Or hunting crocodiles or whatever you locals do in your spare time."

"That would be alligators," I corrected him with a frown.

"Please tell me you're not hunting fae," Ivy said.

"And why would it be a big deal if I am?"

"Why? You're not trained, Bri. You're not—"

"I am trained." Irritation flushed my system. "I received the same training both of you did."

"But you're not in the field," Ren reasoned, shaking his head. "You have never been in the field, so all that training means shit."

"Listen to Ivy," the King urged. "You cannot interact with Aric or Neal. The fact that they already know you're involved is bad enough."

"I can handle myself," I said. "Pretty sure I've proven that."

"All you've proven is that you're incredibly lucky," he fired back.

"You're not like them." He gestured to the others. "You're not a warrior with years of experience under your belt."

"I'm a member of the Order. I'm trained and—"

"You are a member, but this is not your job," Ivy stated.

"If hunting and killing evil fae isn't my job, then what is?"

Silence greeted me, and damn if that wasn't telling. I focused on Ivy. "I have been in the field. I have been for the last year and a half, and, hello, not once have I gotten myself killed."

"A year and a half?" Ivy screeched. "How? Wait. Was that what he was talking about with the costumes and shit?"

"Yes. I disguise myself. Sometimes it's…elaborate. Other times, not." I folded my arms so I didn't pick up something and throw it. "I make sure no one recognizes me, not even other Order members."

Ivy stared at me.

"*He* recognized you." Ren gestured at the door.

I turned, realizing the jerk King had bailed, along with Tanner and Kalen. How like him. "Yeah, well, he's special," I muttered.

"You're out there, by yourself, without anyone knowing what you're doing?" Ivy asked.

"Obviously, the King of all douchebags knows." Thank God the sleeves of my blouse hid the cuffs because I figured if they saw them on me, they'd both stop breathing.

"He doesn't count," Ivy shot back. And, wow, that would've been funny if I weren't so angry. "Wait. Does Tink know?" Her eyes widened. "He has to know, and he's said nothing to me." She went for her phone.

"Don't drag him into this!"

"Oh, he's been dragged—"

"He didn't tell you because it's not your business!" I threw up my arms. "And I didn't say anything to you because I knew you'd react this way. All of you forget that I'm an Order member. I've had the same training you have, and the only reason I'm not in the field is because I had to be home to take care of my mother." Dragging in a deep breath, there was no stopping me now. I was on a roll. "I know you all think I'm not strong or skilled enough, but guess what, I've fought fae. I didn't need backup or anyone to help me. I didn't need the Order or any of you to tell me that I'm good enough to be out there. I did it all on my own."

Ivy drew back. "It's not that we think you're not good enough."

"It's not?"

"Wait a second," Ren cut in. "You've been hunting for the last year and a half?" He came forward, stopping by the arm of the couch. "Basically, after you had enough time to get back on your feet following the attack."

Pressing my lips together, I said nothing.

"You're hunting the fae who attacked you," he said. "Aren't you?"

"Oh, Bri," whispered Ivy, looking away.

"What is that supposed to mean?" I demanded. When Ivy just shook her head, I was a second away from picking up a chair and throwing it. "You know what? Yes, I have been hunting them. I know who they are, and I've killed four of them."

Ivy's gaze shot to mine.

"Yeah, I did, and I will keep doing it until I kill the fifth," I told them. "And then, after that, I may keep hunting. The Order needs the additional bodies, and I'm good." Swallowing hard, I lifted my chin. "Despite the fact that I wasn't out in the field."

Ivy opened her mouth, then closed it. "I think…it's incredible that you are such a good fighter, and I don't mean that in a patronizing way."

It sounded awfully patronizing to me.

"But I remember what it was like to see you in a hospital bed, hooked up to tubes and fighting for your life. I remember what it was like to go to your mom's funeral—to *all* of those funerals," she said, and I flinched. "We almost lost you."

I softened. A little. "And you almost died too, Ivy. I didn't think you were incapable of fighting afterward. I didn't expect you to quit."

Her chin dipped, and I waited for her to say it was different. But common sense seemed to prevail, and if she thought it, she at least didn't say it.

Ivy's shoulders rose and fell, and then she quieted. "You're my friend, Bri. You're my only friend, actually. I'm just… I'm worried about you."

"Wow," Faye murmured, alerting us to the fact that she was, very much, still in the room. "I thought I was your friend."

"You are." Ivy turned to her. Faye lounged on the couch, looking as if she were missing a bowl of popcorn. "I meant that Bri is my only human friend."

"Do you normally separate your friendships by species?" Faye asked.

"I didn't mean—"

"I'm kidding." Faye laughed. "You're my only human friend, too."

I frowned. Did she not consider me a friend? Damn.

"What about me?" Ren demanded. "I don't count?"

"You always count, Ren. Always." Faye's gaze shifted to me, her stare assessing. "They are just worried about you. You did almost die, but so has Ivy. So has Ren. And you want revenge for what was done to you and yours. That's understandable."

"You're not helping," Ivy snapped.

"And neither are you," Faye replied calmly. "She knows how to fight, obviously. She's killed."

"Thank you," I said, feeling some of the tension ease out of my shoulders. Someone finally recognized that I wasn't book-nerd Willow anymore, friend to Buffy. I was kickass Willow—though not evil, dark Willow.

"But you being out there is a risk." Faye's cool eyes flicked to me. "It's personal to you. Not in the same way it is to other Order members. That makes it dangerous."

I swallowed a truckload of curses, and then round two of why Brighton should just stay safe at home with her nose stuck in a book began. At some point, I plopped back down into the chair, and just…stopped arguing against all the various reasons I shouldn't be hunting in general and let it all sink in. I allowed it to really sink in that even with them knowing that I was capable of killing and defending myself, they didn't believe I was capable *enough*.

And that didn't just make me mad.

It also hurt.

* * * *

I didn't go to the offices of the Order, nor did I go home. After I'd managed to extricate myself from Ivy and Ren—and Faye—I caught an Uber and headed to an apartment in the Warehouse District. I'd run into Kalen while looking for the person who'd not only thrown me under the bus but then backed up over me. Kalen had said he was here, and if he weren't, I would find him.

The King and I needed to have a little chat.

I stalked down the hall of the tenth floor, growing more furious than I even knew was possible. Stopping at his door, I banged my fist on it like I was the police.

Only a few seconds passed before I heard the click of the lock and the handle turning. The moment the door opened, I didn't even give him a chance to shut me out. I barged right in, shouldering past the King as I clutched the strap of my purse.

"Well, come on in," he stated dryly. "And help yourself."

"Plan on it." My gaze roamed over the exposed brick walls and rather bare space. Like the last time I was here, there was only the large sectional couch and the TV. It still didn't look lived in. "Hope you don't have company." I spun, facing him. "If you do, I don't…"

I trailed off, thinking that I probably should've looked at him before I forced my way inside. He wasn't exactly shirtless, but that white shirt of his was completely unbuttoned, giving me an eyeful of his toned chest and a tight, ripped lower stomach.

God, he had the kind of body that wasn't even human.

Probably because he *wasn't* human.

The King arched a brow. "Do you see something you like, sunshine?"

Cheeks heating, I snapped out of my stupor before I started drooling. "Did you forget how to button a shirt?"

A faint grin appeared. "Actually, I was going to change it. However, I was interrupted by someone banging on my door like a madwoman."

"Oh, I am definitely a madwoman." I glared up at him. "How could you do that?"

"Do what?" he asked, leaning against the wall.

"Don't pretend like you have no idea why I'm here."

"Is it because I outed you?" He crossed his arms, which made his pecs do amazing, interesting—*stop it!* "For your own safety."

Dumbfounded, I was momentarily speechless. "My own safety?"

"There seems to be an echo in here."

"There's about to be an ass-kicking in here," I shot back, hands balling into fists. "I don't need you looking out for my safety."

He tilted his head, the grin increasing. "You need someone. Anyone. But a person who is responsible."

"Oh my God." I took a breath. "Do you think this is amusing?"

"How mad would you be if I said yes?"

My nostrils flared.

"Very mad, I see. I can't help it." A full smile appeared. "You're…adorable when you're mad."

"Adorable?" I stomped my foot.

"See. Just there. It's cute."

"I am going to physically harm you."

"Versus mentally?" he queried.

The fact that he was teasing me, that he wasn't taking this seriously at all, infuriated me even more. "You had no right to do what you did." I took a step toward him. "Do you know I spent the last hour or so listening to Ivy and Ren and Faye talk to me as if I've never held an iron dagger before? Do you know that if this gets back to Miles, I could be removed from the Order?"

His gaze sharpened. "Ivy nor Ren would inform on you."

He was right. Ivy would never do that. At least, I hoped not. "That doesn't mean someone like Tanner or Kalen or Faye won't say something to someone that eventually gets back to Miles," I pointed out. "What you did was wrong."

The King pushed off the wall, unfolding his arms. The shirt parted, attempting to distract me. "You left me no choice. You would not stop. I thought maybe they could talk some sense into you."

"Guess what? They didn't." I smirked when his jaw tightened. "And I'm going to repeat this for, hopefully, the last time. You do *not* get to tell me what I can and cannot do. Even if you and I were a thing, which we're not, you still would not get to tell me what to do. I don't know who you think you are—"

"The King?" he suggested.

"—but you have no say over what I do. Stay out of my way and out of my life," I told him. "I mean it. There is no reason for you to interfere."

The King looked away, a muscle thrumming in his temple.

Having said my piece, I started toward the door.

"Has it ever occurred to you that I am trying to protect you? That I'm trying to keep you safe?"

Slowly, I turned to him. "No. It hasn't. For a multitude of obvious reasons. And besides that, I don't need you to keep me safe or to protect me."

"Everyone needs someone to protect them." He tipped back his head, his eyes closing.

"Even you?" I scoffed.

"Even me."

My brow smoothed out. I'd seen what he was capable of, so the fact that he'd admitted that was rather shocking.

"I do not want to see harm come to you." His voice was quiet. "I do not have to be with you to want that."

I flushed to the roots of my hair. "I know that."

"Then why are you being so difficult about this?" he asked.

"Because..." I toyed with the strap of my purse. "Because I need to do this. I can't sit by, not when Aric is still alive. You have to understand that."

The King was quiet for several moments, and then he looked at me. "If you knew that someone you...you looked fondly upon was doing something that would surely lead to their demise, would you not try to stop them?"

"Are you saying you look fondly upon me, *King*?"

His head tilted, and then he looked away.

I laughed, but the sound lacked any real humor. "Yeah, okay. But to answer your question, I wouldn't stop you, even if I knew it was dangerous."

The King's gaze cut back to mine. "But you'd still look fondly upon me."

I gave him a tight-lipped smile. "No. Because it would get you out of my hair."

"Now, Brighton, you and I both know that's a lie." His chin dipped. "If something were to happen to me, you'd be devastated."

I didn't even want to think about that. I didn't want to acknowledge how thinking about that made me feel and what it meant. "You value yourself a little too highly."

"And you don't value your life enough."

My hand tightened around my purse strap. "I value my life. And I don't think of myself poorly." I took a step toward him. "Aric and those fae took more than just my mom that night." Something in my chest cracked open as I spoke. "They took..."

"What did they take?"

I bit my lip. "They took my feeling of security, my belief that I could protect myself and my mom—that I was capable of taking care of her. They took my purpose."

"Your purpose?" He faced me fully.

Swallowing the lump in my throat, I shook my head. I was not getting into this with him. "I've said what I needed to say. You don't have to like that I'm out there, but you can't stop me. If it ends with me getting myself killed, then so be it. And I don't say that because I don't value my life. I say that because at least I would die taking back what they stole from me."

"I can... I can respect that," he said, his gaze meeting mine. His eyes were pools of golden fire. "But I won't."

For a second, I didn't think I'd heard him right. "You won't?"

He shook his head as he approached me. "I will watch you. I will have others watching you. Every time you step foot on that street in some silly disguise or near any location where Neal has been sighted, I will intervene."

My lips parted as disbelief swirled through me.

"I will become your shadow, always present. That is what I'll do."

"You…you are…"

"Determined to keep you alive? Yes."

"You are out of your mind!" I didn't stop to think. I cocked back my arm and swung my fist—

He caught my wrist with shocking speed. "See how easy that was? I didn't even blink."

Fury erupted in me like a volcano. I swung my purse around like a bat toward his big, egotistical head—

It never made contact.

The purse flew off my arm and from my grip as if an invisible hand had grasped it.

"And now?" he asked, his grip on my arm firm but not painful.

I twisted, angling my body to his as I jerked up my knee, aiming for his groin.

The King shifted, using his thigh to block my strike. The impact caused him to grunt. "And how about now? What else are you going to do?" He flipped me so my back was to his front. An arm clamped around my waist, yanking me back against him.

The heat of his skin seeped through the thin material of my blouse, scorching my flesh as his other hand curved around the underside of my jaw. He forced my head back against his chest, causing my back to arch as I met his gaze. "Do you know how easy it would be for me to snap your neck? Just like that?" His thumb slipped over my thrumming pulse. I reached both arms up, one hand fisting the soft strands of his hair. "Are you going to pull my hair, sunshine? Is that your—?"

The soft click of my blade sliding out of the cuff silenced him. His eyes widened slightly.

I kept the edge of the blade a scant centimeter from pressing into his jugular as I smiled at him. "What are you going to do, King? I can't decapitate you from this angle, but I can make a hell of a mess out of your throat."

His eyes flared with heat as he stared down at me. I felt his chest rise and fall against my back. I saw his gaze move to where my breasts were straining against the delicate strip of buttons along the front of my blouse.

It happened so fast.

One second, we were fighting. The next moment, it all changed. I didn't protest as he lowered his mouth to mine, utterly unfazed by the iron at his throat. I didn't say a word or pull away. Anger and frustration crashed into something far stronger, something rawer, and the moment his lips touched mine, I was lost.

He was no longer the King.

He was Caden.

Chapter 5

The kiss…

Caden's mouth moved against mine with lust-soaked intensity. He kissed—God, he kissed like a man starving. He kissed as if he were going to devour me, and I wanted that. I *needed* it. It was all I could think about. Or maybe I wasn't thinking at all. Instead, I was feeling. I was just letting myself feel.

"You drive me insane," he growled, sliding his hand down my throat. "And even worse, I think I like it."

"There is something wrong with you." I gasped as his hand cupped my breast. "There's nothing wrong with this." He squeezed gently, causing a hot shiver to curl its way down my spine. His arm loosened around my waist, and I felt his fingers at the buttons of my blouse. There was a light tugging motion, and then the sound of buttons hitting the floor. "I hope you didn't like this shirt."

"I did."

"You'll forget about it soon enough."

Caden was right. I did. He turned me in his arms, tugging the cups of my bra down, and the hem of my skirt up. Before I had a chance to think, his lips moved along the scar Aric had left behind, kissing the faintly pale, slightly raised skin.

And then he drew my nipple into his hot mouth. I gasped as pleasure rolled through me. His free hand slipped between my thighs, his fingers brushing over my panties before making quick work of them. I had no idea if he tore them off or if they'd simply fallen to the floor.

He lifted his head, nuzzling my neck under my ear. "I don't think you have any idea how badly I want you." His fingers brushed along the center of my core once more, this time with no barrier. "I can't stop thinking about *this*." One finger slipped inside, just a little. I moaned. "About how you felt around my fingers. How tight and wet. How you rode my hand."

My entire body clenched. Hot, tight shudders racked my body. Caden's fingers were barely in me, and I already felt like I might tip over the edge. This was insane. I was mad at him, and he was beyond frustrated with me, but this… God, this felt right, and I was so full of raw, painful need that I didn't care what came next.

"Do you want this?" he murmured against my cheek, pressing his finger in just a little farther. "Just say the word, and I'll make you forget everything."

I knew I should say no. I should stop this. But I didn't. I said, "Yes."

Caden moved so fast, my breath got stuck. He lifted me up as if I weighed nothing, and then he was laying me down. It took a moment to realize that I was in his bedroom, on his bed, stripped bare. And then he was naked above me, his erection thick and hard.

His mouth was on mine once more, his tongue dancing with mine, and then he trailed kisses down my throat, over my breasts, and…then he kissed each of the scars on my stomach with his tongue and his lips. The silent, small act was monumental and brought tears to my eyes.

I was lost all over again, and it wasn't just the pure seduction he wrought as his mouth made its way around my navel and then moved lower. It was him.

Lightning burst through my veins as he grasped my hips, and I felt his breath brush over where I ached the most. There was no time to feel self-conscious, to think that I'd only done this twice before, and both times I'd been so caught up in my own head and the shocking intimacy of the act that I hadn't enjoyed myself.

There were no thoughts here.

Caden captured my flesh with his mouth, slipping in with deep, firm strokes of his tongue. I cried out, trembling as raw sensation threatened to drown me. My fingers curled in his hair as my back arched. I couldn't move, not with the way he held my hips down. There was no escaping the blissful torture. Not that I really wanted to, not with the way the tension was building and building. Finally, it shattered. My body liquefied as I climaxed, kicking my head back as I moaned his name.

His head lifted at the sound, and through half-open eyes, I saw that his gaze was luminous. "Say it again. My name."

"Caden," I whispered.

Never breaking eye contact, he lowered his mouth once more, lapping at the slick moisture. I panted, my eyes widening as he lifted his head and licked his lips.

Dear God.

He climbed over me, his attention feral and possessive. Slipping an arm under my hips, he lifted me up. The fine hairs of his chest teased the sensitive peaks of my breasts. His lips claimed mine as I felt him reach between us, and then I felt his thick head pushing in. His skin felt like fire—his *bare* skin. Concern flared, but reality swept in. Fae couldn't pass diseases to humans, and pregnancy was so rare that it wasn't an issue.

I clutched his shoulders, lifting my hips as he sank in an inch and then two. Caden groaned into my mouth.

His hips flexed, and then he slid in all the way. The pressure and sudden fullness wrung a gasp from me. It had been a while, like years and years, but the bite of pain gave way to pleasure as he started to move, slowly at first, and then faster. He *took* me, and I didn't realize until then how badly I wanted that from him. He pressed his lips to my temple the moment before his thrusts lost all rhythm as his hips plunged into mine. The sounds of our breathing and our wet bodies making contact surrounded us until I couldn't hold back. Moans I didn't even know I was capable of left me, and his answering groan was like a match to kindling. I went up in flames all over again, breaking into a thousand tiny pieces. I cried out his name over and over as he drove into me, his arm tightening around me until there was no him or me, just us. He thrust deeply, stilling as he came, shouting my name, his large body trembling with the force of his release until he collapsed, his weight shifting to one arm beside me on the bed.

His breath was ragged as he rested his forehead against my temple, and I had no idea how long we lay there. Could've been minutes, could've been hours. Finally, he slid out of me and fully onto his side. He didn't pull away, though. With his arm around my waist, he tugged me against him so that my chest was pressed to his.

I could feel his heart pounding just as fast as mine.

The reality of what had just happened was slow to take hold as his hand slid up and down my thigh and hip. The only thing I could really focus on at first was how callused his palm felt, but then my brain finally pulled itself out of its multiple orgasm-induced stupor.

We'd had sex.

And not just normal, everyday sex, but sex that had started with us arguing and, somewhere in the middle had turned into me pulling a dagger on him, and then… He'd kissed me, and it was like a switch had been thrown for both of us. How all of that had come about, I really had no idea, but I…I didn't regret it, even though the logical voice in the back of my mind told me that everything could change in a matter of moments. I just…I couldn't find it in me to lambast myself for this at the moment.

But I didn't know what to say or do as my fingers rested on his side. Did I get up, thank him for the orgasm, and then remind him to stay out of my business? Or did I linger? I couldn't do that. Tink was leaving this evening.

"You okay?" Caden asked.

I leaned my head back so I could see him. Those amber-colored eyes were only half open as they focused on me. "Yeah. Are you?"

"Barely." His full lips tipped up in a half-grin that did funny, crazy things to my heart. "You haven't been with someone in a while, and I wasn't…particularly gentle."

His concern caused another round of funny things to happen in my chest. My gaze lowered to his mouth. "It was…you were perfect."

"What? Is that a compliment? From you?" He paused. "The same person who threatened to cut off my balls?"

"Can I take that back?"

"The cutting off my balls part?"

"No. The compliment part."

"Harsh."

I grinned, finding it surprising how…comfortable I was with him, even though I was lying there buck-ass naked with all my flaws on display. And there were a lot of them. Not just the scars, but the many, many nights of eating pizza, ice cream, chips….

"It's been a while for me, too." His voice was quiet.

That didn't shock me. I looked up. "Not since the Queen's spell broke?"

"No. The night you allowed me to feed, the night you saved me was the closest I've been to anyone really."

"Why me?" The question left me before I could stop myself. "God, that sounded terrible. I mean, there is no shortage of women or men who'd light themselves on fire to be with you. And you and I, we are…"

"Complicated?"

My gaze searched his face. "That would be one word I'd use."

"I don't know, Brighton. I didn't think this would happen, and I don't think you came here expecting this."

I laughed. "Yeah, no."

The half-smile returned. "Those people you say would light themselves on fire to be with me? Most of them would because of who I am. The King." His brows lowered as his hand stilled on my hip. "I didn't—"

Although he didn't finish, I thought I knew what he was going to say. "You didn't want to be King."

His eyes met mine, and there was something in them. A brief flash of emotion that traveled across his face but was gone before I could figure out what it was. "No, I didn't. It was one of the reasons I hadn't fed. When I did that, it put this into motion, and when I used the King's sword, that was it. That was when I ascended."

My mind traveled back to when that had happened. Caden had been different afterward. Quiet. And when Tink had seen him, what had he asked? Should I bow? Tink had sensed that the Prince had become the King.

"Why? Why do you not want to be King?"

His gaze shifted then to a place above my head, and he was quiet for a long time. "Certain traditions are…well, they are more like law. The kind that supersedes even biology. And…it was not something I wanted. Not after…"

Supersede biology? That made little sense, but the world of the fae was drastically different than that of the humans, just as it was similar. "You don't think you deserve to be King, do you? Because of what you did while under the Queen's control."

Caden's eyes shot back to mine. "There are a lot of things I don't think I deserve because of that, but the kingdom is not one of them."

"But—?"

"But, this?" His hand slid around to my ass. He squeezed, wringing a gasp from me. "I don't think I deserve this either. Knowing that hasn't stopped me." He shifted suddenly, and I felt his hardness against my hip a moment before he rolled me onto my stomach. "And knowing what I do, it isn't going to stop me now."

My fingers dug into the sheets as I felt his mouth on my spine. He trailed a path of kisses down to my ass before he lifted my hips. "I'm selfish. I don't think you realize that."

A cry of pleasure left me as he entered me in one deep stroke that would've hurt if not for what we'd done before. Bracing himself on his arms, he caged me as his hips moved ruthlessly against mine, plunging in and out at a pace that was almost brutal and yet unbelievably hot. His lips pressed against my temple as he lifted a hand, working it under me. Those agile fingers found my bundle of nerves, and the combination of sensations was like a streak of lightning electrifying my blood. I rose onto my elbows, moving my hips back against him, panting as the release building in me came closer and closer to the edge.

He seemed to know when it was coming because he pulled out and rolled me onto my back again. There was only a brief rush of cool air against my heated, damp skin, and then his body was pressing down on mine, pressing into mine. I tangled myself with him, arms and legs and tongues twined, and when I came, so did he, and it was just as intense as the one before.

This time, after it was over, I somehow ended up sprawled across his chest, my muscles and bones completely gone.

If this was Caden being selfish, I had no problem with it. At all.

His fingers idly moved along my lower back, and I might've dozed off. I wasn't sure. But the feeling of being…content was pure bliss.

I never wanted to move.

But I had to. And then what? Where did we go from here? Part of me was afraid to ask, but we'd just shared bodily fluids, so I needed to get over that.

"Caden?"

"Yes?" he rasped.

Keeping my cheek against his chest, I swallowed. "Where do we go from here?"

His hand stilled for a fraction of a moment. "I imagine you will continue hunting for Aric."

That wasn't what I had been asking about, but since he mentioned it… "Yes, I will."

Caden's chest rose beneath my cheek as he let out a heavy sigh. "I wish you would let me handle this. I plan to kill him, and I will make it slow and painful. I will make sure that he begs for your forgiveness before I end his life. Isn't that enough?"

I lifted my head and propped my chin on his chest so I could look at him. "It's not enough. It's not the same."

His eyes closed. "What else did they take from you that night?"

I pressed my lips together as I sorted through what I wanted to say. "Ivy and Ren don't think I'm capable enough to be out there hunting. Like, at all. Not even run-of-the-mill fae. They just want me to be the Brighton I was before, one who was content to be on call doing research. I was happy that way."

Caden's hand started to move again. "And that changed?"

"Yeah." I returned my cheek to his chest, staring at the dark wall. "They took that. My contentment. My happiness with the way things were. I saw value in my purpose before, and they took that, too." I closed my eyes. "And they stole what I thought I knew about myself."

"Were you happy before?" he asked. "Truly?"

I opened my mouth, but I found I couldn't answer that question.

"You were afraid," he stated, and my eyes opened. "You were afraid of me before. You helped my brother, but you were afraid of him, too. Even Tink. You blended then. Or at least tried to. You didn't want to be seen. You just wanted to exist in your own corner of your world."

My breath caught.

"Afterward, you were no longer afraid. You stopped trying to blend in. Now, you're seen, and you're heard. You stand up for yourself. You're living. They did take a lot from you, Brighton. Your mother. Your contentment. But it also seems like you gained a lot. Not from them, but from yourself."

Chapter 6

Tink didn't end up leaving Monday night. Supposedly, he'd read on the internet that Tuesday was actually the best and safest day to travel. I had no idea if that was true or not. But it'd worked out because I'd spent Monday evening with him and Fabian marathoning the *Avengers* until one in the morning. We'd only made it through a handful of the million movies, but at this point, I was just grateful that Tink had moved on from *Harry Potter* and *Twilight*. Not that I had anything against them. I loved them with all my heart, but I was confident that I could quote at least half of those movies at this point.

I was just happy to spend a little more time with them and Dixon. It really was going to be weird waking up without a cat sitting on my chest or Tink singing made-up songs about eggs and bacon. I was happy for him, though. This trip would be good not only for him and Fabian, but Ivy was also right. It was far past time for Tink to see something other than the Amazon website.

Having them to help occupy my evening had also stopped me from obsessing over what had happened that afternoon—and what hadn't.

Luckily, Tink and Fabian had been squirreled away in Tink's room when I returned from Caden's. Otherwise, it would've been hard to explain why I was wearing an oversized man's shirt with a skirt.

Caden had never answered what came next for us, and that left me…unsettled. I wasn't naive enough to think that sex—even great sex—equaled a relationship. But for me, well, it sort of did. I didn't care what it meant or didn't mean for other people, but for me, that was how I operated. That was why I was so shocked that I had done it at all. Surprised that there hadn't been a moment where I'd thought we should pump the brakes. It also stunned me that I had been so comfortable with him afterward. In the few previous relationships I'd had, I didn't lay around naked to chat. I was always quick to cover up. But with Caden, I never felt like I had anything to hide or any reason to.

After he'd dropped that little truth bomb about how much I'd given back to myself after the attack, he'd received a call from Tanner and had to return to Hotel Good Fae. He'd kissed me goodbye, but there'd been no promises of any sort. The only thing I think he finally accepted was that I wasn't going to quit looking for Aric.

I'd come this far, and I wasn't going to stop now.

When I finally did go to bed that night, I'd ended up falling right to sleep. The multiple orgasms probably had a lot to do with that, along with the popcorn-induced food coma. But throughout the day, while I searched my mother's books for anything about Devil's Breath and headed into the offices to comb through all the papers filed away there, my thoughts kept drifting back to Caden's apartment. To what he'd done, what I'd done, and I came to a realization. It…it had to mean something. All of it had to. Why he didn't want me out there looking for Aric. The reason he felt like he needed to protect me. Caden wanted me, whether he liked it or not, and that had to mean something. Because he had only been with me since he came out of the Queen's spell, and I hadn't been stroking his ego by stating that he could have anyone he wanted. He could, and he…he wanted *me*.

As I thumbed through dusty papers, scanning them, I wondered about the traditions he'd spoken of that he wanted to avoid enough to not want to be the King. Part of me still believed that he didn't feel worthy enough after what he'd done, and I hated that for him because I knew how it felt.

My mind shifted to Ivy and Ren, who I hadn't seen yet today.

I knew what it was to not feel good enough.

My research was about as fruitful as stressing over Caden and myself. Nothing came out of either. By the time I returned home, I had a headache from sneezing over the dusty papers that no one had looked at in ages.

I passed a small army of fae outside my place loading up suitcase after suitcase as I walked inside. I stopped counting at six bags.

Dropping my keys and purse on the foyer table, I found Tink in the living room with Fabian. Dixon sat on the couch, staring at the carrier with his ears flat. He wore a little kitty shirt that read *WORLD'S WORST BACKSEAT DRIVER*.

I grinned at that as I walked over, scratching the little guy's head. "How many suitcases are you guys taking?"

"The better question would be how many suitcases is *Tink* taking," Fabian answered with a smile. He looked so much like his brother, except his hair was much longer, and he wasn't as big. Then again, most people, fae or human, weren't as big as Caden.

"I need to make sure that I have everything I could possibly want," Tink defended himself. "Plus, I had to pack Dixon's toys—"

"And his cat house and cat tree." Fabian smiled. "Along with a cat bathing suit."

My brows lifted. "They make cat bathing suits?"

Tink's eyes glimmered. "I found it on Amazon, and I cannot wait to see him in his swim trunks."

I glanced down at the cat, wishing I could be there when Tink attempted to introduce Dixon to swimming. Poor cat.

"My Prince," a fae said from the doorway. "Sorry to interrupt, but there is a message for you from the King."

My stomach did a stupid little tumble at the mention of Caden.

Fabian nodded at us as he stepped around the coffee table. "Please excuse me."

I waited until he was out of earshot. "He's always so polite."

"I know." Tink widened his eyes. "It's annoying."

"Shut up," I laughed. "It's a breath of fresh air."

"It is." Tink scooped up Dixon. "But his politeness makes me feel uncivilized, like I was raised by animals in the wild."

"Well..."

He shot me a look as he placed Dixon in front of the carrier. The cat seemed to sigh but climbed in. "By the way, I think that's the first time someone said 'the King' around you where you haven't muttered 'asshole' under your breath. Turning over a new leaf?"

"No. He's still an asshole," I said without much heat.

Tink looked at me over his shoulder. "He is trapped by duty. That is what he is."

"What kind of duty?" I asked, thinking of what Caden had said about the traditions.

"Lite Bright, there is not enough time to talk about all his duties." Locking the door on the carrier, Tink met my stare. "But suffice it to say there are a lot of things that he has to do and say because of that. He had to sacrifice what he cherished most to become King."

"What would that be? Freedom to do as he pleases?" Which would be a lot.

A faint, almost sad smile appeared on Tink's face. "In a way, I suppose."

Fabian returned then. "It is time for us to leave, Tink."

My heart grew heavy at those words, and as I looked around my living room, it already felt emptier. "Have fun." I plastered what I hoped was a bright smile on my face. "And take pictures and send them to me."

"I'll take so many pictures, it'll blow your phone up!" My laugh was cut off as Tink all but tackled me with his embrace. We held onto each other for so long, I didn't think he'd ever let go, but he did, and I saw that his eyes appeared damp when he pulled back. "Tink," I whispered, sliding my palms down his arms until I reached his hands. I squeezed them. "I'll see you soon."

"And you'll be okay?"

"Of course. Do not worry one second about me."

He opened his mouth as if he wished to say something, but then he just nodded. "I suck at goodbyes." He popped forward, kissing my cheek, and then he hurried to Dixon's carrier, all but running out of the house. "Oh, there's a package coming from Amazon with the name *Peter Parker* on it," he yelled. "Don't open it! Just put it in my room."

I laughed, shaking my head as I turned to Fabian. "I don't even want to know what's in that package."

"Strangely, neither do I." Fabian came forward, hugging me. "You know, you are welcome to join us if you find yourself with free time. I would love to have you there."

"I'll think about that."

"Please do."

"Take care of him," I whispered as I hugged Fabian, thinking how strange it was that a few years ago I never would've considered embracing a fae.

"Always," he replied, pulling back. "I imagine you will be heading out yourself, to the meeting my brother called."

Meeting?

"I do believe Ivy and Ren are on their way," he added, reaching down and picking up a tote. "They received word that they believe will lead them to the Ancient who wishes to free the Queen." His gaze caught mine with meaning. "Be safe, Brighton."

I turned, watching him leave. Something told me that he knew I was unaware of the meeting and was telling me about it. My stomach knotted. Caden had information about Aric and didn't tell me. I wasn't exactly surprised by that. While he may be more accepting of me being out there hunting, that didn't mean he was going to help me find Aric. But it still stung.

The silence of the house settled around me.

Snapping forward, I hurried to the foyer and snatched the keys off the table.

Uninvited or not, I was not being cut out of this meeting.

* * * *

I knew exactly where to find them.

There were several rooms used for meetings on the main level of Hotel Good Fae, and we often moved from one to the other. But the two male fae standing outside the closed door with their backs rigid and their hands clasped was a dead giveaway.

The Knights were always present when Caden was here. I imagined he must stop them from following him when he was at his apartment. Or if they did trail him, they remained well-hidden.

I stopped in front of them, and one of them must've seen the look on my face because he stepped aside with a sigh.

"Thank you," I said sweetly, opening the door.

Ivy and Ren sat across from Caden. Ivy was perched on the table, one leg curled up to her chest. Ren was sitting in the chair beside her. They looked over. Ren's face went expressionless, but Ivy's lips thinned. Faye and Kalen were also present, both standing by a window. The latter looked uncomfortable, but Faye looked well…annoyed. Like usual.

Caden was speaking. "Even though he was seen alone…." He trailed off, and without even turning around, I knew he knew it was me. "I see my brother has loose lips."

The rather cold greeting after yesterday did more than sting, even though I told myself that this meeting wasn't about us. It burned a hole right through my gut, but I lifted my chin. "I figured you just forgot to tell me."

"Brighton," Ivy began.

"Nope." I held up my hand as I stalked across the room. Sitting down in one of the chairs, I calmly placed my purse on the floor. "I'm here. You all have some sort of information, and I'm a part of this whether you like it or not."

Ivy looked down at Ren as if he were supposed to do something.

"We were discussing a possible lead." Caden looked over at me, and our gazes met. Nothing could be gained from his expression, but heat bloomed across my cheeks nonetheless. His lashes swept down, concealing the amber hue of his eyes.

"Oh, so now you're okay with bringing her in on this?" Ivy demanded.

Faye sighed, muttering, "Here we go again."

Kalen stared up at the ceiling.

"I'm not okay with it," Caden answered, refocusing on Ivy. "Not remotely. But it does not appear that any of us, no matter what we do, will change her mind."

Did including having sex fall in the whole *no matter what we do* equation? My eyes narrowed on him as a seed of illogical and ridiculous suspicion took hold.

"This isn't okay." Ivy unfurled her leg. "I won't be party to you—"

"Stop." Ren placed his hand on her leg. "He's right. Nothing is going to change her mind. And at this point, we're just beating a dead horse, and we don't have time for that."

Ivy looked as if she wanted to argue. "Fine," she snapped, sending me a look that said this wouldn't be the last time I'd hear about this.

Great.

Kalen stepped forward at Caden's nod. "We've learned that Aric is still in the city," he explained. I stiffened. "He was seen this afternoon."

"Where?" I breathed.

Kalen looked at Caden before answering. "He was seen exiting Flux."

"What?" I twisted in the chair and turned toward Caden.

"Before you ask, yes, we've had eyes on Flux. He was not seen going in, but that doesn't mean he wasn't well-hidden." He paused. "Like some do when they go to Flux."

I ignored that. "And where did he go?"

"That, we don't know," Ren answered. "They were able to tail him for a couple of blocks, but they lost him on I-10." Based on Ren's tone alone, I knew how ridiculous he thought that was. Yeah, depending on the day, traffic sucked, but…come on. "But he's here. We'll let Miles know so all Order members are on alert."

"And we're increasing our own presence," Faye added. "Between the two groups, we'll form a net that can sweep the entire city. We will find him."

My gaze shot back to Caden, and I knew without a doubt that he would be out there tonight and every night until Aric was found. "I will—"

The door opened, and I looked over my shoulder. It was Tanner and a younger man that I'd never seen before. They weren't alone. There was a tall, lithe, dark-haired female fae with them. She wore a pretty, off-the-shoulder, pale blue and gold dress that would've looked great on a beach and terrible on me—someone who actually had hips. She was gorgeous, with delicate features, and whoever she was, she didn't attempt to conceal the quicksilver tone of her skin. The male beside her didn't glamour himself either.

"My King." Tanner bowed slightly before correcting himself and slipping into a full bow. His gaze flicked to me and then away. He swallowed, probably worrying that I was going to start screaming curse words at his King at any second. "I am sorry to interrupt, but I was sure you would want to know the moment our guests arrived."

Caden stood, but he did not speak as his gaze flickered across the two standing behind Tanner. A hardness settled across the King's features, and tiny balls of unease formed in my stomach. I took a closer look at the two new fae, sensing that Caden was either not thrilled with the interruption or not exactly happy to see them.

"This is Sterling," Tanner advised. "And his sister Tatiana."

"I am pleased to meet you, my King." The woman stepped forward, hands clasped under her breasts as she bowed deeply with the grace of a dancer. As she straightened, she smiled. "And I am honored to become your Queen and serve our Court together."

Chapter 7

I couldn't… I couldn't have heard her right. Honored to be his *Queen*?

A sharp blast of icy panic sliced through my stomach as I stared at the beautiful fae. No. No. There was no way I'd heard those words or understood them correctly.

Because if I did, that would mean…that Caden was to be *married*. That he was engaged and belonged to someone else while…while I'd had him in my arms and inside me. If what I had heard was correct, that meant I'd never had him at all because he already belonged to someone else.

My chest rose and fell with short, quick breaths as disbelief ripped through me. Knots formed in my stomach, and a tremor started in my legs, traveling rapidly throughout my entire body.

"As I am honored to be joining my family with yours," the brother spoke, bowing as gracefully as his sister.

My heart started thumping harder, and then it was racing. Pressure seized my chest as I slowly turned my head toward Caden. He was speaking. I knew this because I saw his lips moving, but I couldn't hear the words over the pounding of my blood in my ears.

Caden was…he was to be married.

I was going to be sick.

Nausea twisted up my insides. I could taste bile in the back of my throat. I needed to get out of there. I needed to be far, far away.

Placing my hands on the arms of the chair, I started to stand but couldn't. The muscles all along my calves and thighs seemed to have turned to liquid.

Caden looked at me then, and our gazes connected. I saw… I saw *nothing* in his expression, and I knew he saw everything in mine. He faced the door. "Give us a moment, please."

There was a brief hesitation. Tanner murmured words I couldn't understand. Then Ivy and Ren shuffled out when they realized that Caden was asking them to leave. I felt Ivy's stare, but I couldn't look away from Caden as what we'd done the day before played over and over in my mind. I felt like I couldn't breathe. That every breath I took did nothing to inflate my lungs or push oxygen through me. Faye and Tanner leaving momentarily blocked Caden from my view, and I…

I hadn't known what to think about yesterday or what it had meant. I'd been too wary about allowing my heart to run away from me. But I'd loved him before we had sex and I loved him afterward.

And he belonged to someone else.

Caden's amber gaze collided with mine once more. My fingers began to ache from how tightly I was clutching the arms of the chair.

God, I was so incredibly *stupid*, so recklessly naive to believe that him not wanting to feel what he felt for me meant that he felt more than he should, not that he only wanted me physically. Never once had I considered that perhaps he'd been fighting what he felt for me—whether it be more than the physical or not—because he was already committed to someone else. Obviously, this wasn't the first time he'd heard about this…engagement. As if he weren't involved in the whole damn process up until a handful of minutes ago. I doubted even the fae operated that way. Caden knew he had been promised to another when he kissed me, when he stripped my clothes from me and *fucked* me. Because that's what he'd done, right? We hadn't made love. We'd screwed. We'd fucked.

And I was the other woman.

"Say something," he said.

I opened my mouth, then closed it before I tried again. "What do you want me to say?" My voice was too hoarse, but I couldn't clear my throat.

His gaze searched mine. "Anything."

A sharp giggle tittered out of me. "You want me to say something? Me? You…you're engaged?"

"I am."

The blow his words landed knocked the wind out of me. My fingers eased off the arms of the chair. "How long?" I heard myself ask as if I didn't already know the answer or that it would somehow change things.

"Shortly after I ascended." Caden looked away, his gaze fixed on the window. "It was…" A muscle flexed along his jaw. "It's what's best for… The Court wants their King and Queen united," he replied, his voice monotone. "I am their King. It is my duty to serve them."

I stared up at him, anger slow to break through the disbelief, but it was there, heating my skin and my blood. "Was it the best for your Court when you fucked me yesterday?"

Caden's shoulders tightened.

"Twice?" Anger solidified the muscles in my legs. I stood.

"I told you before that there could be nothing between us," he said.

"Yeah, and then you fucked me—"

"I didn't fuck you." His gaze shot to mine, and those amber eyes now burned. "That is not what we did."

"It's not? What the hell do you call screwing someone who is not the person you're engaged to."

"It was…" He looked away again. "It should not have happened. Yesterday is on me. Not you. You did nothing wrong."

"I *know* I didn't do anything wrong. I'm not fucking engaged to someone else."

"All I can say is that I'm sorry, Brighton."

"You're sorry?" My chest felt as if it were caving in on me. "Which part are you sorry about? What happened between us? Or the fact that you failed to mention that you're engaged?"

His jaw flexed once more. "All of it."

My heart fissured into millions of pieces. I'd been a lot of things in my life, but I'd never been a mistake. I'd never been a mistake with the same person twice. What did my mom use to say when I was younger? "*Fool me once. Shame on you. Fool me twice. Shame on me.*"

"You don't understand." He glanced at me. "You cannot possibly understand—"

"Because I'm not a fae?"

His eyes met mine, and an eternity stretched between us as a wild array of emotions flickered across his face. And then it all went away as if he'd shut down whatever he was feeling. "Yes, because you are not like me. I am a King. I must have a Queen, and you… You're a distraction. A weakness that I will not allow to be exploited."

I jerked back a step. Deep, wounding hurt collided with fury. My legs knocked into the chair. Thrown off balance, I stumbled. Caden stepped toward me, reaching out.

"Don't touch me!" The sound of my voice was shrill to my ears as I straightened myself. A burn crawled up the back of my throat and then entered my eyes. "Don't ever touch me again."

Caden—no, he wasn't Caden. He was *the King*, and I shouldn't forget that. The King pulled his hand back, and our gazes connected once more. The pressure in my chest continued to expand until it felt like something might burst.

And then words did break free of me. "I want to tell you I hate you. I want to tell you that I despise you, but you would know that it's not true."

He remained quiet, and a long moment passed between us as a hundred quick, in-complete thoughts flashed through my mind, forming all the things I thought I wanted to say to him.

But only one fully formed.

"I never once thought you were terrible for all the things you did while under the Queen's spell. I hated that you held yourself responsible for things you had no control over. It killed me a little, but this…." A shudder racked me. "You did this. You led me on the first time, and you did it again. No, you didn't make me any promises, but you know me better than most. You knew before yesterday that it was going to mean something to me. And you turned around and made me the other woman. You made me feel shame and regret, and for all of that, I think you're terrible."

The King closed his eyes.

Turning away from him, I picked up my purse and walked out of the room with my head held high, but my heart broken, and my body weighed down.

It was only when I left the room that I realized it was the same one we'd stood in weeks before when he'd carved out his first piece of me.

* * * *

The trip back home was nothing but a blur of trees and concrete, people and cars. Ivy called. Three times before I silenced my phone. I didn't know if she was calling because she'd sensed that something had happened between…the King and me, or if she was calling about my hunting. Either way, I couldn't deal with her at the moment.

I was strangely numb after I walked out of Hotel Good Fae and all during the ride home. Even as I pushed open the iron gate and walked toward my front door, I felt nothing. Or maybe I was feeling so much that it had overwhelmed my senses to the point where I couldn't feel anything. Like I had reached some sort of internal meter where the gauge had been blown.

But my hands trembled as I unlocked the front door, and they shook as I placed my purse and keys on the foyer table.

I stood there for…I don't know how long. Seconds? Minutes? I was supposed to be at work, but I didn't think I could do that. Face Ivy. Miles.

Stiffly, I turned from the foyer and walked through the silent house into the living room. Dixon wasn't scampering across the hardwood floors. Tink and Fabian weren't there to distract me with movies or silly conversations. I swallowed, but my throat seemed to lock up. I forced myself to take a deep breath—

"I hear you've been looking for me."

Heart jumping into my throat, I spun around.

A male stood a few feet behind me, brown hair clipped short, his cruelly handsome face just as I remembered. The faint smirk he wore twisted the scar that cut through his lip.

Aric.

Instinct kicked in. I sprang back—

He was horrifically fast and on me before I even had a chance to engage the iron cuffs. He caught my wrists, locking them behind my back as his other hand clamped down on my throat.

Seconds.

Within seconds, he had me.

"So, I thought I should come find you," he said.

I twisted, but his grip tightened. My eyes widened as he lowered his mouth to mine. I knew what was coming. Oh, God, I knew what was—

Aric inhaled.

My entire body jerked as if a tether had been formed between us. I was hooked to him, deep in the very core of my being. My insides flayed as he fed. The pain was like icy fire, burning me from the inside out, and I couldn't break free as it dragged me down into an abyss of nothing but searing coldness.

Chapter 8

I was cold.

That was the first thing I realized when I slowly drifted out of the black fog that consumed every part of my being.

Shivers skated up and down my body. I didn't know I could be *this* cold. My skin was chilled to the bone, and icy dampness seeped through my dress. How…how could I be this cold? It had been chilly earlier, in the low sixties, but this felt as if I were lying in a mound of fallen snow.

Confusion swept through me as I tried to remember what I'd been doing before I…before I fell asleep. That was what'd happened, right? No. That didn't make sense. I tried to open my eyes, but they were heavy and felt as if they were glued shut as cloudy images of my living room flickered through the fog in my mind. I'd been there…

What was going on?

I willed my eyes to open, but the concentration sent a sharp burst of pain bouncing around my skull. Wincing, I kept my eyes closed as the throbbing slowly dulled. Did I have an injury? That would explain the confusion and pain, but how did it happen? I was in my house, having…

I'd come home and…

Aric.

My heart rate kicked up as the lost memories crashed through the wall of nothingness and flooded me. He'd been waiting for me when I came home. He'd been so fast, on me before I even had a chance to scream or release my blades.

He'd fed on me.

Oh, God. That bastard had used me like I was a juice box. My lips tingled from the memory of his icy breath and the horror of the feeding that resurfaced. It had felt nothing like when Cad—when *the King* had done it. That had been orgasmic, but this…this had felt like frigid claws reaching deep into my very core, tearing through bone and tissue and yanking out what made me who I was. Now I remembered. The tide of pain had sucked me under into an abyss.

How much had Aric taken from me? Based on the way my head felt, more than enough.

I needed to get up. I needed to figure out where the hell I was, and then I needed to find that bastard and kill him a million times over.

Turning my head, I stopped suddenly when something hard bit into my neck like a frigid vise. My eyes flew open as I lifted my hand to my neck. Metal—cold and unforgiving—encircled my throat. I pressed my palm against the band, my fingers digging into the narrow space between it and my skin as I jerked upward and scanned the…

"What the hell?" I croaked out, my voice hoarse.

I wasn't home, that much I knew, and that was about *all* I knew. The flames did very little to beat back the shadows, but what I could see reminded me of… God, it reminded me of some kind of underground tomb.

A *tomb.*

Pressure clamped down on my chest as my wild gaze darted around the circular chamber. Two torches jutted out from a grayish brick wall, spaced several feet apart. Dark and ropey lines climbed from the low ceiling and down the walls, forming a network of veins. Vines? Across from me was a slab of stone standing about five feet high. The center was stained with something…dark.

That was when I realized that I was on a similar rectangular stone bed.

Holy crap.

I was in a damn crypt, chained by the freaking neck to a stone slab that had quite possibly been used to murder people based on the stain. My hair fell forward and slipped over my bare shoulders as I lifted my arm. Dread exploded. Part of me already knew what I was going to see when I looked down, and I wasn't wrong. The bracelet that held the four-leaf clover was missing. Without it, I was susceptible to a fae's glamour.

Jesus.

Squeezing my eyes shut, I struggled to stay calm. I was trapped by a psychotic creature, and I knew how this was going to end.

Not with me breathing.

No. I couldn't think like that. I dragged in a deep, musty breath as I struggled to push back the creeping panic. I couldn't focus on that scenario. If I did, I'd have no chance of surviving this.

Opening my eyes, I ignored the pounding of my heart as I drew up my legs and swung them off the edge of the slab. A wave of dizziness rolled over me, and I took another deep breath before I picked up the heavy chain and stood, wincing as my bare feet touched the floor. I didn't think about how I'd lost my shoes since those suckers would've had to be removed as I followed the length of the chain to the metal hook embedded in the stone floor. There were several feet of chain, allowing me to edge toward the darkened area of the chamber, but not long enough to reach what appeared to be a wooden door.

"Damn it," I snapped, stepping back between the two slabs.

I refocused, looking around the room until my gaze stopped on the vines. It seemed like the chamber was underground, but it was rare to find such a place in New Orleans and the surrounding areas. Had I been taken out of the city? And if so, how far? Or was this a place designed to appear as if it were below ground?

If I was still near the city, I had complete faith that I'd figure out where I was the moment I got outside. If I knew anything, it was the layout of New Orleans and the surrounding areas.

I'd just have to get out of this tomb first.

Tightening my grip on the chain, I looked down at the heavy metal. My thumb smoothed over a rusted section, causing some of the oxidation to flake off.

Wait.

That wasn't rust.

It was dried *blood.*

Jesus.

Stomach churning, I almost dropped the links as I lifted my gaze to the door. The chain freaked me out, but it was also a weapon. An image of Princess Leia choking the ever-loving crap out of Jabba the Hutt formed.

I could do that. In fact, the scene of me strangling Aric to death replaced the one from *Return of the Jedi*, and it filled me with a rather unhealthy amount of glee. Twisting the chain around my hands, I waited.

I didn't have to wait long.

The sound of footfalls was like a breath of air along the back of my neck. Darting toward the slab, I shifted the chain behind my back and leaned against the stone, hiding the chain. Every muscle in my body tensed painfully.

A stuttered heartbeat later, the door creaked open, and fresh air rushed in—rose-scented air. I was either near a garden or, if I was underground, I couldn't be that far. I filed that little piece of information away. Aric stood in the doorway, appearing alone. His broad shoulders nearly took up the entire width of the opening as he ducked and stepped through the door.

A whoosh went through the room, startling me. Fire sparked, and the remaining torches flared to life, nearly a dozen of them casting flickering light into the chamber.

I'd been right about the vines, but now I also saw that there were chains mixed among them.

"I thought you'd still be asleep," Aric said, his deep voice tinged with amusement.

The links of the chain I held pressed into my palms. "Sorry to disappoint you. I'm wide-awake, asshole."

He chuckled as he straightened. The door behind him swung shut, cutting off the flow of fresher, warmer air. "Don't apologize, I am thrilled that you're awake."

I lifted my chin, forcing myself to breathe steady and sure. "Where am I?"

"Where I want you to be."

"That doesn't answer my question."

Aric smirked as he stopped just a few feet inside the chamber, out of my reach. "You're right outside the city. I believe this used to be an old tomb that has partially sunken underground."

Shock splashed through me.

"You seem surprised that I told you." He inclined his head. "I'm not worried about you escaping. Not at all."

Fury quickly replaced the surprise, prickling at my skin. "I wouldn't be too confident about that."

His gaze flickered over me. "Your courage is…admirable, but I have no reason not to be overconfident."

I forced out a laugh even though my heart raced. "There's a very fine line between confidence and arrogance."

"True." He smoothed an imaginary wrinkle on his white, linen shirt. "But there is a difference. Not that you'd know anything about confidence."

"Really?" My spine stiffened. "You know nothing about me."

"I know everything about you, Brighton Jussier," he replied.

"You're thirty years old, never married, and childless. Once devoted to taking care of your poor, unstable mother, you're now devoted to finding and killing me."

My chest rose with a heavy breath. "Did you read my Facebook profile or something?"

He laughed. "You were born into the Order, but you're not a true member. Other than hunting me, you do not hunt fae. How do you mortals put it? You were put out to pasture before you even grazed. They do not see you as remotely useful to their goals. You're simply allowed to be because of who your parents were."

I flinched as his words landed a blow on the still open wound left behind by Ivy and Ren, both who doubted my ability to do anything more than read a map. There was too much truth to what Aric said.

"The only reason you ever even came onto my radar was because you were seen aiding the wounded Summer Prince."

He was talking about Fabian, and the night the Queen had been forced back into the Otherworld, when I'd helped transport the Prince back to Hotel Good Fae.

"Other than that, you're fairly unremarkable. Well, with the exception of fucking the King," he remarked, and my breath caught. "Then again, at one time, he was known for having very little taste when it came to his partners."

That would've stung if I weren't currently chained up in a tomb.

"So, do you still think I don't know anything about you, little bird?"

"Don't call me that."

"Why not? Isn't that what Caden calls you?"

The sound of his name was like a shock to the system, one I couldn't afford to be distracted by. "No. He doesn't call me that."

"Hmm." Aric folded his arms over the dark shirt he wore. "That's what he called Siobhan. Do you know who that is?"

"No." I kept my gaze glued to him, ordering myself to wait until the perfect moment to strike. "And in case you're wondering, this is my I-don't-care face."

"She was his lover, and his would-be mate."

I sucked in air. Another fiancée?

"'His little bird' is what he called her. Because she was as light as air and just as constant and steady. Always perched on his shoulder when they were young. And she would sing—oh, she sang so beautifully." Aric chuckled lowly. "I can see you didn't know that."

Pressing my lips together, I said nothing because there was nothing to say. The King wasn't Caden to me any longer. Pretty sure he'd driven that point home the last time I saw him. Blood rushed to my cheeks, making the skin prick with the reminder of *that* humiliation. He was just the King to me now, and I didn't care if he'd been engaged once or five times.

"Siobhan was his soulmate. His one, true love. They grew up together, were promised to one another from birth. She was groomed to be his Queen. They shared their lives and their bodies for well over two hundred years. She was beautiful. A stunning creature, tall, and full of grace. She had blond hair like you, like spun *sunlight*." His lips curved into a taunting smile as my body jerked. "That's the only thing you share in common with her. Other than the hair, you're…pathetically, uninspiringly human."

I didn't care. The sting that crawled up the back of my throat had nothing to do with anything Aric was saying. "I don't think uninspiringly is a word."

His smile was tight-lipped. "Do you know what happened to Caden's little bird?"

"No, but I'm betting you're going to tell me."

"I snapped her wings and plucked all her feathers." His upper lip curled.

Revulsion morphed into sudden understanding. This was the loved one the King had spoken about losing. *This* was why he wanted Aric for himself. Not because the psycho was trying to bring the Queen back to the mortal world or because he'd stabbed him in battle. Because the bastard had killed his fiancée. And I could understand the King's need for revenge. I totally did because of what this monster had cost me.

"It's what led to the war between our Courts," Aric continued. "Well, one of many, but this was the big one. We had years of peace. The Otherworld was thriving, but my Queen…she wanted this world, and she needed Caden for that. You know the prophecy."

Of course, I did. The child of the Prince and a halfling—who happened to be Ivy—would undo the spells that kept all the doors to the Otherworld sealed. Because the ideology, the basic fundamentals of our world and the Otherworld, would be challenged, and, therefore, collapse because a halfling shouldn't exist, and a Prince was never supposed to be in our world. It was the whole insane baby prophecy that had been hard to believe when I first heard about it.

Aric unfolded his arms as he walked away from me and moved toward the wall near the door. "My job was to goad the Prince into war, where he'd be weakened in battle. I knew exactly what would provoke him. Taking Siobhan was a part of getting the job done." Aric reached out, running his fingers over a vine. The thick, ropey strand blanched and withered under his touch. "But one I thoroughly enjoyed."

"You're messed up," I snarled. "Seriously. A one hundred percent psychopath, but I'm not the King's little bird. I'm not anything to him, so I don't know why you're telling me any of this. It doesn't hurt me." A lie. "At all."

"True," Aric murmured, looking over his shoulder at me. "You'll never mean to him what Siobhan did."

I flinched, hating myself for it—hating *him* for it.

"Perhaps you don't mean much to him. You are human, after all, but you mean something." Lowering his hand, he faced me. "Enough that I'm sure I'll also enjoy our time together even though you won't last nearly as long as Siobhan."

Nausea twisted my stomach as he took a step toward me. The chain practically hummed against my palms.

"And when I'm done with you, I'll make sure Caden knows exactly where you've been and what was done to you, even if he doesn't realize you're missing."

Just a few steps closer. That was all.

"And if he doesn't care now, he will," the Ancient continued, his voice low and taunting. "Because when I'm done with you, all he will be reminded of is his little—"

Snapping forward, I lifted the chain above my head, prepared to wrap it around the bastard's neck and squeeze until I ripped his head right off.

Except that wasn't what happened.

Aric was like a cobra striking, ripping the chain from my hands with such force that the flesh on my palms tore. I jerked as the burning pain shot up my arms, stumbling back. He yanked the chain toward him, and I had no choice but to follow. I slammed into him just as he placed his hand around the band circling my neck.

"What did you think you were going to do?" he asked, pale blue eyes gleaming. "Hurt me?"

"Kill you," I gasped.

"Really?" Aric laughed, lifting me onto the tips of my toes. "Do you really have that in you? Because the last time you and I were alone, you gave up pretty quickly. Trembling and crying on the ground while that old hag bled out beside you."

"I'm not that girl anymore."

"Good." He sneered. "I'd rather you fight me than give up. Weakness is boring."

Before I could say another word, he lifted me off the floor by the band around my neck. The metal pressed in, cutting off my air flow before I even took my last breath. Panic exploded like a bomb in the pit of my stomach. Turning, he slammed me down onto the slab, knocking whatever air was still in my lungs out. The moment he let go of my throat, my training kicked in.

Don't get stuck on your back. Don't get stuck on your back.

Swinging out a fist, I jerked upward, but he was still holding the chain and pulled it back. The back of my head cracked off the stone as he caught my fist and then my other hand. Tsking under his breath, he pressed my wrists together as he transferred them into one hand.

"Keep fighting me," he said. "I find it greatly amusing."

Lifting my hips, I twisted toward him, kicking out. The heel of my foot connected with his thigh, causing him to grunt. The burst of satisfaction was short-lived when he drew my arms up over my head.

"Kicking is not nice, little bird," he admonished. Panic choked me just as badly as the band had earlier when cool metal clicked around my wrists, securing my hands to the stone. "You wouldn't like it if I did it to you."

"Fuck you." I kicked out again, catching him in the stomach.

The blow to the side of my head stunned me. I hadn't even seen him move, but I felt the explosion of pain. White crowded my vision as I breathed through the agony.

"Didn't like that, did you?" He had a hold of my leg as he moved down to the end of the slab. "I can do much, much worse."

"You…you hit like an…underdeveloped five-year-old," I said, blinking to clear the starbursts from my vision.

Cool metal snapped around my right ankle and then my left, and the only good takeaway was that I wasn't spread eagle. But when I dipped my chin and peered down, I could see that the hem of my dress was riding up. Not like it had far to go to begin with.

Aric stalked back toward me. "I didn't know you had such a mouth on you."

"Surprise."

He gave me another tight smile as he placed his hand over mine. "I'm going to have to teach you how to be mindful of what you say to me."

My heart tripped over itself as he trailed his hand down my arm. "Good luck."

"I won't need it." His hand left my arm, and he gripped my cheeks. "You will, but you will find none of it."

I forced myself to meet his pale eyes. "I'm not scared of you."

His smile increased as did the pressure on my face. "That is a lie. Do you know how I know that?"

He was right. God, he was. I was terrified of the Ancient, but I'd be damned if I gave him the satisfaction of admitting it. "You're a super special, know-it-all fae?"

"Cute." His chuckle dripped ice down my spine as he guided my head up. "I can smell it in your sweat. It reminds me of kerosene."

"Sorry I…"—I swallowed back a groan as the pressure on the joints of my jaw increased—"I don't smell better for you."

"Don't be too hard on yourself." Using his grip on my face, he pulled me upright as he held the chain in his other fist, shortening the length until the cuff pressed into the front of my throat. My back bowed painfully, and my arms stretched. "I love the smell of fear. It gets me hard."

My heart stuttered and then sped up. A whole new horror swamped me. There were a lot of things I could deal with. At least, that's what I kept telling myself. Pain. Humiliation. Fear. None of those were new. But this possibility? I didn't know how to deal with that.

"You're sick," I gasped out.

Aric aligned his face with mine, causing my hands to open and close. When he spoke, his icy breath coasted over my nose. "Not sick enough to fuck you, if that's what you're worried about."

A rush of relief pounded through me so fast and hard, I almost lost it. A burn in my throat crawled upward—

"Don't be too relieved to hear that. It offends me, and"—he tilted his head, his gaze traveling over the length of my body, lingering in areas that caused my skin to crawl—"well, I can always be swayed."

Revulsion threatened to choke me as he lifted his gaze to mine. I glared back at him, my hands trembling as they curled into fists. Once again, I found myself wishing I was wearing anything but the sleeveless sheath dress. Then again, I had a feeling if I were wearing a parka or a head-to-toe shapeless jumpsuit, I'd still feel stripped bare.

One side of Aric's lips kicked up. "But right now, there is something else I want from you."

"I'm not going to tell you a damn thing about the Order."

"Silly girl." He jerked the chain, snapping my head back. "There is nothing about the Order that I don't already know. They are no threat to me."

Whether that was true or not, I had no idea, but I couldn't really focus on that. Not when the strain of the chain was sending jagged shards of pain down my neck. "Then I'm of no use to you."

"Not true." He leaned away from me, reaching behind him. "You have so many uses to me, you have no idea."

Aric pulled something out of his back pocket. In the golden light of the torches, my heart stopped in my chest when I saw what he held. A long, slender blade that came to a wickedly sharp point.

My gaze flew to his, and my breath caught as his hand and the blade it held moved out of my line of sight. "What are you doing?"

He continued to smile at me. "Pulling out your feathers."

There was a good chance my heart stopped.

"Scream as loud as you like," he offered, and I felt the tip of the blade press into my skin. I bit down as the slight pressure turned to pain. "Because no one is coming for you."

Chapter 9

My body was on fire, and for once, I wished for that bone-chilling coldness that had greeted me when I first came to in the chamber.

And when was that?

Had to be…days ago. Definitely days. Maybe five if I based it on when Aric arrived. Twice a day, I believed. Possibly the morning and the night, and each time he stayed…long enough to do what he needed, which was to take me outside to do my business like a dog on a leash, and then do what *he* wanted, which was to turn me into a living, breathing pincushion.

And to feed.

He generally fed on the second visit, and I was always left unconscious when he left, waking the same way I had the first time, my head throbbing and feeling disoriented. And each time, it seemed to take seconds longer for me to remember how I had gotten here.

Why I was here.

My painfully empty stomach grumbled as I stared at the withered vines by the door. It had to be at least three days since Aric had tossed a bag of cold McDonalds at me. I'd scarfed that grease-soaked crap down and then promptly vomited it all back up. Now, I'd probably murder someone for a stale and cold cheeseburger.

Working on a dry swallow, I tipped my head back. Water would be nice, too. I was given enough to survive, but nowhere near enough to quench my thirst.

A full-body dip in lidocaine would be great also.

I sighed, not daring to move too much. The heavy chain pooled on the floor beside where I was propped up against the base of the stone slab. My wrists and ankles were always unlocked after the feeding, allowing me to roam as far as the chain would allow.

Which wasn't all that far.

The only thing I knew was that Aric had no plans to kill me. At least not yet, and despite how…horrific all of this was, alive was better than dead.

I kept telling myself that. Repeatedly.

I probably shouldn't be sitting on the floor, considering my body was one giant, open wound, and God only knew what kind of dirt and water was getting into the hundreds, if not thousands of tiny slices that covered nearly every inch of my body. I was probably going to contract some kind of flesh-eating bacteria.

Dragging my gaze from the vines, I looked down at my legs and winced. Purplish bruises mottled the pale skin, left behind when Aric had bored of me fighting back and secured my legs and arms. They were all pretty gnarly, but they were by no means the worst. The cuts were worse.

Dozens and dozens of them on each leg, on the front and the back, all methodically two inches long and carved into neat lines just a touch beyond shallow. My arms were the same. So were my chest and a good part of my back, which was why I was on the floor and not lying on the slab.

The back…those were fresh.

Another grumble echoed through my stomach. I'd thought I'd known what hunger pains felt like. I, of course, had been foolishly naive to think that skipping a meal could cause these gnawing, strong contractions that nearly doubled me over.

I was *starving*, and thinking about food was surely the worst thing I could do. So, I focused on my butchered arms and counted the slices starting at my shoulder.

One. Two. Three. Four….

I hadn't given Aric what he wanted. Not the first or the second time.

Ten. Eleven. Twelve. Thirteen….

I'd nearly cracked my molars from not screaming. But by the third time, Aric had started with the more sensitive areas first, and there hadn't been any numbness to soften the shock to the system.

Twenty-five. Twenty-six. Twenty-seven….

When he cut along the back of my knees and elbows, I'd screamed.

I'd screamed until my throat felt as raw as my skin.

I stared at the smudges of dried blood as another shudder rolled through me. Aric had been right about something, though. No one had come when I screamed.

Thirty-five. Thirty-six. Thirty-seven. Thirty-eight….

The next breath I took was shaky as I continued counting. *Forty-one. Forty-two. Forty—*

Footsteps drew my attention and I jerked up my chin. He was back. Lurching to my feet, I winced as my skin stretched. The room swayed a little, a kaleidoscope of flames and gray walls as I steadied myself.

The door swung open, and Aric strode in like he was taking a walk in a park and not strolling into a torture chamber. I wanted to shout at him, but I saw that he carried a white paper bag. I inhaled, catching a faint whiff of meat.

My knees felt weak.

"Look at you, standing when I arrive." The door swung shut behind him. "I'm impressed."

All I could do was stare at the bag of food.

Aric followed my gaze. "Hungry?"

I didn't nod or speak as he stopped a few feet from me.

"Is that why you're not lying in wait or pouncing on me like an inept buffoon?"

I didn't think my tactics were that of an inept buffoon, but he could say whatever he wanted as long as I got what was in that bag.

"You *are* hungry." Smirking, he unrolled the top of the bag and reached in, pulling out a loosely wrapped sandwich. "Sorry. I forgot how often you humans need to eat."

My mouth started to water.

He peeled back the wrapper, revealing what appeared to be a breakfast sandwich. So, I'd been right. It was morning. "Actually, I didn't forget."

Shocker.

Stepping forward, he dipped his chin and smiled. Every muscle in my body locked up. Aric was…well, he was an Ancient fae. So, of course, he was strikingly handsome. And when he smiled, it transformed all those angles into something truly majestic.

And something entirely evil.

Because he smiled like that when he cut into my skin, and he grinned like that when I screamed. He beamed like he was right now when he led me outside, when it was too dark for me to get my bearings while I went to the bathroom.

"I just want you to know that I control everything," he said as if he were suggesting that I check out a new TV show. "When you're awake.

When you rest. When you expel. When you eat. I control your every waking second."

His words burst through my fog of hunger. Words rose to the tip of my tongue. I wanted to tell him that even though he may control all of that, he still didn't control me, but I was hungry, and I needed to eat so that I had some sort of strength. It would be stupid to mouth off, so I wisely kept said mouth shut even though it ate away at a part of me.

Aric offered me the sandwich.

I eyed him warily, resisting the urge to snatch it out of his hand.

"Come on," he coaxed. "It's going to get cold, and I hear this stuff tastes even worse when it's not hot. Be a good girl."

Hatred swarmed me, hot and heavy. The tips of my fingers itched to dig into his skin, to rip at his flesh. Pushing all of that down was one of the hardest things I'd ever had to do, but I managed to do just that as I reached out to take the food.

The stinging blow seemed to come from nowhere, knocking me back. My legs went out from under me as the room spun. I went down, my knee cracking on the hard floor. Stunned by the taste of metal flooding my mouth, I planted my hands on the floor and lifted my chin.

Aric wiggled the sandwich in my direction. "You didn't say please."

* * * *

Scratching at the slab with the tiny rock I'd found near the wall of vines at some point, I worked and worked until my fingers ached and cramped, but a thin line the length of the ones that marked my body eventually took form.

My name is Brighton.

Friends call me Bri.

Tink has christened me Lite Bright.

Caden calls me sunshine.

My name is Brighton, and I will kill Aric.

That was my mantra as I finished, dropping the stone and then counting with one functioning eye. The other was swollen shut.

Thirteen. Thirteen days. I didn't quite recall exactly when I started doing this or if I had counted the days before I had begun marking them into the stone, but thirteen days had passed. Knowing that seemed important.

Just as important as forcing myself to remember who I was and why I was here every time I woke up and couldn't…couldn't recall a single thing.

Almost as important as remembering that I would kill Aric.

Footsteps echoed outside the tomb, causing my empty stomach to drop. I pushed the rock back so it was hidden and remained where I was, learning that it was safer to do so.

The door inched open, revealing Aric. He carried food, a platter covered with plastic, but it did very little to stop the aroma of roasted beef wafting its way toward me. A grumble rattled my insides as dread exploded in my chest. The dueling reactions ratcheted up the unease. Sustenance shouldn't equal fear, but it had begun to.

But the fact that he had food wasn't the only reason alarm rang its way through me like a siren.

Aric wasn't alone.

Behind him was a female fae, and this was the first time anyone besides Aric had entered the tomb. And when he took me aboveground, I never saw a soul, even though I could hear traffic. The female was tall with a blunt, icy-blond haircut, and she carried something, as well. A tote.

Was Aric going to let her get in on the fun of torturing the ever-loving hell out of me?

Knowing my luck, probably.

Aric approached me, kneeling down a foot away as the female stayed near the door. Smugness crept into his disgustingly handsome face, as did a sick look of pleasure. "How are you feeling today?"

I said nothing as I glared at him.

"You do not want me to ask you twice, little bird."

My wounded fingers spasmed as I croaked out, "Dandy."

He tilted his head. "I'm happy to hear that."

I'm sure.

"You surprise me each day, you know? That you're still alive, still *there*. It's impressive."

"I live to impress you." My gaze darted to the plate of food.

His chuckle was low. "Hungry?"

Every muscle in my body locked up as my eyes shifted back to him.

"Oh. Are you not hungry?" He lifted his brows as he peeled back the plastic wrapping. "Here." He held out the plate as I zeroed in on the meat. The hunk of beef sat in its own juices and looked so good, it made my stomach ache. "Take it."

On reflex, I reached up, touching the split in my lower lip.

Aric smiled as if I were a child showing him a report card with straight *A*s. "Come on, it's just food. It won't hurt you."

That was a lie.

My hand trembled, and I quickly hid it in the folds of my stained dress. The female fae remained quiet, still standing by the door.

"Be a good girl," Aric murmured.

Anger flushed me as my gaze flew to his. *I'm going to kill you.* A shudder rocked me as I forced myself to take a breath. *I'm going to rip your fucking head off.* Slowly, I lifted my hand and reached to the plate—

He tipped forward suddenly, and I couldn't stop my reaction. Flinching, I pressed back against the stone, waiting for the blow.

This was why food equaled fear. Why hunger had truly become painful and something to dread. It was another form of torture, one both physical and mental. I was Aric's messed up version of Pavlov's dog, but instead of salivating at the sound of a bell, I saw food and experienced horror.

Classic fucking conditioning at its finest.

"Take the food," he ordered when I didn't move. "Take the food, or I will take from you."

Ice dripped down my spine as I found myself stuck between a rock and a more messed up rock. Reach for the food and most likely get punched or kicked or slapped or grabbed? Don't reach for the food and he'd feed.

I chose the former, lifting my arm once more.

His other hand whipped out, catching mine. My heart jerked to a stop as he squeezed—squeezed until the bones of my hand ground together. I gasped back the cry of pain.

"You do not learn, do you, you stupid cow?" His smile twisted into a snarl that made him look more rabid animal than human. "What are you supposed to say?"

What he wanted tasted of bitter ash on the tip of my tongue.

"Say it."

I knew what was coming.

His lips peeled back. "Say it."

I said nothing because all I had left was my will, and I clamored to preserve that even when I knew he was going to take that, too.

"Say it!" he roared.

I swallowed hard. "Make me."

Letting go of my bruised hand, he grasped my chin, digging his fingers into the skin. He yanked me up onto my knees with his grip. His eyes caught mine, and there was no looking away, no blinking as his pupils seemed to constrict to pinpoints.

Without the four-leaf clover, I was like any other mortal, fully susceptible to a fae's glamour, and it took nothing for Aric to seize control of my mind.

And in a sick way, it was sort of a relief the moment I felt the icy brush against my consciousness. Because then, I felt nothing. No fear. No hate. No dread.

Nothing.

"Say it," he whispered, but his voice echoed throughout me. "Say *please*."

"Please," I repeated.

Aric's smile returned. "Good girl." Letting go of my chin, he dropped the plate of food in front of me. "Eat."

I ate, using my sore fingers to pull apart the cooling meat.

"When you're done, you will be bathed," Aric explained. "You reek of sweat and humanity."

Pausing mid-chew, I glanced over at the female fae who remained silent by the door. Was that why she was here? There was a niggle of concern as if the idea of being bathed should concern me, but the sensation floated away, and I resumed eating.

Once the plate was empty, the female hurried over, placing the tote beside me. She went back to the door, disappearing for a moment only to return with a small army of fae. They carried a copper tub, dropping it in the space between the stone slabs. Water sloshed over the edges, hitting my legs. I jerked my feet back. The liquid was cold.

Aric snapped his fingers, and the other fae quickly left. Only he and the female remained. He turned to me. "Stand."

I climbed to my feet.

Aric tilted his head, his pale gaze flickering over me. "You're so much easier to deal with like this." He approached me, curling his fingers around my chin and tilting my head back. "Which means, this will go so much more smoothly. Because I know the minute I release my hold on you, you're going to fight this."

I blinked slowly as he reached around, unhooking the band secured to my neck. He placed it on the stone.

"Because I know you'll find every second of this utterly humiliating, being stripped and tended to as if you are nothing more than a child. I want to see that. The red flush of embarrassment, and the futile attempts to cover yourself." His eyes closed as he sighed. "It would truly be a marvelous sight to behold. But alas, I fear it would break you, and since you're my favorite new pet, I'm not done playing with you."

He opened his eyes. "Plus, I have important business to do today." Slipping his hand from my chin, he stepped back and motioned the female forward.

I stood still, waiting.

Aric pivoted, reaching into his pocket and pulling out a cellphone. He stared down at it as the female picked up the tote and began taking out items. Removing two pitchers, she filled them with the water from the tub.

"Undress," she said, her voice sharp as an icicle. "And get in the tub."

My gaze flicked from her to the Ancient's back.

The female beside me sighed with annoyance. "My lord."

He glanced over his shoulder and, a moment later, he chuckled. "Undress and get in the tub, little bird."

I did as he requested, letting the soiled clothing fall to the floor. The water was a shock, stunning me into immobility as the cold shot straight up my legs and my spine. There was no time to adjust. Hands landed on my shoulders, forcing me down so I was sitting. Gasping, I reached out, clasping the sides of the tub.

The female got to work, working a lavender-scented bar of soap against my skin. The sting against the raw cuts warred with the numbing properties of the frigid water, and eventually, the water won. The smarting pain faded as the female moved to a cloth, dragging it down my arms as she knelt behind me. Quickly, the once-clear water turned murky.

Aric moved to the other slab of stone, stretched out on it, reclining as if he were lounging by a pool. "Ask me what business I have to take care of, little bird," he said, looking up from his phone.

Teeth chattering, I winced as the female dragged the soapy cloth along my back. "W-what business d-do you have to t-take care of?"

"Well, since you asked." He returned to thumbing through his cell. "I have a very important meeting with a…certain member of the Summer Court who, like me, wishes to see the return of the Queen. For very different reasons, but reasons nonetheless."

My head jerked back as the female scrubbed at my tangled hair, lathering the oily strands.

"I'm so close to reopening the doorway and freeing my Queen."

Looking up from his phone, Aric glanced over at me just as the female tugged on my hair once more. One eyebrow rose as his gaze dipped. The corners of his lips tipped up. "Do you know how I will succeed? Answer me."

My spine bowed as the female guided my head. She picked up the pitcher. "No."

Swinging his legs off the stone, he stood and approached the tub. "Obviously, the likelihood of the King having a child with a halfling is slim, but there is one way that the gateway could be opened. The King himself can do it."

He dropped to his knees in front of the tub, snapping his fingers. A moment later, he held the pitcher. "But why would he?"

Shivering, I waited for him to continue.

He curved a hand around the nape of my neck. "Tip your head back," he coaxed, and I obeyed. "The King wouldn't unless he was forced. After all, he would do anything to protect his *mortuus*. The Summer fae can bring me the King's weakness, and with that, I will be able to make him do whatever I want."

The cold water pouring over my head wasn't as much of a shock as it had been when I first climbed into the tub, but it still caused me to jolt.

"And as more younglings and Summer fae taste the Devil's Breath, the Order will be too busy wrangling them as I force the King to open the doorway." He picked up the other pitcher, rinsing the remaining soap from my hair. He placed it aside. "When that happens, this world will finally become the Queen's, and nothing will be able to stop her this time."

Drops of water blotted his white shirt as he slid his hand to the front of my throat. "You'll most likely be dead by then."

His fingers followed the stream of water coursing down my shoulders and then lower. His gaze tracked his hand. "Perhaps you will make me a liar. You are strangely resilient, and I have yet to bore of our time together. I'm not ready to silence your screams."

I sucked in a sharp breath at the sudden pinch.

"You're surprisingly…pleasantly developed for a mortal," he murmured, the coolness of his palm branding my skin. "I am starting to understand why the King became interested. Then again, he was, how do I say? Always virile before he was mated to Siobhan. His escapades were rather legendary."

The pale gaze remained fixed below my shoulders, as did his hand.

"Your skin here is soft. Unmarred. We shall have to fix that, won't we, little bird?"

"Yes," I whispered.

Chuckling, he slid his hand down my stomach and then under the water. I jerked at the contact. His smile grew as his gaze finally lifted to mine. He held my stare for a moment and then looked at the female who waited behind us silently. "Finish with her."

Aric withdrew, and the female fae did as ordered, making sure the rest of me was clean. Then I was guided from the tub and dried off with a small linen that did more to irritate the numerous cuts than it did to soak up any of the water. A clean slip was tugged over my head, and when I looked down, I saw that it only reached to mid-thigh and offered little coverage or warmth.

Still shivering, I waited where I had been left as the female went back to the door, and both male fae returned, taking the tub and exiting. Suddenly, I was alone with Aric.

"Much better," he commented, lifting a hand. He crooked his finger. "Come to me."

I went to him.

His touch against my cheek was almost gentle if not for the pressure against the tender skin there. "I think it's time to let you free, don't you?"

Unsure, I nodded.

He bent, picking up the band and securing it around my neck. His eyes caught mine again, and he whispered something. The icy brush of fingers retreated from my consciousness. It was like a retractable leash. Free will snapped back into place with such force that it drove me back away from the Ancient. Slamming into the edge of the slab, I stared at him, gulping air.

"Welcome back, little bird."

Chest heaving, I pushed off the slab. "Fuck you."

He smirked. "Oh, how I missed that mouth. But I wished you knew what I missed"—his gaze dipped in a way that made my skin crawl—"most of all."

I knew what he missed. I could still feel his hands on my skin, touching me. And what he didn't realize was that I remembered *everything.* What I did. What he said. I didn't know how or why, and while there was a whole lot I wished to forget, I now knew how he planned to free the Queen.

So I smiled.

Chapter 10

Fingers brushed my cheek, drawing me out of the abyss of nothingness.

"Open your eyes," a voice beckoned, one painfully familiar. "I need you to open your eyes, Brighton."

I knew that deep, smooth voice.

Gasping, I opened my eyes and found myself staring into eyes a shade of pale blue—eyes and a beautiful face framed by blond hair. I couldn't believe who I was seeing. "Caden?"

The King smiled. "There's my sunshine."

My sunshine….

"I don't…I don't understand." I blinked, thinking he'd disappear, but he was still there when I reopened my lids, those full lips curved. "You…you came for me?"

"Of course, I did." He touched my cheek again, his touch so gentle that I barely felt it. "How could I not?"

Confusion clouded my thoughts as I stared at him. "How?"

"I've been looking for you. We've all been looking for you. We didn't give up on you," he said, dipping his head. "*I* didn't give up on you."

Caden kissed me, and the touch of his lips against mine was a jolt to my system. Not because it caused the swollen, torn skin to sting, but because it was like a rush of fresh air. And because it tasted like the sun.

"We need to hurry." He lifted his head as his fingers found mine. "We have to get out of here, now."

Stunned by his presence and the kiss, I didn't resist as his hand folded around mine and he pulled me up. I stood on shaky legs, throat burning and eyes stinging. "You…you came for me."

"I will always come for you," he replied. "I love you, Brighton."

Tears filled my eyes as I stared up at him. He…he'd come for me, and he…he loved me.

Caden let go of my hand and went to the door. The hinges creaked as he opened it. The faint glow of dusk crept into the chamber. Inhaling deeply, I caught the faint scent of roses reaching me. He turned back, stretching out his hand—

Wait.

His…his eyes weren't a cool blue the last time I saw them. They were a warm, fiery amber, but his eyes were now blue. I didn't understand.

"Come," Caden urged. "You must follow me. Quick. Before we run out of time."

Realizing that he was right and the whole eye thing wasn't important, I started forward, hurrying toward freedom, toward life—

Jerked backward by the neck, my feet slipped out from underneath me. I went down hard on my ass, grunting as a bolt of pain jolted up my spine. My hands flew to my throat. Cool, hard metal greeted my fingers.

"What…?" Confusion swamped me as I twisted toward the stone slab.

The chain….

The tether was still there, bolted to the floor, and the chain was still…. It was still connected to the band around my neck.

Why didn't Caden take that off? He had to know that I couldn't leave with it still attached. Rising to my knees, I turned back to Caden—

He wasn't there.

Where he stood was now just the wooden door—the closed, locked, wooden door.

I fell back onto my ass, my hands dropping to the floor. "He's not here," I said to the empty chamber.

He was never here.

Realization slammed into me, punching a harsh cry from my chest. Caden had never been here. The door had never been opened, and I was awake. This wasn't a dream. This was a…this was a hallucination. I lifted a hand, touching my lips. A very real hallucination because I could still feel the press of his soft kiss.

"Oh, God," I whispered, curling my hand into a fist.

Memories of my mom surfaced. Many of them flipping together, forming a whirlwind of the hours where she was utterly detached from reality. Episodes where she spoke to people who weren't there or when she believed that she was still being held by the fae. All those times when it was like I wasn't even there with her. When it was like she couldn't even see me.

I had just experienced that. A hallucination so real I had mistaken it for reality.

God.

It was official.

I was losing my mind.

* * * *

I didn't know where I was or why…why I hurt so badly. I was cold, and yet I was hot as I lay on my side on a hard table of stone and stared at the still flames across from me. They didn't even seem real to me, barely flickering. I was in a tomb, that much I knew, and there was a chain secured to my neck. And I hurt.

My gaze dropped to where my fingers lay limply in front of me. They were covered in tiny, stinging cuts.

I hurt all over.

I was also hungry.

None of these things pointed to anything good.

I started to shift onto my back but stopped with a wince. The skin there felt raw too, because…because there were cuts there also.

Disjointed images and memories took form. The glint of a blade. Pale blue eyes. Screams…screams and laughter—cold, malicious laughter.

Closing my eyes, I inhaled the musty air and sifted through the cotton that seemed to take up space in my head. There was an odd sense of having done this before as I started with my name because that seemed like a good place to start.

My name.

I had one. I knew I did. A moniker tied to a past, to memories, to a duty. A name that was often shortened.

Lite Bright.

The two words popped up in my head. Someone called me Lite Bright, because my name sounded like that—sounded like light.

Bri.

Brighton.

My eyes opened, and I focused on the dark, low ceiling. Brighton was my name, and…and my friends—I had friends—they called me Bri, but *he* called me sunshine. A whoosh swept through my chest, twisting with sadness and…and love. Love that wasn't…returned by him? I saw him suddenly, golden hair brushing broad shoulders and eyes the color of honey set in a face so exquisitely fine that he didn't seem real. But he was real, and his name was Caden. He was the King, and he'd wanted me…and then he didn't. The twisting motion inside me returned at the memory of what I knew in my bones was the last night I'd seen him. We'd been together. It hadn't been planned, because I…I had been angry at him, and he'd pushed me away until he pulled me to him. We'd made love. Or at least I thought we did, but then something…something happened.

Dampness crowded my eyes, and the back of my throat burned. What had happened?

"I am honored to become your Queen and serve our Court together."

The words returned with a jolt, along with the face of…of the Summer fae who'd delivered them. His chosen. His soon-to-be Queen. He'd made love to me and yet was promised to another who was worthy, a beautiful fae creature—

I cut those thoughts off as my cheeks became wet. Reaching up, I wiped the tears away. The stinging of my fingers, salt in open wounds, cleared more of the fog. What had happened with the King wasn't important now, because I was here….

It took me what felt like forever to remember how I had ended up here, and even once I did, some of the details were still missing. Like where I'd been when Aric had taken me, and how long I'd been here. It felt like…weeks, but I wasn't sure if that was the case or not. I slowly realized that more was gone though as my history stitched itself back together, forming a puzzle that was missing pieces. I could remember Tink and his cat, but no matter how hard I tried, I couldn't recall the cat's name. I knew who Ivy was, but her last name was just out of reach, as was her boyfriend's first name. Or was it her husband? I could only remember his last name, but not his first. And saying Owens over and over didn't magically make his first name appear. I knew there was something important I needed to remember, something that Aric had said, but I couldn't recall it. I knew who had killed my mother but couldn't remember when or how it had all gone down. I knew something had happened to me that night too, but that was just outside my grasp. There was more I knew was gone, because….

Because parts of me were being stripped away, peeled back and discarded with each feeding.

Was that what had happened to my mom before she was killed, back when she'd been held captive by the fae? She'd been fed on so much that she'd lost a part of herself...and lost touch with reality from time to time.

Was that what was happening to me each time I had to backtrack through what had happened to remember, each time recalling less and less? Would I eventually stop remembering altogether?

I shuddered.

Panic forced me upright, and I ignored how every square inch of my body protested the movement. I let my legs dangle as dizziness swept through me, and the right side of my face throbbed. Gingerly, I prodded at the swollen skin along my jaw. The flesh around my left eye felt the same, and as I stared down at my legs, there were fresh bruises and cuts there, a map of slices and ugly shades of red and purple. I remembered how the cuts had gotten there, but I had no idea why I had the injuries.

I couldn't think about any of this. I couldn't dwell on it. Not when I still had parts of myself, which meant that there was still an opportunity to escape.

Steely resolve finally settled in my stomach like a lead bullet. Purpose returned, driving home the need to keep going, to keep living.

I would not die in this place.

I would not die by Aric's hands.

I would not give him that.

A hollowness opened up in my chest even as I repeated those three sentences over and over. My gaze tracked to the side of the slab of stone, and I saw tiny scratches there, likely marked by the rock lying on the floor next to it, a shard no bigger than my thumb.

I counted the marks. Twenty-nine. A sense of knowing led me to my feet and over to pick up the sliver. I worked at the stone, scratching a slash over the last four ragged lines. Thirty.

Thirty days that I was aware of. That was at least how long I'd been here, and I knew in my bones that I had to escape because this wasn't like when Ivy had been taken back when Caden had been the evil Prince, hellbent on opening all the doorways to the Otherworld. She'd had help from the inside, and people were looking for her. People who cared enough to risk their lives. They'd found her the night she had been aided in her escape. How long had she been held? Three weeks? An incredibly long time, but she had been found.

A sudden memory surfaced—the hallucination of Caden freeing me. That hadn't been real.

The hollowness spread, threatening to choke me with bitter

hopelessness that seemed to linger like a heavy, oppressive shadow.

I dropped the stone, and slid to my knees, curling inward.

"They care," I whispered to myself. I knew that Ivy did. So did Tink, and Ivy's man. I knew they cared. Maybe even Caden. He liked me, just not *enough*. But the truth was, I knew how the Order operated. I knew enough to know that if Caden, the King of the Summer fae, was looking for me, they'd have found me by now. Ivy's…boyfriend—husband?—had nearly torn the whole city apart looking for her.

And I was still here.

Because no one was coming.

Chapter 11

"I'm amazed. Really, I am." Aric held the dagger, turning it so the flames reflected off the blade. It was streaked in red. "You're still alive."

There was a part of me that also couldn't believe I was still alive. How long had I been here now? My thoughts were sluggish as I tried to remember how many little nicks I'd carved into the stone. Forty? Forty-five, maybe. There was something about that time frame that seemed important. Something that should've happened in that time.

"I must say, it thrills me that you're still here. You came to me as a little bird I couldn't wait to break, but now, you're my pet." Lowering his head, Aric's lips brushed the curve of my cheek, sending a wave of revulsion through me. "My most cherished one. How do you feel about that?"

"Like…like my life is now complete," I rasped.

"Do I detect a hint of sarcasm?" His breath now danced over my lips, so I turned my head away. Lately, he seemed to be…getting way more into this, so much so that I feared he was beginning to change his views on whether he found mortals attractive. "I hope so. It warms my heart to know you still have so much fight left in you."

Letting my eyes close, I searched for memories to lose myself in. There was the time my mom had taken me to the Gulf. I'd been a teenager, and I knew I'd loved it there, but I couldn't remember what the sand felt like between my toes. I focused as hard as I could on what the water looked like, but as soon as the picture began to form in my mind, the image scattered like smoke.

It was so hard to remember the details of…of anything.

"You're obviously incredibly strong, bizarrely so for a mortal." My muscles clenched as I felt the cool press of the blade's edge against the skin of my inner thigh. "Unbelievably so, really."

I kept my eyes closed, my heart thumping as I waited for the sharp, stinging bite of pain to come. At some point, he would run out of skin to carve up, and then what? Would he start on my face? Probably. He'd already covered my stomach with those tiny slices, and now those scars mingled with the ones he'd left behind before, the old, shiny, pale teeth marks and deep grooves that Caden had…worshiped with his lips.

Forty-five days.

Days that sometimes included feeding, sometimes included baths in cold water. Days where I couldn't recall what exactly occurred, moments that left me feeling that perhaps it was better that I didn't remember.

"No one has ever lasted as long as you." The blade moved swiftly across my skin.

A hoarse scream left me as I pulled against my bonds, trying to escape the blade—the pain—even though I knew it was useless.

His pale eyes glowed. "I've had men twice your size die within weeks and lose their minds in days, and yet you and I have had weeks together. More than a month, and you're still here."

My head lolled to the side, and I found myself staring at the other stone slab, the one stained in the center. Had men twice my size died there? Members of the Order? Helpless humans? Other fae? Aric was truly a psychopath, so I imagined he was equal opportunity when it came to whom he tortured.

Forty-five days, and I should have had…I should have had my period by now. A frown tugged at my brow. I hadn't. As far as I could tell, at least. And I figured Aric was the type to have pointed it out if there was more blood than normal. He was an asshole like that.

Probably was the stress of being slowly cut to death and the lack of food and water. Aric seemed to continue to *forget* to feed me on any sort of regular basis, and I had no idea how much weight I'd dropped, but my stomach was sunken instead of rounded, and I knew my ribs were beginning to jut out, even when I stood, as were my hipbones. I could feel—

He gripped my chin, forcing my gaze back to his. "What I'm trying to tell you, if you'd pay attention, is that I'm beginning to think there is…something different about you."

I glared at him.

Aric bent over so that our faces were only inches apart. "You shouldn't be alive, and that makes me very, very curious. Come to think of it, I was somewhat stunned to discover that you'd survived our first meeting. You should've died then."

I should've.

His pale gaze flickered over my face, and then he moved away. I tracked him, my heart stuttering when he lowered his head again, this time to where he'd just sliced open my skin. I tried to pull away, but there was nowhere to go. Bile crept into my throat as I felt his tongue against my skin.

He lifted his head, smirking. "You taste like a mortal."

My hands opened and closed into tight fists. *I'm going to kill you. I'm going to rip out your tongue and kill you.*

"But I no longer believe that you are an ordinary human." He moved back to where his face was just above me, his head tilted to the side. "Tell me what I don't know."

"You're a fucking psychopath," I croaked out.

Aric chuckled. "I said something I *don't* know."

Nice.

He lifted the blade, placing it against my cheek just under my eye. The tip was wet as he dragged it down, smearing blood from the cuts he'd made on my thigh. "Tell me, pet. Tell me how you're still alive. How you survived before."

"I…I don't know," I said, and that wasn't exactly true. I knew how I'd survived our first little meet and greet.

"Hmm." He slid the edge of the knife over my chin and down my throat. "I don't believe you."

I held still.

"And I don't like it when you lie to me. I thought we'd moved past all of that," he said. "That you and I were better than lies."

"You're insane," I choked out.

"I'm a lot of things, pet. Insane is not one of them." The pupils of his eyes dilated. My breath caught as I started to close my lids. "Don't," he commanded, and it was too late for me to do otherwise. "Tell me how you survived."

My lips and tongue moved, giving sound to words. "Caden saved me."

His head straightened, and he frowned. "How did he save you?"

"I don't know."

"You have to know." He cupped my cheek, smoothing his thumb over the trails of blood. "Think hard about it. What was he doing when he saved your life?"

I did what he asked, thinking back to when Caden had saved me. It was like wading through muddy waters until I came to vague images of a hospital room and beeping and…. "I felt the sun. I tasted…tasted sunlight."

"Tasted sunlight?" Aric was still for several moments, and then he jerked upright. He stumbled back, dropping the dagger. It clattered off the floor. "He gave you the *Kiss*." His eyes widened. "He gave you the *Summer Kiss*."

* * * *

Scratching the rock against the stone, I carved another mark.

Forty-seven.

Today was day forty-seven, and it was different. Aric had not been to see me. Not yesterday or today, and I knew this because my thoughts were clearer, even though I was hungrier than I'd ever been.

But I knew there was something important that I needed to remember, something that Aric had shared, and that was what I focused on while I worked on the mark.

He'd told me something about the Summer fae, something that had been…unexpected.

My gaze drifted from the stone to the floor as my thoughts wandered to all-you-can-eat buffets and gumbo and beignets and—

I dropped the rock and tipped forward, my eyes narrowing on the floor under the slab. Something was lying there. What was it? Scooting onto my knees, I stretched until my fingers brushed cool metal.

The dagger.

"Holy shit," I whispered, curling my hand around the hilt. How had it gotten there?

Part of me didn't even care to know the answer, because this…this was my chance. My vehicle of retribution. My payback. It was everything, better than a juicy steak and a mountain of mashed potatoes.

My stomach grumbled in disagreement.

Okay. *Almost* as good as a juicy steak and a mountain of mashed potatoes, but this was…this was my chance.

Tears flooded my eyes as I stared at the dagger. Aric was an Ancient. I still remembered how to kill one. Head shot or sever the brain stem. Fae be gone, right there.

I rocked back, lifting the dagger toward one of the torches. The blade was stained red—with my blood. I looked down at the cuts all over my legs and my arms. This was Aric's weapon, the tool he used on me. He…he'd *dropped* it the last time he was here.

That was super careless of him, but he'd been…shocked about something. My grip tightened on the dagger as I tried to recall what had led to him dropping this. Even though my head felt less woolly than normal, it was still full of empty spaces. He'd been asking me questions, wondering how I'd survived—

The sound of footsteps outside the chamber forced me into jerky action. I needed this dagger, so I knew to hide it and pray that he hadn't realized he'd left it behind. Shoving the blade back under the tomb until it was hidden by the shadows, I then took a deep, slow breath, preparing to stand. I knew I'd be dizzy and winded, but I needed to get to my feet. I needed to do everything possible to keep my wits about me and keep that dagger hidden.

Slowly, I pulled myself up, and I swayed like a reed in the wind. My heart was racing from the effort, but also because of my find.

The door opened as Aric entered. Anticipation and dread clashed like thunder within me. He had food, and I was starving, but eating never came without a price. And he wasn't alone. The same icy female fae as before was with him. My stomach sank.

Bath time.

I thought—no, I *knew*—he glamoured me when this occurred. Sometimes, I remembered it. Sometimes, I didn't. But I knew he always fed afterward, and then…then I remembered nothing.

Oh, God, what if I forgot about the dagger? Dread quickly turned to panic. I couldn't forget the weapon. I couldn't—

"Did you miss me?" Aric strolled forward, platter in hand. "I missed you."

I took a step back. The female remained by the door as she usually did, but she carried more than just a tote with her this time. A long, dark bag was draped over her arm.

"You don't want to admit it, but I know you've been wondering where I've been, what I've been doing." He placed the covered dish on the slab. The scent of meat reached me. "I've been very busy, my pet."

My pet.

God, I couldn't wait to tear his fucking head off. It took everything in me not to grab the dagger and do just that.

Twisting toward me, he picked up the chain, tugging on it until I stumbled toward him. Once I was close enough, he curled his arm around my waist, drawing me to his side as if we were lovers.

I wanted to vomit.

"I cannot wait to tell you all about it. You will be so very interested in what I've discovered," he went on. "But first, I've brought you gifts."

Gifts? My hungry gaze found its way to the silver platter.

"Not that," he murmured, skimming his fingers over the many tiny abrasions marking my arms. I winced at the contact, and his eyes took on a heavy-lidded quality. "At least not the gift I'm most excited about." He snapped his fingers at the female. "Show her what I've brought her."

Pulse skittering, I watched her lift the bag. The sound of a zipper being lowered filled the chamber. It was only then that I realized she was holding a garment bag. The folds of the bag parted as she stepped forward, revealing what lay beneath.

A gown. It was a gown. One made of some kind of silvery material that reached the floor. As the female fae pulled the garment bag away, I saw that the dress was sleeveless and nearly translucent. It was like spun moonlight, even in the dim lighting of the crypt, and utterly beautiful.

My stomach twisted with nausea. "You expect me to wear that?"

"Ah, she has found her voice." Aric chuckled, squeezing me like it was some kind of inside joke between friends. "I do expect you to wear this, and I expect you to be honored to do so."

I stared at him, dumbfounded. He couldn't be serious.

Aric motioned the female forward, and she obeyed without a word, laying the gown over the slab but keeping it on the garment bag so my blood did not reach it.

"You see, this gown is very special." Aric slipped his arm away from me, and I exhaled raggedly. Reaching for the delicate material, he traced the deep v-neck of the dress. "It is not of this world, but a token of mine. It was to be a wedding gown. *Mathing*," he said, speaking fae. I thought the word meant mating. "You would not be the first to wear this, but I believe you will be the last."

Stepping back, I wrapped my arm over my waist as I followed his fingers down the center of the dress. The material seemed to respond to his touch, darkening into a slate gray.

"Do you know who wore this gown last?" he asked.

My throat dried while my suspicions threatened to sink me.

Aric glanced over his shoulder at me. "Answer me, my pet, or I'll make you."

Even though I wanted nothing more than to disobey him, I couldn't risk being glamoured or fed on. Not when I needed to remember that dagger. Swallowing hard, I lifted my chin. "Who…?" I cleared my throat. "Who wore it last?"

"Thank you for asking." He refocused on the dress while the female slipped silently back to the doorway. "Siobhan wore it on her wedding day."

Oh, God.

I closed my eyes.

"Well, she wore it *to* her wedding. I caught her before she arrived," he added. When I reopened my eyes, Aric was staring down at the dress. "Caden never saw her in it, but he'll know it was hers when he sees you in it."

A jolt ran through me as my arm unfurled.

He tilted his head to the side, his pale eyes opening to meet mine. "Funny how history repeats itself."

"I…I don't understand."

"You don't?" He faced me fully, and I tensed. "You don't remember, do you? What you told me the last time I was here." A smirk graced his perfect lips. "You're strong, and you've held on longer than any mortal should've. All those lovely moments when I've taken your essence from you have done their damage, but it should've fried that little brain of yours. *If* you were fully mortal."

Part of me wondered if my little brain was fried since I knew I couldn't have heard him right. "I am fully mortal."

"You *were* fully mortal," he replied. "But that all changed when Caden gave you the Summer Kiss."

The Summer Kiss? "I—"

"Have no idea what I'm talking about? You don't remember our conversation? About how he saved your life after we first met? After I was positive that I'd killed both you and your mother?" he explained, and a shudder rolled its way through me. "He placed his lips to yours and, instead of taking your essence, he gave you his. That is the Summer Kiss, and only an Ancient can bestow such a gift."

"What…what kind of gift?" I asked, wondering if I could return or exchange it.

One side of Aric's lips tipped. "The kind that will make it extra hard to kill you, and one that will ensure you will have a very odd lifespan by mortal standards." He took a step toward me. "You'd figure something out as the years went by and you looked the same as the night I tore into your flesh with my teeth and nails. You'd begin then to realize something had been done, as would the Order. They'd either make damn sure you were put down, or they'd study you to figure out what was done. But you, my pet, are no longer simply mortal. You're not a halfling either. You are something else entirely."

My mouth opened, but no words came out. He couldn't be saying what I thought he was.

"It's rare for a fae to bestow the Kiss upon another. It's an ancient practice used only in the direst circumstances, but it is unheard of for one to do so with a mortal," he continued, his eyes gleaming. "A great offense, one punishable by death. If we were in my world, you'd be dragged before the Court and slaughtered while Caden watched—something he witnessed the few times a fae gave the Kiss to a mortal. So, for him to do that with you can only mean one thing."

Through the fog of memories, Caden's lack of reasoning for his actions came back to me. I'd believed… "I did something for him," I said. "I think…I helped him somehow. That's why."

Aric approached me, placing his fingertip on my chin and tilting my head back. "That is not why he did it, my pet. He gave you the Kiss because you are what I've been searching for. You are his *mortuus.*"

Chapter 12

Pulling away from Aric, I stepped back. Even if I hadn't spent the last forty-seven days being tortured, starved, and fed on, I would have had trouble processing the news that I wasn't quite mortal and that I didn't have a normal lifespan.

Then again, there was a good chance that Aric was lying just to mess with my head in a rather creative form of torture.

"I can tell by the dumb look on your face you have no idea what a *mortuus* is or how it plays into what I need," he said. And, yep, that was as offensive as it sounded. "I'm not all that surprised. You've forgotten my plans, and it is doubtful that Caden would ever share with you what *mortuus* means."

The cogs and wheels in my brain finally started turning. "I don't see how I can be his *mortuus*. I don't—"

"You don't know anything, my pet. But your knowledge isn't what makes you valuable." Aric turned to the slab with an air of flourish. "Come. You must eat and then bathe."

I didn't move. "I want to know why you think I'm his—" My words ended in a shriek.

Aric moved so fast that I couldn't track him. Suddenly, he was in front of me, his hand clamping around the nape of my neck. "I don't care what you want to know. I don't care if you're confused or even if you believe me." His grip tightened, forcing my head back as his fingers tangled in my hair. Pain flared along my scalp, but it was nothing compared to what I was used to. "All I care about at this moment in time is for you to not cause me any problems. Do you understand me?"

Fury ripped through me like a tornado, and any plans I had of keeping him happy jumped right out the window. Jaw locked, I met his gaze and said nothing.

"Do not make me ask you again. You will not like what happens if you do, and I am confident that you think you know what I'm capable of, but you have no idea." The alabaster skin seemed to thin over his bones. "I need you alive, but there are far worse things than a slow death."

There wasn't a single part of me that doubted what he promised, and common sense dictated that I answer him. It was just one word. *Yes*. I had a dagger, and I just needed to get him alone. Fighting him now wasn't going to help.

It was just one word, but it was about control and stripping away every ounce of free will I had without glamouring me. It was all about submission and humiliation, tiny acts stacked upon each other, and each one carrying the weight of shame and dread until I collapsed under them. Until I was truly bent and broken, and all that was left of me belonged to him.

It was just one word, but he hadn't broken me yet.

I lifted my chin, met his stare, and said nothing.

Aric's lips curved up on one side. "I could almost respect you."

The punch connected before I could even formulate a response, catching me in the stomach and doubling me over. I tried to suck in air, but it was like my entire chest had seized up. Gagging, I struggled to lift my arms as the years of training dictated, but he was too fast, and I was too tired and hungry and weak. The next blow took me to the floor, and then…there was nothing but pain.

I didn't know how long it lasted or how many blows he delivered. At some point, I thought I might've blacked out because when I opened my eyes—no, my one eye—his blurry face had replaced his fists.

He was staring down at his hand. "You've dirtied my knuckles with your blood."

A hoarse laugh parted my lips. It was slightly crazed-sounding to my ears, but then again, there was a strange ringing in them now, so who knew.

His head tilted to the side. "Glad you find that amusing, but I'm sure it won't be as funny to watch you try and eat with those busted lips."

Eat? I almost laughed again because the beating had pretty much knocked the hunger right out of me. I wasn't even sure my jaw would work. I tentatively moved it, wincing as sharp pain darted around my skull. It hurt like holy hell but, impossibly, the bones seemed intact.

No longer simply mortal.

Could Aric be telling the truth? And if so, was that why I was still alive without a multitude of broken bones? The questions did matter.

Aric grabbed my arm, yanking me to my feet. Pain flared along my ribs. "Eat and then bathe. I do not have all day."

He shoved me toward the slab, and I stumbled, catching myself on the side of the stone near where the dagger was hidden in the shadows.

I focused on what I planned to do with that dagger as I lifted my head, dizzy. Aric strode toward the platter, lifting the lid. It was beef in some kind of stew like before.

"It's grown cold," he remarked. "If you hadn't delayed things, it would've been a worthwhile meal. Eat."

Slowly, I inched my way toward the food and reached out—

The slap nearly toppled me over. Skin stinging, I drew back my hand. Nausea rose as I stared at the food.

Aric sighed. "You will never learn, will you? Even with the Summer Kiss, you're as stupid and mindless as any other mortal. Eat," he spat. "And do it in a hurry."

I didn't move, not until he went over to the doorway. I'd forgotten that the female was in the room. With distance between us, I hesitantly reached for the meat, knowing that he could move fast. When he didn't, some of the tension eased from my shoulders. Without a fork or knife, all I had were my fingers, and I used them, eating what was provided even though each bite hurt, and I was no longer hungry. I ate because I knew I needed the strength.

Cutting off a head wasn't going to be easy.

Before I finished, the copper tub was brought in and filled up, and I added those two male fae to my *To Kill* list. The female was already on it. The plate was taken away, and I knew what was coming next. Aric would glamour me so I didn't put up a fight, and then he'd feed. Between the two, I ran the risk of forgetting the discovery of the dagger. I knew I couldn't prevent him from feeding, but I could prevent the glamour, and if history were any indication, he'd return to me alone and then….

Then I would kill him.

But the dress.

I glanced at it. The dress could mean that his schedule would change. That he wouldn't feed, or that he wouldn't return alone.

I couldn't risk not trying to keep some of my wits about me.

So, I did what I had to the very second the female fae approached me with her damn tote. Focusing on the tub, I didn't give myself time to dwell on what I was doing as I reached up and grabbed the thin straps on the shift, shimmying them down my arms.

Aric made a soft sound, alerting me to the fact that he was paying attention. "Aren't you eager to strip bare?"

The statement wasn't worth a response.

This wasn't the first time he'd seen me naked, and at this point, what was there to see but scars and skin? That's what I kept telling myself as I stepped into the tub. The water wasn't frigid, more like room temperature, which was a vast improvement.

I sank down quickly, seeking the little privacy the wall of the tub provided. Bathing with the chain still attached to my neck wasn't exactly the easiest thing. The female got to work, as gentle as a wild boar as she scrubbed at my raw and bruised skin. I found myself staring at the dress where it lay waiting on the slab.

Aric had moved closer. "I didn't tell you why you'd be wearing such an exquisite gown, did I?"

The female yanked my head back as she lathered the strands with lavender-scented soap.

"You will find out soon enough, and I have a feeling you'll be pleased."

Doubtful.

A sense of deja vu swept through me. The Ancient fell silent, and my mind wandered, sifting through foggy memories as the female fae finished up. There was something he'd told me while I was bathed before. I'd been glamoured, but I'd been aware of what was happening. Images surfaced of Aric kneeling in front of the tub, his white shirt dotted with water. He'd told me something. Something about the *mortuus* and—

My head was dunked without warning, and when I resurfaced, I sputtered as I gripped the rim of the tub.

My thoughts were effectively scattered. There was nothing of any value floating around in my head anymore as I was yanked from the tub and then roughly dried off.

The gown was lifted over my head, the fabric settling around me. I caught the two sides of the chest as it began to gape. There were laces along the back, left undone. The material of the dress felt indulgent, and it pooled like liquid around my feet. Even in the poorly lit chamber, I could tell that the fabric played peekaboo with what was hidden beneath, and I imagined that in brighter light or in the sun, there would be little left to the imagination.

Siobhan had worn this to her wedding? In front of people?

"The gown complements you, my pet." Aric jerked his chin toward the female. "That is all."

My heart seized as the fae gathered up her tote and scurried from the chamber, closing the door behind her. I knew what normally came next.

Holding the front of the dress closed, I stepped back.

Aric's gaze roamed over me as he approached. "With your hair, you could almost be mistaken for her." He walked behind me, lifting the chain. "Hold this."

Swallowing down a wave of trepidation, I shifted the front of the gown to one hand and took hold of the chain with the other. Aric in front or behind me was equally bad.

"She was beautiful." His fingers brushed over my back as he picked up the laces, causing the sensation of a thousand spiders crawling over my skin to surface. "Stunning in her silver gown…and out of it." There was a pause as he began tying the back. "Siobhan was always beautiful, even when she cried. Loosen your grip on the front."

I forced my hold to ease. The material slid across my chest, forming a deep vee that went all the way down the front of my stomach, ending in a point just above my navel.

"She saw no one but Caden, even when he dallied with anything that breathed," Aric went on. "He did not deserve her."

I turned my head to the side, ignoring how my face throbbed. The way he talked about her…" Understanding filled me. "You…you loved her."

The waist of the dress tightened on my bruised ribs, causing me to gasp. He chuckled. "Love? Did I love her?" He scoffed. "If my Queen were to ever hear that, she'd gut me."

Oh, if only I could get so lucky. "Did you?"

Aric was quiet as he tied up the remaining laces. Once secured, I was surprised to discover that the dress truly fit. Definitely would not have before my forced dieting. The soft material didn't chafe the countless cuts, which I supposed was better than the coarse shift.

Aric's hands settled on my hips, and he turned me so I faced him. "I was obsessed with her," he answered, staring down at me. "I feel as if there is very little difference between love and obsession."

I thought there was a whole world of difference.

"I wanted her. So, I took her." His hand skimmed up my sides. "Just like I took you."

A wave of revulsion choked me. "I'm not her."

"You aren't." His fingers drifted up and over my arms to settle on either side of my neck. "And you are."

"I'm—"

"You are his *mortuus*, and he will come for you," Aric said, pressing his thumbs under my jaw. He lowered his head. "He will do anything to save you."

Panic exploded like buckshot. He was going to feed. "He's not coming for me." No one was. At this point, that was beyond evident. "Whatever you think, you're wrong—"

"I'm never wrong."

I tore at his grip, but it was no use. His mouth came down on mine. Shock splashed through me. His lips had never touched mine before, at least not that I remembered, but this—this time was different. This wasn't normal. It was a kiss—a rough, brutal one that was like a kick to the teeth. I tried to twist away, but then his head tilted, his mouth opened, and his chest swelled in an inhale.

My world exploded in fire.

* * * *

I didn't…feel right.

Sitting on the stone slab with my arms curled around my stomach, I shivered as I stared at the floor. I'd come to a little while ago, having no idea how much time had passed, only knowing that it felt like it took longer for me to remember…

Remember who I was and how I was here, why my body was covered in slices and bruises and why one eye didn't open all the way, but I…I didn't feel right. I ached all over like I was coming down with the flu, and my stomach churned like a ceiling fan on low speed.

And I couldn't recall exactly why I was wearing this silvery dress. I had a vague idea that it was for something important.

There was something I needed to remember, but I knew what I needed to do.

Standing, I bent down and found my rock. My eyes crawled over the marks in the stone as I counted them. Forty-seven.

My skin turned clammy as I worked at the next mark, scratching in number forty-eight. Resting my forehead against the cool stone as a sudden knot settled in my stomach, I dropped the shard. I focused on taking slow, even breaths as I tilted my head to the side—

Then I saw *it.*

Memories slammed into me with the force of a freight train. The dagger. I was going to kill Aric with the blade when he returned—

Pushing back from the stone, I rose as my stomach shifted violently. I spun, careening wildly toward one of the walls. My stomach contracted and then heaved as I went down to my knees, my hands digging into the vines. Everything I ate and then nothing at all came up, and the retching was painful against my ribs and stomach.

Only when I thought I was done, did I move. Rocking back onto my ass, I dragged the back of my hand across my mouth. The taste of bile threatened another round of vomiting, but after a couple of moments, the nausea eased off enough that I was able to push myself back up.

The dagger.

I needed to get the weapon.

Staggering over to the slab, I knelt down and grabbed the grip of the blade. The bitter taste in my mouth increased when I saw the dried blood.

My blood.

I needed a plan.

Turning to the closed door, I sucked in a reedy breath as I struggled to pull my fleeting thoughts together. All I knew was that I needed the element of surprise, and that I needed to be fast with a perfect strike. My gaze dropped to the dagger as my pulse pitched. I'd only have one chance. One. And if I failed?

He'd kill me.

I need you alive.

Aric's words were a jolt to the brain. I was important to him. It had to do with this dress and with…Caden. Aric was going to use me for something, but what that was, existed outside my grasp.

I had no idea what Aric thought I was to Caden, or how he imagined he could use me. The King… I doubted he wished me harm, but he didn't care—not enough to come for me, and surely not enough for me to be used as leverage against him.

None of that mattered. Aric could show at any moment, and I needed to be ready. I needed to kill him. And afterward? I dragged the chain over my shoulder as I climbed back onto the stone and lay on my side, hiding the dagger in the folds of the dress. I wasn't sure if I had realized this when I discovered the dagger, but there was no *after* once I killed Aric. I rested my heated cheek on the stone, my eyes glued to the door.

I'd promised myself over and over that I would not die by Aric's hand, that I would not die in this tomb. One of those promises I could not keep.

I would kill Aric, but I would not leave this crypt. This was where I'd die, either by the hands of the other fae when they discovered what I'd done, or by starvation. The only chance I had was if Aric took me outside. But he'd stopped doing that many days ago, bringing in some kind of pot for me to use instead. It was unlikely that he'd release me from the bonds, and it was too much of a risk to wait and see if that would happen.

Part of me hoped it was the former, because lingering any longer than I already had was just too much to bear.

But I would have the satisfaction of Aric's death. I couldn't allow any other thought to creep in.

My grip on the dagger didn't loosen for even a second as I waited for the moment. And then it came. The sound of footsteps could be heard. I remained still even as my heart pounded as if it were going to explode out of my chest.

The door opened, and through the thin slit of my one good eye, I saw only one pair of legs enter the room before the door closed.

Silence filled the space between us, and the seconds ticked by. Every sense of my being became hyper-aware of where Aric stood just inside the chamber. Why wasn't he saying anything? Or coming forward? Paranoia sank its claws into me. Did he know what I had planned? Impossible, unless he realized he'd lost the dagger.

Then he moved.

Aric quietly crossed the chamber, stopping beside me. My heart rate skyrocketed. "Why do you lay so still, my pet?" he asked, touching my cheek with icy fingers.

A sensation surfaced, one of his cold fingers elsewhere.

"Are you unwell?"

Knowing if I didn't answer, he would become suspicious, I said, "I…I don't feel well, no."

That was not a lie.

"Hmm." His fingers caught strands of my hair, lifting them from my cheek. He tucked them behind my ear as a lover would. "Well, that's a shame."

Wait, I told myself.

"Perhaps I took too much from you," he remarked. His fingers drifted back to my face, tracing the line of my jaw. It took everything in me to hold still. "All of this has taken a toll, hasn't it?"

He almost sounded genuine. His tone was right, as were the words, but I knew better. There was nothing kind or gentle about Aric.

I sank into myself, cowering so that I could draw the dagger upward, keeping it hidden.

"I'm not going to hurt you," he said, lowering his head toward mine as he brought his fingers down over the band circling my throat. "At least, not right now."

Wait.

"Later," he mused. "Well, we'll have to see about that, won't we?"

Wait.

"I suppose it will all depend on how you behave." His head tilted to the side, and I felt the brush of his cold lips against my cheek. I opened my eye. "How long it takes you to pull yourself together now, for example."

Wait.

"Admittedly, I have no patience for invalids or those who—"

Jerking upright, I swung out with the dagger and slammed it into the side of his throat. Warm liquid sprayed against my hand and face, telling me that I had struck true.

Aric roared, rearing back, but I followed, scrambling off the slab as he tore his head to the side, free of the dagger. I latched on to him, my knees clamped to his hips as he wheeled backward.

"You fucking bitch!" Blood and spittle hit my face. "You stupid, fucking bitch!"

His fist connected with the side of my head as I swung the dagger again, missing his neck but hitting his cheek. He shouted and went down as I tore the dagger free from his flesh. He hit the floor on his back, and my knees cracked off the floor. I slammed my other hand into his forehead, forcing his neck back and holding it there with everything—

His head snapped up, breaking my hold. His teeth caught my forearm, ripping through flesh. I screamed, my body spasming as he rolled me. He tore his mouth free, spitting in my face as he gripped my neck, digging his fingers into my windpipe. I felt the air charge around us, and I knew he was about to use abilities I couldn't fight.

"I'm going to gut you," he swore, blood racing across his face. "I'm going to fuck you and gut you right—"

I swung again, this time catching him in the other side of the neck, and I didn't let up. Using all my strength, I dragged the blade along his throat from ear to ear.

Aric's eyes went wide as he rocked off me, grabbing his neck. Blue-ish red, shimmery blood poured down his hands and over his white shirt. He tried to stand, making it onto one knee.

"I'm not done with you," I growled, shoving to my feet. The world seemed to tilt and sway, but I ignored it as I limped toward him.

His mouth opened, but all that came out was a gurgle of blood.

"Finally." I gripped the top of his hair, yanking his head back. "You're fucking quiet."

He grabbed for my arm, but I evaded him as I jabbed the dagger in for the final time. The grinding of bones giving way and the fleshy noise of sinew and muscle snapping turned my stomach as I jerked my arm, carving my way through the bastard's neck until I reached the other side.

My gaze met his. The luminous glow of his pale eyes flickered. "I hope you can still hear me." My tongue felt thick, and my voice sounded mushy to my own ears. "I never submitted to you."

The pale blue light flared as his pupils constricted.

I jerked my arm, severing his head from his neck. His body toppled onto itself, and his head fell behind it, thumping off the stone.

I did it.

Aric, the Ancient who'd murdered my mother, was dead.

I did it.

Chest rising and falling heavily, I took a step back from his body. Violet-hued blood ran down my arms and over the stone as I stumbled back. Eyes wide, I watched it fill the crevices between the stones, branching off as the viscous liquid crept across the floor.

I looked down at myself. The front of the stunning gown was splattered with blood.

The dress was so ruined.

My lips parted, and I laughed as the dagger slipped from my blood-soaked grip. I laughed as my legs buckled and I folded like a paper sack.

And I laughed as the blood flowed.

Chapter 13

When a normal, run-of-the-mill fae is stabbed with iron, they're sent back to the Otherworld instead of killed. Their bodies are sort of sucked into themselves and…poof, they're gone. No mess. No cleanup. Same happens when you kill them. They just evaporate almost immediately.

The same cannot be said about Ancients.

When you kill them, their bodies remain, at least for a little while. They decompose like mortals, but it's rapid in comparison.

I sat on the stone floor, watching Aric's skin darken and start to flake, his stomach sinking in instead of bloating, and his body shrinking inside its clothes. That took minutes. The rest took hours. But on day forty-nine, the following day, he was nothing more than an oily, clumpy stain on the floor, and the seeping wound on my arm left behind by his bite had finally stopped bleeding. I had a feeling that it needed stitches, and would probably get massively, grossly infected without them and some antibiotics.

Unless there was a doctor hidden among the vines, there was nothing I could do about that.

There was nothing I could do about any of the pains or the weird, random waves of nausea that ended in another round of vomiting either.

But I waited.

My knuckles ached from how tightly I held onto the dagger, knowing that there was no way I could take two or three fae at once, even if they weren't Ancients. But I refused to go out without a fight.

No one came.

Not the female fae who bathed me, or the male ones who carried the tub in and out of the room. There were at least three of them that had to be aware of where I was held, who I assumed would come looking for Aric at some point, especially since he appeared to be their leader.

Eventually, my attention shifted from the stain to the door. I imagined it wasn't locked. Freedom was just a few feet from my reach, and I tried, stretching as far as I could. I did this for hours, and then I used the dagger, prying at the bolt in the floor and then the clasp that connected the chain to the band around my throat until I felt the blade about to break, and then I stopped. I couldn't risk losing my only weapon if other fae did finally show.

But no one did.

Hours turned into another day, and that day slowly churned into more. I'd lost my grip on the dagger, letting it rest in my lap.

Hunger set in, overshadowing the aches and the nausea, and all I could think about were burgers and steaks, leafy salads, and chocolate cakes. I even fantasized about all-you-can-eat buffets, and then I stopped thinking about food. Either my body and mind had become used to the hunger, or I just no longer felt it. I no longer really felt the coldness or the throbbing either.

Bone-deep tiredness set in, a lethargy that wrapped around me like a heavy blanket, weighing down my limbs. I stopped tracking days after forty-eight, unable to rally the strength to pick up the shard of rock or use the dagger to scratch the mark into the stone. I didn't know if it was the hunger or all the feedings or the wounds finally catching up to me, but I slept where I sat, propped against the slab. And then I couldn't sit up any longer.

I wasn't sure when it had happened, but I only became aware of lying on my side when I opened my eyes again. The dagger had slipped from my lap, resting a few inches from me on the floor.

I needed to get it, keep it close, but I simply could not do it. And as I drifted off again, I told myself that it would be okay if I didn't wake up. I'd killed Aric. I'd completed what I'd set out to do two years ago. I had honored my mother's death. Dying in the stale, damp chamber didn't matter. Not anymore.

But then I lost more than my grip on the dagger. I lost my grip on…everything.

I did wake up again. Or maybe I dreamed. Or I was awake and hallucinating. I wasn't sure, but I saw people. My mother pacing in front of me, dressed in her pink housecoat flapping like wings behind her. She was speaking, but I couldn't hear her, and when I called out to her, there was no response. And then she was gone. Later, it was a girl with curly, fiery red hair, and a man with wavy brown hair. I knew them. I thought I did, but their names were lost to me as the chamber faded and was replaced by a restaurant lit by warm, twinkling, white lights.

The group was talking, but I wasn't listening. I was thinking about…Christmas mornings and hot cocoa and the good moments with my mother, times where she remembered where she was and—

Fingers snapped, drawing my attention.

"*Sorry*." My lips moved, my voice hoarse. "*I spaced out. Were you saying something?*"

"*I was saying that I was about to strip naked and run outside*," the girl said.

The male smiled as he stared at the girl. "*I am so down for that*."

"Of course, you are." She grinned, pointing to a menu. "*Did you want dessert, Bri?*"

Bri.

Only she called me Bri.

Bri stood for…Brighton. That was my name, and she was…

I blinked, and they were gone. The restaurant was gone, replaced by the round, vine-covered walls and flickering torches. Then I faded out, and there was nothing until I heard someone again.

"*I'm sorry*."

My eyes fluttered open, and he was standing there, dressed in a dark shirt that was like a second layer of skin, clinging to his chest and tapered waist. His blond hair brushed the width of his broad shoulders as he bowed his head.

He wouldn't look at me.

"*You're sorry?*" I heard myself say, and my chest… God, it hurt. It broke. "*Which part are you sorry about? What happened between us? Or the fact that you failed to mention you're engaged?*"

A muscle tensed along his jaw. "*All of it*."

What broke then cracked wide open, shattering. "*God*," I whispered.

"*You don't understand*." He looked over at me. "*You cannot possibly understand—*"

"*Because I'm not a fae?*"

His eyes met mine, and an eternity stretched out between us as a wild array of emotion flickered across his face. And then it all went away, as if he shut down whatever it was he felt. "*Yes, because you are not like me. I am a King. I must have a Queen*."

The word was a stab to the heart. My cheeks dampened, and the world around me seemed to shift again. He wasn't in a hallway anymore but standing in a brightly lit room that smelled like crisp apples. And there were others. The girl with the red hair and people with no faces, no names.

"Listen to Ivy," he urged. *"You cannot interact with either of them. The fact that they already know you're involved is bad enough."*

"I can handle myself," I said, repeating what felt like a script—one I didn't want to read. *"Pretty sure I've proven that."*

"All you've proven is that you're incredibly lucky," he fired back. "*You're not like them.*" He gestured at the others. *"You're not a warrior with years of experience under your belt."*

"I'm a member of the Order. I'm trained and—"

"You are a member, but this is not your job," the girl said.

"If hunting and killing evil fae isn't my job, then what is?"

Silence from them, from the others, and in the silence, I heard Aric say, "*You were born into the Order, but you're not a true member.*"

Confusion swept through me as the room and everyone in it seemed to flicker in and out. Aric was dead. I'd killed him. He couldn't be here—

Caden faded out and then back in again. *"You're a distraction. A weakness that I will not allow to be exploited...."*

"I'm not weak." The words scraped against my throat. "I killed Aric. I…killed him."

The space in front of me was empty.

He was gone.

And then I was gone.

* * * *

I wasn't sure what stirred me, tugging me out of the emptiness, but I could feel the coldness of the tomb when I'd felt nothing before. A distant part of me acknowledged that I didn't feel as cold as I should, and that perhaps that was concerning, but I was too tired to care, and too grateful that I didn't hurt. That I felt…okay, just tired. So very tired. I started to slip away again when I heard it.

Footsteps?

No. It was too loud, too many thumps coming too fast. Banging? Yes, it sounded like banging. Was it the other fae finally checking on Aric? The Ancient would be pissed to realize it had taken so long. It was sort of insulting. A small grin cracked my dry lips. There was a burst of pain as if the flesh were too thin or raw, but it was okay.

I needed to open my eyes, but my lids were too heavy. I just wanted to sleep. That was all I wanted.

Voices.

That's what I heard next, or at least *thought* I heard. I wasn't sure. Shouts. Names that teased at the disjointed memories. Pounding footsteps followed—

The world seemed to explode. Wood cracked and splintered, and air—fresh, rose-scented air—flowed into the chamber.

"Brighton?"

The voice. *His* voice. I recognized it. The deep, melodious baritone that had whispered against my skin. But it sounded different now, full of relief and horror, fury tinged with desperation.

A curse was uttered, and then warmth flowed over me like sunlight breaking through the clouds. The air stirred.

"Brighton?" He was closer, and I tried to open my eyes, but it was of no use. A moment passed, and then I felt warmth against my cheek. Fingertips. Warm hands smoothing back the matted strands of hair—"Dear God."

The two words sounded as if they took the speaker to their knees. My eyelids fluttered. Finally, I was able to open both of them halfway. The blurry image of a man dressed in black formed.

He was on his knees.

I knew him. I knew I did, but I couldn't remember his name.

Blond hair shielded his face. He wasn't looking at me, but instead reaching for the strap of the dress, pulling it back and then fisting a handful of the skirt, tugging it up and over one leg. I didn't want him to do that. I knew I didn't want him to see what had been done to me. That much I knew.

"Fucking Christ," he snarled. "Fucking Christ. I'm going to fucking kill him."

I flinched.

His head whipped in my direction, and I jerked away from the rage that filled every pore and plane, making his strikingly beautiful face more animalistic than human. The pure violence radiating off him was terrifying.

He seemed to rein it in, the anger and the power, wrapping it around himself like a cloak. Dropping the dress, he reached for me, and every muscle in my body locked up. I closed my eyes, waiting for the pain that was sure to follow.

"Brighton," he spoke, his voice softer. "It's okay." The warm touch returned to my cheek, brushing my hair back. He seemed to freeze, and then he spoke again, the words hoarse. "It's going to be okay now. I'm going to get you out of here. I'm going to…"

He trailed off as a chain rattled. A wave of heat entered the room, stirring the material of my dress.

"It's okay. It's okay," he repeated. His hand moved—

"Don't," I croaked, recoiling out of instinct, managing to draw back a few inches.

There was a tense silence and then, "I'm not going to hurt you. I could never hurt you." His touch returned, slow and measured. He slid his hand along thc side of my head, his palm becoming a barrier between me and the floor. "Open your eyes for me, Brighton. Please. Open your eyes, baby. See me and know I'm not going to hurt you. Open your eyes for me, sunshine."

I saw you smile once, and it was like the sun finally rising.

He'd said that to me before. When I asked why he called me sunshine, he'd said that to me. He'd said that, and he…he'd told me that my hair was like sun rays.

Caden.

The King.

I knew him.

He wouldn't hurt me, but…but it felt like he had. Deeply, but differently.

Drawing in a shallow breath, I cracked open my eyes and found him in the darkness and he… He couldn't be real. He couldn't really be here.

"There you are." He smiled, but it seemed off. Like I knew what his real smiles were like even if they were rare. This one looked sad. "Keep your eyes open for me, okay? I'm going to get you out of here, but I need you to keep your eyes open so I know you're still here, and so you know that this is me."

My lips parted to speak again, but my tongue was heavy and useless. Some innate part of me told me that I needed to tell him about Aric, that he needed to know.

"I…I did it," I said, wincing as the words scratched at my throat.

"Did what?" His thumb moved along my temple.

"I killed him… I killed Aric."

Caden's eyes widened slightly, and then he looked to his left, over his shoulder, to the stain on the floor. He refocused on me, and a long moment passed as what looked like awed pride filled his gaze. It quickly gave way to despair. "Good."

Uncertainty filled me. I swallowed again.

"You don't need to speak right now." His eyes searched mine. "I'm going to break this chain, and then we'll get you out of here and go home."

Home?

"Caden?" A familiar male voice filled the chamber, hesitant.

"She's here," he spoke, and his gaze remained fastened to mine.

"Is she…?" The new voice was soft. Female. Red hair came to mind.

Caden's jaw hardened. "She's here," he repeated. "She's chained." There was a curse from somewhere in the chamber, and I shivered. "Keep it cool," he said over his shoulder. "Keep it quiet—don't. Stay back. Just for right now."

"But—" the female protested.

"Ren, go find a blanket or a jacket. Something warm and soft," he cut the woman off. "We need to get her warmed up. She's too cold. And call Tanner. Tell them they're going to need to get the infirmary ready."

This Ren must've listened because Caden refocused on me. "I'm going to break the cuff around your neck, okay? I'm not going to hurt you, but this may startle you, and I'm going to need help, so please be still. No one is going to hurt you."

I took another breath, but it felt like it went nowhere.

His chest rose. "Ivy, I need you to come over here and hold her head, but walk over slowly."

Ivy. Ivy. Ivvvvvy. The name. I knew it, but I couldn't remember her. I knew I should. My heart rate kicked up as uncertainty sprang to life. Why couldn't I remember?

"It's all right," Caden soothed. "I promise you. You're safe now."

Light footsteps approached, and then I heard a sharp inhale. "*God.*"

Caden's head snapped in the redhead's direction, and whatever she saw quieted her. She moved out of my line of sight, and I tensed.

"She's just going to hold your head. That's all," Caden assured me. "And then I'll get this cuff off you, and we'll be out of here."

"I'm going to touch you," Ivy said from somewhere behind me. Seconds later, I felt her hands on either side of my head. "I've got her."

"Thank you," Caden replied, and I had the distinct impression that wasn't something he said often. "Just a couple of more seconds, sunshine, and that's all."

He folded his hands around the metal band, and there was a strange flaring of heat as his chin dipped. The muscles under his shirt along his shoulders and arms flexed. Slight pressure encircled my throat, setting off warning bells. I tried to pull away, but Ivy held me in place. My stomach twisted with panic—

Metal groaned and gave way, and when I swallowed, there was no longer anything pressing against my throat.

"There," Caden murmured, placing the snapped cuff aside. He tipped forward. "I got her."

"Do you?"

His gaze lifted from mine to the woman behind me. "I do."

"You better," she said.

I had no idea what their exchange meant, but she said nothing when he slipped an arm under my shoulders and then under my legs. Only then did she let go. He pulled me against him, and the contact jarred me. I gasped as a wave of sensation rippled through me.

"Sorry," he said gruffly, rising fluidly. He turned, and my gaze swiveled around, landing on the patch of floor that was dark and stained.

Caden was speaking, but I wasn't tracking what he said. I wasn't even sure if he was talking to me or not. I shifted my gaze to him as he started toward the door. I'd been here before. Or it felt that way, like it had happened in a dream. A knot formed in my throat as we neared the opening. I locked up, waiting for the catch, the obstacle that blocked me from leaving, the tug on my neck. The reveal that none of this was real, just another elaborate ruse produced by my mind.

Caden crossed the threshold, still speaking in a low, soft voice as we entered heavy darkness. He climbed the stairs, and then…then I saw the silvery glow of moonlight.

Moonlight.

I drew in a broken breath, and the air was fresh and clean. Was this…? Tears clouded my eyes, blurring the rays of moonlight that filtered through the trees.

I swallowed again. "Are you…are you really here?"

"Yes." Caden stopped, looking down at me. "I'm here. I'm really here, sunshine."

Chapter 14

Things were hazy from the moment Caden carried me into a vehicle and wrapped a blanket around me. Between the warmth of the throw and the heat his body was throwing off, I couldn't do what he kept asking of me and keep my eyes open.

Bits and pieces of the conversation floated around me as he held me in his lap, keeping me steady as the wheels bumped along. He held me gently, keeping an arm around my shoulders and my cheek pressed to his chest. Every so often, I felt the soft-as-air brush of his touch on the side of my head or down the bones of a finger. Like I…like I meant something to him, like I was precious and cared for. But there was something that lingered at the fringes of my consciousness that wanted me to pull away, to put distance between us because it was needed. I couldn't remember why, and I was too tired to figure it out.

Ren was speaking from the driver's seat when I came to. His name was familiar, as was his face. I knew him and the redheaded woman next to him, and I knew they were together. Their names and faces were like the framework of a house, but the walls and the floors and everything in-between hadn't been installed.

"How bad?" Ren asked.

The arm around my shoulder tightened and then relaxed. "Bad."

"Did she say she killed him?" Ivy asked. "I heard that, right?"

"You did," Caden answered as a weird feeling started in my toes. It wasn't exactly unpleasant, more like a low burning that reminded me of a sunburn.

"Damn," muttered Ren. "Well, now we know why Dumb and Dumber hadn't seen him."

Dumb and Dumber? Wasn't that…wasn't that an old movie? The burning crept up my calves.

"They said they hadn't seen him in four days," she said. "Could she have been down there alone?"

"She's been gone for almost two months," Ren said, and a flicker of surprise scuttled through me. Had it really been that long? I'd stopped counting after day forty-eight. How many days had I missed in the beginning? "I can't believe we found her after all of this time."

"She had to think…" Ivy trailed off, and then she spoke again. "Did you see her? Her skin?"

"I saw." Caden's voice hardened.

"That sick bastard—" She cut herself off. "I'm glad she killed him. I hope she made it hurt in the worst ways."

"I'm not glad she did," Caden stated.

The uncertainty returned. Why wouldn't he be glad? They were enemies, and I knew that Aric had done things to Caden—horrible things to people the King cared about. He was going to use Caden to return… I lost track of the thoughts, my mind seeming to power down like a shut-off button had been pressed.

Caden didn't reply to that, and then I must've faded out for a few moments because when I came to, the burning sensation had reached my shoulders, and I didn't like it. I squirmed as it reached my throat.

"Hey," Caden's voice was soft in the darkness. "It's okay. We're almost there."

It wasn't okay. The heat swept over my head and then my skin turned *prickly* as if a million pins and needles began dancing over my flesh. "It hurts," I told him, opening my eyes. "My…skin."

Caden shifted me slightly, and his face came into fuzzy view. "It's your temperature rising."

I tried to untangle my arms in an attempt to push the blanket off.

"Don't." His arm curled, keeping the throw around me as he placed his palm on my forehead. I flinched. "You need to keep the blanket on."

"It's hot," I whispered, stretching out my leg. Pain flared all along my skin and sank deep into the muscles. I gasped. "It hurts."

He made a sound in the back of his throat. "I know. I'm sorry, baby. I am, but you have to keep the blanket on. You're still not warm enough."

I didn't care. Fire ants were chewing their way through my flesh. I twisted, moaning as my ribs protested. The numbness had vanished, and I yearned for the return. "Why…why does it hurt now? It…stopped hurting. It had finally stopped."

"I'm sorry," he whispered. "Your body is warming up, and blood is moving like it should. It's going to hurt, and then it'll be better."

It wasn't going to be better. There was no way it could be when every long-forgotten cut began to sting, and every bruise started to throb incessantly. I couldn't hold still, even as the King tried to keep me immobile. I became a twisting mess of aching, moaning flesh. Everything hurt, inside and out. Each breath was like breathing fire. Tears crowded my eyes.

"Not much longer," Caden murmured over the top of my head. He said that more than once. Repeating it over and over. And then it became too much.

"Can't you do something?" Ivy demanded, her voice pitched with worry. "Glamour her?"

"I can't do that to her. Not now. Not after—"

"Please," I begged, each breath coming in short, painful pants. "Please do something."

"I know he's done it to you multiple times. I can tell. I hate this. It's killing me."

"It sounds like it's actually killing her," Ren snapped. "So, why don't you get over yourself and help her out?"

"You don't understand," Caden growled. "She's on the brink of not coming back. I can see it in her eyes. She didn't recognize either of you. She didn't know me at first. Why do you think that's the case?"

"Please," I whispered. "Make it stop. Please."

"I can't." His voice gentled as his hand curled around the back of my head. "One more feeding. One more glamouring, and that could be it. I will not do that to you."

"I'll drive faster," Ren muttered.

"Please." My voice cracked. "Stop it."

"I'm sorry," Caden said as I shuddered. "I'm sorry this happened to you. I'm sorry."

My skin felt like it blistered and then burst. My muscles felt stretched until they snapped. Every bone felt brittle and sharp-edged. There was no escaping this—

Sudden clarity flowed through me, pushing away the fog, and I remembered all that had been done. All of it. And I couldn't deal with it.

I kicked my head back as a hoarse scream tore from my throat. Voices poured from the front of the car. Agony contorted my body, further inflaming the bruises and raw skin. My voice gave out, and finally, it was too much. I slipped into blissful nothingness, and the last thing I heard was Caden shouting my name.

* * * *

A stranger stared down at me, a female wearing a pale blue shirt. Others were moving around, tugging at the straps of the dress I wore as the fae's mouth moved, but I couldn't hear her over the rushing sound in my ears.

"Stop," I rasped, swatting at the hands. "*Stop.*"

"I'm a healer. I work for the King." She caught my hand, carefully lowering it to the table. "We need to get this dress off and assess your injuries."

Her words made sense but also didn't. The material slipped down my shoulders—

The female jerked back, her eyes going wide. There were several gasps, and then the healer snapped into action, firing off orders at a rapid pace. "Get the IV in and use the morphine. Start her with four milligrams and then get some fluids in her. Get Ringer solution on board. Check to see what kind of antibiotics we have, and get one of the mortals ready to make a possible run."

It happened so fast. The dress was removed, replaced by a warm, soft blanket. I felt the needle go into the vein in the top of my hand, but it was nothing compared to everything else.

"You're going to feel a rush of warmth in a few moments. Maybe taste something weird in the back of your throat, but don't worry. It's just some medicine to take the pain away," the woman said. "We're going to look at these injuries, okay?"

I didn't know who she was—who these people were. What had happened to Caden? Heart thumping, I started to sit up, and then a buzzing wave swept through me, somehow beating back the fire, cooling it down by degrees with each passing moment. Suddenly, I wasn't struggling. I wasn't….

People moved around me, and the woman was talking again, but I wasn't following. My head lolled to the side, and my gaze connected with eyes the color of liquid amber.

Caden stood off to the side, his normally golden skin paler than I'd ever seen. All others gave him a wide berth, and he did not move, but I thought his lips did.

I thought he mouthed, *I'm here.*

* * * *

There were two things I became aware of.

The steady sound of beeping was the first thing I heard when I, well, stopped floating around out there in the fuzzy ether. The second thing was that I didn't hurt all that much, and that was the most important part. I felt…a little sore and achy, but that was such a marked improvement that I wanted to cry.

I didn't.

Instead, I tried to open my eyes. This time, it didn't take an act of Congress to do so. Still took a while because my lids felt crusty and swollen, but I did it, and the smooth, white ceiling I stared at wasn't the dark interior of a car or the stone ceiling of the chamber.

Another massive improvement.

I was alive, and I wasn't in the tomb, chained to a stone slab, waiting to die.

God.

I swallowed, wincing at what felt like razor blades in my throat. *I'm alive*. I kept repeating that in my head because it didn't seem real or even possible, but I was lying on a comfortable mattress, and the room was filled with soft, filtered sunlight. Memories of how I had gotten here were like sifting through a photo album of faded, distorted pictures. But I remembered Caden and Ivy and Ren, and the pain as my skin had warmed up…. Yeah, I wasn't going to forget that pain anytime soon.

I also remembered the fae healer. Before I started floating away on a cloud of nothing matters, I had heard her talking to others—to *him*. Concern about infection and scarring, the latter almost making me laugh because I was already scarred. What was a handful—or a couple of hundred—more in the grand scheme of things? Blood had been taken. Words like *dehydration* and *malnutrition* were thrown around, as was concern about other things—things I didn't really want to think about.

Looking back, I thought that it was quite inappropriate that they had allowed him in the room. Then again, he was their King, and they probably allowed him to do just about anything.

My arms felt heavy, glossy with some kind of ointment, and there was a bandage covering the bite mark on my left arm. Oddly, I felt clean as if someone had bathed me, but based on the itchiness of my scalp, I knew my hair hadn't been washed.

God, I would kill for a shower, one where my skin wasn't being scrubbed raw, and someone—

Closing my eyes, I cut off that train of thought as I sucked in a sharp breath. No good could come from thinking about that right now, not when there were so many things that would surely haunt me.

The shuffling sound of someone shifting in a chair drew me from my thoughts. I turned my head to the left, my breath catching as the left side of my cheek throbbed.

Ouch.

All right, pain meds only worked to a point. Good to know.

Opening my eyes, a shock rippled through me. Caden was stretched out in a chair next to the bed, his bare feet resting on the footboard, crossed at the ankles. His eyes were closed, his cheek pressed against his fist, his hair hiding half of his face. He was dressed as I recalled. Black shirt and dark denim jeans. He appeared to be sleeping.

How long had he been in here?

How long had I been out?

Better yet, why was he even here at all?

I didn't know the answers to those questions, and I didn't want to wake him. Instead, I lay there and I… I stared at him, soaking in the sight.

Caden was…he was as beautiful as I remembered, a visage of otherworldly perfection that bordered on being unreal. I wished for the hundredth time that he wasn't so nice to look at. Good thing his royal jerkiness attitude dampened some of that attraction.

Yeah, right. Who was I kidding?

I still loved him. I was still *in love* with him, and even though he was promised to someone else—could already *be* with someone else—and had failed to mention that on top of all of the other stuff, my feelings for him were still there.

I loved him.

I just didn't like him.

Strange how one could feel those two conflicting emotions, but love was odd like that.

The moment those thoughts finished, awe flickered through me. I was surprised that after everything I'd gone through, I could still…I could still think about *normal* things—stuff that was important but also wasn't compared to being tortured and starved. That I could think about the night we'd spent together, the things he'd done to me, and what I'd done to him, and feel my insides warm. That felt beautifully *normal* because I…

I honestly never expected to see him again. I hadn't expected to see sunlight either or breathe in fresh air. In the end, I hadn't thought I'd survive.

That was a lot to process.

As I lay there, watching the steady rise and fall of Caden's chest, I realized that it was also a lot to process the fact that there were huge gaps in time where I couldn't remember what had happened while Aric held me, even though I could still feel the…the fear and the hours of nothing but pain. I remembered what he did to me with the dagger I'd killed him with, and I recalled his fists, but a lot was missing that still carried feelings of panic and humiliation.

I sighed, glancing around the room. I wasn't in the infirmary but one of the spacious hotel rooms. I had no idea how I had gotten up here.

Caden stirred, his thick lashes lifting. His gaze found mine. Slowly, he lowered his hand and straightened. He didn't speak, not for several long moments, and then he said, "How long have you been awake?"

"Not—" I cleared my throat, working on getting the painful hoarseness out. "Not very…long."

"So, in other words, you haven't been watching me sleep for that long?"

"I wasn't watching." My cheeks heated at the blatant lie.

"Uh-huh." A small grin played at his lips as he pulled his feet off the foot of the bed and placed them on the floor, leaning forward. "How do you feel?"

I thought about the way he'd held me in the car, trying to calm me as I screamed. "A lot better."

"You look better."

"I bet I look a mess."

"No," he said softly. "You look beautiful."

I rolled my eyes—well, one eye. "I don't need…a mirror to know that's not remotely true."

"You don't need a mirror at all."

Having no idea how to respond to that, though liking the tiny flutter in my chest, I decided it was time to change the subject. "How long have I been out of it?"

"Today is Thursday. We brought you in Monday night. So, about two days," he said. "You've woken up a couple of times."

Two days? God. "I don't remember that—the waking up."

"The healer has kept you on some pretty good pain medication. You were a little…out of it, but able to walk to the bathroom."

Well, that explained why it didn't feel like my bladder was about to burst. Wait. "Did you help me to the…bathroom?"

Seriously, if he confirmed it, God hating me would be official.

"No." He shook his head. "Ivy and Faye helped. They also changed the bandages on your arm and your legs."

"My legs?" The corners of my lips turned down, tugging at the flesh of my lower lip in a way that told me it was still healing.

"There were some cuts there that were deeper but did not require stitches." He tucked a strand of hair back from his face.

"Oh." I shifted my gaze to my hands, finally looking at them. Both bore signs of fading bruises. I blinked slowly. "You…you've seen what it…what it all looks like?"

Caden seemed to know what I was asking because he tipped forward even farther. "I've seen most of it, Brighton. I've seen enough."

I closed my eyes. A prickly heat crept over me, a flush of shame that I knew I should have no ownership of. What I looked like now shouldn't matter. For the most part, it didn't because I was alive, and *that* mattered. But where my body had been a faint sketch of what had happened to me before, I knew without even seeing it that it was now a roadmap of all the horrors. I'd already known that some of what I'd seen would scar, and I guessed I just hadn't been all that concerned about it while in the tomb, given that I had more important things to worry about.

I still did.

But knowing that Caden had seen what was left of me still cut as deep as that edge of the dagger.

"It'll get better." His voice was quiet, so much so that I had to look at him. "You will heal. All of this will fade. Remember that."

"Yeah," I whispered.

His gaze searched mine. "Do you think you can drink something? I think food is off the table until the healer sees you."

I nodded, thinking that water would be lovely. Caden rose from the chair, walking into the adjoining living area. He returned quickly, a small glass in hand. I started to sit up but stopped when pain flared along my ribs. I took a deeper breath as I reached down.

"Your ribs are bandaged. Some of them were broken." He set the drink aside. "Let me help you."

Tension poured into me as Caden neared. *It's okay. It's okay.* I kept repeating that as I stared at his chest while he carefully slid an arm under my shoulders, lifting me as he shoved extra pillows behind me. *It's okay. It's okay.*

"This okay?" he asked.

I nodded.

Caden slipped away, picking up the glass. I looked up as he turned to me, offering the drink. I reached for it, and without warning, terror exploded inside my chest. The logical, functioning part of my brain knew that the reaction was unnecessary, but it was a reflex I could no longer control. I jerked back my hand, closing it in a fist against my chest.

"Are you okay?" Concern filled his tone. "Is it your ribs?"

I opened my mouth but couldn't find the words. A logical part of my brain knew that Caden wasn't Aric. He wasn't going to hurt me, but I…

Tremors coursed through me as I stared at the glass, incredibly thirsty, but my throat choked with dread.

"What's wrong? Tell me, Brighton. I can go find the healer." Out of the corner of my eye, I saw him reach for me.

"Don't!" I jerked sideways, flinching. Understanding dawned, quickly followed by a pained expression that settled into his striking features. I averted my gaze, feeling the swampy heat of embarrassment. "I'm okay. I just… I need a minute."

Caden fell silent, and I took a minute to calm my racing heart. Then I took more than a minute to reassure myself that no blow was coming.

It's okay.

Drawing in a deep breath, I held onto it as I lifted my hand and reached for the water. I flinched as my fingers brushed the cool glass and when nothing happened, I curled my fingers around it. Caden immediately pulled back, returning to his chair.

I couldn't look at him as I stared down at the drink, finally exhaling. Tears pricked the backs of my eyes as I felt heat invade my neck. Lifting the glass, I caught a slight fruity scent. "What…what is in it?"

"A type of elderberry found in the Otherworld," he answered, his voice rough like sandpaper. "It helps with inflammation and is good for an upset stomach. Many of my kind claim it can help with anxiety, too. It's perfectly safe for humans."

Anxiety?

I was going to need some man-made pharmaceuticals for that. "Upset stomach?" I took a tiny sip and almost moaned at the blissful coolness and the light taste of berry that eased the scratchiness of my throat.

"You were sick one of the times you woke up. You were already in the bathroom, and Ivy was with you."

"Oh," I murmured, taking a longer drink. When I swallowed again, it was easier. "Sorry, um, about how I freaked out. I'm just… I don't know."

"Don't apologize. There's absolutely nothing you need to apologize for."

Peeking over at him, I found him watching me. I took another drink, wishing it would remove the flush staining my skin. When I was finished, I wanted more but figured I should probably see how my stomach handled it.

"How did you all find me?" I kept the glass between my hands because it felt normal to do so.

"I'd been looking for you. All of us were."

Surprise rose, and then so did guilt.

"You didn't think we were looking for you? I can't blame you for that. Not after what happened before…before you disappeared, and with how long Aric had you. But we were. Every day, we were. Every night. I knew in my bones that he had you, but we couldn't find him or Neal." Caden's voice hardened. "We captured and questioned every Winter fae we came across. Either they knew nothing, or they refused to talk. We never gave up. I never gave up hope that we'd find you, but…"

"But you didn't expect to find me alive," I finished for him.

Caden tilted his head away from me, his lips pressed into a firm line. "The more time that passed, the more I knew the chances were unlikely or that if you were still alive…" He tipped his head back, his throat working on a swallow. "I feel I need to be honest. After a certain point, I was no longer sure what would be worse. That you were alive and with him, or that you were gone."

My grip tightened on the glass.

"You being…you being gone would be far worse. It would be like losing the sun."

Chapter 15

I opened my mouth, but I had no words. That was incredibly—well, it was just an incredible thing to say.

"I haven't thought of anything else but finding you. I don't think any of us has," Caden continued, facing me once more. "But I know that no matter what we felt or feared, it's nothing compared to what you've gone through."

Yet again, I had no idea how to respond to any of that or what to think. So I pretty much ignored it. "And the Order? Miles? Did they…look for me?"

"They did in the beginning."

I knew what was left unsaid. "But they stopped? Assumed I was dead and cut their losses."

"I'm sorry."

"Don't be." I smiled, and it felt weird and wrong. Probably because I hadn't done so in…well, a long time. "It's thc way it is, and I was not an essential member of the Order."

Caden's gaze flew to mine. "That was their mistake. And ours."

I looked away as conversations from the past resurfaced. Caden. Ivy. Ren. Both of whom I now remembered. All of them telling me that I needed to stay out of it.

"Aric sent a message. He wanted a meeting with me, said he had something that I was looking for. I knew immediately that it was you. He was right." Caden exhaled heavily, and something stirred on the fringes of my memory. "I had no idea if you were going to be alive or not, but I went. He never showed. Two of his Knights did. Both claimed that they assumed Aric would meet them there."

Dumb and Dumber, I thought. The ones who'd carried the copper tub.

"One of them didn't crack. The other did, told us where you were being held. Unfortunately, it took a while to get that information from them."

I had a feeling I should know this. "How long did it take?"

"Four days," Caden said.

Flashes of those days danced in front of me. The hunger. The exhaustion. The hallucinations. "Are they dead? The two Knights?"

"Yes."

"Good," I murmured.

"How did you kill him?" Caden asked after a moment.

"He left a…dagger behind. I can't remember why he forgot it." I frowned. "I think he was surprised by something and left it, but I remembered when I…. When I woke up." I glanced over at him. "I remembered it, and I knew to wait until it was only him. Those two Knights carried the tub into the chamber so I could bathe. There was also a female fae."

Caden's head tilted slightly. "He made you bathe in that chamber?"

Returning to staring at the glass, I nodded. "Yeah. Anyway, I used the dagger the first time he was alone. I cut off his head with it." I thought of the dress. He'd called it a gift. "I think he was coming down to take me…" Holy crap, something occurred to me, and my chin jerked up. "I think he was coming down to take me to you. That's why he put me in that dress."

Caden's jaw tightened.

"He was going to release me and take me out of the chamber. I could've killed him then, and I would've had a chance to escape." My eyes widened. "Then I…I wouldn't have been in there."

"You had no idea what he was planning. You did what you thought was best at the time," Caden told me. "You did nothing wrong."

I'm not glad she did.

The King had said that in response to Ivy saying that she was glad I'd killed Aric. "You said you weren't happy that I killed him."

"You heard that?" When I nodded, a faint smile appeared and then disappeared. "Besides the fact that I wanted the absolute pleasure of tearing him apart myself, I rather you had never been in the position to do that. That's why I am not glad that you did."

"Oh," I repeated for the umpteenth time. "Well, he suffered. A lot." A real smile graced my lips then, the kind that probably would concern therapists across the nation. "Cutting off someone's head isn't exactly easy."

One corner of his lips curved up. "But you did it."

"I did. I had to." The smile faded from my lips, and the next breath I took felt harsh. "It's the only thing I *had* to do. He is—he was…" Trailing off, I shook my head. "He was evil."

"I know he was."

The way he said that tugged a memory loose, an image of Aric's taunting smile and something about… Whatever was there slipped outside my reach. Exhaling loudly, I looked over at Caden.

He had sat back, his hands resting on the arms of the chair. He made the simple seat look like a throne. "What did he do to you?"

The question was a loaded one—one I wasn't sure I could even answer. My brow knotted.

"You don't have to answer that. I'm sorry. I shouldn't have—"

"He did whatever he could," I whispered, the glass trembling as more memories wiggled free. "When I didn't cave or when I…I didn't scream, he made sure I did. He took his time. The cuts…he did it for hours. I don't know. He…wanted to make sure I knew he was…in control—when I slept, when I was awake, when I…when I ate or drank."

"He did something with the food and drink?" Caden asked.

Looking over at him, I saw that his hands had curled around the arms of the chair. "He didn't…" I twisted, ignoring the dull flare of pain along my ribs as I placed the glass on the nightstand. "He didn't make eating easy. I'd be…"

"What?" His voice had softened. His knuckles had started to bleach white.

"I never knew how you could desire something so much and dread it at the same time." Without realizing what I was doing until I did it, I lifted my fingers to my lip, feeling the swollen skin there for the first time. "I'd be so hungry because I didn't get a lot of…food, but I…I *hated* eating."

"Brighton." His voice was still so soft, but it had a rough quality to it that I didn't want to hear.

I worked my neck to the side, lowering my hand to my lap. "He just did a lot.

"Did he…?" Caden's shoulders tensed as if he were bracing himself. "The healer said you had bruising in areas that concerned her. That there may have been other assaults that happened. Ones that she could not see."

I knew what he was asking, and my breath hitched in my throat.

Our gazes connected for the briefest of seconds, and I couldn't hold his stare. Instead, I found myself inspecting the bandage on my arm. "I don't… I don't think so," I said, picking at the edge. "I mean, I don't remember him doing something like that. Not even when I bathed or—"

Cold lips against mine. Frigid hands. An image flashed in my mind of Aric kneeling in front of me while I was in the tub. His hand under the water, his icy fingers—

Squeezing my eyes shut, I held myself perfectly still. I remembered that. I'd been glamoured, and he'd touched me as he talked, as he told me—

"You don't have to think about it," Caden said, drawing me from the disjointed images. "You don't have to remember right now."

"What if I remember later?" I whispered.

"Then we'll deal with it then."

We? My gaze darted to him. His expression was stark and…*violent.* A shiver danced over my skin. He'd let go of the chair and had scooted forward on the seat. The arms of the chair looked strange. Was the wood…dented? For some reason, the dress appeared in my mind, the one Aric had me wear. There was a distinct feeling that there was something incredibly important about it—something I needed to tell Caden, but no matter how hard I tried, I couldn't figure it out.

Thinking was hard.

Leaning back against the cushions, I closed my eyes. What if I didn't remember? What if I did? I wasn't sure which was worse, to be honest.

I realized in the silence that I hadn't thanked Caden, and I had no idea if I'd thanked Ivy when she was up here. "Thank you," I said.

"For what?" He sounded genuinely confused.

"For…for looking for me. For finding me," I said, fighting the hollowness that was building in my chest. The grief of thinking that no one was coming for me still lingered. "I would've died there if you hadn't found me."

"You never have to thank me for that, Brighton. Ever."

"Well, I just did."

A sound of frustration rose from him, and for some reason, it made my lips twitch. "I wish you never had to doubt that I would come for you."

"Caden—"

"I wish for *you* that you never had to spend a moment thinking that no one was coming for you." His voice was low, urgent. "That you were never put in the position to feel as if you were not wanted or cherished or loved enough that people would not come for you."

In the back of my throat, a burning knot formed. I couldn't hear this now. I didn't think I could hear it at all. It made me want to cry. It made me want to ask why he was saying these things. It made me want to believe that it wasn't the guilt and regret I saw in his expression that made him say them.

"Before I forget to tell you, I think you have a new fan club among the Summer Court," he said, shifting the conversation. It was obvious that he'd picked up on my discomfort with his super special fae senses, but at that moment, I appreciated it. "Perhaps even rivaling Tink."

That sounded unlikely and surprising because I faintly recalled being treated like I carried a contagious disease. "Why?"

"They learned that you killed Aric. In their eyes, that makes you a bit of a savior."

"Ah." I opened my eyes. "It's not over, though. Right? Neal's still out there. Younglings could still be taken."

"He is, but he's not as powerful, dedicated, or smart as Aric. He gets word that Aric is gone—which I will make sure happens—he'll most likely tuck tail and run."

I exhaled a long breath of relief, but just as I inhaled, unease filled my lungs. I didn't understand why. If Caden were right, then it was over. No more worrying about the Queen returning or younglings being taken. The Summer fae were safe, and so was our world.

But I couldn't shake the feeling that this wasn't over. It was only getting started.

Chapter 16

"Hey," Caden called out, drawing me out of my rather foreboding thoughts. "What are you thinking? Don't say 'nothing.' I can tell you went somewhere."

I didn't know how to tell him what I was thinking because I had no idea. As his gaze searched mine intently, it occurred to me that he wasn't so much questioning what I was thinking, but more if my mind had taken a vacay and left the building. I returned to staring at the bandage. "I'm still here."

"Bri—"

"Anyway, this is good news for you, right? The threat with the Queen basically being over?" I asked. "You can get to doing whatever a King of fae does. You can get married to your Queen." The words tasted like ash on my tongue, but they also brought forth an odd sense of deja vu. Like there was something more to that. "I'm sure Tatiana is ready to be Queen. Or maybe you've already done that."

"I haven't."

The flash of relief couldn't be stopped, and I didn't even want to acknowledge that. Accepting that I still loved Caden was one thing. Being happy to hear that he hadn't gotten married was a whole other level of WTFery. "Then you should probably get on that. 'The Court wants their King and Queen united,'" I parroted back what I knew he'd said to me. Bizarre how I could remember that but still not remember Ren's last name.

"We'll talk about all of that later."

My brows furrowed, and the dull flare of pain smoothed it right back out. "There's nothing to talk about."

"There's a whole lot to talk about." He rose from the chair. "But you need to get some rest and get better before Tink gets back and realizes that we all lied to him about you."

"You did?"

"We didn't tell him that you were missing. Ivy knew that if we told him, he would be out there looking for you. Him falling into the hands of a Winter fae is too much of a risk," Caden explained, and that made sense. For someone as goofy as Tink, he was incredibly powerful. "We told him that you'd been sent on assignment with the Order."

"Really?" I replied dryly.

"It was Ivy's idea. Tink believed it."

"He's…he's going to be so mad when he finds out you all lied."

"Yes, he is."

"Going to be mad at you." My gaze shifted to him.

A small, lopsided grin appeared. "I'm the King."

"Doesn't that make you an even bigger target for people to be mad?"

"Not in my world."

I sighed.

"Plus, he loves me. So, I figure he will direct his anger at Ivy and Ren."

"Nice."

His gaze flickered over me, lingering on the left side of my face. I had a feeling that side looked particularly messy. Sadness crept into his warm eyes, along with what I easily recognized as guilt.

"This wasn't your fault," I told him.

"We're going to have to disagree on that."

"No, we don't. You…" I blinked rapidly as an image of Aric formed. "You didn't do this to me. Aric said…he said he knew I'd been looking for him."

"This wasn't your fault either." Caden sat on the bed, planting a hand on either side of my hips, startling me. I tensed as my heart turned over. He pulled back, lifting his hands. "Nothing that was done to you was your fault, Brighton. It wouldn't matter if you walked right up to him. *He* did this."

"And it's not your fault either."

Caden turned his head. A muscle flexed along his jaw. "I know why he took you. I knew why before I saw you in that tomb, in that…" He trailed off, releasing a rough breath. "I wish he was still alive so I could rip him apart, finger by finger, limb from limb."

Part of me thought I knew why, too. That Aric had told me, and it was important. All of it.

"There is something… I can't remember." I moved my head from side to side like it would somehow jar the memories loose. Of course, that didn't work. Frustration rose. "I can remember things that don't matter, but I know there is more."

"As you begin to heal, your memory should also mend itself."

I barked out a short laugh. "I know that's not always the case. My mom…" I pressed my lips together, ignoring the pain. "She had good days, and then days where it was like she wasn't there. She didn't really know who I was or that she was at home. And her memory? It was never the same. Whole years were forgotten, and they only had her for a few days. Aric fed on me…" I swallowed at the blast of heat that rolled off the King. "It was a lot, and there were times in that chamber where I…I had no idea where I was, how I got there, and I'd have to remember who I was. That could happen again, and there'll be nothing I can do. Even if it's just a couple of hours, I'm going to lose parts of myself."

"That's not going to happen to you," Caden swore.

My gaze shifted back to him. His face blurred. "You can't say that. You don't know that."

"You're right." Caden slowly reached for my hand, and when I didn't react, he picked it up, holding it loosely in his warm grasp. "But I was wrong."

"Really? You're admitting that you're wrong? About what exactly?"

That small smile returned. "I doubted your strength. Instead of forcing you out of the hunt for Aric, I should've included you. I was…it doesn't matter right now what I was trying to do, but none of us should've forced you out. That includes Ivy and Ren, and the Order, and any of our warriors. We were wrong."

Hearing that meant a lot. It really did.

"I don't know everything you suffered, but I know enough to confidently say that very few people could've gone through what you did and be here right now. Not only that, to kill him…your only source of potential freedom without believing anyone was coming from you? That was not only strong, but also incredibly brave. The latter is something all of us need to face," he said, and I opened my mouth, but he continued, his voice rough. "You were willing to sacrifice yourself. In a way, you did. I believe you will heal far better than you fear, but even if you don't, you will be okay. I will ensure it."

He would ensure it? How? He was the King, one I imagined had duties beyond taking care of me if or when I roamed off in a state of confusion. And besides, he was about to get married.

MARRIED.

I doubted his soon-to-be Queen would be thrilled about that, and the last thing I needed in my life was one more pissed-off fae becoming psychotic and gunning for me.

And I really didn't need to be reminded days, weeks, or even years from now of why Caden felt he needed to ensure that I was okay.

Staring at our hands, I welcomed the burn in the center of my chest only because that sensation was a dose of reality. Caden wasn't here because he felt for me what I did for him. He wasn't promising to be there for me while I dealt with the consequences of…of what Aric had done. We weren't partners in the way that made people stick together through sickness and health and all that jazz. What I felt for him wasn't returned, at least not to the same degree. That much was obvious since he was engaged to someone else. He was here because he felt guilt, because he felt pity.

And he felt responsible for me.

It took nothing to see his expression when I freaked out over the glass of water. I squirmed a little, embarrassed.

Out of all the things I was having trouble remembering, I hadn't forgotten how he had looked at me before. Even when he was angry with me or we were arguing, he stared at me like he could barely restrain himself from leaping on me and taking me to the ground—or against a wall. I shivered.

Now, he looked at me with a mixture of pity and horror, guilt and regret, and seeing that sat like a lead ball in the pit of my stomach.

And that was the worst part about everything that had become of us. I'd gone from respected and desired, even if reluctantly, to someone Caden pitied. I didn't need time to recover to see that clearly.

I already saw it.

Uncomfortable in my own skin, I pulled at my hand, and he let go. I clenched the blanket. "I really am tired. I think I need some sleep."

Caden was quiet for several moments. "I'll be back with something to eat in a few hours after the healer sees you."

"You don't have to. "

"I know." He placed his hand over mine, gently prying my fingers loose. "I want to."

My gaze shot to his. "More like you need to."

"That, too."

"I'm sure someone else can bring me something. You have to be busy, and Tatiana—"

"We will talk about that later," Caden interrupted. "I'll be back." Lifting my hand, he kissed the top of it, surprising me once more. "Get some rest."

Caden was standing and already at the door before I had the chance to process what he'd done. He stopped and looked over his shoulder at me. "I was wrong about a lot of things, Brighton. Things I don't expect you to ever forgive me for, but things we will discuss when you're better. When you're ready."

* * * *

I really had no idea what Caden thought we needed to talk about. What kind of paper he and his soon-to-be Queen were going to use for their wedding announcements?

Did fae even send invites?

I had no idea, but about five minutes after Caden had left, there was a knock on the door, and Ivy poked her head in.

"Hey," she said, stepping inside. "It's Ivy—"

"I know who you are." My cheeks flushed as I toyed with the blanket.

"Sorry." She cringed.

"It's okay."

Her face smoothed out. "We ran into Caden, and he said you were awake. You up for a quick visit with me and the doc? She wants to check you over."

I nodded. "Sure."

Ivy smiled as she moved aside, and the tall female fae entered. My first thought was that she looked like a mortal doctor, white lab coat and all, and even though the four-leaf clover had been taken from me, I could still see the blond female for what she was. Silvery skin and ears slightly pointed. She walked to the bed with the innate grace of all the fae.

"I don't think I got a chance to introduce myself. I'm Luce."

"Hi," I murmured. "I'm Brighton."

The fae's pale eyes lightened. "How are you feeling?"

"Okay."

Her head tilted slightly. "There's no way, with your level of injuries, that you're feeling okay. No one would expect that of you, and the most important thing right now is that you're honest with me so I can make sure you *are* okay. If not, I'm pretty sure our King will have me drawn and quartered."

Uh.

I glanced at where Ivy had plopped into the seat Caden had occupied. All her wild, red curls were pulled back in an impressive bun. Widening her eyes, she nodded in agreement to what Luce had said.

Alrighty then. "I feel better than before."

The fae smiled. "And your pain?"

"Not bad."

"Good. I'm going to check some of these wounds and do a quick check-up," she explained. "Then we'll see about getting some real food in you."

The exam was rather quick and only a little painful. Sitting up wasn't exactly fun, and it was only when she lifted the hospital-type gown that I really got to see how the cuts were healing.

My legs and stomach looked like someone had been counting the days on my body like I had been on the stone.

When the healer was done, I was sitting completely upright, my feet resting on the floor, focusing on taking slow and even breaths.

"Everything looks like it's healing up just fine," Luce told me, slipping her hands into the pockets of her lab coat. "Actually, you're healing better than I would've anticipated given the number of wounds and the lack of nutrition combined with dehydration. I am aware that can be particularly dangerous for humans."

"Luce works part-time in a human clinic," Ivy explained, apparently noting the way I was staring at the doctor.

"Just a couple of hours a week," she said. "Humans fascinate me. Sort of like how I imagine wild animals fascinate zoologists."

I blinked.

Ivy pressed her lips together, expanding her cheeks as she widened her eyes once more.

Unabashed by the human and wild animal comparison, Luce continued, "Have you had any more nausea? Vomiting?"

I shook my head and then said, "Not that I remember."

"Not since yesterday," Ivy confirmed.

"Good. I think we can get some food sent up. Something light. We'll see how that goes."

Exhaling, I nodded again. "Can I take a shower? I really want to wash my hair."

"If you feel up to it and keep the wounds on your legs and arms bandaged, I don't see why not." The fae jerked her chin in Ivy's direction. "I do think you should have someone here while you do it just in case you get tired."

"I have ample time on my hands," Ivy offered.

My gaze shifted between the two women. "When can I go home?"

Luce's smile remained firm as she glanced at Ivy. My brow puckered. "We'll see how you're doing in a day or so, okay?"

I opened my mouth.

"In the meantime, I'll have some more pain meds sent up," she moved on. "There's something else I want to talk to you about."

Ivy started to rise. "I'm just going to go see if I can rummage up some food for you."

Understanding flared. I knew what the healer wanted to talk to me about. "You don't have to leave," I said, and Ivy halted. "I know what you want to talk about. If I was sexually assaulted."

Luce nodded. "As you know, there are no diseases that can be transmitted between human and fae, nor is pregnancy common. It's rare and has to be done without compulsion, but that does not rule out physical force. Even so, it's still extremely rare, but there are people that you can talk to. Humans I know that specialize—"

"I wasn't raped," I cut her off. "I mean, I'm pretty sure I wasn't. I don't remember anything like that happening." My stomach soured. "He did get…handsy a few times, but I think he was actually disgusted by humans."

At least until the end.

In the end, I had a vague sense that he'd begun to admire me and had started to view me in a different light, as twisted as that sounded.

Luce nodded. "There were bruises on your inner thighs and hips, the kind that are sometimes found in victims of assault."

Victims.

I closed my eyes, took a breath, and then reopened them. "When I said handsy, I didn't just mean in a sexually unwanted way. He liked to hit and kick. Those bruises could be from anything."

Luce smiled faintly as she nodded. It was one of those well-practiced smiles designed to make a patient feel at ease. "Okay, but if you happen to remember something, please do not hesitate to come to me or someone else."

"I will," I said, hoping that would be a non-issue. "Thank you for helping me and for…well, making sure I'm okay."

Luce left after mentioning that she'd pick up the routine blood work that she'd sent into the clinic soon, leaving Ivy and me alone. Things were oddly awkward between us as Ivy found a pair of loose pants and a shirt that I could wear. Ivy was too *smiley* and too nice. Not that she hadn't been nice before, but she was like Positive Polly now, and that wasn't her.

"I'm still Bri," I told her.

She was in the process of yanking a shirt out of the dresser. Who the garment belonged to, I had no idea. She looked over at me. "You are."

"And you're still Ivy. I'm not like my mom," I said. Ivy cast her gaze to the shirt. "At least, not right now. Maybe I was earlier. I don't remember you helping me. Thank you for that. Seriously. And for looking for me."

"You don't need to thank me for that—any of it."

Caden had told me the same, but it still needed to be said.

She lowered the shirt as she drew her lower lip between her teeth. "I don't mean to act weird."

"I know."

Ivy glanced over to where I sat. "You know I loved your mother. She was a bit…brash at times, but I loved her."

The corners of my lips turned up. "Brash would be an understatement."

"True. So, you know when I say this, that I say it with all the love in the world." Her lower lip trembled. "I don't want what your mom went through for you. I don't want to see you go through that."

Tears filled my eyes. "I don't either."

She inched toward the bed, balling the shirt in her hands as she sat beside me. "But if you do, Ren and I will be here for you. So will Tink."

"That is if he doesn't turn you all into troll dolls first," I joked. "I heard that you guys told him I was on assignment."

She grinned. "Yeah, he's probably going to max out my credit card or something." Her grip on the shirt loosened. "You have a lot of support." She cocked an eyebrow. "Even royal support, and I'm not talking about Fabian."

"Ivy—"

"Caden nearly lost his mind when I told him that we couldn't get ahold of you. Pretty sure he actually did lose a little bit of it, and I'm also sure he holds the record for the most Winter fae kills." Ivy smoothed the shirt. "I know there was something going on between you two."

"There's nothing—"

"Everyone knows that there is or was or whatever, including Hotel Good Fae." She slid me a long look. "You know I have my issues with him *even* though I know he wasn't responsible for my kidnapping," she added when I opened my mouth to, well, defend him. "It's just…when I see him, I remember."

I could understand that.

Unfortunately, it took being kidnapped myself to do so.

"But he did everything to find you. Nearly tore this city apart. And when days turned into weeks, and weeks into months, I saw what it did to him. We all did. I don't think he slept more than a few hours a day. Every waking second was spent looking for you," she said. "Whatever was going on between you two doesn't seem to be in the past."

"It is," I told her. "He's engaged. To be married. Like forever and eternity kind of married. Like I said, he just feels responsible and guilty. That's all."

Ivy lifted a shoulder. "All I'm saying is that he earned some brownie points with me, and even Ren."

With Ren, too? Wow. That was unexpected.

And it also didn't matter. "I'm glad he's redeeming himself with you guys, but it's…there's nothing going on. Not anymore," I added.

Ivy just stared at me.

"Anyway…" I drew out the word. "I just wanted to make sure that you knew you don't have to treat me like fragile glass. If I break, then I break. There's nothing anyone can do about that."

Ivy held my stare, nodding. "Okay. Now it's time for me to make sure you know something. If you need someone to talk to, you can talk to me. I know what it feels like to be held against your will. I didn't go through what you did, but I still understand on some level."

And she did. "I know. Thank you."

She smiled then, and it wasn't a weirdly forced one.

We decided that a shower came first, and then I'd eat something. She helped me to the bathroom, and even though I wanted to do it on my own, I had to lean on her for support. It wasn't until I was stripped down, and the bathroom was filled with steam that I saw why.

I hadn't just lost weight, I'd lost muscle mass. My legs felt like jelly and looked like tenderized meat. My reflection was no better.

Seeing myself for the first time was a shock, even though I knew it would be bad.

My hair was a matted, limp mess, slicked back from my forehead, but that looked decent compared to the rest of what was going on.

I'd been right. The left side of my face was a mess of swollen, reddish-purple hues like I had a plum shoved in the side of my mouth. The left eye was open, but it was more purple than pink, and the lid was so heavy it drooped. The right side was only marginally better, and there was a half an inch split in the center of my bottom lip.

There was a bluish band of skin around my throat.

Sucking in a sharp breath, I let my gaze drop. My shoulders and the upper part of my chest were covered in slices, as were the rises of my breasts. Aric had stopped there, moving to my stomach, but I imagined he'd planned to revisit that area.

Farther down, my flesh was a patchwork of old and new scars. Some of the fresher, redder ones would fade, but the others...

They'd be there, always. And even if they didn't serve as a constant reminder, I would bear other scars. Deeper ones.

"*Say it*!"

Gasping, I jerked back from the mirror, clasping my hands over my ears. Aric's roar was so sudden, so real, I closed my eyes. *He's not here. He's not here.* I could smell it, the roasted meat. Shudders overwhelmed me as my knees knocked together.

Nausea rolled through me, driving me to my knees. My stomach clenched, and everything I drank came back up, burning my sore throat. I stayed there, shaking as I kept telling myself that there was nothing left in me to throw up.

"Bri? You okay in there?"

Wincing, I lifted my head. "Yeah. Just…just getting in the shower."

There was a pause. "Yell if you need me."

"Will do," I shouted weakly, shifting back from the toilet as damp warmth curled around me. I let my head fall back.

"I'm okay," I whispered. "I'm going to be okay. No matter what."

That's what I told myself.

That's all I could do.

Chapter 17

Showered and dressed in the soft pants and shirt Ivy had found, I was back in bed, utterly exhausted while Ivy went off in search of food.

I didn't tell her about the puking thing because, despite the round of throwing up my guts, I *was* hungry.

I had no idea how I knew that when the knock at the door came, it wasn't Ivy, but some inherent sense told me that it was Caden. A disconcerting mix of anticipation and dread surfaced in me. I wanted to see him, yet I didn't—the latter for a multitude of reasons, but mostly because I *wanted* him to be here.

I wanted him to be here for me, and that was wrong. I knew that, and I still wanted it, which was one of the reasons he *shouldn't* be here.

And the other reason? I knew how he was likely going to look at me. After seeing what I looked like and then throwing up my guts, I really didn't want to face his mournful gaze.

Caden entered, and I focused on either his chest or his legs. He'd changed. Gone was the black shirt, replaced by a pale blue one, though his jeans were still dark. Maybe he'd showered, too.

"How are you feeling?" he asked, stopping just inside the doorway.

"Better." I fiddled with the bedspread, finding a stray thread and tugging at it. "The shower really helped. Now I just need to get the million knots out of my hair."

"Do you think you can eat something?"

My empty stomach rumbled despite my praying to the porcelain gods for a small eternity earlier. "I think so."

"Good." I saw his legs move back toward the doorway, and then he returned, caring a tray.

I sat up gingerly. Or at least I started to sit up, but the stiffness around my ribs protested once more.

"Here." The King placed the tray on a small table that sat behind the couch. "Let me help." He reached for me—

My body recoiled as it had been trained to do when hands that could become claws or fists got too close. I tried to stop it, but it was a reflex beyond my control.

"I'm not going to hurt you," Caden said.

"I know." I closed my eyes and then opened them. "I'm sorry—"

"Don't, Brighton. Remember?" His voice was soft. "There's nothing to apologize for. Okay?"

I drew in a deep breath. "Yeah."

"Do you want me to help you sit up, or do you want to do it yourself?" he asked. "I'm hoping you'll let me because I don't want to see you in pain."

I glanced at him and saw that all those thick, golden strands were pulled back from his face, and the whole situation struck me as funny even if I didn't laugh.

The King of all the Summer fae was serving me soup in bed.

Weird.

"You don't have to do this," I told him, lifting my gaze to his face. His expression was devoid of any emotion. "You don't owe me—"

"Did you forget that I can scent your emotions?" Caden interrupted, and Christ, I sort of had. "That I know what you're feeling? That I knew the whole time I was in here earlier?"

"Okay. Do you want a gold sticker or something? The kind with a little smiley face on it?"

He cracked a grin. "God, how I missed your attitude."

I frowned.

"I know you think I'm here because I feel guilt or a responsibility to you. I don't even have to have my 'super special fae abilities' to know that. You said it, but I can feel it. Your distrust of my motives, and your fear that I pity you is like burnt rubber."

My frown started to increase. "Now I really do feel like I need to apologize for offending your sensitive nostrils."

One eyebrow cocked. "I need you to understand something, Brighton. I'm here right now because I want to be. I'm here because I need to be—let me finish," he said when I opened my mouth. "That need is not drawn from some sense of guilt or remorse. Don't get me wrong, I feel a whole lot of that, but it is not what drives my actions."

"Then what does?" I challenged, feeling the prickle of irritation, which was far better than anything else I was feeling. I latched on to it, wrapping the anger around me like the fuzziest, softest blanket. "You're engaged, Caden. Something you failed to tell me before you fucked me, both literally and figuratively."

"I did not fuck you. Not literally. You did not fuck me."

"Oh, okay. What then? We made love?" I coughed out a harsh laugh. "Pretty sure you don't make love when you're going to marry someone else."

Caden's jaw hardened. "This is not the time to talk about this."

"Damn right," I snapped, pushing myself upright because arguing while lying prone in a bed really made me feel like I was at a disadvantage. It cost me, though. The flare of pain told me it was time to investigate that pill bottle that had been sitting on the nightstand after I'd stepped out of the shower. "There's no point talking about any of this at all."

"Oh, there's a whole lot of points for why we need to talk about this." Making a sound under his breath, he stepped forward and then halted. "Can I help you?"

"No." I moved again, gasping. I slumped back, my heart pounding from the exertion of *sitting up* and failing.

Caden crossed his arms. "Do you not want me to help because you don't want to be touched or because you're angry with me."

Both, but mostly the angry part at this point. I was being ridiculous. To eat, I needed to sit up. And I needed to eat because I was hungry, and I needed to get my strength back. "Fine. Whatever. You can help me."

"You sure?"

I shot him a dark look that promised murder.

He smiled at me, and it was a real one. The kind that softened the beauty of his face and brought fire to his amber eyes.

My breath caught.

I hated myself.

Caden chuckled under his breath, but then he moved toward me. I braced myself, but when Caden carefully slid an arm under my shoulders, I didn't freak, so bonus points there. He lifted me up, helping me lean against the fluffed pillows.

"Thank you," I muttered, about as gracious as a spoiled child.

"You're *very* welcome."

Caden backed off, retrieving the food. "Luce wanted you to start with something light." He placed it down, and with its little, sturdy legs, the tray was the perfect height. "It's chicken soup with rice mixed in, and Luce said if you tolerate this well, we can move onto something more substantial."

Staring down at the bowl, I realized there was cutlery. God, when was the last time I'd even used silverware? I could almost see the stewed beef staining the tips of my fingers. I started to reach for the spoon but stopped when I became aware of my arm shaking. Tremors coursed throughout my entire body.

I stared at the bowl, unable to move for several moments. The fear was irrational. I knew I could eat with no problem, but the emotion was so potent it choked me.

Heat crawled up my neck, and I looked over at Caden, expecting to see him watching me, expression haunted.

He wasn't.

Caden wasn't watching me at all. Instead, he was over at the small table, pouring a glass of the berry water.

Sweet relief swept through me. He wasn't anywhere near me, and while I suspected that he'd done that on purpose, I didn't care. The tremors lessened, and when I finally picked up the spoon, it wasn't like I'd forgotten it.

A little of the broth spilled as I lifted the utensil, but at the first taste, I closed my eyes. It didn't hurt, and it was so good.

I ate.

Caden stayed back, silent as he turned on the TV. I had no idea what he was watching because he had the volume turned down low, but he appeared engrossed in it.

At least that was what I thought until I placed the spoon in the empty bowl, and he turned immediately. "Thirsty?"

Belly warm and full, I nodded.

Walking over to me, Caden set the drink on the nightstand, within my reach. "I'm going to grab the tray," he announced, doing just that. Placing it on the table, he then returned to sit in the chair that was next to the bed.

I stared at him for several moments and then picked up my glass, taking a sip. "So…" I drew the word out.

"Yes?"

"Are you just going to sit there?"

"Yes."

I looked at him. "Why?"

Caden leaned back, hooking one leg over the other. He looked completely at ease. "Because I want to."

"What if I don't want you here?"

"Then I'll leave."

I stared at him pointedly.

A grin appeared. "But you don't want that."

I started to ask why he thought that, but it was true. Only because I didn't want to be alone. I'd spent enough time in that crypt by myself.

That's what I told myself.

But also, I was…afraid to go to sleep. Part of it was the nightmares I was sure would find me, but a lot of it had to do with my mother. Things were always the hardest for her in the mornings, especially when she had her spells where she had no idea where she was, or when she believed she was still trapped with those fae.

What if that happened to me?

Shoving those fears aside wasn't exactly easy. "Aren't you tired?" I asked, wanting to distract myself.

He shook his head. "I feel more awake than I have in centuries."

"Well…" I placed the glass back on the nightstand. "You were under a dark spell for a lot of it, so…"

"True." Humor danced in his eyes, which was something I'd never thought to see when time under the Queen's spell was referenced. "Is there anything I can get you?"

I thought about that. "A comb? I think there's one in the bathroom."

Caden rose, retrieving the comb. Instead of handing it over, he did what he'd done with the glass, placing it on the nightstand.

Murmuring my thanks, I picked it up, but the moment I attempted to lift my arm to my head, I knew it wasn't going to work.

I sighed. "Who would've thought that broken ribs would be such a pain."

"Anyone who has had broken ribs," he replied.

"Have you?"

"More times than I can count."

"Really?" Disbelief filled me as I thought about what Tink had said and also…something that Aric had said about Caden, giving the impression that the King had been a bit of a playboy in his day. Actually, Tink had said the same thing once.

"Would you like me to help?" Caden asked, and my gaze shot to his. "I'm actually quite accomplished at combing the knots out of ornery females."

"I have so many questions, starting with how in the world you have that experience."

A faint, wistful smile appeared. "Fabian and I had a younger sister."

"Oh." *Had* being the keyword. "I…I didn't know that." I dragged my thumb along the teeth of the comb. "Maybe I'll just cut it all off and start over."

"Let me help you instead?" he offered. "It won't take very long at all, and then I'll leave you be."

I looked at the comb and then at him. "You promise?"

"Promise," he murmured.

I had a feeling he was lying, but there was no way I could comb the knots out, and waiting until Ivy returned was just going to make them worse. A little embarrassed and a whole lot unsure, I handed over the comb.

He took it so quickly that I didn't even see him move. "I'm going to move behind you, but I'm going to hold you up so it doesn't jar your ribs."

I nodded, and then Caden did just as he said, somehow rearranging me and the pillows so that he was behind me, one long leg hanging off the bed, and I…I was sitting between his thighs, leaning onto one of the pillows, holding it close to my chest.

This was so inappropriate.

But I didn't say anything as Caden began to separate my hair into three sections. He didn't note the tremors that had picked back up in my body.

"My sister was the baby of the family," he said, beginning to work at the knots in the center section. "She was born two hundred years after Fabian and I were."

Goodness.

It was easy to forget how old Caden and his brother were.

"Scorcha was…she was the kindest and most beautiful soul," he said, gently tugging at the rat's nest that was my hair. "Far better than Fabian or I could've ever hoped to be, except when it came to getting the knots out of her hair. You see, she had long, thick hair, and was constantly running about after Fabian and me. It was a constant battle between our mother and her to get her to sit still long enough, but she always did it for me. No matter what."

I hugged the pillow. "Sounds like she wanted your attention."

"She did. She wanted both Fabian's and my attention, but we'd just gone through puberty, and well, we were concerned with other things," he said. "Funny how you think you'll learn from the knowledge that time can be fleeting, even for our kind, and come to realize that as fickle as time is, it also makes you forget."

I didn't know how to respond to that. "What happened to her?"

He was quiet, and a part of me wished I hadn't asked. "We do not suffer from many illnesses, but there are a few that are similar to cancer or…heart failure. Some of the older fae believe that these sicknesses are curses, while others believe there are genetic reasons. Either way, Scorcha came down with what was called The Long Sleep. It's a…wasting disease. Appetite and stamina are lost, and eventually, one slips into a sleep they don't wake from. She was only ten years old, very young, even by human standards."

"That is so young. I'm sorry."

"Thank you." Finished with the center section, Caden moved on to the right. "You asked how I got broken ribs. I was a Prince, but I was always a warrior first. Before the big war, there were skirmishes, and I often found myself embroiled in a tavern fight—or five."

"That I can easily see."

"What? The tavern fighting?"

My lips twitched. "Well, yeah, but also the warrior part. I didn't think you just lay around all day and…." Something prodded at my memories, but I couldn't reach it. My eyes had drifted shut. There was something incredibly relaxing about having your hair brushed.

"I could be lazy and indulgent, but I always did my duty," he said after a few moments. "My parents used to think that was one of my admirable traits. However, I have come to realize that it's a flaw."

"How so?"

"Duty should never supersede what is right," he said. "No matter the cost."

Before, I would've argued that duty always came first. It was everything to those raised in the Order, but that was before learning what Ivy was, before meeting the Summer fae and learning that not all of them were evil creatures hellbent on destruction. That was before meeting and…and falling for Caden.

Now I knew that duty often dictated things that were not right. Duty was too black and white, with little to no gray area.

Caden fell quiet as he worked at my hair, moving on to the left side. Not only was this incredibly soothing, it was also…kind and so sweet. And if I believed him, believed what he'd said about why he was here, then why was he—?

I cut those thoughts off. There was no reason for me to go down that road. A knot lodged in my throat anyway.

His hand stilled. "What are you thinking, sunshine?"

"Don't call me that." My voice rasped.

"Why wouldn't I?" The comb started moving again.

Why? I almost laughed, except nothing about this was funny, and considering that he was pledged to another, the nickname was cruel in a way.

"You shouldn't be doing this," I whispered, blinking back tears.

"There is nothing wrong with what I'm doing. You need help, and I am here, where I am supposed to be."

"But—"

"Let me help you. That is all," he coaxed. "Then you can rest. Later, if you're feeling up to it, you and I can talk."

I turned my head to the side. "There's nothing to talk about. I already told you that."

"And I already told you that there is a lot."

"Then talk to me now."

His chuckle somehow rumbled through me, stirring parts of me I'd rather ignore. "Now is not the time, Brighton. Not for a conversation like this."

No matter how much I insisted, he wouldn't tell me what he thought we needed to discuss, deflecting each question by changing the subject. He talked about the tavern brawls, which always surrounded some sort of perceived insult, and then he told me about the little-girl games his sister would make him and Fabian play. It all seemed so…human. I imagined if I had older brothers, I would've forced them to play with dolls and eat pretend food. I would've chased after them just like Scorcha had with Fabian and Caden.

When Caden finished with my hair, I could actually run my fingers through it, and like I had suspected, he didn't leave. After helping me lay back down, he got me one of those pain pills and refilled my glass. Then he pulled up his chair as close to the bed as he could get it and told me more stories about him and his brother like he had before. And when my eyelids got too heavy to keep open, his voice softened. I fell asleep knowing that he would remain and that he'd be there when I woke up.

And I wasn't afraid.

Chapter 18

When I woke the following morning, I *remembered.*

In my sleep, I had shifted to my side, and I was surprised to find that it didn't cause my ribs to hurt all that much. Opening my eyes, I found Caden asleep in the chair beside the bed, just like I had the last time I woke up. He was closer than before, the chair right next to where I slept, and not only were his legs propped up on the bed, but his left hand…his fingers were threaded through mine.

We were holding hands.

If I'd done that in my sleep or if Caden had, who knew? But it was as sweet as him brushing my hair the night before, and just as wrong.

In the moment, none of that seemed to matter.

I didn't know why or how, but I remembered bits of what Aric had told me about Caden—about the *mortuus* and about Siobhan…and about the Summer Kiss.

Important bits.

I remembered why Aric had dressed me in that gown, and that he had planned to use me to force Caden to open the gateway, something that, at the time, hadn't screamed how much of a big deal it truly was.

Because Caden was the King. He could open those gates, releasing the Queen and God only knew what else. That was something I doubted Ivy and Ren were aware of, and I also knew it would unsettle them and the Order.

I stared at our joined hands. I also knew that if the Order ever became aware of what Caden could do, they'd put a hit out on him. I knew it to my very core. They wouldn't care that he wasn't evil and hated the Queen more than anyone else. He'd be viewed as too much of a risk.

And being a member of the Order, even if one undervalued, it was my duty to inform Miles of what I knew. If I didn't, and they were ever to discover that I knew the truth, they wouldn't just remove me from the Order, there'd probably also be a hit placed on me.

Hell, if they learned I'd had relations of the forbidden kind with Caden, they'd probably boot me right out of the Order. The fact that Ivy still remained a member even though it was known that she was a halfling wasn't something that all Order members supported. She had Ren's support, and she was also a hell of a fighter. The Order needed her.

They didn't need me.

I thought about what Caden had said the night before about duty and how following it wasn't always the right thing to do.

Reporting what I knew about Caden was my duty, and to the Order, it was the right thing to do. But it wasn't. They wouldn't care what had been done to him or how he'd been forced to do the Queen's bidding. They already didn't like or trust him, and Caden…well, despite what had happened between us, he was good.

He didn't deserve to be hunted down.

Caden stirred, his lashes lifting. Eyes the color of amber jewels met mine and then drifted to where our hands remained clasped. The corners of his full lips tipped up.

"You're awake," he murmured, voice thick with sleep.

"He said I was your *mortuus*," I blurted out.

I'd never seen someone wake up as quickly as Caden did. He slipped his hand free from mine as he pulled his legs off the bed. All traces of languid sleepiness vanished. "What?"

"Aric told me that I was your *mortuus*," I repeated, sitting up and finding that I could do it without too much pain, which reminded me of something else I now remembered. "He told me you gave me the Summer Kiss, and that was how I was still alive after everything he did. It's probably why I'm healing so quickly now."

Caden swallowed, saying nothing.

"He told me that I wouldn't age like a normal human, that…I was only *mostly* human now," I said, shifting so I wasn't leaning too far to the side. "Is it true? Is that how you healed me? With the Summer Kiss?"

"It is."

Even though I already knew it, it was still a shock to the system. Possibly because I'd totally forgotten about all of it. "Were you ever going to tell me? I mean, eventually, I would've figured out that something was up. Or what if I was injured and went to the doctor? They'd see—"

"They would have no way of knowing. Your blood work would not show anything abnormal. They do not have the technology to test for that," he explained. I gaped at him. "Aric didn't explain it to you completely. The Summer Kiss healed you, yes, but I had no way of knowing that it would have long-term effects on you. It doesn't always, and I wouldn't have known until you were injured again or—"

"When I stopped aging?" I suggested because I was helpful like that.

"You will age, Brighton, just at a much slower rate."

"How much slower? Like I'll have to leave before people start asking questions?"

"Yes," he answered bluntly.

I opened my mouth and then closed it.

"You won't live forever. Neither will I. But from what I know,"—he exhaled heavily—"for every fifty years, it will be a year for you. Give or take a few."

"Oh, my God."

Caden sat back. "I didn't tell you because if Aric hadn't done this, I wouldn't have wanted you to worry unnecessarily. But once I knew for sure, I would've told you."

Nodding dumbly, I admitted to myself that I believed him, but it was still a lot to process. Everything was a lot. Silence fell between us as I gathered my thoughts. There was more we needed to talk about, and right now wasn't the time for me to freak out.

Apparently, I'd have a lot of time for that later.

"He told me about Siobhan and what…what he did to her," I continued, heart thumping. "And how that started the Great War. It was why he put me—"

"In the dress," Caden said, dragging his finger over his brow. "I know. It was her wedding dress. Or it was supposed to be. Aric took her on our wedding day."

Empathy crowded out the anger and confusion, taking center stage in my chest. "I'm sorry. What he did… He was truly evil."

Caden nodded. "It was a long time ago, Brighton."

"That doesn't make it easier to deal with."

"No, you're right. I knew what he did to her. He made sure I did. And the rage…it made me vulnerable to the Queen."

I shifted carefully, letting my feet touch the floor. Like this, we were only inches apart. "I understand why you wanted to be the one to kill him."

"It wasn't just because of what he did to Siobhan. Don't get me wrong. That was part of it, but it was also what he did to you and your mother. It's what he's done to countless others. His death was a long time coming."

That was true.

I drew in a shallow breath. "He said I was your *mortuus*. That through me, he could've forced you to open the doorway and free the Queen. What does that mean?"

His gaze lifted to mine. He was quiet for so long that I didn't think he'd respond. "You are my *mortuus.*"

The breath I took seemed to go nowhere.

"It means you are…you are my strength. My sun. You are my heart."

My entire body jolted.

"You are also my greatest weakness," he continued. "It is not an object or anything tangible. It is the source of my power and my weakness. Through you, complete and utter control of me is possible. That is what *mortuus* means. There was only one before you. That was Siobhan."

I drew back, shaking my head. "I don't understand. How is that possible? You…" I swallowed the lump that formed in my throat.

"I love you."

Those three words were like a bomb.

And Caden wasn't done. "I love you, and that is why you're my *mortuus*. My everything."

"You love me?" Happiness I didn't know I could even experience rushed through me in a wave that left my skin tingling. Then it was squeezed too tightly by the grips of reality, turning my entire being numb. "How can you love me? You're engaged—"

"Not anymore. I broke the engagement before I even knew you disappeared."

"What?" Thunderstruck, I stared at him.

"When we were together, that wasn't planned. You know that. I wouldn't have set out to sleep with you while still marrying Tatiana, but I…I wanted you. I've wanted you from the first time I saw you. Before I even knew you. And I don't know why. Our elders say—" He cut himself off. "That doesn't matter. My duty is to take a Queen of my kind, but that isn't right. It's not what I want, and it would not be fair to

Tatiana. To marry her when I love and want another."

My heart was pounding so fast, I feared it would come out of my chest.

"I thought I could go through with it. That I could keep you away. I tried. The moment I became King, I tried, and I failed. Obviously." His eyes closed. "I knew what you were to me. Not when I saved you after Aric's attack that night years ago, but not too long after that. I watched you, watched you heal and then hunt. From afar, I saw you grow braver and stronger, and I admired you. I respected you. I…knew after I found you in that club, pretending to be someone else."

Oh.

Oh, wow.

"But I also knew that if Aric or Neal or any of my enemies realized that you were my *mortuus*, you'd be at constant risk." His gaze held mine. "I thought it was best to marry Tatiana and keep you safe."

His words came back to me. *You're a distraction. A weakness that I will not allow to be exploited.*

I'd thought he meant that I was nothing more than a distraction that could be exploited, not what he was saying.

"That's all I was trying to do, but I couldn't… I couldn't go through with it, being with someone else and knowing that you'd eventually find another. I'm too selfish for that. I couldn't do it. I broke the engagement and then went to you. You weren't home, and you didn't come home. That's when Ivy reached out to say that no one had heard from you."

"You…you told me that you needed a Queen of your kind and that what we did was a mistake. You said it was nothing. All of that was a lie?"

"It was," he said quietly.

"Do you have any idea how much that hurt me? How much that sliced into me because I—" I cut myself off. "If it wouldn't hurt me so much, I'd totally punch you in the throat right now."

"I'd deserve it. I hurt you. I thought it was the lesser of two evils. I was wrong."

"You were so wrong." My hands curled into fists. "Because Aric figured out anyway. There was…" Something tugged at the fringes of my memory. "I don't know… I don't know what to say."

"There's nothing you need to say." Caden leaned forward, his eyes snagging mine. "Not right now."

But there was. Because, damn it, I was tired of lies. "I love you. I'm *in love* with you."

A half-grin appeared. "I know."

I blinked. "Excuse me?"

"I can sense it." His grin turned to a smile that took a little of my breath away. "I could feel it."

I snapped my mouth shut, blowing air through my nose. "But you hurt me, Caden. You hurt me twice now, and I'm just supposed to be okay with that? Take that risk again?"

Sadness crept into his gaze, and his smile faded. "I know. I don't expect you to be okay with it. Not right now. But I plan to prove to you that there will be no risk. I will not take from you like I have. Never again will I hurt you."

God, I wanted to believe that—so badly that it almost hurt. But I… "I don't know what to think right now. About anything. I don't even know what is going to happen to me." Tears pricked my eyes. "If you had told me this before…before what happened with Aric, things might be different. I wouldn't just be learning this."

"I know," he repeated. "All of this was what I needed to talk to you about, but I knew it wasn't right. Not after everything. Some time needed to pass. You needed to heal. I had no idea that Aric told you any of this."

I believed him, and maybe…maybe if this conversation had come later, it would have been easier to process. Right now, it was like being handed what you wanted most after suffering a great tragedy. And that was what had happened in a way.

"I need you to know something." Caden reached out, taking my hands. When I didn't flinch away, he threaded his fingers with mine. "I am here. I know you need time, and if it takes a hundred years, so be it. I'll wait. What I feel for you is not going to change. Not today. Not next year. Not fifty years from now. You tell me when you're ready, and I'll be there."

My throat closed off, and now I really wanted to cry, because…God. That was exactly what I needed to hear. What I needed to know. That he'd be there when I was ready. That I could have time to piece myself back together, to find myself again, and then I could find him.

"I need to check in with Tanner and see about getting some food sent up to you," Caden said after a couple of moments. "Then, if you're feeling up to moving around, maybe we can go outside. Get some fresh air. What do you think?"

The breath I took was shaky, but it felt good. It felt clean. "That sounds good."

"Perfect." A smile appeared, and then what happened next surprised me.

Caden rose and then lowered his head, kissing my forehead. I hadn't expected that. I also was surprised that I didn't recoil or flip out.

"See you in a little bit."

I might've nodded. I didn't know. But he left, and I just sat there. I didn't know for how long. I just absorbed everything he had told me.

Caden loved me.

The King of the Summer fae loved me.

In a daze, I rose from the bed and showered, wrapping the fluffy robe around me. And when I returned to the bedroom, sore and more tired than I wanted to be, I was still caught in the grasp of confusion, but an intense rush of emotions brimmed just under the surface.

The King loved me.

I stopped in the center of the room, behind the cream-colored couch.

Caden had ended the engagement before he even knew that I was missing.

None of that changed how badly he'd messed up, but I…I loved him, and that hadn't changed. And the most wondrous thing happened. Just like when I realized how awe-inspiring it was to still feel attraction, a sense of hope rose for the first time since…since Aric had taken me. I knew that I could move on from what had happened, even if moving on took a long time. Because I could still feel love, and Caden—

A memory surfaced, one of Aric and I when I was bathing and glamoured but aware of what he was saying.

A certain member of the Summer Court who, like me, wishes to see the return of the Queen.

Oh, my God.

There was someone within the Summer Court working with Aric. Someone who claimed that they could bring Aric the *mortuus*.

I needed to find Caden. I started toward the door just as a knock sounded. Expecting it to be Ivy or Caden, I called out, "Come in."

The door opened, and my lips parted. It wasn't Ivy or Caden.

Tatiana stood in the doorway.

Chapter 19

Although I'd only seen Tatiana briefly, she was as beautiful as I remembered.

Raven-haired and statuesque, her skin tone was a deep silvery hue, and her ears were delicately pointed. Tatiana didn't attempt to glamour herself as she stood before me, hands clasped in front of her. She wore an off-the-shoulder dress the color of buttercream that hugged her breasts and waist before flaring out at the hips.

Tatiana looked like an ethereal princess straight out of a Disney movie, while I looked like I'd gone a few rounds with a meat grinder and was currently starring in a horror flick.

Not exactly how I wanted to look when I came face to face with Caden's fiancée—*ex*-fiancée.

I stared at the would-be Queen, wishing that there had been clothes for me to wear. Maybe a head-to-toe bodysuit. Anything would be better than the lumpy, shapeless robe I currently wore.

"I hope I am not intruding," she said, her voice carrying a soft lilt that reminded me of someone who was from Great Britain. "But I was hoping you had a few minutes to spare."

Wondering how rude it would be to say no, I looked around the room like an idiot. Based on what Caden had told me this morning, I had a good idea of what this conversation would be about. And considering that I hadn't even had a drink of anything other than the berry water, I really wasn't mentally prepared for this. But more importantly, I needed to find Caden and tell him what I remembered.

Instead, I said, "Sure. Would you like to sit?"

She nodded, and I limped my way to the couch. I was a little too relieved to be sitting. The shower really took a lot out of me, so I plopped down like a horse falling over.

Tatiana sat on the other side of the couch, as graceful as a ballerina, crossing and tucking her ankles and resting her hands in her lap. "How are you feeling?"

"Um, better than I look." Which was true.

A faint smile appeared. "I'm relieved to hear that. Your injuries are…frightening."

I blinked.

"I mean, they don't frighten me, but you must have suffered greatly," she rushed to correct herself. "I am glad to hear that you killed your tormentor."

"Yeah," I said, curling my fingers around the sash of my robe. "I am glad…I killed him."

Did that sound as dumb as it did to me?

"Aric has haunted the King for far too long," Tatiana added, surprising me. "What he did to the King's fiancée all those years ago was an act of pure evil."

"You…you know about that?"

"Everyone knows what Aric did." Her head cocked to the side as a frown pinched her brow. "Well, the Summer fae know."

I stiffened. There was a good chance I was just being sensitive, but that sounded an awful lot like a jab.

"What he did to you was also horrific," she continued, and I realized that the posture was perfect. She inhaled deeply, appearing to brace herself. "The King was beside himself with worry for you."

There was a part of me that wanted to pretend like I didn't know where this conversation was headed, but that would not only be pointless, it would also be cowardly. And I had faced much, much worse.

"Not to sound rude or impatient, but I imagine you're here to talk about Caden," I said. Her pale blue eyes widened ever so slightly. "He told me he broke off the engagement."

Her chin lifted. "Yes, I am here to talk about him."

"I don't know what there is to say." I twisted my fingers around the sash. "I had…I had no idea he ended the engagement until this morning, and I…well, this is super awkward."

"That it is." Another small smile appeared. "The entire Court was in the midst of preparing for our mating, and they have no idea it has ended."

"You haven't told them?" Admittedly, I didn't like that. If Caden were so sure about how he felt about me and ending the engagement, why not tell his Court?

"He wanted to wait until I returned home," she explained. "So that I could avoid any possible embarrassment. While I appreciate the attempt, his refusal will follow me no matter where I go."

I opened my mouth to apologize but stopped myself. Some innate knowledge told me that she wouldn't appreciate that. I wouldn't either. In a way, I was… God, I *was* the *other* woman. Unknowingly, but still.

Damn it.

Now I was pissed at Caden all over again.

"But what the King intends has a far greater impact than causing me embarrassment," she continued. "That is what I wanted to talk to you about. I doubt you fully understand what it means for him to refuse a Queen of his own kind—and I mean no insult by that. You are most likely not aware of our most intimate and political customs."

"I'm not," I admitted as a tiny ball of unease formed in my stomach.

"Once a Prince ascends to the throne, they have certain responsibilities that they must complete within a year of doing so. They must assign a council and choose the best warriors of their Court to become their personal Knights." Tatiana's gaze skittered to the curtained window. "A King must also choose a Queen, one of their kind deemed worthy enough to bear the next generation."

"And what if they don't want to be with the opposite sex?" I thought of Fabian, and suddenly I remembered what Tink had said about how Fabian could not be King or did not want to become King.

"Our kind do not limit…sexuality to one sex." Her nose wrinkled. "That is an entirely human concept, but a King would still be required to marry a female. He may choose to keep a lover."

I guessed being forced to marry and sleep with someone he was not attracted to wasn't—understandably—high on Fabian's to-do list.

I shook my head. "And what if the King chooses not to marry a female fae?"

"What if Caden chooses you, you mean?" Her gaze met mine then. There was no malice in her stare. Nothing but…sorrow. And that made me even more uncomfortable. "He has already chosen you, but you cannot become his Queen."

"I don't want to be his Queen."

Her dark brows lifted. "You do not want him?"

"That's not what I said," I replied before I realized what I was saying. "I…I love him. I was in love with him before he became King."

Swallowing, I shook my head. "I didn't think he loved me, and I didn't even know…well, none of that matters right now. I *do* want him."

And that was true.

I wanted him, even with his mistakes and flaws and stupid decisions. And he wanted me, even with my scars and bitchiness and even though I wasn't ready.

"Then I am sorry," Tatiana said.

I jolted. "What for?"

"My Court. You have no idea what will happen if Caden gives up his throne to be with you. And that is what he will have to do to have you," Tatiana said. "He knows that. I do not believe *you* know that."

"No," I whispered, clearing my throat. "I didn't. Why must he give up his throne?"

"Because he would not fulfill his duty by taking a Queen."

"That…that is incredibly stupid." Letting go of the robe sash, I pushed damp strands of hair back from my face. "Why does having a Queen have anything to do with his ability to rule?"

"Because a King does not rule alone," she stated.

I stared at her, really having no words. That didn't sound like a reason. Not a real one, anyway. "The Queen rules, doesn't she? Morgana? She doesn't have a King."

Tatiana paled at the mention of the Queen's name. "She rules through dark magic, and she had a King when she came into power. One that she slaughtered as he slept. And because she has not remarried, her powers are limited. If she ever does marry again, she will be unstoppable."

Uh.

Good to know.

"You don't understand." Tatiana leaned toward me. "This is not just some silly rule we follow out of tradition. The entire future of the Court depends on Caden keeping his throne. The responsibility can no longer be given to his brother, not after Caden ascended. Prince Fabian could only take Caden's place if the King were to die."

My unease grew. "What do you mean the future of the Court depends on him?"

"I am glad you asked. Without a King, we would be powerless as we were before he ascended. Our Knights would be weakened, and we would have to return to hiding. The Winter Court could overtake us, and you know what they're capable of," she said, lips trembling. "Not only that, but Caden would be weakened. He would no longer be King, ostracized from the Court, and unprotected. Although he would no longer be King, he would still carry royal blood—blood that the Winter Court could use for unfathomable reasons. The entire Court would be vulnerable."

"How is that even possible?" I exclaimed. "You had no King for how many years?"

"And as I said, we had to hide during that time. We were weak and could do very little to stop the Winter Court from hunting and hurting humans, from plotting to release the Queen," she returned. "But not only that, we were not…fruitful."

"Fruitful?" I repeated.

The centers of her cheeks flushed. "Our Court has not been as plentiful as it once was when we had a King and a Queen. Our…fertility is tied to theirs."

Oh.

My.

God.

Did these people not believe in science?

Did science not exist for them?

"I can tell you do not believe me." Tatiana shook her head sadly. "But we are not governed by the biology humans share. There is a…an essence to us that connects us to the King and Queen. When we had a King before, families had six or eight children over the course of their lifespans."

Good God.

"Now, we are lucky if we have two or three, but that has already begun to change. Without a King or Queen, our race will die out."

I lifted a hand and then dropped it back to my lap as I refocused on Tatiana.

"I came here to implore you to do what the King cannot. Not because I love him. I don't. I do not know him well enough to feel that. But because I love my Court. He could still keep you. If that is what you both wish," she continued. I jerked. "Or he could choose a fae other than me, as long as he chooses one of us. He needs a Queen."

Unease had rapidly spread like a weed, tangling with every part of me. I had no idea what to say. Caden knew this, knew what a risk it would be to choose me, and he still did.

That was…flattering, and also batshit insane.

"I hope that because you are a member of the Order, you will understand the danger Caden will place us in, the risk he will place all of mankind under." Her eyes glimmered with tears. "If we fall to the Winter Court, mankind will fall next. You know that to be true. Is love really worth that?"

Looking away, I took a breath, but it seemed to go nowhere as the implication of what Tatiana claimed settled over me. Was love really worth that? *Yes*, screamed a selfish, not-so-tiny voice inside of me.

But the potential downfall of the entire Summer Court? And mankind?

I closed my eyes.

"I wish I was here to wish you well, but…nothing good will come to my people or to the King if he gives up his throne," she said quietly. "So, I ask a better question. Do you love him enough to save him?"

The breath expelled out of me in a harsh cry. How could I answer that? How could I be with him if it would weaken him and put him at risk?

I already knew the answer to that.

I just couldn't speak it aloud.

I really didn't even want to think it.

How could I go from feeling hope to crushing dread in the matter of an hour? To having something ripped away before I even had a chance to hold it?

Because that was how it felt. Knowing what I did now, there was no way I could allow Caden to do this.

"I think…I think I need to be alone," I said, my voice hoarse as I opened my eyes.

"I understand." Tatiana rose. "I am sorry."

My gaze cut to her. She turned, walking toward the door, her steps light. I started to look away as she pulled on the handle, but her startled gasp stopped me.

"Oh. Sorry!" Luce exclaimed. "I was just about to knock. Would've been your face had I done it a second earlier."

"I am glad you didn't." Tatiana glanced over her shoulder and nodded. "I was just leaving."

Luce glanced over at me, her brow knitted. She waited until the female had left. "Are you okay?"

"Yeah." I cleared my throat. "Yes. Are you here to check on me?"

"I am. Kind of." Luce closed the door behind her. "I need to talk with you."

I wanted to throw myself on the floor and scream, so the last thing I wanted to do was talk to Luce or be checked out.

"I feel fine. A thousand times better than yesterday," I told her as she came around the couch. "I think—" I squared my shoulders. "I think I can go home."

Her forehead wrinkled as she took the seat Tatiana had just vacated, much to my dismay. "We'll talk about that later. There's something more important to discuss."

A laugh burst out of me. Something more important than learning that the man I loved could end up risking not only his life but also the lives of his entire Court and mankind by being with me? Unless I chose to be his…his side piece while he married a fae and fathered a whole litter of children.

Luce frowned. "Are you sure you're okay, Brighton?"

"I am." I stopped the next laugh from bubbling up. "What did you want to talk to me about?"

She looked down and then up. "Remember when I said that I was waiting on some blood work to come back? I wanted a full workup to make sure there were no hidden infections."

I nodded. "I'm guessing it came back?"

"It did, and there was something noted that required further testing to confirm."

"What? I have sepsis of the heart or something?"

Luce's brows crinkled once more. "I do not think that is a thing, but I will have to check—"

"I was kidding," I said. "What did you find?"

"The blood test picked up an abnormality in a hormone, an increase in HCG." Her eyes searched mine. "After seeing that, I ran a quantitative blood test just to confirm the levels that were present and what it meant."

"Can you just give me antibiotics for it?"

Her frown increased. "You cannot take antibiotics for this."

"Okay." I stared back at her. "Then what do I do?"

"Well, there's a lot to do, actually. Another test just to be sure, and then—wait." She drew back. "You don't know what HCG means, do you?"

"No. I mean, maybe I did, and I've just forgotten it."

Her shoulders tightened. "HCG stands for human chorionic gonadotropin, a hormone that is produced when someone is pregnant."

"Pregnant?" I repeated.

Luce nodded. "You're pregnant, Brighton. And based on the levels, you're at about eight weeks. Maybe a little more, but you're definitely pregnant."

My brain stopped working.

"That means you conceived before you were taken. And, somehow, by some miracle, you're still pregnant," Luce continued. "I would like to do some more testing. Your body has been through a lot, so there are a lot of risks that this…this fetus will not hold or may be..."

It was like an out-of-body experience.

I was sitting, but I felt like I was floating, and I knew Luce was still talking, but I couldn't hear a word she said.

I was… I was pregnant?

Possibly eight weeks or more pregnant?

That was….

"… I have to ask you this because it could change everything—the tests I need to do, what you can expect," Luce was saying as I refocused on her. "Is it possible that the…?" She paled, much like Tatiana had earlier when I'd spoken Queen Morgana's name. "Is it possible that the King is the father?"

Possible?

It was the only likelihood.

I was pregnant with Caden's child.

The Queen

1001
DARK
NIGHTS
THE QUEEN
A Wicked Novella
NEW YORK TIMES BESTSELLING AUTHOR
JENNIFER L.
ARMENTROUT

Acknowledgments from the Author

Thank you to Liz Berry, M.J. Rose, Jillian Stein, Chelle Olson, Kimberly Guidroz, and the amazing team behind 1001 Dark Nights for allowing me to tell Caden's and Brighton's story.

None of this would be possible without you, the reader. Thank you. Thank you.

Chapter 1

Pregnant.

Eight weeks pregnant. Maybe a little more.

The most common response in the history of womankind was dancing on the tip of my tongue, threatening to make me sound like an idiot.

That's not possible.

But the logical and sane voice in the back of my head whispered that it was as I stared at the silvery-skinned fae doctor. The same voice that also whispered, *that's what happens when you have unprotected sex, Brighton Jussier.*

That voice sounded a lot like my mother's during those moments when she had been herself and not the confused, lost shell of a woman the Winter fae attack had left behind.

"Are you okay?" Luce asked and then wrinkled her nose. "That's probably a stupid question. I doubt this was news you were expecting."

A strangled laugh escaped me. This wasn't even in the realm of things I'd expected. So many thoughts swirled as I sat on the plush couch of what could be considered a luxury suite in a place commonly referred to as Hotel Good Fae. Hidden by glamour, to human eyes, the building appeared to be a rundown and abandoned factory on South Peters Street, but the hotel was actually a stunning, massive community complex to all Summer fae who refused to feed on unwilling humans.

Right now, it felt like the entire building was made out of cardboard and could collapse at any second.

"How?" I whispered. "How is this possible?"

The blond fae who apparently worked part-time in a human clinic because, according to her, being intrigued by humans was similar to how wild animals fascinated zoologists, frowned. "Well, I imagine it happened during sex—"

"I know that." I cut her off. "But how could I survive being pregnant…after what I went through?" I couldn't even fathom how it was possible that a…pregnancy had survived the time I'd spent as Aric's captive. The psychotic Ancient fae who had killed my mother and left me for dead two years ago, had tortured me for weeks. For *months*. And it wasn't like I'd gotten three square meals a day.

"Your body has been through a lot," Luce repeated carefully. "Even for a fae, a viable pregnancy would be nothing short of a miracle. But for a human? It would be highly unlikely—"

"Then are you sure?"

"I cannot think of any other reason why you would have such an increase in that hormone. I want to do more testing. An ultrasound, for example. Some more blood work."

"I'm… I'm pregnant."

She gave a quick nod.

"Pregnant," I repeated, the information sort of sinking in. A child was growing inside me, right at this moment. I was… I was going to be a mother. My heart stuttered. Could I even be a mother? I was relatively organized and responsible. I was smart, and I'd had to take care of *my* mother from a very young age, but that was not the same thing as having to take care of a tiny human being. I had no idea what my future held.

Now my heart raced. Aric had…he'd fed from me repeatedly, just like the fae had done to my mother all those years ago. The trauma that had left her spontaneously going in and out of reality. I'd already had moments of being sucked into a world that seemed to exist only in my mind. There could be a chance I would wake up tomorrow and spend the entire day stuck in a world of terrifying memories and haunting hallucinations. I might spend days that way. Mom had sometimes spent weeks like that, and I…I didn't want to do that to a child. I knew what it felt like to see someone you loved, who was supposed to be the person that supported and took care of you, become trapped and unreachable. I wasn't bitter nor did I regret being there for my mom. Not at all. But when she was herself, I knew the knowledge that she needed constant care killed her.

I didn't want to repeat that cycle.

God, that was the last thing I wanted to do.

Luce's pale blue eyes searched mine. "It would help to know who the father is. That could possibly explain how this is likely."

I pulled myself from what felt like a downward spiral into flailing panic and drew in a tight, shallow breath.

Her shoulders squared as if she were preparing herself. "It

is…obvious that the King cares for you deeply. When you were gone, he nearly tore the city of New Orleans apart looking for you. He's barely left your side since he found you, and sleeps only for a few hours here and there."

My heart squeezed painfully, and I closed my eyes. So much had happened since I woke up, no longer chained to what I believed would be my tomb. I'd just remembered what Aric had insinuated. That a Summer fae had been aiding him. I needed to tell Caden this. Not only that, I was still trying to process everything that had happened with Aric, what had come before that and after. And just an hour ago, I'd felt a sense of hope for the first time since Aric had taken me. The feeling had nearly stolen my breath.

Caden loved me. He'd ended his arranged engagement for me, but the awe-inspiring part was that I could still feel attraction and love after being trapped by Aric. The pain and the humiliation and the god-awful fear hadn't stolen the capability to desire, want, or love from me. Realizing that was life-altering. I knew that I could move on from what Aric had done, even if doing so took days or months or years. And I knew that Caden would be waiting for me, no matter how long it took.

That hope had crashed and burned spectacularly when Tatiana, the would-be Queen of the Summer Court, sat right where Luce was sitting now and explained what would happen if Caden didn't marry a fae of the Summer Court.

A King must choose a Queen to bear the next generation. Without doing so, the entire Summer Court would be weakened, and so would Caden. He would be dethroned, ostracized, and unprotected. Although he would no longer be a King, his blood still could be used by the Winter Court to commit unimaginable horror. Not only that, if what Tatiana claimed was true, the entire Court's fertility rate would continue to decrease until the entire race died out.

Caden must have known all of that when he ended the engagement with Tatiana. And while that was overwhelming in a way I had little experience with, it was also terrifying.

Because without the Summer fae fighting back against the Winter fae, mankind would fall. The Order I worked for wouldn't be able to hold them back.

It wasn't just the future of the Summer Court that relied on the King choosing his Queen. The entire world did as well.

I'd always dreamed about the kind of love where someone was willing to risk everything. I never thought I'd be on the receiving end of it, but I wanted it—wanted it so damn badly.

But was that kind of love worth everything? The downfall of the Summer Court? Mankind? I shuddered as the back of my nose burned. A part of me wanted to scream that yes it was, but could I really live with myself—live happily ever after for however long Caden and I had—while the world fell apart around us? Until the Winter Court came for him, and he wasn't able to fight them off?

Could Caden really live with that?

He might think so now, but months and years from now? I didn't think so.

I knew I couldn't.

And now, with the knowledge that I could…that I *was* bringing a child into a world that would definitely have an expiration date stamped on it? I couldn't do that.

Luce had tipped forward when I reopened my damp eyes. "Is it possible, Brighton, that the King is the father? Or could it be someone else?"

"Aric didn't…he didn't rape me."

"You said you didn't remember anything like that," she clarified gently. "I would think it would be unlikely for it to be him, based on the stage of your pregnancy. But if it happened at the beginning of your captivity, it wouldn't be wholly *im*possible."

I was pretty sure Aric hadn't forced himself on me. To be honest, he'd seemed pretty disgusted by humans, especially me. But toward the end, I'd thought he started to respect me, as messed up as that was. If I hadn't been able to kill him when I did, I had a horrible, sinking feeling that this conversation might be different.

I shook my head. "It's not him."

Luce's gaze met mine. "Then the King is the father. Or possibly someone else?"

The breath I exhaled punched out of me. "There's no one else. It has to be him. We had…well, we were together, and there wasn't protection. I didn't think it would be a concern."

Luce didn't move for several moments. I wasn't even sure if she breathed, but then she swallowed and sat up straight. "It's extremely rare for a human to become pregnant by a fae, but it happens."

I knew that. A halfling could be born from such a union. Ivy Owens was a prime example of that—

"The prophecy." I jolted, heart leaping into my throat. "The one that could cause the gates of the Otherworld to open—"

"You're not a halfling," Luce interceded calmly. "Your child most likely wouldn't even be one."

Yes, she was right. The prophecy that would tear open the gates between our worlds, freeing the demented Queen Morgana, required a Prince or Princess or a King or Queen to procreate with a halfling, creating a child that should never exist. I knew that. I wasn't a halfling, but I also wasn't exactly human anymore, was I? The King had given me the Summer Kiss, something that no one else knew. Well, no one who was alive. Aric had figured it out, but—

"Wait." My brain had finally processed everything she'd said. "M-my child most likely wouldn't be a halfling? It would be human?"

"No." Luce leaned forward again, pressing the tips of her fingers together. "The child would most likely be completely fae."

I opened my mouth, closed it, and then tried again. "How is that even possible? I'm human." Mostly. "And he is fae. His genetics can't cancel out mine."

"Actually, for the King or for an Ancient, they would."

I stared at her. "Does science mean nothing to you people?"

A faint smile appeared. "Only to a certain degree, Brighton. We are not human, and we are not bound by human science, biology, or genetics. We are far more superior than that." A pause. "No offense meant."

I blinked at her.

"This could explain why the pregnancy is still viable despite the trauma to your body," Luce went on, a look of curiosity creeping across her face. "A child of a King would be incredibly strong, even at this stage and inside a human incubator."

"Human incubator?" I repeated. "Can you please never refer to me as that again?"

"Sorry." She dipped her chin. "I know you are more than that. Sometimes my mind is far too…clinical for the comfort of others."

"Really?" I said dryly.

Seeming to miss my sarcasm, she nodded. "The King being the father lessens some of my concerns over what risks you'll face. I would even be willing to suggest that the pregnancy might continue to be viable."

Viable.

I was beginning to dislike that word. I looked down, realizing I was still wearing the fluffy white robe. "What…? I mean, will this pregnancy be different from a normal one?"

Luce appeared to think that over. "It's hard to say. Not many Ancients have impregnated a human before. But I can tell you what a pregnancy for a fae is like."

Unsure if I really wanted to know, I nodded anyway.

"Pregnancy terms are about the same as humans. Nine months. Not many fae are born prematurely without there being a physical cause, like an injury," she explained. "Most fae only experience sickness during the first two or so months."

The vomiting spells were suddenly brought to a whole new light. I'd thought it had been the trauma and my stomach adjusting to food.

"The threat of miscarriage also usually only exists in the first two to three months," she went on. "We are extremely lucky compared to human women in that sense."

Yes, they were.

"The progression of the fetus is relatively the same as it is for a human." Luce loosely clasped her hands together. "Come to think of it, our pregnancies are rather uneventful compared to humans'. I imagine yours will be too."

I slowly became unaware that my hand was pressed to my lower stomach. I hadn't realized that I'd even placed it there. My stomach felt flat—flatter than it had ever been.

Luce studied me like I was some strange creature she'd never come into contact with before. "You're handling the news well."

"I am?" A brittle laugh parted my lips. "I think it's because none of this seems real, and I… after what I've gone through? I don't know. I don't think I've truly processed any of this." My gaze shifted to the closed door. "It's not like there's anything I can do about it."

"There are options, Brighton."

My head jerked back to her.

"The same ones available to human women," she added quietly.

Shock flickered through me. Not because of what she was suggesting. I was relieved to hear that fae women had a choice, but I was stunned that she would even bring it up, considering who the father was.

But then I thought of how her face had paled when she first asked if the King could be the father. "What will happen if the King doesn't take a Queen?"

The only visible reaction was the tension around Luce's mouth. "He would be dethroned, and since he's ascended to the throne already, his brother would not be able to take it. We would be without a King."

"And the entire Court would fail—would become vulnerable to the Winter fae," I said.

Luce inhaled sharply through her nose and then nodded. "It would be very…catastrophic for all if that were to happen."

Tatiana hadn't lied.

Then again, I hadn't thought she had.

"Is that why you're telling me I have options?" I asked, knowing that Luce had no idea that Caden had already ended his engagement with Tatiana. "Because the child and I might get in the way of Caden marrying a fae?"

Her eyes widened slightly. "I'm letting you know you have options because, as a healer that is my duty. What I personally feel has no bearing on what you decide to do."

I believed her. Luce seemed too, as she said, clinical "But do you think it will get in the way?"

"What I think is not a part of my duty, Brighton."

"But what is happening could impact your future," I persisted.

She looked away, lips pressing into a flat line. She was quiet for so long that I didn't think she was going to answer. "I believe that our King knows how important it is to the entire Court. He will not fail us."

My heart did a weird thing. It swelled because even knowing how important his duty was, the King had chosen *me*. Then it sank all the way to the pit of my stomach because he was going to fail them.

Her gaze slid back to mine. "Tatiana was here before I arrived. I imagine she has become more than aware of the King's feelings for you. I do not believe he has spent more than a handful of minutes with her. I also imagine it was she who filled you in on what would happen if the King doesn't choose a Queen."

Seeing no point in lying, I nodded.

"Did she tell you that while some fae choose to be monogamous, we are accepting of relationships which do not start with one person and end with a second. Especially for someone like our King, whose duties may not align with his heart."

"She did, but…" My mind was all over the place. "But you're suggesting that Caden could marry a fae while keeping me and…and our child in the picture?"

"Yes. However, he would also need to provide an heir," she said. Before I could question that, she added, "I'm sure your child with him will be a full-blooded fae, but only a child between the King and Queen would be recognized as a Prince or Princess."

"This is some medieval bullshit nonsense," I told her.

She lifted her hands helplessly. "Be that as it may, would that kind of arrangement be suitable to you?"

"Basically, being a mistress with a child that wouldn't be recognized—"

"I am sure your son or daughter would be welcomed warmly and would be loved and taken care of," she interceded. "We are not *that* medieval."

Never in my life did I think to even answer a question like this. "No," I said, and it rang true. "It's not like I think unorthodox relationships are wrong. I couldn't care less. It's just not something I could do. I couldn't even try."

Luce opened her mouth and then closed it. Several moments passed. "You don't have to decide anything right now."

"But I do." I closed my eyes briefly. "I mean, I already have. I will keep the b-baby." I rose swiftly on unsteady legs, causing Luce's gaze to turn wary. "I'm pro-choice and pro-mind your-own-business. But I can't do that."

And I couldn't.

I looked down at the fluffy robe as a knot of raw emotion choked me. I was pregnant. This was my child. This was Caden's child. *Our* child. And he or she would be the only thing I would have of Caden. A small, beautiful piece of him. Proof that our love for one another was real, even if we hadn't the chance to explore it.

Because I could not risk the world.

Not even for love.

Chapter 2

Luce watched me as if she expected me to topple over at any second, which was possible. As I started to pace in front of the couch, I felt as if each step were as uncertain as a child learning to walk.

Something that I would have to help this child learn.

Oh God.

I would need to teach the child how to eat, brush their teeth, sit up, and—

"So, what are you going to do then?" Luce asked.

That was a good question. What *was* I going to do? Who could I even ask? I had very few friends, and none of them had any baby-making experience. But I knew I couldn't stay. Leaving here would be hard. I'd never been anywhere before, but I would have to move. Where? No clue. I felt pretty confident that the Order would approve a transfer, especially after everything that had happened. Then what? I'd be a single mother to a full-blooded fae?

A single mom who may or may not lose control of her senses?

That would be problematic.

Rubbing my brow, I continued pacing. "I don't know exactly what I'm doing, but I can't…I can't stay here."

Her brows lifted. "During your pregnancy? I imagine that the King would want you to stay with him—"

"Caden can't know." I stopped walking and lowered my hand.

Luce blinked once and then twice. "You're not planning to tell him?"

My heart thumped against my chest. "No. I can't."

"Do you think he wouldn't be receptive to news of a child? I don't know him well at all—"

"No. It's not that." Honestly, I had no idea if he would be

amenable or not. It wasn't like we'd had a chance to talk about any of this.

She frowned. "I know this is shocking news, and on top of everything else. You have to be experiencing a lot of confusion."

I was definitely feeling a decent amount of confusion, but I knew one thing for sure. Caden couldn't know. "I'm not confused about this. He can't know. You're just like a human doctor. You told me that what I say to you and what my condition is stays between us. You won't tell Caden."

"I would never betray a patient's trust by doing so, but I also won't betray my King," she stated, and pressure clamped down on my chest. "You want me to hide his child from him?"

The judgment and disbelief in her tone were evident. "You just said what you feel has no bearing," I reminded her. "And you're obviously feeling something right now."

"You're right." Luce rose with the grace of a trained dancer. "But if you're planning to keep this child, bring him or her into this world, you cannot expect me to keep that from the King."

"But you would keep an abortion from him?" I challenged.

"I never said that."

My mouth dropped open. "I don't think you understand what patient-doctor confidentiality means."

"And I don't think *you* understand what being the subject of a King means."

She was right. I didn't. But that didn't change anything. I needed to convince her to keep her mouth shut, and that wasn't easy when I honestly had no idea what I was going to do. "Just give me a moment. I need to think."

"You need to take more than a couple of moments, Brighton."

I pinched the bridge of my nose as I raced over the possible options like I did when I mapped out the best possible routes for Order members to take when they were needed. "I don't plan to keep the child from him forever. I wouldn't do that," I decided, and that was true. "That wouldn't be fair to Caden or the child."

"I'm relieved to hear that." She crossed her arms. "But that's very contrary to stating that he cannot know."

"He just can't know right now."

"Brighton—"

"You don't understand, Luce. He can't know right now. Okay? I will tell him, but not now."

"When will you?"

"When the time is right."

Luce stared back at me, and then her gaze lowered as she nodded. "All right."

Instinct flared. I knew she was lying. Everything in me said so. She may not go straight to Caden, but she would whenever I passed whatever time limit she set. I was angry that there was really no confidentiality here, but I also understood that I had no grasp of what it meant to have a King or to be fae. Human norms couldn't be expected. I still needed to stop her, and I only knew of one way.

"He's already ended his engagement," I told her.

"What?" Her gaze sharpened.

"He already ended his betrothal to Tatiana." I sat down, suddenly so very tired. "He…he chose me. Only me." My voice cracked as I scrubbed my palms down my face. "He's already made his choice."

Luce stumbled back a step and then plopped into the chair. Any other time, I would've laughed at seeing a fae being so ungraceful, but there was nothing funny here. She understood what I was saying.

"Tatiana told me. That was why she came here. She didn't come out of jealousy. At least it didn't appear that way to me. She was even open to me being a part of his life so long as he married a fae—any fae." Tears blurred my eyes. "No one else knows. Caden wasn't going to announce it until after Tatiana had left."

Her lips parted.

"I knew then that I…I couldn't let him do this. I love him—" I sucked in a sharp, burning breath. "I want him. I want to be his only choice. But I can't be the reason the entire world goes to hell."

Luce said nothing.

"The moment what Tatiana said sank in, I knew I had to…I don't know, make him think that I didn't want to be with him or something. I knew that I needed to leave." I brushed a fat tear off my cheek. "Having his child can't change that. It can't, Luce. And I really don't think him learning that he's about to become a father is going to push him in the right direction."

She remained silent.

I took another breath that went nowhere. "So, once he c-chooses his Queen and is married, then I can tell him about the child. I swear I will. Because, like I said, it wouldn't be fair to the child or to him." My heart felt like it was cracking and splintering. "I didn't want to say anything, but you have to understand why he can't know right now.

Please tell me you understand."

Luce stared at me.

Seconds ticked away, and I started to worry. I sat back. "Are you…are you okay?"

Finally, she moved—well, she blinked, but that was definitely better than sitting there and staring at me. Then she spoke in a voice barely above a whisper. "You're his *mortuus*."

My heart skipped a beat. I was Caden's *mortuus*. His heart, his everything, and his greatest weakness. Through me, all manner of things could be done to Caden. Aric had only realized what I was when he figured out that Caden had given me the Summer Kiss. "Why would you say that?"

"It's the only reason he would be willing to forsake his entire Court." Luce lifted a trembling hand, smoothing down hair that was already pin-straight. "That goes beyond love, beyond what most of us can even fathom." Awe filled her pale eyes. "It's a connection of two souls and two hearts. It's rare for any fae to find their *mortuus*, but to do so with a human? I…" She trailed off and then gave herself a little shake. The shock cleared from her face. "No one can know what you are to him. That kind of information is far too dangerous. You're safe here, but if it were to get out—"

"I know." Aric could've told Neal, who was still somewhere out there. And if someone from the Summer Court was aiding him, he could've told them. Aric might have told me that he told them. Perhaps I simply didn't remember. The feedings…

I pulled myself out of those thoughts.

Luce was now really staring at me, like I was some sort of new creature. "Fate can be so cruel sometimes."

"It really can," I whispered.

She lowered her gaze, falling silent.

"Am I wrong?" I asked, genuinely curious. "Am I wrong to walk away from him? To keep this from him until he marries?"

"No, you're doing the right thing." She rose and then sat beside me. A jolt of surprise went through me as she picked up my hand. "You are quite admirable, Brighton. More than most fae could ever be. You've survived what I am sure many have succumbed to—too many to count. And to put my people before your own needs, to sacrifice what you must feel for the King for people who will never know what you were willing to give up? That makes you as brave as any warrior, if not more."

Speechless, I blinked back tears. I didn't think she knew what that meant. So many people didn't. They didn't believe in my competencies or strength, that I was capable of acts of bravery. The Order didn't. Not even Miles, who ran it. It took me getting captured and surviving for even Ivy to realize that I was no longer the quiet, shy Brighton who was only good for research.

Luce squeezed my hand and said, "I won't say anything, and I will help you in whatever way I can. But, Brighton, I must be honest."

I tensed.

"I don't know if it will be enough. I fear that what is done is done."

Unease blossomed. "What do you mean?"

Her gaze locked onto mine. "I don't think you'll be able to walk away from the King. That there will be anything that you can do to cause him to choose a Queen that is not you. You're his *mortuus*, the other half of his soul, his heart. And it is very unlikely that he'll give you up. Ever."

Chapter 3

After a drawn-out battle of wills between Luce and I, she promised not to protest my leaving Hotel Good Fae as long as I agreed to stay for the remainder of the week for observation and met her at the clinic she worked at next week for an ultrasound and bloodwork. Since it was Monday, that meant five days before I could go home. Five days where I would be in the same building with the man I loved but couldn't have.

I wasn't exactly happy, but I relented. My body had been through a lot. So had my mind, and with the latest development, I needed to be somewhere Luce could easily check in on me.

Relief that she was going to stay quiet overshadowed the irritation of being stuck here. But what she'd said sat heavily on my chest as I pulled on a pair of loose sweats and a shirt Ivy had left for me.

Could Luce be right? Caden would never let me go?

My hands shook as I pulled my hair back into a ponytail. Part of me was thrilled to hear that Luce believed Caden felt that strongly for me. That he wouldn't let me push him away. That was the incredibly selfish part of me that was doing jumping jacks at the prospect of Caden fighting for me. For us. The other half was terrified over what was at stake.

Stopping in the middle of the room, I looked down. *I'm pregnant.* A wave of shivers skittered over my skin. Hands still trembling, I reached down and lifted my shirt. I tried to see past the way my stomach caved in and the old, pale scars left behind from Aric's first attack as well as the fresher, angry red cuts that covered nearly every inch of my midsection. There was a…a baby in there, right now, *growing*. My child.

Our child.

A wealth of emotions rose, so many that I could barely decipher the unexpected excitement from all the fear of the unknown and what needed to be done.

If things were different, I would still be scared out of my mind. I never really thought hard about having children. I'd had to take care of my mom, and then there had been my need for revenge. There hadn't been any serious relationships in the last several years. It just hadn't been something I thought about. So, I would still be afraid. I'd be wondering if I was capable of caring for a baby. I would still have no idea if I'd be a good mother. But that burst of excitement I'd felt a few seconds before wouldn't have been squashed by all the fear. It would continue to grow, and maybe some of that trepidation would lessen over time. Instead of thinking about how I was going to make Caden understand that he had to be with someone else, I would be obsessing over how to break the news. I wouldn't be trying to figure out how to leave, or where I could go. I would be worrying about normal things like how Caden would take the news. Would he be happy? Scared? Disappointed? If things were different, I wouldn't be spending one moment hiding the pregnancy from him.

God, that hurt. I hated the whole idea of hiding it. That wasn't who I was. But things weren't different. I was pragmatic enough to realize that these were the cards I had been dealt, and it didn't matter how unfair that hand was.

I pressed my palm against the skin of my stomach, wincing as the many slices stung. Here were the facts: I was pregnant with the King of the Summer Court's child. He loved me, and I loved him. But the fate of the actual world rested on him choosing a Queen from his people. I knew I didn't have it in me to share him, even if he married someone and eventually slept with them only out of duty. I couldn't do it. We had to put the world before ourselves, and I needed to somehow get Caden to see that. More importantly, there were more immediate, pressing concerns. Aric was dead, but Neal was still out there. He may not be as powerful or as smart as Aric, but I didn't think he'd tuck tail and run like Caden thought he would. Even if he did, there was still the issue of someone within the Summer Court working with the Winter fae. I needed to find Caden and tell him what I'd remembered. I had to do that before I even tried to talk some sense into him or find a way to get him to do the right thing.

Letting go of my shirt, I watched the soft fabric flutter back into place. It was then I realized that I was crying. I wiped at my cheeks a little too roughly. It hurt the still-healing bruises.

"Pull it together," I said, forcing myself to take a deep breath. "You need to pull it together, Bri."

And I did. It took a while, but I was able to do what I'd done while being held captive by Aric. I shut my emotions down and locked them away. Only then did I toe on a pair of flip-flops Ivy had brought and leave the room.

The hall to the elevator was blessedly empty. I stepped inside, hitting the button for the first floor. I had no idea which room Caden was staying in, but if he was up and moving about, I figured he'd either be in or near Tanner's office. If not, Tanner could probably tell me where he was. I rode the elevator down, not letting myself think of anything.

A mysterious sugary scent hit me the moment the elevator doors opened to the wide hall that split in three different directions. My stomach grumbled. There was a bakery in the cafeteria area, and they must've put out a fresh batch of something. With great effort, I forced myself to turn right instead of walking straight toward the cafeteria. I headed down the brightly lit hall. Reaching the corner—

I came face-to-face with several silvery-skinned fae. I didn't recognize any of them, but there was no mistaking the shock on their faces as they got an eyeful of me. I had no idea if they knew who I was, but it was obvious that they saw someone who looked as if they had gone toe-to-toe with a professional boxer and lost. My left eye was open, but it was more purple than pink, and the lid felt incredibly heavy. The swelling had reduced a little along my cheek, but I still looked like I had food shoved in there. The cut in my bottom lip didn't nearly look as bad as it had this morning, but it was still angry-looking.

Then there was the band of bruised skin around my neck.

One of the fae, a younger male, stared at that, and I realized I probably should've left my hair down. Or found a turtleneck. And a ski mask.

They hurried around me, saying nothing, and I trudged on, seeing the open door to Tanner's office up ahead. Above me, one of the recessed lights flickered—

Say it!

I jerked to a stop, air lodging in my throat as Aric's voice thundered in my ears and all around me. He wasn't here. I knew that. He was dead, and I wasn't in that awful place. I was safe. I'd killed him. I was—

Say it!

Clapping my hands over my ears, I tried to silence the roar of

Aric's voice, but the hallway around me darkened. The walls became damp, moldy bricks. I inhaled sharply, no longer smelling sugar but mold and decay. Blood. I staggered forward. *Chains clinked.* The weight unbearable around my neck. *I'm not there. I'm not there.* The floor shifted under my feet, and I felt my knees connect with the stone, but the pain barely registered. Aric's cold breath was against my cheek.

"Say it," he demanded, his voice echoing around me, through me. "Say please."

"No. No. No," I whispered, doubling over.

Hands touched my shoulders, and I jerked back, expecting biting pain to follow. I couldn't take anymore. I couldn't—

A voice broke through the haze of panic, a timbre that was deep and smooth. Comforting. I thought I recognized it. Whoever it was said something. A name. *Brighton.* More words. *Open your eyes.* My fingers curled into the hair above my ears. I'd heard those words before. *Open your eyes, sunshine.*

Sunshine.

That…that meant something. Meaning was attached to that. Emotions. Happiness. Sadness. Safety.

Arms shifted around me, and I felt as if I were floating for several seconds before being settled against something warm and hard. It moved. Rose up and down steadily against the side of my body as a voice whispered, "It's okay. I'm here. I've got you. I've always got you."

Fingers curled around my wrists. They were warm, not at all like Aric's. His skin was ice cold. I focused on the feeling of those fingers as they slowly pulled mine away from my ears. This wasn't Aric. He was dead. I'd killed him. I wasn't there. I knew that. My arms were lowered to my lap. I didn't want to look because I had the distinct feeling that I'd heard this all before. And once…once it hadn't been real.

What if none of this was real?

Maybe I was still in that cold, damp, and dark place, chained to the stone slab. My heart stuttered as a hoarse sound crawled up and out of me.

Those warm fingers touched my right cheek, and I started to draw back, but a gentle touch followed. "Open your eyes for me." The voice came again. "Please open your eyes so you can see me and know that it's me holding you, touching you. That you're safe. Open your eyes, sunshine."

I did, and I found myself looking into two amber jewels. Not Aric's icy eyes. Not the pale blue of a normal fae. Hot, golden eyes thickly fringed with heavy lashes. My gaze moved over the straight, proud nose and the full, expressive lips, to the sculpted jaw and blond strands of hair that rested against high, sharp cheekbones.

He cupped my cheeks, careful not to put pressure on the left side of my face as he guided my gaze back to his. "Your name is Brighton Jussier. Your friends sometimes call you Bri. Tink calls you Lite Bright," he said, those beautiful eyes searching mine. "I call you my sunshine. Do you know why? It's because I saw you smile once, and it was like the sun finally rising after centuries of nothing but night."

A deep shudder started inside me and then rippled out over my skin. With the next breath I took, the scent of summer rain and long, hot nights surrounded me.

It was like waking up from a nightmare with your eyes already open. I was stuck somewhere, and then I was here.

I knew who I was.

I knew where I was.

And I also knew who held me.

The King.

Caden.

Chapter 4

Impossibly, all thoughts fled the moment Caden smiled.

He was a stunning man, but when those full lips curved into a grin, he became breathtakingly beautiful. Everything that had led to this moment took a backseat. It was just Caden and me, his warm body against mine, and his hands ever so gently holding me.

I'm carrying his child.

I didn't know who moved first. If it was him. If it was me. Or both of us. What mattered was that our lips met. My breath snagged. He was more than aware of the cut along my lower lip, knew just the right pressure so it wouldn't cause even a second of pain. And it felt like a first kiss. In a way, it was. Our last kiss like this had been weeks ago—months ago. An eternity. Before Aric, before things I knew were important but couldn't pull from my scattered thoughts.

There was no thinking. Only sensation as I felt as if I sank into him. Caden was so incredibly careful, avoiding the numerous areas of aches and pains. He sipped from my lips in slow, drugging kisses that sent a flush of heady warmth through my body, chasing away the iciness of what had just occurred.

He tasted rich and lush as one of his hands lowered to my hip. I could feel the tension in his lax grip, as if he wanted to grab me, hold me tight but held back.

Caden and the kiss…they were both so incredibly gentle, so *loving.* A swelling motion rose in my heart, and a rawness appeared in my soul. I no longer had to fantasize about how it felt to be kissed by someone who didn't just love me but also cherished me. Because that was how I was kissed right then. It was one of the most beautiful and painful realizations.

All those scattered thoughts were piecing themselves together, reminding me of what exactly had just happened and everything that had come before.

I shouldn't be doing this—allowing this. Too much was at stake. I needed to distance myself from Caden. Not make out with him.

Caden ended the kiss before I had the common sense to do so. He pulled away just enough that his forehead rested on mine. Against my arm, I could feel his strong heart pounding. "I missed that little catch in your breath," he murmured. "I missed the taste of you on my tongue."

Heat swamped me, and I wanted to let it drown me. Then I wouldn't care about the consequences.

God.

I shouldn't have let him kiss me.

Or I shouldn't have kissed him.

My lips still tingled. Other parts of me were also doing that, and I didn't need the reminder to make what I had to do even harder. I had to put as much space between us as I could, but my body and heart had different ideas. I tipped forward, resting my unbruised cheek on his shoulder. There was no hesitation from Caden. His arms swept around me, and a sigh I couldn't hope to hide parted my lips. He held me so very carefully, mindful of all the hurts. In his arms, I felt as if nothing could reach me—not the past or the future, not even the horrible dread that I would become just like my mom, or the knowledge that I had to walk away from Caden. I felt cherished and protected. Safe.

Caden drew a hand over my head, down the loose ponytail, and then over the line of my spine. The steady sweep of his hand was soothing. I didn't know how much time passed as I soaked up his warmth, his closeness, but then he spoke. "I just missed you, Brighton."

My heart squeezed as if a hand reached inside and gripped it, and all that warmth from before was chased away by cold, harsh reality.

Caden lifted his head then, his gaze coasting over my features as if they were flawless. He smiled again, but I realized it didn't quite reach his eyes. A wealth of concern rested there, and I hated seeing that. "How are you feeling now?"

I dragged my gaze from his, focusing on the patch of golden skin above the collar of his black shirt. "I feel okay."

"Truly?"

I nodded, having a feeling that he knew better.

"I have a lot of questions."

Not exactly surprising.

"Starting with the most important one," he continued. "What are you doing out of bed?"

I blinked. That was the most important thing? He'd found me in a hallway, having what was definitely a hallucination, and he was asking why I was out of bed? I started to move, reminding myself that we definitely needed space between us, but the hand at my back held me in place.

I didn't fight him. I could've, and I believed if I pushed, he'd let go, but I didn't. *Just a little longer*, I told myself. "I was looking for you," I admitted.

"Flattered," he murmured, smoothing down the wisps of my hair with his other hand. "But you should be resting and taking it easy. Neither of those two things includes roaming around the hotel."

"I wasn't roaming around." I looked up at him. "And I feel fine."

Caden stared at me.

I sighed. "I mean, I physically feel okay."

He sat back a little, and I realized we were in one of the meeting rooms near Tanner's office, sitting on a couch. Well, he was sitting on the couch. I was sitting on him, my legs resting on the cushion next to us. "You want to tell me what happened out there?"

Not really, but he'd seen me worse than this. When he found me in that underground chamber, I had been much harder to reach. "I don't know what happened. I was coming down to tell you something, and one of the ceiling lights flickered." My nose scrunched as I looked away again, focusing on a bouquet of purplish-pink irises. "Actually, I'm not even sure if the light flickered or not."

"They did in Tanner's office. A power surge, I believe," he said.

Knowing I hadn't hallucinated that part brought forth a small measure of relief. "After I saw the light, I…"

"What?" he asked softly.

My cheeks heated. "I heard Aric's voice." Aware that the movement of his hand had halted at the mention of the Winter fae, I forced myself to keep talking. "I knew he wasn't here, but it was like being sucked into this…this hallucination. I don't know if the light triggered it or what. With Mom, I don't think there was anything in particular that caused her to lose the sense of who she was. But I couldn't pull myself out of it. And I…I knew who I was." A shiver worked its way through me. "Mom always did, but it was like I didn't know where I was or what was real. I can't…" I exhaled roughly as I gave a little shake of my head. "It wasn't the first time I'd heard his voice or hallucinated. When I was there, I thought I saw a lot of things. And with Mom, it wasn't as bad when she first came back. But it steadily got worse."

Caden's hand started moving again. "I know you're aware of this. Too many feedings can fracture a human's mind. It doesn't take much."

I did know that. Even if I hadn't seen it firsthand with my mom, I could see it every day on the streets of New Orleans. Humans who stumbled around mindlessly, some easily mistaken for addicts while others became uncontrollable, violent creatures. It also happened when a fae bent human minds to their will too often.

"I know you're afraid that you're going to become your mom, but you're stronger than that."

"Mom was the strongest woman I knew."

"I don't know that, but you're different. You're not entirely human," Caden said quietly. Slowly, my gaze lifted to his. The Summer Kiss. "You're going to heal from this. All the bruises and the cuts will heal. Your mind will heal. You just need time. And you have time."

God, I wanted to latch on to that and believe him, but I wasn't sure if he was telling me that so I'd have hope, or if he was being truthful. But I really didn't have time. There were important things to deal with.

Namely one that would be arriving in roughly seven months—give or take a week.

Pressure settled on my shoulders, and I had to change the subject. If not, I was likely to blurt out everything.

"What is it?" he asked, curling his fingers around my chin. He guided my gaze back to his.

My heart tripped over itself. "What do you mean?"

"Something is bothering you," he said. "Something that's not about what just happened. What are you not telling me?"

Panic flared in the pit of my stomach as my throat dried, and it became difficult to swallow.

"You're scared. That, I understand." His thumb swept over the curve of my chin. "But there's sadness there too. I can feel it drenching your skin. You've been through a lot. I know, but this is different. You weren't like this when I left you earlier or any other time."

I froze. He couldn't know. Caden could sense emotions, which meant hiding anything from him was difficult, but he wasn't a mind reader. There was no way.

My mind rapidly searched for an explanation. Luckily, I remembered why I'd set out in search of him. If what Aric claimed was true, that would give me a reason to be sad. I latched on to that and ran with it. "It's what I came down to tell you. I remembered—"

A soft knock on the door interrupted me, followed by Tanner's voice. "My King? Is everything all right?"

Caden's gaze didn't leave me as he all but growled, "Everything's fine. I'll be in to see you when I can."

"Wait!" I shouted, scrambling out of Caden's lap. He frowned, but I ignored that and the flare of pain that shot through my body.

"I'm…I'm waiting," came Tanner's tentative response through the door.

"We're not done talking," Caden told me.

"This involves him." And it did. Also, I seriously doubted that Caden would pursue his earlier questioning while Tanner was present. The older fae was also the perfect buffer. "Please come in."

The door didn't open. Confused, I looked at Caden, who sighed. "It's okay," he announced, draping an arm along the back of the couch. "You may come in, Tanner."

My brows lifted. "Really?"

He winked. "I'm the King."

"Whatever," I muttered as the door opened.

Tanner entered, dressed as if he were about to go out for a round of golf. Beige, pressed trousers and a light blue polo shirt, wrinkle-free. All he was missing was a glove. He couldn't look more…human. The silvery hair at his temples was spreading, proof that he didn't feed from humans. Sometimes I wondered if my mom had developed a bit of a crush on Tanner, one that had been reciprocated. Mom liked him, so I trusted Tanner.

He wasn't alone.

A dark-haired fae followed him in. Faye's silvery skin was darker than Tanner's, often reminding me of a stunning pewter shade. While Faye had the most impressive resting bitch face I'd ever seen, and I often wasn't sure if she actually liked me, she had a no-nonsense mentality, and I trusted her. She, like Kalen, another fae, were warriors. They didn't feed on humans, so they could be killed a lot easier than those who did, but they were still faster and stronger than any human could ever hope to be.

Faye's cousin Benji was one of the missing younglings, and I suspected that he wouldn't be returning to the hotel. There was a good chance that he, like the others, had somehow gotten ahold of Devil's Breath, a liquor laced with a drug derived from the *borrachero* tree. It turned humans into virtual zombies, and the fae into evil creatures controlled by the Winter fae.

"We're sorry to interrupt," Tanner said, clasping his hands behind him as he glanced over at me. "We were just worried."

"We heard you shout in the hall," Faye explained.

Well, that explained how Caden had found me. "I'm fine."

Faye lifted a dark brow. "You don't look fine."

I couldn't be offended by Faye's bluntness. "I feel better than I look."

"I would hope," Tanner murmured.

Faye walked to where I stood, her gaze coasting over my face. My muscles stiffened as I forced myself not to flinch or take a step back. It had nothing to do with Faye, but with the fact that Aric had been really good at teaching me to be wary of anyone getting too close. Oddly aware of the tension radiating off Caden, I held myself still as she placed a hand on my shoulder. "I heard that it was you who killed Aric."

"It was."

Her eyes glimmered. "The next time I need backup, I know who to call."

Pride swept through me like golden fire. Out of everyone, Faye never doubted my ability to fight and defend myself, even though she saw my thirst for revenge as a risk. She hadn't just seen me as the *Willow* to the *Buffy*, something that had taken a while for Ivy to recognize.

"I'm not sure how I feel about that," Caden said.

"It's a good thing you don't have a say in what I do," I retorted.

Tanner's eyes widened while the glimmer in Faye's deepened.

"But I do have a say in what she does," Caden remarked.

I shot him a look, to which he simply grinned. Then I remembered what Caden had told me. Ivy and Faye had helped to change my bandages while I was unconscious. "Thank you for helping to take care of me."

She inclined her head. "You would do the same for me, would you not?"

"Of course."

"Because that's what friends do for one another, even human and fae friends," she said, and a hint of a smile pulled at her lips when I rolled my eyes. "More importantly, that's what warriors do for one another."

Warriors.

She was talking about *me*.

Twice in one day, someone had referred to me as a warrior. I liked that. A lot.

Tanner replaced Faye and took my hands in his. "I am relieved to see you here. We didn't lose hope that you would be returned, but that hope didn't lessen our fears. After what happened to you and…and Merle, I couldn't…" He trailed off, lips tightening in a grimace as he cleared his throat.

A ball formed in the back of my throat as I squeezed his hands. "I know."

His pale eyes searched mine. "I am relieved to see you up and moving about, but are you sure you're ready for that?"

"You know," Caden began as Tanner let go of my hands, "I was saying just the same thing to her."

"I'm ready. Besides, I think getting up and moving around will help with the whole healing thing. Anyway," I cut in before Caden could reply. "I hope I didn't interrupt your meeting,"

Tanner appeared as if he wished to say that I had, but he seemed to know better than to say that in front of Caden. "Not at all." His lie was so smooth, it brought a faint smile to my face. I knew that Tanner liked me—well, liked me when I wasn't calling Caden names. But I also suspected that he would not be pleased to learn that there was a relationship between Caden and me. Then again, I imagined he already knew that something was going on. "We were discussing a few important details—"

"That can easily be discussed later," Caden interjected. I had a feeling it was about Caden's impending engagement. I doubted that Tanner knew it had been canceled.

The male fae nodded. "Of course."

"I'm actually glad you guys came by," I said, moving so I sat on the chair across from a square ottoman. Caden's head tilted to the side as he watched me. "I remembered something that Aric said—something I think you all need to know."

Tanner sat in the other chair, and Faye moved to stand behind him. "What is it?"

"I wish I'd remembered this sooner," I said, almost apologetically. "But things have been…" *Kind of a mess in my head?* I didn't say that.

"It's okay. I understand," Caden said. "They understand."

I lowered my gaze and took a deep, steady breath, clearing my thoughts. "Aric said that someone within the Summer Court has been helping him."

Tanner went stiff while Faye became alert, but it was Caden's reaction that I saw the most. He'd gone impossibly still, his chest barely rising as his jaw became as hard as granite. The air above his head seemed to ripple, reminding me of how flames distorted the air. My breath caught as the faintest outline of a…of a crown began to appear on his head.

"Go on," he said, his voice deceptively level.

My heart thrummed as I stared at him. I'd only see the flaming, burnt crown and sword once before. Both seemed to have appeared out of thin air, and then disappeared again into it. The near presence was both fascinating and unsettling.

I swallowed. "He said that it was a member of the Summer Court who wished to see the return of Queen Morgana," I told them. "I think…I think he went to meet with this fae while he had me."

"Impossible," breathed Tanner. "No Summer fae would ever want such an atrocity as she to breach this world."

"Did he ever say how he planned to do so?" Caden asked.

I remembered, and I wasn't sure if telling him would cause that crown to make a complete appearance. "He said that it was unlikely for you to complete the prophecy, but he believed he could force you to open the gates. Is that possible? Can you open the gates without the prophecy?"

A muscle ticked in Caden's jaw. "I can."

That seemed to be news to both Tanner and Faye. "How?" she asked.

"If properly motivated, I could open a gateway," Caden said, the air settling above his head as his gaze held mine.

"You mean you could simply open one?" Faye asked. "Like turn a doorknob and…bam, it's open?"

My heart started pounding as flickers of memories surged. Aric had been searching for the King's *mortuus*, believing that he could use the person to force the King to open the gateway. It wasn't until he figured out that I'd been given the Summer Kiss that he realized I was the *mortuus*.

"Yes," Caden answered. "Obviously, that is information not widely known, and it needs to stay that way."

"Obviously," Tanner sputtered. "Especially with the Order. They would view you as a threat—"

"And that would be the last thing they ever viewed if so." Caden snarled, and a shiver of goosebumps spread across my flesh. His golden eyes burned. "It's not something I would do."

Unless.

That one word wasn't spoken, but I knew it hung in the silence between us.

And that was the moment I knew Caden's reaction had more to do with what Aric could've shared with this Summer fae. Aric could've told the fae traitor that I was the King's *mortuus*. His greatest weakness that could be used to control him.

"You can't stay here," Caden said. "You will stay with me."

My mouth dropped open in surprise. Partly because I hadn't thought he'd say something like that in front of Tanner and Faye, and also because he thought he could just state that and I'd go along with it.

"I'm not planning to stay here forever," I told him. "Luce said I just need to stay the rest of the week, and then I can go home."

"I don't want you to live here. I want you at my place where I can make sure you're safe. If you don't want to go to my place, I'll take you to yours. Luce will just have to deal with that."

A tumbling motion swept through my stomach. Caden and I staying together couldn't happen. I obviously didn't have the willpower necessary to keep from kissing him within five seconds of seeing him. There was no way I could do what I needed to do if he was living with me. No way at all.

Caden's eyes narrowed.

I squared my shoulders as I lifted my chin. "I don't recall asking you to stay with me or giving you permission."

"I don't recall needing either of those things."

"Are you serious?" I demanded, rising to my feet. "Of course, you need my permission to stay at my house."

He glared up at me. "Under normal circumstances, yes. But when it's to keep you out of harm's way, I don't."

"Yeah, that's not some unspoken law or something. And even if it were, I don't need to follow it. I'm not fae. You're not my King."

"Um," Faye murmured, shifting from one foot to the other uncomfortably.

"I know exactly what I am to you." Caden rose to his full height, but he didn't step toward me. I gaped at him. "This isn't up for discussion."

"That we can agree on, because you're not staying with me."

His smile was slow, predatory. "Then you're staying with me."

"No, I'm not!" I shouted. "I'm staying here until I can go home at the end of the week and sleep in my own bed—"

"I like where this is heading," he cut in.

Tanner made a choking sound.

I stepped forward. "By myself. I'm going home at the end of the week. By myself."

He quirked a brow. "We'll see."

Anger flashed through me hotly. "We won't see crap. You're not--"

"Okay. Let's all take a breather." Tanner had stood, holding up his hands. "No matter where Brighton decides to go at the end of the week, I am sure that she is not in any danger here. Aric is dead, and if what he said was true, which is unlikely, no Summer fae would seek to harm her, especially not here."

"I will rip the skin from any fae who even has the smallest inkling of looking at her in a way I do not like," Caden bit out.

My eyes widened. "That's a bit excessive."

Caden didn't take his gaze from me. "That's your opinion."

My hands curled into fists. "That's a mentally healthy opinion."

"You know damn well that it's not excessive," he all but growled.

"If you're worried about Brighton's safety, I'm sure that Ivy or even Faye would be willing to stay with her after she leaves. I will also make sure she's watched while here," Tanner tried again, and Faye nodded while I bristled at the idea of being under surveillance, even if necessary.

"I will make sure she is safe here," Caden replied.

Tanner appeared beyond flustered. "I mean this with all due respect, my King, I know that Brighton is important to you, but you must think about how this will look to Tatiana and her brother."

Caden's head snapped in his direction. "Do I appear as if I remotely care how it looks?"

The breath I took was as sharp as the one I knew Tanner inhaled. "You should care," I told him, and I had no idea how he didn't crack his neck with how fast he turned those furious eyes on me.

I had a feeling that whatever was about to come out of his mouth would be tantamount to me taking out an ad announcing that I was his *mortuus*.

Thank God that Faye spoke when she did. "Not to interrupt this very awkward conversation, but a Summer fae wanting the Queen to enter the human world? Do you really think one of our own would be working with Aric? With the Winter fae?"

"As if it hasn't happened before," Caden snapped. "Let's not forget that Aric was one of my closest confidants. He was my Knight. So, it's not just possible, it's extremely likely."

Chapter 5

I hadn't believed that Aric had lied, but knowing that Caden saw it as highly likely was like watching a pall of death settle over the normally warm hotel.

Tanner was in shock. I couldn't blame him. Faye looked as if she wanted to start a Fae Inquisition, and Caden looked like…

Well, I was doing my best not to see what he looked like by studiously ignoring him. Wasn't exactly doing much since I didn't need to see him to know that he was mad. His fury was in every clipped response and the tension that bled from him. I didn't know what he was angrier about—that someone in his own Court had betrayed him, or that I had pushed back on the idea of him staying with me.

There was no way I could allow that to happen.

I kept trying to leave while Tanner and Faye discussed who the traitor could be. Still, every time I moved an inch, either Faye would ask if there was anything else I could remember, or Caden sent me a look that froze me in my tracks.

Which caused my irritation to skyrocket to uncharted territories. I would've loved for Caden to stay with me. For him to be there with me. But that was beside the point. Even if things were hunky-dory between us, I wouldn't be cool with his high-handed attitude. I had a say in this. The final say. And he needed to get that through his thick, albeit sexy, skull.

Finally, after it was agreed that Kalen, another fae, and Ren and Ivy would be advised about the potential traitor in our midst, Tanner and Faye headed for the door. It had also been decided that it would be best to keep the knowledge of Caden's ability to open the gateway limited to those in the room. As Tanner had said, there was no need to cause undue distrust and weaken the fledgling bond between the Summer fae and the Order…if one could call the sliver of a thread brought about by an agreement to work together a bond.

I rose, my gaze fixed on the door as if it were a lifeline. It was far past time to act like the entire future of the human and fae race, of our child, depended on us—or me—making the right choice. *Our child.* Those words caused my heart to start pounding. I made it about two steps.

"Brighton."

A tiny, childish part of me wanted to pretend as if I hadn't heard him. I was a lot of things, but a coward wasn't one of them. I stopped.

Okay. Maybe I was a little bit cowardly, because I didn't face him. I could feel him though. He couldn't be standing more than a few feet behind me.

"Talk to me."

"About what?"

"Don't pretend that you don't know." He was closer now. I could practically feel his heat against my back, and it took everything in me not to turn around and throw my arms around him. To revel in that warmth and comfort once more.

I stayed where I was. "Maybe I just don't want to talk about what I know you want to discuss."

"And maybe I don't want to stand here and talk to the back of your head, but that's what I'm doing."

"You stopped me," I pointed out.

There was a beat of silence. "What is going on, Brighton?"

Sighing, I faced him because he didn't deserve to talk to my haphazard ponytail. Even though I'd been sitting in the same room with him, had been in his lap and had been kissing him just a bit ago, I still felt a little breathless when I met his gaze. There was such openness in his striking features, not at all like when I'd first gotten to know him.

"Why are you so resistant to coming home with me or staying with you?" he asked. "You know damn well it's necessary. If Aric told anyone that you're my *mortuus*, you're in danger."

My chest hollowed. I didn't want to be in danger. Not after what I'd gone through, but it wasn't like my life hadn't been risky before. As a member of the Order, even one that wasn't expected to patrol like the other members, I still had a target on my back, as history had proven. "We really don't know if Aric told this Summer fae traitor anything. It wasn't like he lived long after realizing what I was."

"But it's also not like you killed him the moment after he realized what you meant to me, right?" he challenged.

I hadn't. "All that means is that we don't know."

"And that is why we need to be extra cautious. I will not allow harm to come to you. Not again." His chin dipped as those fiery eyes met mine. "Never again."

His words brought forth too much pleasure. "I can protect myself, Caden."

"Didn't say you couldn't, but why should you have to do that by yourself?"

I folded my arms over my chest, mainly to stop myself from looping them around his neck. "Because I always have."

He took a small, measured step forward. "But things are different. You have me now. You have all of me."

It felt like a knife being shoved straight into my heart. His words shouldn't make me feel that way. They should bring me nothing but happiness.

This isn't fair.

It really wasn't, but that didn't change reality. "I don't want you to protect me," I forced out, each word stinging and scraping at me. "I don't want you at my house. I don't—I don't want you."

His brows lifted. That was the only response he showed.

I drew in a shallow, burning breath. "Thank you for everything you've done for me, but I can't… I can't do this with you. I care about you, but I…I don't want to be with you."

"You don't?" His tone was flat.

Another sharp, piercing stab to the chest as I said, "I don't love you."

"Is that so?"

I blinked at the response, unsure how to proceed. I didn't know how he'd react. Maybe argue? Get mad? Sad? The deadpanned replies threw me off. Would it be this easy? If so, did he even really love me?

It doesn't matter.

It did, though.

Confused and irritated with myself, I took a step back. "I'm sorry."

His head tilted slightly. "For what?"

"Everything," I whispered.

Caden's jaw tightened. "Are you done now?"

"Done what?"

"Done lying?"

I jolted. "I'm not lying."

"Bullshit," he said, and I tensed. "I don't know what's going on, but I know there's something. You're not telling me something."

Ice drenched my skin. "I'm telling you how I really feel—"

"And I'm telling you that you don't even believe the words coming out of your mouth. Neither do I. What you're saying is not what you want."

"It—"

"It's not the truth," he continued, the fire in his eyes flaming. "I *know* it's not."

I snapped my mouth shut as the walls around me seemed to press in. Was it possible that what he sensed of my emotions could betray me that much? I wasn't sure, especially since I could barely make sense of everything that I was feeling.

Turning into the coward I didn't think I was, I said, "I can't do this right now. I'm really tired and just want to go lay down."

Caden appeared as if he wished to continue, but after a moment, he said, "This conversation isn't over, Brighton."

How I wished that it wasn't. "But it is," I whispered, and then I walked out of the room, my heart in tatters.

* * * *

I'd gone straight to my room and climbed into bed, curling onto my side and squeezing my eyes shut against the flood of tears that threatened to burst free.

I hurt. My heart hurt. And I couldn't think about what I'd just done and how incredibly wrong it'd felt. I forced myself to sleep, thinking that would be better than lying awake and feeling what I did now. So I slept the day and night away. I woke in the morning to find a covered plate of scrambled eggs and toast sitting in the chair Caden had occupied. I'd devoured the food by the time Luce showed to check on me. She was pleased and a bit surprised by how quickly my injuries were healing. I'd asked about the food, thinking she'd had it sent up, but she hadn't. I tried not to think of who had while I asked if it was possible for Luce to pick me up some prenatal vitamins. Already ahead of me, she pulled a small bottle from the pocket of her white lab coat. According to Luce, a pregnant fae didn't need the extra vitamins, but considering that I was human, and given the lack of nutrition I'd experienced in the early weeks of pregnancy, she believed it would be wise for me to take them.

I hid them in the dresser drawer.

After, I'd slept for most of the day, waking once when Ivy came to visit and then again in the late afternoon. The first thing I looked at when I opened my eyes was the chair.

Caden wasn't sitting there, but another covered dish was.

Sitting up far more easily than I had the day before, I lifted the lid and found a warm bowl of soup that smelled of rich, flavorful herbs. There were two slices of thick, toasted bread beside it. My stomach grumbled.

Did Ivy bring this up?

Had it been Caden?

I stared at the food for what felt like a small eternity, just like I had that morning. A sense of unease mingled with the hunger, leaving me vaguely nauseous. Trepidation was acid in my veins. A fine tremor coursed through my arm as I reached for the food. I didn't realize what I was doing until I caught myself looking around the room, making sure…

Making sure it was empty.

No one was here. No one was going to hurt me. Aric was dead. I was safe.

I still hesitated.

God, I hated this—hated that I associated food with pain now. Eating was…well, it was a favorite pastime of mine. I *loved* to eat.

Cursing under my breath, I snatched up the plate. Creamy soup sloshed over the side of the bowl. I grabbed the spoon and started hauling the liquid into my mouth, not even slowing down to really enjoy it. I shoveled bread in next, chewing enough that I didn't choke. Every time thoughts of Caden, Aric, of *anything* began to creep in, I shoved them aside. By the time the bowl was empty and only crumbs remained on the plate, the unease had faded to a shadow.

I placed my hand on my stomach. I needed to get over this whole food thing. I was eating for two now.

That thought caused a half-hysterical-sounding giggle and a stunning realization. I wanted a family. A husband. A child. It wasn't something I'd ever really consciously acknowledged, and it wasn't as if I believed one needed a significant other or offspring to make a family, but that was what *I* desired. I wanted to give a child what I didn't have—a father who was alive and not just present or active in a child's life, but also *there*. I wanted to be the mother that mine couldn't be—at no fault of her own. The realization brought forth a wave of aching yearning for what I wanted so badly but could not have.

I waited until I was sure my stomach wasn't going to revolt and then I rose, leaving the room. I already knew I couldn't just sit in here like I'd done. If I did, my brain would start going down roads best not traveled. I needed to move around—do something. The faint glow of sunlight still crept under the blinds. Moving to the dresser, I rooted around until I found a cardigan. I slipped it on and then made my way to the first floor. I kept my eyes downcast as I passed fae going in and out of the cafeteria and the common areas. Reaching the glass doors, I looked up as they parted. Cool, early evening air washed over me as I stepped out into a courtyard that was so beautiful it often seemed unreal to me.

I secretly believed that this had to be how the Otherworld looked, at least at some point in time. Tall trees rose up in the deep blue sky. Vines climbed trellises, and a variety of flowers bloomed, unaffected by the chillier temperatures as they scented the air with sweet and musky undertones. Paper lanterns hung from the branches, always lit. String lights crisscrossed over the stone pathway and led to little sitting areas hidden away.

This was a favorite place of mine, and whenever I visited Hotel Good Fae and got the chance to explore the courtyard, I did.

Reaching out, I skimmed my fingers over the slick vines. No matter what I did with my own courtyard, I could never hope for it to look like this. Not even when Mom was still alive. Gardening had seemed to ground her, keeping her in this world. If Caden weren't correct about my mind being stronger due to the Summer Kiss, maybe I could seek refuge in the garden as well.

God, I hoped he was right. Glancing up at the sky, I prayed that he was. The child I carried in me needed a mother—

"Lite Bright?"

That voice. That name. Heart leaping into my throat, I spun around. "*Tink*."

Chapter 6

Standing several feet back on the pathway, the brownie was in his full-sized form. He was well over six feet tall, and even in the fading sunlight, I saw that he looked different. I'd have to be missing my eyeballs not to notice it.

His normally shockingly white hair was a dark brown.

"Your hair!"

He stood there, arms at his sides, and I knew with his vision, he could clearly see my face. "Who cares about my hair right now," he said, and then he moved.

Tink crossed the distance between us, and in a nanosecond, he swept me up. My feet left the ground as the right side of my cheek was planted to his chest. My ribs and the numerous bruises protested the embrace, but I didn't say a word as I hugged him back just as tightly.

I'd missed him so much.

Sure, he could be a handful sometimes—okay, most of the time. His short stay with me had turned into more of a permanent roommate situation, unbeknownst to me. I was constantly tripping over the numerous boxes shipped from Amazon, he almost always left some sort of mess behind, and on more than one occasion, he'd given me a minor heart attack by hiding while in brownie-sized form under the covers or in cabinets. But I'd missed him.

Slowly, he lowered me to my feet and pulled back, keeping his arms around me. His gaze searched my face in the waning light. "I didn't know."

"Tink—"

"I was lounging on the beach, drinking super fruity cocktails, getting my suntan on, and enjoying being treated like the last brownie in this world and any other. And I had no idea." His eyes glistened. "I had no idea this was being done to you."

My chest ached. "It's okay."

"No, it's not," he replied softly. "Each time I called and either Ivy or Ren or the King answered, my super-brownie senses told me something was up. But they assured me you were fine, and that the Order had you working on a special project or some shit. I should've known better. The Order hardly uses you for anything."

"Well, that's not necessarily true…"

"But Fabian told me I shouldn't worry, and he suggested that we stay longer," he continued as if I hadn't spoken. "I believed him. I wanted to believe him, even though I knew something was wrong. I was living my best life, and you were fighting for yours."

"That's not your fault." I gripped the front of his shirt. "They didn't want you to worry when there was nothing to be done."

"I get that. I do. That's the only reason I haven't killed any of them, including Fabian. And trust me," he said, voice hardening, "I am more than capable of killing each and every one of them."

I blinked. Sometimes it was easy to forget that Tink wasn't just an amusing Otherworlder able to change sizes. He was one of the most powerful Otherworld beings alive, who happened to have an addiction to Amazon Prime, *Harry Potter*, and *Twilight*.

"I could've done something. I could've looked for you. I could've found—"

"No one was able to find me. Not even the King until…until he did," I said, tugging on Tink's shirt. "You would've just been worrying and—"

"And that's what I should've been doing. You're my Lite Bright. I'm your Tink. I should've known. And I may or may not punch Ivy when I see her."

"Don't punch Ivy."

"Not even a little?"

"No."

"How about a love tap?"

A sob settled in the back of my throat as I shook my head no.

"What about when I'm tiny Tink-sized with teeny, tiny fists?"

I choked on a laugh. "Ren would still skewer you with a toothpick."

"I'd punch him first. He's had it coming since I had to unexpectedly see his junk in Ivy's kitchen."

Another laugh left me. "I've missed you," I said, face-planting against his chest.

"Of course, you did. I'm awesome." He cleared his throat. There was a pause, and I felt his lips brush the top of my head. "Fabian told me what really happened when we were about an hour out from here. I almost caused a massive pileup on the interstate."

My lips twitched.

His hands settled on my shoulders and he guided me back. "He said you killed him. Aric?"

"I did," I whispered.

"Is there anything left of his body?"

"Um, no. He sort of just disintegrated, like most Ancients."

"Not even ashes?"

"I don't think so."

"I'll ask the King."

I frowned. "Why?"

"Because I want to take a shit on his remains."

"Oh my God." I laughed again. "That is so disgusting."

"I know. It's the most disrespectful thing I can think of," he explained and then led me toward a loveseat that often reminded me of a birdcage sliced open. "Tell me, Bri. Tell me everything you can."

As we sat on the thick cushions, and the gauzy curtain draped over the chair rippled in the breeze, I told him everything I could remember. It wasn't the first time, but there was a sense that the weight was lifting, just a little this time around. It was like letting out a breath.

"The King is most likely right," Tink said after I told him about the hallucination I'd had earlier. "Your mind is stronger."

"I hope so."

"It could have nothing to do with the feedings." He was toying with my hair. Somehow, it had come out of its ponytail. "It could be that post-traumatic syndrome thing that sometimes causes people to hoard things in their houses."

I arched a brow. "You watch way too much television."

"But I could be right. You experienced some trauma. Hearing voices, reliving the events is pretty common afterwards, according to Dr. Phil."

I stared at him.

"After I saw Ren's junk, I kept seeing it. Sometimes, it would talk to me—"

"You're a mess."

He grinned at me. "Fabian told me something else."

"What?"

"He told me how the King nearly tore the city apart looking for you," he said, and every muscle in my body tensed. "Wouldn't give up on finding you. He also said that Ivy told him he's barely left your side since he found you."

I looked away. "You know that I helped him when he was wounded. He felt like he owed me—"

"Are you forgetting that I saw him kiss you like you were a snack?"

My cheeks heated. "No, I'm not forgetting that, but you know he's the King and I'm…it doesn't matter. Tell me about your hair. Please?"

Momentarily distracted, he ran his hand through his locks. It wasn't spiky but fell over his forehead. "Do you like it?"

"I …I do." The color matched his brows now, and somehow made him appear more adult. Which was weird, but the darker color suited him. In all honesty, any color fit him. Tink was gorgeous. "It's just a shock."

"I didn't recognize myself when I saw my reflection. It was strange." He lifted a shoulder. "I sort of got bored with it, you know? Fabian suggested I should color it, and since I was bored, I thought YOLO, bitches. Fabian did it for me." His voice lowered. "He didn't wear gloves. It took days for the dye to fade from his hands."

"Oh no." I grinned. "But he did a good job."

"He does a good job at everything. It's annoying, and I mean that in the best way." The smile on his face faded. "Lite Bright…"

"I'm okay. I really am. I know I don't look it, but I'm fine." I changed the subject once more. "Where's Dixon?"

"Fabian has him. Carrying him around in the sling."

I sort of wished I could see that.

"I know he loves you."

"What?" I squeaked, my gaze shooting back to his.

"He spoke to Fabian before we got here. I don't know exactly what he said, but Fabian knows his brother." Tink lightly touched my arm. "He also told Fabian what he did."

There could be several things that Caden might've told him.

"He ended his engagement."

I closed my eyes. Why did it have to be that?

"I honestly thought that when I got here, I'd find you with him. So, color me surprised when he told us you were out in the courtyard by yourself."

My eyes opened as my lips pursed. I couldn't say that I was

shocked that Caden knew exactly where I was.

"And here you are, acting like nothing's going on when the motherfucking King of the Summer Court is in love with you." He tapped my arm again. "I know you like him. You like him a lot, and you were hurt when he pushed you away."

"Things have…they've changed. I've been through a lot," I said, hating that I was using what'd happened to me as an excuse.

"Bri, you've been through a lot. But, girl, you'd already been through a lot. You're a fighter. You're a survivor," he said, and my gaze lifted to his. "What you've gone through is terrible. But I don't think it sucked out your ability to love and the ability to recognize the feeling. Or your common sense."

"My common sense?"

"Yes. Your common sense seems to have taken a vacation," he said, and my brows lifted. "You have the love and devotion of a King. Granted, he's not human, but who in their right mind would swipe left on him?"

"That's the problem, Tink. He's the King."

"So? That should fall under the pro category," he reasoned.

I stared at him. "Do you know what will happen if he doesn't choose a Queen from his people? I know you do. That's why you got all quiet and weird after you saw him kiss me. That's why you tried to get me to understand that he had reasons for pushing me away."

"You're right, but he still chose you. He chose you over his Court, over—"

"And you know what that means." I couldn't hear how he chose me. That wasn't helping. "You know what will happen."

"Is that why you're saying things are different now?"

"Why else would I say it?" I admitted, shoulders slumping.

His gaze roamed over me, and his chest rose with a heavy breath. "You love him, right?"

"That doesn't matter."

"It's the only thing that matters," he responded. "Despite what and who he is, you still fell in love with him. Is that not true?"

I wanted to be able to say no, and maybe that would be the right thing to do. I needed to get better at saying it because perhaps then I'd believe it. But I couldn't lie to Tink. "Yes," I whispered. "But you can't tell him that."

He arched a brow. "You think he doesn't already know?"

"It doesn't matter what he knows or thinks. He needs a Queen, and the last thing he or I need is for someone to confirm how I feel."

"You mean confirm what he already knows." Tink looked out over the darkened courtyard while I debated punching him, but since I'd just told him he couldn't punch Ivy, I couldn't turn around and do it to him. "I know what could happen. Sure, the Court would weaken, and they'd be without a King, but that doesn't mean fae will start dropping dead everywhere." He sat back against the thick, cream-colored cushion. "It doesn't mean that the King will become so weakened that he can't defend himself. It doesn't mean that you should both sacrifice what you deserve. Love is more important."

"You really believe that? That Caden and I being together is more important than the survival of the fae? Of the human race and our—?" I cut myself off as my stomach dropped.

His eyes shot to mine. "And what?"

"Nothing."

"Liar. What were you going to say?"

Shaking my head, I looked away. "It's nothing, Tink."

He was quiet for a moment. "What are you not telling me?"

"Why does everyone keep asking me that?" I threw up my hands in frustration. Okay. Only he and Caden had said that, but whatever.

"Maybe because there's obviously something you're not sharing." There was a pause. "I'm offended."

"Are you now?"

"Yes. I'm Tink. We're roomies. We have joint custody of Dixon."

My brows puckered. "We do not have joint custody of your cat."

"Not true. He sleeps in your bed. That means we have joint custody whether you're aware of it or not," he said. "And you're keeping something from me. You're not telling me the truth, and I've just spent weeks with everyone keeping the truth from me. I expected better from you."

My mouth dropped open as I stared at him. A trickle of guilt crept into me, which I was sure he'd intended. "That is so manipulative."

"Is it working?"

A short laugh escaped me as my gaze traveled to where my arms were folded over my stomach. I opened my mouth and then closed it. The need to confide in Tink—in anyone—hit me hard. It hadn't even been a day, and I was bursting to tell someone.

And Tink…if he was still living with me in a few months, would know. It would eventually become noticeable. I couldn't hide it from everyone. I needed someone who knew. I could confide in Ivy, but she was prone to outbursts, and there was her own messy history with Caden.

Lifting my hands, I scrubbed them down my face, covering my mouth. "If I tell you this, you have to promise me you won't say anything."

"I promise," he agreed quickly.

"I mean it, Tink. You're going to want to say something, but you can't repeat this. Not to Fabian or Ivy or even Dixon."

"What in the hell would Dixon do? He's a cat."

"I don't care." Lowering my hands, I looked at him. "You can't repeat this. If you do, I will…" I searched for the worst possible thing that could happen to Tink. "I will find a way to blacklist you from Amazon, and until then, I will throw every single one of your packages in the garbage. I will cancel your orders. I'll discontinue the internet."

His eyes widened as he pressed his hand to his chest. "That's harsh."

"I know." I held his gaze. "Do you still want to know?"

Tink tilted his head. "I can keep a secret, Bri. You have no idea how many secrets I already keep. I'm practically the keeper of secrets. You all don't even know my real name."

I frowned. "What is your real name?"

He smirked.

"Does Fabian know?"

"Nope."

"For real?"

"For reals."

I was kind of surprised that he hadn't told Fabian. There was power in knowing a fae's true name. I nibbled on my lip and then it sort of just spilled out of me. Two simple words that were incredibly life-altering. "I'm pregnant."

Tink blinked slowly. "With a baby?"

"What other thing would I be pregnant with?" I asked.

He gave a little shake of his head, and then a wide, beautiful smile broke out across his face, briefly stunning me. "Does that mean I get to be a godfather? I've always wanted to be a godfather. I can babysit. There are so many things I can show this child. I can make his or her toys come to life. Did you know that? I can teach them the wonders of *Harry Potter* and *Twilight*. Oh! And *Game of Thrones*. Well, that will probably have to come later. But think of all—" He came to a grinding halt while I gaped at him.

Tink drew back from me and then stood, lifting his hands. "I'm about to ask a potentially obvious question here. Bear with me while I collect myself."

"Yes, it's Caden's child," I stated dryly.

"You didn't bear with me!"

"Tink."

He clasped his hands together under his chin. "You are having his child?"

I nodded.

"You are carrying a baby inside you right now that has your and his DNA?"

"Yes."

Tink bent at the waist so we were at eye level with each other. "You are impregnated by him?"

"Yes. Yes, Tink. I'm pregnant. He's the father. Caden's the dad," I told him, exasperated. "The King is the father."

"Holy shit."

I snapped my mouth shut.

Tink blinked.

My heart stopped as my belly rolled all the way to the tips of my toes.

Neither of us had said that.

Tink straightened.

I looked over his shoulder.

And I saw not one, not two, but *three* fae staring at us in utter shock.

Chapter 7

It was the fair-haired Kalen who'd spoken. He looked as shocked as I felt. Standing beside him, Faye looked as if a slight breeze might knock her flat on her back. And of all people to be here, Tanner was with them.

He looked like he was seconds away from vomiting.

The five of us just stared at one another in silence while my heart pounded against my ribs. I thought I might hurl. Tanner and I could go puke together.

Tink was the first to break the silence.

"I dyed my hair," Tink announced. "Do you all like it? I think it complements my skin tone."

For the first time in, well, forever, Tanner ignored Tink. "You're pregnant," the leader of the hotel said. "By…" He seemed as if he couldn't bring himself to say it.

My throat dried. "I…"

"We heard her," Faye said, blinking as her features settled into their typical blandness. "I don't think we need her to repeat it."

This couldn't possibly be any worse.

Well, if Caden had been with them, that would have been worse.

"I knew…" Tanner paused for a rough inhale. "I knew there was something between the two of you. It was obvious even before your abduction. I thought it was a passing fancy, but the way he behaved while you were missing told me it was more."

"Told everyone it was more," Kalen muttered under his breath.

"Now I understand his reaction earlier, why he demanded to be with you—"

"Wait." I shot out of the chair. "He doesn't know."

"What?" Faye's brows lifted.

"I haven't told him. I don't plan to tell him—"

"What?" Tink echoed in a demanding tone.

Kalen pinched the bridge of his nose. "I have a feeling I'm going to regret coming out here tonight."

"What do you mean you're not planning to tell him?" Tanner asked.

"In other words, are you out of your freaking mind?" Tink cried.

"This is like one of those daytime talk shows," commented Faye.

Kalen glanced at her. "You're thinking of *Maury*?"

The female fae nodded.

"Love that show," Tink chimed in.

"He behaved that way and doesn't know you're carrying his youngling?" Tanner asked.

"I'm going to be the godfather," Tink announced.

"Thoughts and prayers for that child," Kalen said.

"I know humans have their own views on these types of matters." Tanner lifted his chin. "But we believe that the father has the same rights as a mother—"

"Okay, everyone needs to shut up for a second, stop judging me and listen," I snapped, a fine sheen of sweat dotting my brow. "I just found out today, and I am planning to tell him eventually. But not right now. None of you are going to say a word to him. For two reasons. Number one—it's none of your business."

Tanner sucked in air, looking absolutely affronted. "He is our King."

"And this is still not your business," I told him. "The second reason is because I'm trying to do the right thing, and that does not involve giving him a congratulations card at the moment."

Kalen's brow wrinkled.

"I'm about to tell you all something that I hope shines a whole new light on this situation. Caden chose me. Not his betrothed. Not any other fae. He ended his engagement with Tatiana." The stunned gasps from the three fae echoed like thunder. "I don't think he's going to pick another fae, and I'm sure as hell not into a party of three. He loves me. I love him, but I know what will happen if he doesn't choose a Queen. I know what's at stake. I assume each of you understands as well."

Tanner was slow to nod, even though he looked a little green under his silvery skin.

"So I know that no matter what I want, what he wants, it can't be." My voice warbled, and when Tink opened his mouth, I pointed my finger at him. "I do not need to hear how love is worth everything. Do you think I don't want to run in there and throw my arms around him and never let go? This isn't easy for me, but I am pregnant. I am going to have a child. And even though I have no idea how to even raise a kid, I know I don't want to bring him or her into a world that will go to hell in a handbasket. I know Caden needs to marry one of his own. I know the entire fae race and all humans depend on that. So, no. I'm not telling him anything until he's happily married. Then, I will tell him."

Breathing heavily, I willed the knot of emotion swelling in my chest to fade. It had to. "So if any of you have any hope of preventing a catastrophe from happening, then you will keep your mouths shut about this, and you will do everything in your power to make—" I tried to swallow, but the knot had crept into my throat. "Everything in your power to make sure he marries Tatiana or another fae. That's what you should be doing. But if you tell him what you overheard… I don't know what he'll do." Pressing my lips together, I shook my head as I remembered him talking about his sister Scorcha. I tried to push away the image of him brushing the knots out of a little girl's hair. I tried to forget how careful and gentle he was when he did it for me. I cleared my throat. "I have no idea what he'd do, but it won't help to make sure the right thing is done. That much I do know."

No one spoke.

Not even Tink. Not for a long time.

It was Tanner who finally did.

"You are doing the right thing," he said. At his sides, his hands were opening and closing.

Finally! Finally, someone realized that I was doing the right thing. There was no relief, though. No joy. Just a heaviness that threatened to drag me to the ground and then through it.

"It gives me no pleasure to hide anything from my King, nor does knowing what you must be going through. But the future of our Court and of this world is paramount and trumps our needs and desires," he continued. I felt myself nodding slowly. "We'll keep your confidence, Brighton."

Sitting down in the chair, all the energy went right out of me. "Thank you."

His mouth tightened.

"Neither Faye nor Kalen will repeat a word of what was overheard or discussed here," Tanner announced, and for the first time, I saw his mask of civility slip a little, revealing the deadly creature underneath as he looked to the two of them. "Do you understand me?"

Faye looked uncomfortable but she nodded. "I do."

"I was right. I regret this." Beside her, Kalen thrust a hand through his hair. "I don't like this. He's our King."

"I'm not asking if you like it." Authority bled into Tanner's tone. "None of us do. But we must do things we don't like to protect the future, no matter how distasteful we find them." His hands stilled as his gaze met mine. "And I promise you that what you're doing will not be in vain. I will do everything in my power to ensure that."

I nodded again because I felt distasteful. I felt wrung out. I felt everything and nothing as Tanner bid us goodbye. The others followed, but Kalen stopped and whispered something in Tink's ear. The brownie nodded solemnly. At any other time, I would've been curious to know what was said, but right then, I didn't have the brain capacity for it.

Tink sat beside me. "So…"

Wearily, I looked over at him.

"That was awkward."

I laughed, but it didn't feel right. "Do you think they'll keep silent?"

"I believe so."

"And you?" I whispered.

"Of course. I don't want you to throw away my packages."

I smiled at that.

He leaned in, resting his forehead against mine. "You know what I think?"

I was half afraid to ask. "What?"

"I think you'll make a good mom. After all, I'm one hell of a test run."

* * * *

I spent the following two days with Fabian and Tink as my shadows. If I wanted to go out into the courtyard, they went with me. If I stayed in my room, they kept me company by either joining me on the bed to watch bad reality television or a movie in the living room area of the suite. I didn't think I'd ever spent that much time in bed with one man before, let alone two. I knew they were there because Caden wasn't, and I had a feeling they were with me at his request. Not that I believed they didn't want to spend time with me, but it wasn't like I was great to be around. I was the living embodiment of morose.

I hadn't talked to Caden since I'd told him I didn't love him, but I woke in the middle of the night, swearing that his scent was in the room. Often, when I was in the courtyard with Fabian and Tink, a shivery wave of awareness broke out along the back of my neck and over my skin. I'd turn, fully expecting to find Caden there, looking at me in that intense way of his. But he was never there, just like when I woke in the night—the room was empty.

I couldn't make sense of how I felt. I didn't know what to think or feel. A stupid part of me had been pleased to know that Caden had possibly been the one to deliver the food or could be watching me while I was in the courtyard. The other half of me wanted to punch myself in the face.

Tanner and the others had kept their vow so far. I figured I would know if they'd told Caden about the pregnancy, but when I walked out to the courtyard with Fabian and Tink Friday evening, I saw that he was diligently working to make sure that Caden chose a Queen.

Stepping out into the courtyard, I felt as if I'd been sucker punched in the heart when I saw Caden standing to the right, under several softly glowing paper lanterns. Wearing black trousers and a white button-down shirt, with his hair loose and brushing broad shoulders, he looked as if he'd stepped off the cover of a magazine or out of some fantasy. He wasn't alone. Tanner was with him, as were several other fae, including Kalen. So was the tall and elegant, raven-haired Tatiana. Her brother, who was equally striking with his dark hair and deep, silvery hued skin, was also there.

There was a slight smile playing across Caden's face as Tatiana said something to him. She reached across the scant distance between them and touched the forearm exposed by the rolled-up sleeve of his shirt.

There was no mistaking that Caden and Tatiana would make a stunning couple found only in fairy tales and seeing them together made me painfully aware of the fact that no one in their right mind would ever believe that he'd chosen me over someone so flawless. So graceful.

The bite of jealousy took a huge chunk out of my heart even as I told myself I should be relieved. I should be happy to see him speaking with her. It wasn't like him finding another fae to marry would lessen the blow if he rekindled the arrangement with Tatiana.

Tink had taken my hand the moment we spotted them and began talking about sea turtles. Or possibly opossums. I wasn't sure. Caden appeared wholly unaware of us. The only person who seemed to know we were there was Sterling, Tatiana's brother. His gaze tracked us until I could no longer tell if he was watching.

The courtyard had lost some of its beauty that night, and I hadn't lingered long. Caden and the group of fae were gone when we went back inside, but based on the amount of activity behind the frosted glass of the common room, I had a feeling the King was in there. There was a lot of laughter, and I thought I even detected music. I'd heard that they often threw parties, sometimes for birthdays or weddings, and other times just because. Envy joined jealousy, and the moment I was in my hotel room, I managed to get Fabian and Tink to leave. I hoped they joined whatever was going on downstairs. They belonged there. I didn't. And while I knew I wouldn't be unwelcome—well, I doubted Tanner would be thrilled if I made my presence known since he was obviously working hard to reconnect Caden and Tatiana. But I also knew that I was an outsider, no matter my relationship with Tink or Prince Fabian.

Feeling older and wearier than I had in a very long time, I pulled on a sleep shirt that Ivy had retrieved from my house. It was lightweight and long, reaching my thighs. I climbed into bed, shamefully early for a Friday night, beyond thankful that tonight was my last night here.

"I got this," I reminded myself as I had every night since Monday. As I placed my hand against my belly, I repeated, "We got this."

Drifting off, I wondered why it was so easy to fall asleep now when I'd always struggled to do so before. Was it the pregnancy? I'd read once that it could make you more tired. Or was it my body healing and recovering? The bruises and the cuts had all faded. My eyes were no longer swollen, and most of the slices had become only faint pink marks. Or was it depression? It was probably all of it.

The darkness of a dreamless sleep slowly broke apart, revealing damp bricks covered by thick, ropey vines. Two torches struggled to beat back the shadows of the…tomb.

My eyes widened as my heart stuttered. Under me, the stone was like a sheet of ice. I jackknifed up, but pressure around my neck choked me. Gasping, I pressed my fingers to my throat. Cool, hard metal.

No. No. No.

I wasn't there. I wasn't in the tomb. This had to be a nightmare. Shaking, I looked down at myself, recognizing the faded image of a mound of beignets on my sleep shirt. My gaze shot to where the door to the tomb was located and saw nothing but a void of nothingness. The abyss rippled out. Thick tendrils licked over the walls and drenched the floor, rapidly swallowing the tomb and me.

Wake up. Wake up. I need to—

"Miss me?"

The sound of Aric's voice in my ear sent a bolt of fear straight through me, and a scream tore from deep within me. I twisted, hands pushing out—

My palms connected with something hard and warm. Aric was never warm. His skin was always cold, his touch painfully frigid.

"It's me. Brighton, you're okay." A deep voice scattered the darkness. "You're safe."

Caden.

I opened my eyes, wincing. A bedside lamp had been turned on, casting the room in light that was normally soft. My pounding heartbeat accelerated as I realized that the hard, warm surface under my palms was the white button-down shirt covering Caden's chest.

Scrambling back to the center of the bed, my gaze flew to Caden's face. He was right there, perched on the edge of my mattress, several strands of hair falling forward to rest against his cheek.

He didn't blink as he stared back at me. "Brighton?"

"Yes?" I whispered, disorientated.

His gaze searched mine. "Are you all right?"

"I…I think I was having a nightmare."

"You were. You screamed."

"You heard me scream?"

He nodded.

Some of the fog lifted. "How did you hear me scream?"

"I was outside your room."

I started to ask what he had been doing there, but then it struck me. "You've been keeping watch during the night?"

Caden said nothing as he tucked the strands of hair back from his face.

My heart started pounding for a wholly different reason. "Have you've been doing that every night since…?"

"Since you lied straight to my face and walked out of the room?" he finished for me. "Yes, I have."

I jolted. "I didn't lie."

One eyebrow rose as thick lashes lifted.

I decided to ignore that look. "Why are you doing that? You're the King. I am sure there are several fae you'd trust to keep watch."

"There is no one I trust enough to keep watch—"

"Besides your brother and Tink?" I interrupted.

"I trust them to a certain degree."

I thought about the sensation of awareness when I was in the courtyard as if he were there. The warring mix of emotion rose again.

"And if you have to ask why I'm the one watching over you, then I don't think I've been clear enough with you," he added.

Oh, he'd been clear, and I was desperately trying not to see the reasons. Maybe that was why the tiny piece of bitterness slipped out of me. "I'm surprised you're not busy right now with—" I managed to stop myself from finishing the sentence.

"With whom?" One side of his lips curved up. "Tatiana?"

I looked away.

"I saw you in the courtyard, Brighton. I wasn't there with Tatiana, but it seems where I go this week, Tanner finds me with Tatiana in tow."

I kept my face impressively blank. "I shouldn't have said anything. I don't even know why I did. And you shouldn't be here."

"I know what I should and should not do. Keeping you safe is something that I should be doing." His gaze lowered. "Checking out your legs at the moment would probably be one of the things I shouldn't be doing."

My legs?

I glanced down to discover that the blanket had slipped to my knees, and a whole lot of leg was visible. Flushing, I yanked the cover up. "I see knowing you shouldn't be doing something hasn't stopped you."

"You know you shouldn't lie to me, but yet you still do," he replied. "Why should you be the only one who does things they know they shouldn't?"

My grip tightened on the blanket. "For the last time, I—"

"Did I ever tell you that my mother always knew when I was lying?" he interrupted, throwing me off.

I shook my head. "No."

"She always claimed that I would look down and smile whenever I told an untruth. I didn't believe her. Who would smile when they lied?"

"Good question," I murmured.

"But then I started to pay attention, and she was right. Every time I lied, I looked down and felt my lips curving upward. It wasn't a large smile, but she was right." He grinned then as he drew a finger over the sheet, idly tracing a shape. "Of course, since I learned that she was right, I've managed to stop doing it. But she could never tell when Fabian lied. Used to irritate the hell out of me."

Unable to pretend that I was disinterested, I said, "Fabian has never struck me as the type who lies a lot."

He snorted. "Fabian lied about finishing his studying or where he was when he was supposed to be training or whatever. He lied as much as I did, but it was never anything harmful."

"Were any of your lies harmful?"

"Only one." His gaze lifted to mine. "But that was a long time after I learned to conceal a lie, and it wasn't all that long ago."

I thought about when he told me that what had happened between us hadn't been real. My stomach churned as all those terrible, sticky feelings came surging back. And now I was doing the same to him.

"My mother would be so incredibly disappointed to learn how good at lying I've become," he commented.

I dared a quick peek at him. "What happened to your mother? And father?"

"They died during the war with the Winter Court," he answered, his voice tinged with sorrow.

"I'm sorry."

"Thank you, but they died fighting for their people. I know both took great honor in that, and I take solace." He trailed off, shaking his head.

"What?"

"I shouldn't even admit this. It shows how incredibly selfish I can be, but I…I take solace in the fact that neither my father nor my mother was alive to see what became of me."

Sympathy squeezed my heart. "What became of you wasn't your fault. You were under the Queen's curse. I don't think your parents would hold what you did while under her control against you."

"They wouldn't have." His eyes met mine. "And that makes it all harder to comprehend."

"I can understand that," I whispered.

He was quiet for several moments. "You look so tired," he said. I didn't take offense. "Have you been having nightmares?"

"Tonight was the first," I admitted. "And I haven't had any more hallucinations."

"It's no surprise that you have nightmares. I have them." There was truth in his eyes when my gaze lifted to his. "Let me stay with you tonight. I know nightmares won't find either of us tonight if we're together."

My lips parted. "Caden—"

"Let me lay beside you so both of us can sleep peacefully. That's all

I want. No expectations. No conversations," he said—pleaded, really. "Let me be here for you tonight."

I knew I needed to say no. This had *bad idea* written all over it, even if all he did was lay beside me, and I honestly didn't expect him to try anything else. Sleeping together was far too intimate. It would mean too much, and it would make distancing myself from him even harder.

But Caden had nightmares too, and no matter how much I wanted to harden my heart, I couldn't. I nodded, knowing I would regret this later, then lay down on my back.

"Thank you," he whispered. Those two words entrenched themselves in my skin.

Caden toed off his shoes and without wasting a moment, turned off the light and then climbed into bed beside me. I might've stopped breathing a little. I felt him even though he didn't touch me, and when I worked up the nerve to look in his direction, I found him lying on his side facing me, eyes closed. I could make out the shape of his hand resting beside his chest, on the bed. I closed my eyes, and after several moments, I rolled onto my side. As if my hand had a mind of its own, it moved beside his, and then I fell asleep.

No more nightmares found me.

Chapter 8

My house looked like it had when I left.

Gray-and-white-checkered throw pillows were fluffed and placed at the corners of the couch. A stack of books was piled neatly on the coffee table. Several tiny stuffed mice had been collected and left by a foyer table where all the mail had been placed. A pair of sandals sat on the bottom step of the staircase leading upstairs. Above them were black and white sneakers that belonged to Tink. The kitchen was utterly spotless, which was almost impossible with Tink living here.

My gaze flickered over the living room. This was where Aric had grabbed me. He'd been waiting for me, and I'd walked right in, having no idea that he was here. I knew that if I closed my eyes, I would hear his voice.

I hear you've been looking for me.

I didn't close my eyes, but his voice was still like a whisper in my ear.

"I tried to keep things the way you had them." Ivy had moved ahead of me, her long, curly red hair pulled up in a messy topknot. "I even dusted."

"Actually, it was me who dusted," Ren said, coming down the stairs. He'd quietly gone up there when we entered, and I knew he was scoping out the rooms, making sure no one was here.

Ivy rolled her eyes. "But I was the one who gave him the supplies."

"It was a joint effort then." I ran my hand along the back of the couch. "Thanks, you guys. I had no idea what to expect when I returned."

"It was no problem at all." Ivy looked down as Dixon pranced out from the kitchen, rubbing against her legs. Bending, she scratched him behind his ear.

Ren leaned against the banister of the stairs. "You sure you're ready to be back here?"

"More than ready." I forced a smile that felt as fake as pleather.

The two of them exchanged a look, and I knew they had questions. Lots of them.

Luce had checked me over this morning, and after setting up a time for me to visit her the following weekend, she'd cleared me to leave Hotel Good Fae. I'd expected Tink to show up then, but come to find out, he was already at the house with Fabian and Dixon. It was Ivy and Ren who arrived as Luce left. All I knew was that Caden had asked them to escort me home, but I had no idea what, if anything, he'd said to them.

He'd been gone when I woke up, but that didn't change the fact that I'd gotten the deepest sleep I had in a really long time. Neither had it erased the moments at dawn when, still mostly asleep, I felt the bed shift and the soft sensation of his lips against my forehead. I told myself repeatedly that had been my imagination.

"Well, if you need anything, you know you got us," Ren said as Dixon meandered over to me, the white tip of his gray tail swishing. "And even if you don't need us, you still have us."

"We'll be making periodic patrols," Ivy said. They'd been filled in about the traitor in the Summer Court, but as discussed, they hadn't been told everything.

"Your phone is on the kitchen counter," Ivy explained while Dixon stretched up, pressing tiny paws into my legs. I picked him up, burying my face in his soft fur as Ivy said, "Oh, and by the way, Miles said to call him whenever you're ready or stop by the headquarters."

Face still planted in Dixon's fur, I nodded. "He most likely wants to see if I'm mentally stable and find out if I spilled any Order secrets."

"He didn't *exactly* suggest that, but…" Ivy trailed off.

I cracked a grin. Miles was the bluntest and most deadpan person I'd ever met. Even more so than Faye. Not one to beat around the bush, his first concern would be if I shared any of the Order's secrets.

"He should be happy to know that Aric didn't seem to care at all about the Order," I told them as Dixon purred.

"Actually, that would probably displease him," Ren commented.

I snorted at that and lifted my head, looking around the sundrenched room. "How did he respond to the news about there being someone in the Summer Court who's working with the Winter fae?"

"The same way Miles takes the news about almost everything," Ivy answered. "He raised his brows, was silent for probably a good minute, and then said something like 'there's always one rotten apple in the bunch.'"

"That sounds like him," I said dryly. "I almost wish we didn't have to tell him, but the members need to be on their toes."

"Agreed." Ren folded his arms. "It's not like every Order member has dropped their guard around the Summer fae, but they have relaxed, and that could be deadly."

And that was why the Order members needed to know.

"I just don't get how any of them could do that." Ivy shook her head, causing a thick curl to fall over one eye. "Them supporting the Queen's return is bad enough, but to aid the Winter Court when they're using stuff like Devil's Breath to destroy the younglings? It just doesn't make sense."

It really didn't. "Aric had said that whoever it was had their reasons. I don't think he said more. Or if he did, I…I don't remember it. But you're right, it doesn't make sense."

"I feel like we're missing something," Ren said. "I've been thinking about this, and I can't come up with a reason a Summer fae would want the Winter Queen to enter this world, especially since they have their bright and shiny King."

A small grin tugged at my lips.

"It's not like they're without leadership or whatever. So, the only thing that makes any sense to me is that it's someone who has a vendetta against the King and would rather risk the whole world to either see him taken out or returned to his former evil glory."

My heart turned over heavily at the thought. "But what kind of vendetta could drive a Summer fae to these extremes? If Caden were somehow placed under the Queen's curse again, they'd have an even bigger problem on their hands."

"So, maybe they were hoping Aric or the Queen would kill Caden," Ivy suggested, and my stomach dipped. "Take him out so another could become King."

I frowned as I thought that over. "From what I understand, only he can be King since he accepted the crown…or whatever. That even if he abdicated the throne, Fabian wouldn't become King. The Court would be without a ruler, but I have no idea what would happen if Caden died." The last word tasted like ash on my tongue.

"That might be a good question to ask," Ren said. "But I doubt we'll get an answer out of Fabian. He'd probably suspect that we were plotting to murder his brother."

"I could ask," I volunteered.

Ivy looked over her shoulder in the direction of the side door that led to the courtyard. "I hate to even ask this, but we don't believe that Fabian has any desire to be King, do we?"

"No. I don't believe that he does," I said honestly as Dixon rubbed his nose against my shoulder. "There are…certain expectations that I don't think Fabian has any desire to fulfill."

Neither did Caden, but that was neither here nor there.

"But why would anyone want to remove Caden as King?" Ivy asked, lips pursed. "I mean, he seems to be doing an okay job, and it isn't like he's unfair or cruel."

She was right, but I didn't think Caden wanted to be King before he took on the role. He'd felt forced, and that was before things really escalated between us. Even now, he was willing to shirk his obligations, but no one knew that while I had been held captive by Aric. And those who now knew about him ending his engagement were the only fae I one hundred percent trusted.

So maybe the traitor's motivations had nothing to do with Caden? If so, that brought us all the way back to square one. Why would a Summer fae work with the Winter Court?

For some reason, I thought of the old leader of the Order. David Cuvillier had betrayed the Order by aiding the Winter Court and Queen. He'd done so out of fear and resignation, believing that we hadn't stood a chance against the Winter Court. Could the traitor within the Summer Court have a similar mentality?

Fear could make some brave.

But fear could also turn others into the worst kind of cowards.

Chapter 9

"Are Fabian and Tink still out in the courtyard?" Ivy asked, drawing me from my unsettled thoughts.

Ren nodded. "Yeah, I have no idea what they're doing. I should probably go annoy them."

Smiling slightly, I watched him walk toward the kitchen, stopping to tip Ivy's head back and brush a kiss across her lips.

A pang of jealousy and envy stabbed me, and I reburied my face in Dixon's fur. He purred louder, like a little engine. After a few moments, I became aware of Ivy moving closer. I looked up, not at all surprised to see the concern in her gaze.

"I want to ask if everything is okay, but I know that's a stupid question. So, I'll try to refrain from asking that," she said, coming to stand beside me. "How are you feeling being back here, though?"

"It's…it's good, but it is weird," I admitted, thinking that if anyone knew what it felt like, it was Ivy. She had been through her own messed-up abduction. "Like it almost seems surreal to be here."

She nodded in understanding. "When I was taken, there were times when I didn't think I'd ever see my apartment again or the people I cared about. The first day home was a weird one."

There had been many moments when I didn't think I was going to walk out of that nightmare.

"Ren and Tink being there for me helped. If they hadn't been, I probably would've eventually dealt with everything, but having them made it easier." She scratched Dixon's ear as she lifted her gaze to mine. "Can I give you some unsolicited advice? Don't shut out the people who want to help."

"I'm not."

Her brows arched.

I sighed. "Things are complicated right now. That's all I want to say about it."

"You don't have to say anything," Ivy responded. "Just remember that I'm here when and if you do."

"I will," I promised.

Eventually, Ren returned inside with Tink and Fabian. It was hard to look at Caden's brother and not see the impossible similarities in the golden hair and cut of Fabian's jaw. After a bit, Ren and Ivy left, and Dixon found his way to Tink. Somehow, and I wasn't even sure how, I ended up on the couch, squished between Tink and Fabian and buried under a small mountain of blankets. There were no questions about how I was feeling or what was going on. Tink turned on what had to be his favorite movie, oblivious to Fabian's long-suffering sigh. *Twilight*. At this point, I'd seen it a hundred times, and I could recite those lines right alongside Tink, but I wasn't complaining. Well, I would draw the line at *Breaking Dawn*. That whole plot would hit way too close to home at the moment. Pizza was ordered for lunch, and since I'd been given the all-clear to eat whatever, I might've gone a bit overboard and eaten half of the pies. For once, Tink didn't comment, but I could tell he was bursting at the seams to make a comment about how I was now eating for two, though was doing his best to keep his mouth shut.

I'd relaxed between them, and by the start of *Eclipse*, I dozed on and off. I didn't know what made me think of the community in Florida, but a plan formed in my mind, one that might actually work.

The moment Fabian left, I twisted toward Tink, who had been combing Dixon's fur. "How big is the fae community in Florida? Is it like Hotel Good Fae?"

"Bigger, I think. There are several thousand there, and they don't stay in a hotel or use glamour to hide where they live. They have several gated subdivisions that are all together, built right by a beach. Super smart what they did by gating the communities." He dragged the small comb down Dixon's back. "Makes the beaches sort of private since you have to come in through the gates. People just think those who live in there are super rich or something."

"Do any humans live there?"

He nodded. "Some of the fae there are in relationships with humans."

That was good. "Did you like it there?"

Tink shrugged as he glanced at the screen as Jacob went full wolf. "I liked it."

"What about Fabian? He normally lives there, right? Does he plan to go back?"

"I think so, eventually." He frowned. "Do you ever wonder why Bella couldn't just have both Jacob and Edward?"

"What?"

"I mean, Edward has been alive for a while, so he's gotta get bored with the same old, same old. And Jacob is a wolf. I'm sure both have seen and done stranger things," he reasoned. "Plus, sharing is caring."

I stared at him and then gave a shake of my head. "No, I've never thought about that."

"You have boring thoughts then."

I ignored that. "Do you think I could go there? To the community in Florida?"

He returned to combing Dixon, focusing on his tail. "Why would you want to do that?"

"I could use the vacation."

Tink glanced at me. "You probably could."

"And…" I took a deep breath. "If Caden doesn't end up picking a Queen soon, I'm eventually going to start showing. It won't be easy to hide."

"Wait a second." Dropping the comb beside him, Tink picked up the remote and paused the movie. He looked at me. "You want to go down to the community to basically hide."

"And to relax. I have enough money saved up, and I'm sure Miles would—"

"You want to go hide in a fae community while becoming obviously pregnant?"

"No one down there should know who I am, right? It's not like Fabian or you told any random fae that I was the human chick the King was hooking up with."

"Of course not. Although, that would've been juicy gossip. But do you really think Fabian isn't going to know who the baby daddy is?"

I opened my mouth.

"He's not going to believe for one second that anyone but his brother is the father," he said before I could speak. "So, you'd be putting him in a position where he'll have to either knowingly lie to his brother or betray you."

I snapped my mouth shut. Shit. "I didn't think about that."

"Obviously."

"I really hadn't." I sank into the couch, surprised that I had forgotten that very important detail. "It's like my brain isn't fully functional or something."

"I just think you're really desperate, and desperate people do and think stupid things."

"Gee, thanks."

Tink was still for a bit and then placed Dixon in my lap. "Can I be honest for a moment?"

I slid him a sideways glance. "I have a feeling you were just super honest right then."

"I'm about to be even more honest. Like really super honest. The realest real kind of honesty."

"I think I get it."

"But you don't." He tipped toward me as Dixon sat up in my lap, watching him. "I get why you're doing what you are. I do. You want to save the world and some shit. Honorable. I'm not going to mess up your need to martyr your warm and fuzzies."

"It's not my need—"

"But it's become clear to me that you really are delusional."

"Wow," I murmured.

"Why else would you think your idea to hide with your baby daddy's brother in a community of fae was good enough to interrupt *Eclipse*? But it's more than that. Do you honestly think Caden is going to marry someone else even if he believes you don't want him?"

My stomach dropped. "He has to."

"He doesn't have to do jack shit, Lite Bright. I feel like everyone, including Tanner and Faye, is forgetting that. He didn't want to be King in the first place, and the last I checked, he's a grown-ass adult. Besides in the highly unlikely event that he's going to be like 'YOLO, let me pick a fae Queen now,' do you really think he's just going to let you walk away? Not fight for you? And I don't mean that in a creepy, super-possessive way either, but in a way we all would want someone we cared about to fight for us."

All the pizza I'd shoved down my throat was starting to settle wrongly in my stomach.

"But I have a really important question for you. One you need to think about long and hard before answering," he went on. "Do you honestly think you're going to be able to shut down the way you feel about him? You're going to be able to stand by and watch him be with someone else? You're going to be able to resist him—resist what you want—when he *does* fight for you?"

* * * *

I hadn't answered Tink's question, and he hadn't expected one, but I had thought about it. I'd spent the rest of the day and a good part of that night thinking about it, and every time I said that, yes, I could resist all of Caden's attempts, there was a little laugh in the back of my mind.

But what other choice did I have?

Restless after downing a glass of orange juice and a small army's worth of eggs, I took the prenatal vitamin and roamed upstairs, my head in a really weird place.

Slowly, I went down the hall of the second floor, past the closed door of the office, beyond the room Tink had commandeered, and to the other closed door—the one my mother had used.

I could use her room for the baby. My stomach wiggled like it always did whenever I acknowledged being pregnant. That was if I was still here then. The community in Florida was a stupid idea, but there were a million other places. If I was here, though, the room would be large, but since the small one that had once been a nursery had been converted into a walk-in closet ages ago, it was the only option. Well, unless Tink ever moved out. His room was smaller. Maybe he'd want the larger one?

Pushing open my bedroom door, I halted just inside the threshold. Last night, I hadn't really paid attention when I climbed into bed, too caught up in my thoughts. Now, I cataloged every square inch as if looking for something to be different. The drapes had been parted, letting in the morning sunlight. The velvety-soft cream bedspread had been smoothed back from the thick pillows. A pair of slippers I always left out but rarely wore waited by the bed. A fluffy and chunky gray throw blanket was draped over the chair by the window. It looked and felt the same. The room even smelled like I remembered. Like pineapple and mango.

But *I* wasn't the same.

My gaze made its way to the closet. I forced my steps forward. Opening the closet door, I switched on the light. What I saw first were the wigs in various colors and lengths, the knee-high boots and spiky heels, and the skintight dresses. They were all costumes designed to hide my identity while I hunted the fae responsible for killing my mother. I didn't need them anymore. I'd succeeded. They were all dead now, and those wigs and dresses…

They'd become a part of who and what I'd been shaped into. I ran my hand over the Lycra material of a red dress that I wouldn't have dared to wear five years ago. The outfits, the wigs, the shoes—all had aided me in finding the fae responsible for killing my mother, but they'd also done something else. They'd given me the confidence I'd been sorely lacking.

But this stuff still wasn't me. They were words written in blood and tears for a chapter that had come to an end.

Pivoting around, I hurried downstairs to the pantry. Black garbage bags in hand, I went back to the closet and started cleaning house. Everything went. The wigs. The shoes. The dresses—well, *almost* everything. I couldn't bear to part with the studded mid-calf boots or the silvery sequined dress. Those boots were surprisingly comfortable, and the dress…

It was the outfit I'd been wearing when I killed Tobias—one of the fae I'd been looking for.

And it was the dress I had on the first time I came face-to-face with Caden in the club.

For that reason alone, I should toss it with the rest, but I hung it back up between the thick, oversized cardigan and the blazer I never wore.

Pulling open the drawers in the center dresser, I breathed a sigh of relief when I spotted the extra sets of iron daggers and cuffs. I closed the drawer and then picked up my makeup case. Setting it on the counter inside the closet, I flipped the switches and rooted around, pulling out the heavier makeup—the stuff I wouldn't even wear for a fancy occasion.

Not that I attended many fancy things.

I dumped the makeup into an old grocery bag and walked out—

Caden stood in the doorway of the bedroom, arms loosely crossed over the plain gray tee shirt he wore as he stared at the garbage bags.

He lifted his chin, and the room seemed to tilt as our gazes connected. His hair was pulled back, and the beams of sunlight seemed to be attracted to all the striking, symmetrical angles and planes of his face.

Upon the unexpected sight, my heart lodged itself in my throat. Now, it was firmly back in my chest, pounding for reasons unrelated to shock.

Caden was…he was gorgeous, his beauty rugged and raw. As shallow as this sounded, I could stare at him all day, and there was a good chance he knew that. Warmth crept into my cheeks and flowed down my throat. It took a moment for me to find my ability to speak. "How did you get in here?"

One side of his lips quirked up. "You know I'm not a vampire, right? I don't need permission to enter a home."

My eyes narrowed. "I'm pretty sure the front door was locked."

"It was."

I lifted my brows.

"Tink let me in," he answered finally, eyes twinkling.

I really needed to talk to Tink about letting Caden in. Not like this was the first time, but that damn brownie knew better.

He unfolded his arms, the act doing interesting things to the muscles under his shirt. "Doing some light spring cleaning?"

"Something like that."

"What are you going to do with all that stuff?"

I glanced down at the overflowing bags. "I thought I'd give them to Goodwill or a women's shelter." My nose scrunched. "Although, they'd probably wonder if an escort had cleaned out their closet."

"A high-priced escort," Caden murmured, and my lips twitched at that. "I have to say I'm glad to see you throwing this stuff away."

I almost said that I didn't care what he felt, but doing so would lessen the significance of what getting rid of these items meant.

"Although…" He reached inside a bag and pulled out a knee-high boot that took an act of God to get off. "I will miss these."

Storming forward, I snatched the boot from his hands and dropped it back into the bag. Caden grinned down at me as if greatly amused by my actions. My stomach did a little flip, and I was reminded of Tink's question. Could I resist Caden?

"What made you do this?" He gestured at the bags with his chin.

I backed up, crossing my arms. Like always, it was almost impossible not to open up. I had no idea why it was like that with him. "They're costumes—the clothing, the wigs, all of it. I don't need them anymore."

"No more late-night visits to clubs then?"

A picture of me in a skintight dress, several months pregnant, formed in my mind, and I snorted. "Not in the foreseeable future."

"What about patrolling?"

That was a good question. "The Order never really had me patrolling, but I…I like being out there." How long I would be able to do that safely was anyone's guess. "I just won't be looking for any fae in particular, I guess."

His jaw tightened as if he weren't all that happy to hear that I still planned to patrol, but he wisely didn't voice his opinion.

In the ensuing silence, I looked at the bags. "Everything that's in those bags isn't me, you know? They really were like costumes, and I don't need them anymore."

"I'm glad to hear that," he replied. "They represent a chapter of your life that's now closed."

I blinked in surprise as he nailed how I felt. He really did know me. Better than anyone else. Panic blossomed in the pit of my stomach, and my mouth dried. "Why are you here. Caden? I know last night might've confused things, but I'm sure I made myself clear."

"Oh, you were clear, all right."

"Then should I repeat my question?"

"If it makes you feel better? Sure. Go ahead."

"It wouldn't make me feel better."

"Good. Because I don't want you feeling bad." He stepped forward, and I tensed. That reaction had nothing to do with my time with Aric. "I want you to feel good. I want you happy. I want you to feel safe and cherished. I want you to feel comforted and comfortable. I want you to feel loved."

Oh God.

All those broken shards of my heart started to piece themselves back together. I needed them to stop. A repaired heart would only hurt worse.

Caden took another step forward, and I moved until the backs of my legs hit the bed. "Did you sleep well last night? I did. Best sleep I've had in years, sunshine."

My heart jumped. *Sunshine.* He called me that because he said he'd seen me smiling once and it was like the sun finally rising. That was possibly the sweetest, kindest thing anyone had ever said to me.

"It's time."

I looked up. "For what?"

"For that talk I told you we needed to have but would be better if we waited until you had time to process everything you'd gone through. But I can see we don't have the luxury of that time," he said. "I know, Brighton."

My breath caught. "Know what?"

Those golden eyes met and held mine. "I *know.*"

Chapter 10

My legs seemed to have given up on me because I was suddenly sitting on the edge of the bed.

He…he knew?

How?

Well, there were countless hows. Four of them had a name. I didn't believe Tink had said anything about me being pregnant, but the other three could've just been convincing when they'd said they wouldn't say anything.

"Know what?" I repeated.

His head tilted to the side like it did whenever he was sensing some sort of emotion I was giving off. I was sure he was picking up on them.

"I know you've been told what would happen if I do not marry Tatiana or a fae of the Court," he said.

My mouth opened as my heart pressed against my ribs. Relief made me dizzy, so much so that I almost laughed. He didn't know. Not really.

His head tipped to the side once again, and I knew I needed to get a handle on my emotions. I dragged my hands over my bent knees, knowing there was no point in lying about what I'd learned. "You mean the basic collapse of your Court and how you'd be dethroned and left to fend for yourself? How the Summer fae would be weakened, and it would eventually lead to the whole world going to hell? How *you* would be weakened?"

Caden's features softened as I spoke, causing warning bells to go off left and right. "I'm honored, sunshine."

I blinked.

He came forward, each step slow and measured. "You don't need to worry about what will happen to me. I'm not worried."

"That's easy for you to say," I replied. "And also concerning that you're not worried."

Caden sat down, his large frame seeming to overwhelm the bed. "I will be fine, with or without the throne. But I won't be fine without you."

My heart gave a happy little jump, and I closed my eyes. "I wish you wouldn't say things like that."

"Why?" His voice was quiet.

"Because it's always so perfect. It's always what I…" It was what I wanted to hear, and that was the problem. "I just wish you wouldn't say things like that."

"I don't think you'd prefer that I lie."

Actually, I would in this situation.

"This is why you've tried to push me away," he said, and my eyes opened on the word *tried*. He was staring down at me, a slight smile on his lips. "It's not because you don't want me. It's not because you don't love me. It's because you think you're doing the right thing."

"Because I am," I snapped.

The smile grew. "Not that I needed the confirmation that I am right, but thank you nonetheless for providing it."

"It doesn't matter if you're right or wrong." I rose, shaking my head. "It doesn't matter how I feel or how you feel."

"It does matter that you believe you're doing the right thing. That you're *willing* to do the right thing. At least to me." He looked up at me, gaze warm. "You know what that says about you?"

"Yes. I'm brave or selfless or whatever." I waved a hand, dismissing that. "I'd rather be selfish."

"But never a coward?"

I didn't even have to consider the answer. "No."

"I didn't think so." His gaze searched mine. "I'm going to ask you something, Brighton, and I want you to be honest. I *need* you to be honest. Do you love me?"

Tension settled on my shoulders as I started to speak—to lie. But he already knew the truth. I imagined he just wanted to hear me say it. Either way, I didn't think I had it in me to force that lie past my lips once more.

"I love you, Caden." My voice thickened as I crossed my arms and gripped my waist. "I think…I think I fell in love with you the moment you walked into Flux and let me pretend I was under the glamour of a fae. I know that sounds weird, but I've always been able to tell you things I couldn't share with anyone else. As crazy as this sounds, I'm comfortable with you in a way I've never been with any guy, even though you're freaking perfect, and I'm the exact opposite of that.

You're smart. You're funny, even when you're annoying the ever-loving crap out of me. You're sensitive in a way I don't think many people would ever expect you to be. So, yes, I love you, Caden."

His eyes closed briefly. When they reopened, it was almost like twin fires had lit them from within. "Do you know that the fae believe that a piece of their soul is released upon birth and finds a home in their soulmate?"

Recalling what Luce had said about two souls and the *mortuus*, I had a feeling that whatever he was about to say was going to make me cry.

"I found that piece of my soul in Siobhan. When she was killed, I didn't believe that I would ever find it again, even though the fae believe that upon death, that piece of the soul is once more released. You see, I was lucky when I found Siobhan. Not all fae find the missing piece of their soul. It doesn't mean that their love for another is any less real. It's just that two souls being connected is more intense and immediate. It can happen with just one look." He pressed his palm against his chest. "What is in here recognizes what belongs. The joining of two souls is an unbreakable bond."

A tremor coursed through me as I fought the urge to both run to him and run from the room.

"I saw you before the night the gateways to the Otherworld were sealed. Just brief glimpses, but each time, I felt this throbbing in my chest. It had been so long since I'd felt anything like it that I wasn't sure what I was feeling. But that night when you helped my brother…" His voice roughened as he tipped forward. "I knew that somehow, someway, the part of my soul that had been released had found another home. I never would've dared to hope I'd find you, the one who held a piece of my soul, but I did."

What he said would've sounded crazy to me a handful of years ago. Soulmates? I would've said they only existed in fairy tales. But now? This made sense.

"I tried to stay away then. I could sense your fear and distrust of the fae, and when I realized that you could be used against me like Siobhan had been, I tried to distance myself from you. Both were mistakes, ones I will spend an eternity trying to make up for."

A breath seemed to shudder out of him. "I love you, Brighton. I know I fell in love with you before we even spoke to one another. That love only deepened when I saw how strong and resilient you became. When I learned how incredibly intelligent and generous you are."

The back of my throat and eyes burned as he continued. "My love for you grew each time you pushed back at me, showing me you weren't afraid, and I knew the reason why you became my *mortuus* when you were willing to look past who I was and saw beyond what I'd done when I was under the Queen's spell. You are my sun, Brighton. I loved you before I found you in that club, even before I gave you the Summer Kiss."

I shuddered, taking a step back. "Caden…" I pushed the tears down. "What you just said, it was beautiful, and I know it's real. There is something entirely inexplicable about us. But hearing that…it hurts."

"It's not meant to hurt, sunshine. I wish you would've come to me the moment you heard what would happen if I didn't choose a Queen. I think I could've saved you a lot of heartache."

I wasn't sure how hearing this days ago would've lessened the amount of pain I was in.

"What if I told you that you could be selfish?" he asked.

Letting out a dry laugh, I shook my head again. "Caden, it's not like I haven't thought about this. About whether either of us could live with ourselves, knowing what we've risked. I know I can't. I know you couldn't."

"I didn't want to be King. You know that," he said. "But that doesn't mean I would let my Court rot and decay."

"See?" I reasoned. "You agree. We can't be together. No matter how badly we want to be. So, this conversation is only hurting both of us."

"This was a conversation I planned to have once you had a little time to process everything you've been through and learned," he repeated. "Because what I'm about to tell you will come as another shock, but I see now waiting was a mistake. Sometimes we think we're doing the right thing when we're not."

Considering what I knew that he didn't, I doubted he could shock me. "What do you have to tell me?"

"I have to tell you that I have chosen a Queen."

My entire body jerked as my heart twisted painfully in my chest. I searched desperately for relief but found nothing but aching emptiness and bitterness. This was what the world needed, but God, it still cut so deeply. "Okay," I whispered, wondering what the hell the point of this conversation was. "Congrats."

One side of his lips curved up. "Perhaps I need to be a bit clearer. I've chosen you, Brighton. I've chosen you to be my Queen."

Chapter 11

"Me?" I squeaked. I couldn't have heard him right. There was no way.

Caden nodded. "You. I've chosen you."

I stared at him for what felt like an eternity, heart racing, and stomach feeling as if I were poised at the top of a rollercoaster. "You can't choose me."

"Oh, yes, I can," he replied. "And I have."

"But the Summer Court, the world—"

"Will be just fine." He reached out, curling his fingers around my elbows. "Because you are my *mortuus,* and I've given you the Summer Kiss."

"What does that have to do with it?" Tears blurred his face.

"Because you're not entirely human any longer." He rose slowly as if trying not to startle me. "You're not fae, either. You have a piece of my soul inside you. That places you above any fae my Court could offer me. The Summer fae would not weaken, nor would the human world. I would not be dethroned." His thumbs slid along my elbows. "I would be whole."

Confusion swamped me as a tiny kernel of something more powerful than hope formed. Some fae knew I was Caden's *mortuus*—Tanner and Luce. I imagined Fabian knew, as did Tink. I didn't think any of them would be particularly dishonest with me. "Is this something well known? That your *mortuus*, no matter if they are fae or human, can be your Queen?"

"It's not just the *mortuus*. It's also the Summer Kiss," he explained, his gaze questioning. "Why?"

"I…" I'd told no one about the Summer Kiss. Luce didn't even know that. Neither did Tanner. Had Caden told Fabian? If so, he must've kept it from Tink because Tink would've told me. The tiny kernel grew, unfurling like a blossoming flower. "Are you…are you for real?"

"Why wouldn't I be?" Caden dragged his hands up my arms.

My brain sort of shorted out. I could have him and the future I wanted so badly and not risk the entire world? We could be together. Our child would have a mother and father who loved each other. My legs started to tremble, and I jerked back from his hold. "Why didn't you tell me this when you told me you ended your engagement with Tatiana!"

"Looking back, I realize I should have, but I figured you'd been through enough, and it seemed like a good idea to wait before I told you I planned to make you my wife. I figured after you had some time to heal, we'd talk," he explained. "I didn't expect anyone to go to you."

My breath came in short, quick pants. What he was saying sounded reasonable. He'd been thinking of what I could handle given that I'd just been held—wait. "You…you want to marry me?"

His lips twitched. "To make you my Queen, I would have to marry you."

"Is this a proposal?"

He grinned then, somehow looking boyish. "I had planned on doing something romantic."

Feeling like I might faint, I pressed my palm to the center of my chest. "You're not lying to me now, right?"

"I would not lie about this." He lifted his hands, cupping my cheeks. I didn't flinch. Everything that had happened with Aric was the furthest thing from my mind. "I would never lie to you about how I feel or our future. Never again, sunshine."

"This isn't…this isn't a hallucination, is it?"

Anguish filled his gaze. "No, sunshine. This is real."

I didn't know what happened next.

It was like a seal deep inside me cracked wide open. I tried to say his name, but all that came up was a deep, soul-shaking sob. The tears I'd been fighting overwhelmed me. Vaguely, I was aware of Caden gathering me in his arms, and then we were on the bed, him sitting with me in his lap, one arm wrapped tightly around me, a hand curled around the back of my head.

And I cried.

It was the ugly kind of crying that shook the entire body. Whatever had been ripped open inside of me had been a Pandora's box of emotions. What spilled out of me was a mixture of the best and the worst of the storm. Some of the tears that fell were for all the wounds Aric had caused, those inflicted years ago, the ones that had faded, and the ones that were never visible. The death of my mother, the way I never felt truly valued by the Order, and even the loss of the father I'd never known fueled the sobs. But there was a different side to the outpouring of emotion as well. A wealth of relief and such potent happiness that all I could do was cry. And I never happy-cried.

But I was now because I didn't have to watch the man I loved bind his life to someone else. I wouldn't have to walk away, knowing I would never feel the kind of love I had for him again, nor would I ever have to worry if I'd find someone who loved me as much as he did. I didn't have to hide our child from him. He could be a part of the child's life from the beginning. We wouldn't have that house with the white picket fence, but we would have each other.

We would have a future together. That realization made me cry even harder, and the whole time, Caden held me. He whispered words to me that reminded me of music. It was a language I couldn't begin to understand. Still, it soothed all the frayed edges until finally the tears subsided, and the tremors stopped.

There was so much I wanted to tell him as I lifted my head from his chest. There was so much I needed to tell him as I looked up and saw the concern in his gaze as he dragged his hand around to my cheek. That I was pregnant. That he was about to become a father. That I loved him. That I now believed in soulmates. That the tears weren't all bad. That happy couldn't even begin to describe the hope, anticipation, excitement, and the hundred other emotions I currently felt.

But as Caden's thumb dragged over my lower lip, I knew that if he felt one-tenth of the rawness swirling around inside me, now wasn't the time for words. Fire replaced the concern in his gaze, and the way his lips parted and his chest rose sharply against my hands was intentional. Tension poured into the air around us, becoming a tangible third entity. I imagined I could almost see the air heating and crackling. A heavy ache settled in my breasts and then moved lower, between my thighs. It was a deep, pulsing throb that I didn't just welcome but reveled in because it was more than just primal physical attraction. It was our love for one another manifesting into something that could not be denied.

Time for words would come later.

Closing the distance between us, I kissed Caden. The touch of his lips against mine was a jolt to the system. It was like brushing up against a live wire, lighting up the network of nerves all across my body. I shuddered as the arm around me tightened, drawing me against the hot, hard length of his body. The taste of him against my lips, on my tongue, was like ambrosia. Every part of me became hyperaware of how his mouth felt against mine, his lips soft yet hard. How he tasted like sunshine and summer against the tip of my tongue.

Giving in to the rising tide of sensations, I rocked my hips against him. The thin leggings I wore were no barrier to the hardness pressing against the material of his jeans. He skated his fingers through my hair, his hand balling in the loose strands. A deep, growling sound radiated out from the back of his throat and rumbled through me. The tips of my breasts tingled, and the kiss went deeper as he managed to hold me even tighter. A moan curled its way out of my throat as he shifted under me, lining his hips up perfectly with mine. My fingers dug into his shirt as my pulse became a heady thrum.

I almost whimpered as Caden broke the kiss, pulling back as his gaze roamed over my face. I didn't care what I looked like after having cried for the Lord knew how long, because I realized he didn't see the puffy eyes or tear-streaked cheeks or the remnants of the fading bruises and healing cuts.

He saw me.

Only *me*.

"Are you sure?" he whispered, his gaze searching mine intently. "Because we can do everything, or we don't have to do anything. I would be happy to just hold you, to just kiss and play, Brighton. I'm satisfied with you being in my arms."

Fresh tears pricked my eyes, but I didn't worry if they fell or not. "That is why I'm sure." His willingness to wait, to do nothing or anything was why I knew I was ready, why it wasn't too soon after everything that'd happened. "I need you, Caden. Make love to me. Please?"

"You never have to say please. Ever." Cradling my cheeks in his hands, he shuddered against me. "All that I am. All that I have. It's yours. I'm yours."

Caden kissed me then, and oh God, no one—*no one*—kissed like him. His mouth moved over mine like he was claiming every hidden part of my heart and soul. My shirt came off. Then his. We stood, our mouths and hands skimming over every inch of exposed skin. His fingers gripped the band of my leggings, tugging them down, along with the panties I wore underneath. I reached for the button on his jeans, hands trembling as I then worked at the zipper. Off went his pants, and then he eased down the tight, black boxer briefs he had on, freeing the rigid length of his cock.

Caden was…he was beautiful. Every part of him, from the broad expanse of his chest and the tightly rolled muscles of his stomach, to the proud jut of his arousal.

So distracted by the sight of him, I hadn't even noticed that he'd unclasped my bra until his mouth closed over one nipple. I cried out, reaching for those silky strands of hair, but he dropped to his knees in front of me.

His lips brushed over the faint pink scars from two years ago. "Beautiful." He tilted his head, kissing one of the many almost-healed slices. "You're so beautiful, Brighton. Every part of you." He sank even lower, his lips searching and tasting, licking and exploring until his breath danced over my most sensitive area. Then his head shifted, and I felt the wet slide of his tongue along my inner thigh, moving up and up until it slipped inside, swirling and tasting. Each time his tongue thrust in, pleasure became a lightning bolt down my spine. "This is especially beautiful."

His mouth closed over the bundle of nerves, and my head fell back. There was no slow build of sensation. He knew exactly what he was doing when he dragged his teeth over my sensitive skin, soothing the bite with his tongue before closing his mouth over the turgid flesh. The release hit me hard. Crying out, my head fell back as pounding wave after wave of pleasure roared through me.

Before the tremors stopped, Caden rose. Somehow, we ended up on the bed, his large body settling over mine and then between my thighs. His mouth found mine once more, and the taste of me mingled with the essence of him.

"I waited several lifetimes for you," he said, brushing the hair back from my face. "I would wait several more if I had to."

"You don't." I touched his cheeks and then slid my hand down the sides of his neck to his shoulders. "You don't have to wait anymore. I don't have to wait."

Caden's body shifted, and I felt him pressing against me. I lifted my hips, and my breath caught and then held. His gaze snared mine. "This feels like a dream. If it is, I don't ever want to wake…" His voice choked off as he thrust in, fully seating himself. The pressure and fullness was unbelievable, and the small bit of discomfort faded as he made a sound, a velvety growl. "Sunshine."

From there, there were only our short, shallow breaths and the sounds of our bodies moving together. His hips rolled and pumped, and I followed, the unbelievable tension building once more.

Caden planted his elbow in the bed beside my head as he shoved his arm under my back and lifted me so my breasts were pressed to his chest. His strength was shocking and wickedly arousing as he moved over me. In me. Each stroke deeper and harder, became more powerful. My back hit the mattress once more. I curled my legs around his waist, and I met each deep and even thrust until I couldn't any longer, until the pace quickened, and his body held mine down. My body tensed around his, and my blood turned to lava as every part of my body tightened at once, all over again.

"That's it." His voice was a heated whisper in my ear.

The most intense pleasure rolled over me in tight, hot waves, and all I could do was hold on as his hips pounded in a tempo that was earth-shattering. Our mouths crashed together His tongue tangled with mine, and the tightly coiled knot of tension whipped through me fiercely, lighting up every cell in my body.

The arm under my shoulders held me in place as he ground his hips into mine. There was one more deep, breath-shattering thrust, and then my name was a rough shout as his body spasmed, his release hot as his hips jerked. My hands glided lazily up and down his sides as one last shudder overtook him.

Caden's lips brushed over my shoulder and then the line of my jaw. Limp and sated, I watched him through half-open eyes. His hand found mine, and he brought it to his mouth, pressing a kiss to the center of my palm. "I have a very important question for you, Brighton."

"Hmm?"

He brought my hand to his chest, over his heart. "Can we stay like this for the rest of the day?"

A slow grin tugged at my lips. "Like *this*?" I asked. He was still inside me, not as hard as he had been, but not remotely soft.

Biting down on his bottom lip, he nodded. "What about all weekend?"

"I would…I would be down for that." My heart was swelling so fast in my chest. "Though I don't think we can stay like this."

"I don't know." His hips rocked, eliciting a sharp gasp from me. His grin became downright wicked. "I'm quite happy to be right where I am."

I started to reach for him when, somewhere from the floor, a phone rang. I looked, brows furrowing. My phone was downstairs. "I think that's yours."

"It is." He bent his head, kissing me. The ringing quieted, and for a few seconds, I got a little lost in him, but then the cell started ringing again.

"I think you should check that."

"I should." Caden cursed under his breath. "Sorry."

"It's okay," I whispered.

Giving me one more quick kiss, he eased out of me and smoothly shifted to his feet. My gaze dropped to his ass as he snatched his jeans off the floor.

That was one lovely backside.

Feeling better than I had in, well, longer than I could remember, I rolled onto my side.

Caden had his phone out and to his ear, answering with an abrupt, "This better be important."

My brows rose, and I started to grin, but I saw the muscles along his back and spine tense. The pleasant languidness vanished.

"I'll be right there," he said, ending the call as he turned to me.

"What is it?"

"It's Benji, Faye's missing cousin. He came back to the hotel."

Sensing the hard edge to his voice, unease blossomed. "It didn't end with a happy reunion, did it?"

"No." The fire had dimmed in Caden's eyes. "He attacked."

Chapter 12

I was already sitting up, scanning the floor for my discarded clothing. "How bad is it?"

"Not as bad as it could've been, but he wounded some of the guards," he told me as he pulled on his briefs and jeans. "And he injured his mother pretty badly."

"Oh God," I whispered, pulling on my leggings. "I assume he's dead?"

"Surprisingly not." His gaze flickered over my chest, lingering in a way that caused warmth to creep into my cheeks. He picked up my bra. "Faye and Kalen were able to apprehend and contain him."

Shock flickered through me as I took the bra from him, quickly donning it. "Holy crap, that's huge, Caden. We may find out where they're getting the Devil's Breath since you guys checked Neal's bar and didn't find any evidence of it."

"It is huge," he agreed.

I pulled on the loose sweater and then shoved up the sleeves. "We just need to get Benji to talk."

"And that's going to be easier said than done." He pulled his shirt on over his head. "You remember how Elliot was."

I thought of the youngling. He'd been crazed, almost as if brainwashed by the Winter Court. "But we have to try."

Caden's gaze flicked to mine, and then he came forward, smoothing my hair back from my face. "You look so delectable right now."

I didn't need a mirror to know my hair looked like I'd been, well, rolling around in bed.

"But *we* don't have to do anything," he continued. "I want you to sit this one out. Stay here, and I'll come back to you as soon as I can."

My brows lifted. "You want me to just sit and wait for you?"

"You don't have to sit and wait, so to speak."

I narrowed my eyes as I stepped back, out of his reach. "Why do you want me to sit this out?"

He lowered his hand. "You're still recovering, Brighton. That's the only reason why."

Taking a deep, even breath, I reminded myself that he was coming from a place of concern, and there was no reason for my head to spin *Exorcist* style. "You took my word when I said I was ready earlier."

His head tilted slightly. "I did."

"And we just had pretty active sex," I said, proud that my cheeks didn't catch fire.

Caden's eyes heated though, and his voice roughened. "We did. I would've loved to do it again." He paused, his gaze sweeping over me. "And again."

A delicious little shiver danced over my skin, and it took me a second to get my mind back on track. "If I was ready for that, why wouldn't I be ready for a questioning?"

"You mean an interrogation."

"Whatever."

"What we did and what I'm about to do are two different things. You won't like what you see down in that room."

"I've seen some really grotesque interrogations carried out by the Order, Caden, but you're right," I replied. "What *we* are about to do will be a hell of a lot easier than what we just did."

"And what you guys just did was very loud and seemed very active." A voice came from the doorway—the open doorway. I turned, finding Tink standing there. "I definitely think Brighton is physically ready…for just about anything."

Oh my God.

"Dixon got scared," he continued. "He's hiding out under the coffee table right now. Traumatized by all the sexing going on."

I had no words.

"By the way, you guys left the door open," Tink explained.

My lips parted as I shot Caden a quick glance. He didn't seem at all perturbed by that fact. Meanwhile, I wanted to bury myself under the bed. How could we have been that distracted?

Well, I knew exactly how we were that distracted.

"I was kind of worried at first. The sounds were interesting." Tink grinned as my eyes widened. "Shouting. Crying. Moaning. A totally different kind of crying—"

"Oh my God, Tink. You can stop now," I exclaimed. "Seriously."

"What?" He lifted his hands. "I'm just happy you finally got some—"

Tink shouted as I picked up my flip-flop and winged it at his head. Caden chuckled, and I had half a mind to throw the other shoe at his face. He ended that thought with one smoldering, fond look.

"Come on," he said, his gaze light despite what had happened. "You need to find better shoes if you're coming with me."

Relieved that he wasn't going to try to keep me wrapped in a bubble, I nodded and started for the closet.

"How about these?" Caden asked.

I looked over my shoulder. He held one of the knee-high boots, all helpful like.

He winked at me. "I have such fond memories of these."

"I'm going to throw that boot at your head," I warned.

Caden grinned. "It would be worth it."

* * * *

Sitting in the front seat of Caden's SUV, with him behind the steering wheel, and Tink in the back seat, I still found it weirdly funny that Caden, the King of the Summer fae, drove. Shouldn't he have a driver or something?

Tracing the outline of the iron cuffs on my wrists that hid the daggers, I wondered if at some point, as the baby grew, I would have difficultly handling iron. I didn't think so since contact with my skin didn't mean contact with the baby, but I supposed that was something I needed to keep an eye on. Wishing there was a guide for expecting fae mothers who were also members of the Order, I wiggled my toes inside my black combat boots. Obviously, I hadn't put on the other boots.

They did, however, end up back in my closet instead of in the bag to donate. "*For later*," Caden had said, which had caused Tink to launch into a discussion about how dressing up kept his sex life lively—something Caden didn't want to hear since it involved his brother.

Tink kept catching my gaze in the rearview mirror, and each time, he raised his brows. I knew he had a lot of questions. I couldn't blame him for that, considering I'd tried to convince him to take me to Florida just hours before. There wasn't time for that at the moment.

There also hadn't been time for me to tell Caden I was pregnant. I had been okay with keeping the truth from him when I had a good reason to do so, but now that there was none, it was pecking away at me. Each passing minute was one more minute where he didn't know he was going to be a father.

How would he take it? I didn't know. He loved me, I knew that beyond a doubt. But even if I'd known from the moment I woke up that I could be his Queen and all would be as well as it was, everything was still new. There'd be no time for just him and me. It would always be him, me, and our child. Though I didn't think we needed the time to get to know each other or to become comfortable. The latter was already there, and it was…it was truly like we were two halves coming together. We may not know every little thing about one another, but we knew each other.

Wait.

I would be his Queen.

My stomach dipped as I stared out the window, the rows of homes and wrought iron fences nothing but a blur.

He hadn't made it super official, but no way in hell would I say no. We would marry, and I would be his wife. A Queen. Would I have like queenly duties? What would the queenly duties even be? I gave a little shake of my head. I needed to focus. Right now, none of that was exactly important. Dealing with it could come later. What we needed to deal with was Benji, and then afterward, I would tell Caden about the pregnancy.

I glanced over at Caden as we turned on South Peters, experiencing a weird little hitch in my chest. A part of me still couldn't believe that this was real—that we could be together.

Caden pulled around to the side of the rundown, brick and metal building that looked like something you'd see on one of those ghost hunters shows.

"This part is so cool." Tink gripped the back of my seat as he popped his head between the two.

Caden drove up to what appeared to be a loading dock for deliveries—two wide metal doors that were covered in splotches of rust—and then right *through* the doors. I didn't close my eyes, but I did tense. I'd entered Hotel Good Fae a few times like this, and it always freaked me out. I kept expecting to crash into a cement wall.

"Magic," Tink murmured in my ear.

"Uh-huh." My eyes adjusted to the fluorescent lighting of the parking garage.

He pulled into the first parking space near the elevator, one I was sure had been reserved for him. Killing the engine, Caden looked over at me, and his gaze met mine. There was a flutter in my chest and then my stomach. I smiled at him.

"Ready?" he asked, and I nodded. He glanced back at Tink. "You?"

"Why, thanks for asking." He sat back, looking between the two of us. "I am ready for some answers to the questions that have been burning me up inside, but with my dark hair comes great responsibility, and a newfound maturity."

I blinked slowly.

"So I realized that now is not the time to ask those questions." He held up his hand. "But as soon as you guys are done with what you're doing, I expect the three of us—no, wait. I'm sure Fabian would also like to be included. The four of us will have a sit-down."

"It's doable." Caden grinned.

"It is." I met Tink's gaze. "But it's going to have to wait a little bit. There's something I need to talk to Caden about first."

Tink's eyes widened, and I was grateful that I could feel Caden's gaze on me. "What do you need to talk to me about?" he said, drawing my gaze back to his. "We can make time now. Benji isn't going anywhere."

Out of the corner of my eye, I saw Tink clasp his hands together under his chin. There was no way I was telling Caden that he was going to be a father in front of Tink. That would be like going on a reality show.

"It can wait," I told him.

Caden's gaze searched mine, and then he nodded. Exhaling roughly, I ignored the pout Tink sent in my direction and climbed out. I didn't make it far before Tink curled an arm around my shoulders, pulling me against his side.

He lowered his head, whispering, "Is everything okay?"

"Everything is more than okay."

Tink pulled back, smiling. "I am going to need an extremely detailed report. You know that, right?"

I laughed. "I do."

"Good."

It was then that I realized Caden hadn't walked toward the elevator. He'd stopped halfway across the parking garage. Tink and I caught up with him. "Where are we going?"

"To a place where Tanner handles certain…unpleasantries."

This is the first I'm hearing of such a thing. I glanced at Tink, and he shrugged. "There is such a place?"

Caden nodded. "Only a few know of it. I'm surprised my brother didn't tell you."

Tink snorted as he shoved his hands into the pockets of his sweatpants. "He knows I abhor violence unless it's violence I'm causing."

I frowned at him as we reached a nondescript white door. Caden placed his thumb against the keypad, and above, the red light turned green. The door unlocked, and he pushed it open. We stepped into a white hallway, and I could already hear Tanner speaking. There were also other voices I couldn't make out. Caden turned to me, extending his hand.

My gaze dipped to his palm and then rose to his. He…he wanted to hold my hand? It was such a simple gesture that wouldn't mean much to others, but it would be huge.

He was the King.

To the others who were here, I was just some human. They didn't know what I was or what he'd done. Him holding my hand was a statement, and obviously, I hadn't the chance to talk to Tanner or Faye or Kalen. They would be so confused.

But I placed my hand in his, and my heart did a back handspring when he curled his fingers around mine, squeezing.

"You guys are so adorable," Tink said, tugging the hair I'd thrown up into a messy bun.

"You are," Caden said. "Especially when you blush."

"I'm not blushing." I watched Tink walk ahead, his long-legged pace taking him around the corner of the hall.

"Your face is the shade of a rose," he told me.

"It is not." I could feel my cheeks heat even more. "We need to focus on what's important."

"I am."

I glanced up at him and felt a little unsteady as my gaze met his. "Benji and finding out where they're getting the Devil's Breath is important."

"It is. But you're more important to me. You will always be the most important thing."

"You…" I swallowed, closing my eyes. "I wish we had time for me to tell and show you how perfect I think you are."

"I'm not perfect." He touched my cheek. "But I don't have a

problem with you showing me later how much you think I'm perfect."

Heat simmered in my veins. I planned on doing just that after I told him what needed to be shared.

But by the time we reached the end of the hall, I'd filed all of that away. What we were about to deal with needed our full attention.

The first person I saw when we turned the corner was Ren. Dressed in black, he leaned against the plain white wall, his back to us, ankles crossed. Tink was beside him. Fabian behind him, his blond hair draped over broad shoulders. He was the first to see us, his expression somber, and then there was a slight widening of his pale eyes.

Ren looked over his shoulder. "I was wondering when you were finally going…"

Either he trailed off, or I just didn't hear what he said because my gaze had been snagged by those remaining in the hall. Faye and Kalen stood with Tanner. There was an older male fae, as well, his silvery skin pale. He'd been pacing while Faye spoke to him quietly.

Maybe it was my imagination, but everyone seemed to stop and notice our joined hands. The message Caden was sending out had been received. We were together.

It was Kalen I zeroed in on because one side of his lips curved up a moment before he bowed slightly. "My King."

There was a flurry of the other fae beginning to do the same, but Caden stopped them with a slice of his hand through the air. "Is he in there?" He nodded at another nondescript door.

Stepping forward, Tanner cleared his throat. He looked shaken, and seeing Caden and I together had to be a part of it. He was likely seeing the crumbling of his entire Court, right in front of him. I wanted to tell him that it was okay, but now truly wasn't the time.

And time always seemed strange like that, because minutes kept ticking by, and they were never the right ones.

"Yes." Tanner sent a quick glance at me. "He's restrained."

"How is he?" Caden asked.

It was the man with Faye who spoke. "He is… He is not well." His voice cracked. "My King, he is not well at all."

Caden's hand slipped from mine as he stepped forward, placing his hand on the man's shoulder. "How is your wife, Balour?"

"Luce believes she will heal, but…" Balour looked away, lips pressed in a thin line. "I don't know who is in that room. He looks like my son. Sounds like him. But it is not Benji."

"I am sorry," Caden spoke, his voice low. "We will find who is responsible. They will pay."

"Thank you." The poor man struggled to take a breath as he looked at the closed door. "Is there any hope for him?

"If there is, we will find it," Caden said. I hoped there was something to be optimistic about, but I doubted there was.

Tanner had inched closer, his voice low. "I…I didn't expect to see you here, Brighton."

"I didn't expect to be here either," I admitted, having no idea what else I could say other than, "We need to talk later."

"Yes, we do." He nodded, watching Caden as Benji's father turned, slowly walking away. My heart hurt for Balour.

Before I could respond to Tanner, Caden turned. "I want to speak with him."

"Of course." Tanner moved to open the door. "Do you want Kalen or Faye to join you? Or Prince Fabian?"

"Brighton will join me."

It took everything in me not to smile because doing so seemed wildly inappropriate given the circumstances.

Tanner looked as if he'd swallowed something that made him ill. "Of course."

"I would like to be a part of this," Faye said, lifting her chin. "He is my cousin."

Caden studied her for a moment and then nodded. Relief didn't flicker across her face. Steely determination lined her features.

Across from me, Ren pushed off the wall. "Be careful, he's a biter."

"Noted." Caden strode forward, stopping in front of me. "Ready?"

"I am."

"Okay." Then he lowered his head, and his lips met mine.

Caden kissed me, right there in front of everyone, hammering home the point that we were together.

The shock of Caden kissing me in front of everyone gave way to the all-too-brief burst of warmth and pleasure, of rightness.

He was mine.

And I was his.

Chapter 13

Benji was young.

He couldn't even be old enough to drink if he were human, and he looked so much like Faye. His hair was the same soft black, his skin a deeper, pewter shade, but those eyes were like Elliot's, the youngling Benji had gone in search of. They were pitch-black, so dark that the pupils weren't even visible.

The moment he saw the three of us, he pulled against the chains bolted to the wall. His hands were secured behind his back, and the length of the chain that connected to his ankles couldn't be more than a foot long, so he didn't make it very far.

He hissed though, the sound so eerily feline that the tiny hairs all along my body rose. His attention was focused on Caden.

"Hello, Benji," Caden said.

The youngling growled, his lips peeling back. "You're going to die."

"Is that so?" Caden replied flatly.

"You're all going to die." Benji looked at Faye and then to where I stood. He sniffed the air. "Especially you, human."

I rolled my eyes but remained quiet. This wasn't my interrogation. Although Caden hadn't said that, I knew I was here to listen. Not to engage. I wouldn't get anything out of Benji.

"And yet you're the one chained to the wall," Caden pointed out.

"For now."

Caden chuckled, the sound dark and cold. My gaze darted to him. "Do you really think you can escape me? Your King?"

Benji snapped at the air. "You're no longer my King."

"So, who do you answer to?"

"The one who gave us this world to rule, who will return humans to their rightful place as cattle," he snarled. "I answer to Queen

Morgana."

Faye sucked in a sharp breath, her eyes squeezing shut.

"How can you answer to someone you've never met?"

"She will rip out your entrails and feast upon them."

"Sounds delightful, but you didn't answer my question, and my patience is already running thin."

Benji threw his head back, letting out a high-pitched whining sound. Jerking forward like a cobra striking, he snapped at the air again. "It doesn't matter if I've seen her. She will be freed, and you will bow to her. You will serve her."

"Thought she was going to rip out your entrails," I muttered.

Caden snorted.

Benji's head snapped in my direction. "She'll flay the skin from your bones, you stupid, fucking cattle. She'll—"

Benji's threats ended in a choking sound as Caden shot forward, clamping his hand down on the youngling's throat. "My patience ended right there. Look at me," he commanded. "Look at me, Benji."

Goosebumps pimpled my skin at the change in Caden's tone. It had lowered, but at the same time, seemed to blanket the room in soft, warm silk. I recognized the power in his words.

Glamour.

He was using glamour on another fae, something only the most powerful Ancients could do. And now I knew why he hadn't wanted me to be here. He'd been worried that seeing him use glamour to compel Benji to speak would remind me of Aric.

It was unnerving to be reminded of how powerful Caden was, but nothing about him made me think of Aric.

Benji quieted, his mouth hanging open as he stared up at Caden.

"Who do you answer to other than Queen Morgana?" Caden asked.

"I…I answer to the Winter Court," he answered numbly.

Faye opened her mouth as if she wanted to speak. I reached over, touching her arm slightly. She exhaled roughly and then nodded.

"Why do you answer to them?"

"Because they are…"

"They are what, Benji?"

"They are my masters."

Caden's head tilted slightly. He asked the question again, and then phrased the same question in a different way, but Benji, even under glamour, couldn't say why he answered to them.

And it became clear that several months of the boy's young life were simply *gone*. He couldn't say when he'd been here last. When he last drank any liquor. All he could repeat was that he answered to Queen Morgana, that he served the Winter Court, and that he only knew one name.

"Who is the Ancient who represents the Winter Court."

"Neal," he said. "I answer to Neal."

* * * *

After we left, Benji returned to his former state of hissing, snapping at the air, and threatening to kill everyone. We'd moved to one of the many meeting rooms on the first floor. Kalen and Faye sat beside Fabian, who was seated at one end of the table. Tink had moved off to the common area, where he could receive his daily dose of unfettered admiration. The fae loved him something fierce and were almost always in a constant state of awe around him, partly due to the fact that many had never seen a brownie. Ren was beside me, and Ivy was supposed to head over once she was done with her meeting with Miles. Fabian sat to my left at the other end of the table, and beside him, across from me, was Tanner. Where everyone was seated seemed to be important because when Caden pulled out my chair, every fae in the room stared as if he'd kissed me in front of them once more.

"Even under glamour, Benji couldn't answer why he serves the Winter Court," Caden told the room. "He doesn't know, not on an conscious or subconscious level."

"He has no memory. It's like his life has simply been wiped away," I said. "The only thing I've seen like that is a few humans who've been fed on and under glamour for long periods, but still, never to this level."

"I haven't seen it either," Ren agreed. "Could it be the Devil's Breath then?"

"It would have to be," Fabian answered. "I cannot think of anything that would strip the will and thoughts so deeply."

"They basically become a minion of the Winter Court without reason." Ren dragged his hand through his hair. "This isn't good."

That was the understatement of the year.

I looked over at Caden. "He knew Neal's name, though. That was the only other name he could say."

Caden nodded. "That doesn't tell us if Neal is still in the city or active. I couldn't get anything else out of Benji."

"And we already knew that Neal was involved and have checked out his bar. There was no sign of the Devil's Breath there," Fabian stated, his fingers tapping on the table.

"We need to find Neal," I said, thinking more in terms of how I would do it if this were something the Order was handling. "He has to be the key here."

"We've been searching the city, as has the Order," Tanner said, nodding at Ren. "If he's still here, he's gone to ground. But with Aric's death, I'm willing to bet he's left the city."

"It's not like there aren't places he can hide that we haven't looked or thought to check," Ren pointed out. "And given how many Winter fae are here, he'd have a lot of help doing so."

"I'm in need of refreshments." Tanner rose. "What would everyone like?"

Ren and Caden asked for water. Fabian and Kalen had gone for a soda, and my tongue tingled at the thought of carbonated goodness. I knew one soda wouldn't harm the baby, so I requested one too.

Tanner nodded. "Faye, why don't you help me?"

She blinked as if coming out of a daze and rose. I nibbled on my lip, watching her follow Tanner out. I wasn't the only one whose eyes were glued to her. Kalen had been like a hawk where she was concerned, his gaze flickering to her every few seconds.

"Do you think she'll be okay?" I asked when the door closed behind them.

"They were close, more like siblings than cousins." Kalen tipped his head back. "She'll be okay. Eventually."

Eventually always sounded manageable, except it could be a lifetime from now.

"So you think there's no hope for this kid?" Fabian asked.

"All of the others who consumed Devil's Breath had to be…put down," Caden said, his elbow propped on the arm of the chair as he dragged his thumb along his lower lip. "I imagine if Benji hadn't been restrained, the same would've happened to him."

"But we have one alive," I said. "That means we can at least find out if this is reversible. Hopefully, in the process, we can figure out how the Devil's Breath is able to make these younglings loyal to the Queen—a person they've never met."

Ren kicked back in his chair, planting a boot on the table. "The *borrachero* drug can make humans compliant, but that's only for a short period of time and when they're under the influence."

"Hopefully the specimens Luce took from Benji will tell us if he's still under the influence." Fabian crossed his arms. "If not…"

"Then there is no option," Caden said. "He will have to be given peace."

His brother nodded.

"He can't be kept here where there's a threat of him escaping, causing more harm." Kalen dropped his hand on the table. "His family will understand that."

"Will they?" I asked. "Truly?"

Kalen's gaze met mine. "No one here will ever risk the whole of the Court for just one. Not even for their family."

That seemed harsh, but I fully understood it.

"Except there is someone here who isn't just willing to risk the Court," Caden said, his thumb stilling under his lip. "But who is actively working against the Court."

"You think whoever that is has something to do with Benji coming home?" Ren asked.

"The youngling didn't indicate as much, but it would be unlikely that they aren't connected," Caden answered.

"So that leaves the question of what the goal of having Benji come back here was," Ren asked. "To cause mayhem? Remind the Summer Court that even though Aric is dead, the Winter Court is still very much active?"

My stomach dipped a little at the mention of Aric.

"Or Benji was acting as a scout. Or at the very least, a test," Fabian said, his gaze meeting his brother's from across the table. "He could've been sent here to see what was going on, in the hopes he'd get back out."

Caden's jaw tightened.

"Or he was sent as a test against our defense systems." Kalen nodded slowly. "But that doesn't seem as likely. Why wouldn't whoever the Summer fae is that's working with them be able to give them that information?"

I thought about the Order, how there was a hierarchy involved. There was one here, as well. "Maybe the fae helping the Winter Court isn't privy to the kind of information that could tell them how weak or strong your defenses are." Several gazes landed on me. Still unused to speaking up, I found being the center of attention unnerving. "It doesn't have to be someone any of us know. It could literally be any fae. And to me, it makes more sense that Benji was a test instead of a scout.

If the Winter Court truly has no idea how prepared Hotel Good Fae is or not, they can't be stupid enough to only expect Benji to make it back."

Ren's lips pursed as he nodded.

"You have a point." Respect flashed in Caden's eyes as he looked at me. "A test does seem more likely."

"Not that any of this isn't important," Ren said, and Caden arched a brow. "But Benji was all hail Queen Morgana, talking like her coming back wasn't something in the distant future but more like an event not too far from now. Was that crazy talk, the dying battle cry of the Winter Court? Or something we need to be concerned about?"

The door opened then. Tanner returned with Faye. Luce was behind them, carrying the bottles of soda under her arm and a file in her other hand. She saw me and did a double-take.

I slid a little in my seat. Yet another person I needed to talk to STAT.

Tanner told Luce who had the sodas in a low voice. She placed one in front of me, her eyebrow raised. I gave her a sheepish grin.

"The Winter Court is nowhere near uttering their final, dying battle cry. Unfortunately," Caden said, nodding his thanks to Tanner as he placed a glass of water in front of him, "even without some of the Ancients, they are so very much a threat, but the doorways to the Otherworld are sealed. They cannot be reopened."

My gaze flicked to Tanner as he sat across from me. The doors could be reopened, but as much as I liked Ren, I would not trust him with that information. I wouldn't trust any Order member with that.

A shock surged through my system. I wouldn't trust any Order member? Wasn't I one? Could I even still be one once married to the freaking King of the Summer fae? Sure, they'd kept Ivy on, and she was a halfling. And Miles was open to things that other sects would've been dead set against. But Caden had…well, Caden was different.

Did I even want to be an Order member?

Being part of the Order was ingrained in my blood and bones. What would I be without my duty? Not that there was anything wrong with being a wife and a mother, but I needed more than that.

But the better question was, should I even still be Order when I wouldn't turn over highly necessary information about how the gates could be opened at any time by Caden?

While I had my little moral crisis, Caden was saying, "Unless she's somehow tripled in power, which is impossible, there is no way for her to physically open the gate."

"They can worship her like she's a god," Fabian chimed in. "But they cannot free her simply by praying for it to happen. What they would need is impossible."

Not exactly…

I wasn't sure if Ren accepted the answer or not, but he quieted as I unscrewed the lid of the bottle. There was no fizz. Was it flat? I sighed, but flat soda was better than none. I took a drink, relieved to feel some carbonation, although it sort of tasted like...like diet? I checked the bottle just to make sure I could read properly. It wasn't diet. Looking up, I saw Fabian frowning at his opened bottle.

"Luce has some information to share," Tanner announced, drawing my attention.

Luce nodded. "I was able to do a rapid test thanks to Benji's affinity for spitting when I went in to see him."

My lip curled as I took another drink.

"I was also able to get a urine sample," she said, and Caden's brows lifted. "You do not want to know how I accomplished that."

"I was there for it. She is right," Ren tossed out.

"I'll take both of your words on that," Caden said, and I grinned a little.

"This isn't entirely comprehensive." She opened the folder. "But from his saliva, I was able to determine that he hadn't consumed any alcohol in the last two hours, but there were trace amounts in his urine."

"What does that mean?" Faye asked.

"It means that he drank at some point in the last ninety days, but not recently, and not a lot. If the Devil's Breath is still being mixed with nightshade and liquor, I don't believe he's consumed any of it in the last couple of days."

Faye started to speak and then stopped to swallow before finding her voice. "But we don't know how long the Devil's Breath influences a fae."

"From what I've learned about the *borrachero*, it's that it only stays in a human's system for four hours and then is utterly undetectable in blood tests," Luce stated carefully.

I recognized that tone. Not the greatest news was coming. I started to drown my sorrow in my soda.

"I can one hundred percent say that it works the same in one of us—that it's only effective in terms of making one susceptible to persuasion for a short period of time. But there were no traces of scopolamine—the drug most similar here—in his system." Luce drew in a shallow breath. "I know these results don't tell us much."

"But what do you think it does tell us?" Caden asked, sensing there was something she wanted to add.

"This isn't my specialty," she started.

"I know. Tell us what you think."

She nodded curtly as she folded her hands over the file. "I think that Devil's Breath is only a part of the equation here. We know certain drugs and food and drinks react differently in us. Nightshade for example is poisonous to humans, but it gives us the same effect as some alcoholic beverages do. We also know that scopolamine, in most forms, is absolutely harmless to humans and fae. It's a common ingredient in motion sickness medication but when it's chemically processed into what we know as Devil's Breath, it's a different story. The fae could obviously be susceptible to it, but I have no reason to believe that it wouldn't have worn off by now. Very few human drugs have any impact on us."

Faye shook her head. "What…what does that mean exactly?"

"What I believe that means is there is a missing link. Something we don't know," she said. "And I know that's not exactly helpful, but there has to be something used or done in addition to this drink. Finding out what that is may be the key to stopping this more long-term influence over us."

"That actually tells us something," Caden said. "More than we knew."

"You don't think he'll come out of this then, do you?" Faye asked.

"I…I don't want to say for sure, but…" She pressed her lips together and then exhaled roughly. "But he's been here long enough for the effects to have worn off, and with nothing showing in his samples, I don't believe it is something reversible without knowing what the missing link is."

Faye closed her eyes as my stomach churned sharply with sympathy.

"I'm not saying he has to be…handled immediately. He's contained," Luce said. "We could wait."

Caden looked to Tanner, who gave a quick nod. "We could."

"No. I mean no offense." Faye opened her eyes. "I know you're suggesting that to be kind. Both of you. But there's no point."

"We can wait," Kalen insisted in a low voice.

"I knew the moment I saw him, he was gone," Faye said. "I knew deep down. There is nothing left of Benji in him. He's already gone, and there is no reason for us to delay this. Doing so won't make this easier for anyone."

A muscle ticked in Caden's jaw. "I can do it whenever you and your family are ready."

My stomach twisted again as I thought of Caden having to be the one to do that. It might be his duty, but who would want that kind of responsibility? What had been done to Benji wasn't his fault. I shifted, uncomfortable.

"I would." Faye's voice steadied. "I would ask your permission to allow either me or another member of his family to carry this out. We are all yours, but—"

"But he belongs to you and yours. I understand," Caden said. "Let me know when you wish to do it. I would like to be there just in case you decide you would prefer that I handle it."

"Of course. I…I need to speak to his father and check in on his mother," she said.

"Go," Caden issued quietly. "I'll await word."

Faye slipped quietly from the room, Kalen's eyes on her as he opened his soda.

"I'm sorry." Luce sat back, hands falling to her lap. "I wish I had more information. Something better than there being a missing link."

"Like I said, that is more than we knew before," Caden told her.

"He's right," Ren agreed. I think it was Ren. Or maybe it was Fabian. I wasn't sure.

I felt…weird.

Like not in a weird headspace, but like I had a few years ago when I'd been out to dinner with my mom. It had been a good night. She'd been herself, and we'd gone to one of her favorite seafood places. The shrimp had gone bad or something. Within an hour of eating, I'd quarantined myself in the bathroom. That was how I felt now.

But I hadn't eaten anything since breakfast, and I didn't feel like I needed to use the bathroom. Sweat dotted my forehead.

"Is it just me," I heard Kalen say, maybe to Fabian, "or does this soda taste weird?"

A sharp cramp sliced through my stomach, forcing me to lean back in my seat. Another knifing pain hit my midsection. It felt like period cramps but on steroids.

"Brighton?" Caden turned to me. "Are you okay?"

"Yep," I forced out, breathing through the rippling pain. "I just…"

Across from me, Tanner frowned. "You don't look well, Brighton."

I didn't feel well. Mouth strangely dry, I reached for the soda.

Caden started to rise, but it was Kalen who shot to his feet, his bottle in hand. "Don't touch that!" he yelled. "Don't take another drink."

Chapter 14

Startled, I drew my hand back. "W-what?"

"What's going on?" Caden demanded.

"The soda doesn't taste right," Kalen said, placing it on the table. "What does it taste like to you, Brighton?"

Heart jumping, I placed my damp hands against my stomach. There had to be a fist in there, clenching my insides. "I don't know. I thought it kind of tasted like diet."

"Like artificial sweetener?" Luce pushed from her seat, her pale eyes wide. "Maybe a little minty?"

"Yeah." I nodded as Caden knelt beside me. "I mean, I didn't taste mint, but..." But now that I thought about it, that could've been what I was tasting but couldn't place.

"Shit." Kalen gasped as Fabian picked up his bottle, sniffing it.

"What the hell is going on?" Ren asked as Luce hurried around the table.

"I second that question," Caden said. "And I want to know what the fuck is happening."

Luce slipped into the space between Ren's and my chairs. "Are you feeling sick?" She placed her hand against my forehead. "Nauseous? Cramps?"

"I..." I found it hard to swallow. "Yes."

Her features tightened and then smoothed out as she looked over at Caden. "I need you to get her to the infirmary."

"What...what is happening?" I whispered as Ren rose, giving us space.

Luce didn't answer. "Let me examine you—"

"I swear," Caden growled, "If I have to ask one more time what is going on, no one in this room is going to like it."

"I know you have questions, but right now, what's important is that we get her to a place where I can monitor her." Luce straightened, calm and collected as her gaze met mine. When she spoke next, there was a world of meaning in what she *didn't* say. "I need to examine you, Brighton. Privately."

Privately.

I looked at Caden, whose features had become stark. *Privately*. Understanding surfaced, and my heart kicked into overdrive.

The baby.

Panic sank its icy claws into me. I gripped the arms of the chair, and then it hit me—the strange sensation of wet warmth.

Standing abruptly, I pushed the chair back. Someone was speaking. It was Caden. His hand was on my arm, worry filling his golden eyes.

My stomach seized. There was no other warning. No stopping what came next. All I was able to do was turn away before my upper digestive system revolted. I doubled over, eyes and throat stinging as everything I'd consumed in the last day made a painful reappearance.

Caden was there, his hand on my shoulder. I tried to wave him away, but the clenching motion swept through me once more. I squeezed my eyes shut.

"I'm sorry—" I gagged.

"It's okay, sunshine." His voice sounded all wrong—panicked. "*Luce*."

I opened my eyes and then tore my gaze away from the vomit. Staring at that wasn't going to help. But suddenly, I was in Caden's arms, and I was staring up at the ceiling. There were voices—shouts, and then I heard Caden.

"She's bleeding," he said, running his hand down my stomach and then around my back. "I don't know from where, but she's bleeding."

In a daze, I saw it. It was small, just a few smudges of red, right where I'd been sitting. I knew what it was even as my legs and arms seemed to no longer be attached to my body.

Blood.

There was blood on the chair.

How much blood did it take for it to soak through clothing? I knew where that sensation of wet warmth had come from—where the blood had come from.

The baby.

Another series of cramps seized me, and I twisted in Caden's arms, gagging. He lifted me off the floor. I must've checked out because the next thing I knew, I was being laid down on a thin mattress. Luce was at my side, my arm in her hand as another fae wrapped a blood pressure cuff around my biceps.

Caden's face was above mine, his hand warm against my cheek as he smoothed the hair back from my face. "It's okay," he said. "It's going to be okay. I promise you. Everything is going to be just fine."

But it wasn't.

You didn't bleed like that when you were pregnant. You didn't have pain like this. You didn't vomit like that.

Something was wrong—very wrong as the fae called out numbers that didn't sound right. There was a pinch in my arm. My head lolled to the side. Luce was inserting a needle. Dark red blood filled a collection tube.

"I need activated charcoal," Luce called out, rattling off milligrams and then fluids as hands lifted up my shirt. I jerked at the cool touch of ECG leads. There was beeping, and I thought it sounded too fast.

"Has she been poisoned?" Caden demanded, and it felt like the temperature of the room had increased. "Has someone poisoned her?"

"I'm not sure." Luce hooked up an IV as she looked over her shoulder. "But you should pull all the drinks you got from the cafeteria, Tanner."

"On it," came the quick reply from somewhere in the room.

Poisoned? Oh God. Panic overshadowed the deep contractions, giving way to terror as my gaze found Luce's. There was only one thought occupying my mind as I tried to drag in air, but the corners of my vision darkened. "Is the baby okay?"

Luce momentarily froze as she stared down at me.

"The baby?" Caden's voice was low, barely above a whisper. "*What* baby?"

Blinking rapidly, Luce's chin jerked up, and then her gaze shot back to mine. Her lips moved, but the beeping from the machines was rapid, and then darkness spread out. The room was suddenly shaking, the gurney creaking—

"She's having a seizure," Luce grabbed my shoulders. "No. Not the Ativan. I need—"

Whatever she said was lost in a roar and a burst of a hundred stars. The last thing I saw was Caden staring down at me in shock

And then I saw nothing.

* * * *

The first thing I became aware of was the steady beep of a machine. My head felt as if it were full of cotton balls so I focused on the sound and followed it out of the nothingness. It took a small eternity for me to open my eyes.

A light from somewhere behind me cast a soft, buttery-yellow glow over the room. I thought this was the same room I'd been brought into it, but it was…quieter. Calmer. On the small table was my iron cuff, blade disengaged.

The baby.

I moved my hand to my stomach, wincing at the pull of the IV. I had no idea what I was feeling for. The act seemed instinctual, but it told me nothing. Was the baby okay? My heart turned over heavily as fear hit my veins. It was strange how quickly I'd gone from being shocked and overwhelmed by the idea of having a baby, to desperately wanting that child.

Now it could be all over—gone before I even had a chance to share the news with Caden. And how could it have survived? I had a vague memory of Kalen yelling at me to not drink any more soda. Had I been poisoned? Grief and confusion swirled through me.

"Brighton."

Slowly, I turned my head to the left. Caden was sitting there, his chin propped on his joined hands. He looked…terrible. His normally smooth hair looked as if he'd dragged his fingers through the strands a hundred times. There were shadows under his eyes, and tension to the set of his lips. A wicked sense of deja vu hit me. It wasn't all that long ago that we'd found ourselves in a similar situation, but this time was different. The way he looked at me was…. It wasn't right.

"How are you feeling?" he asked.

My lips felt dry as I considered his question. My stomach didn't hurt, and I wasn't vomiting. "Okay." My voice was hoarse. "I think."

He reached over, picking up a pitcher and pouring a glass of water. "You should drink this."

I took the water, welcoming the cool rush against my scratchy throat. It helped clear some of the fog that seemed to still fill my brain. I would've drunk the entire cup if Caden hadn't caught the bottom of the glass, tugging it away.

"I think that's enough for right now." He placed the cup on the table. "Luce warned that your stomach might be sensitive."

"What…what happened?"

"You were poisoned."

I tensed. *The baby.* "So hearing that said wasn't a figment of my imagination?"

"No." He sat forward, hands falling to the space between his knees. "It was done with a flower similar to Pennyroyal found in the Otherworld. Fae often use it as a powder for inflammation or bruises. We believe it was placed in the sodas."

I tried to process what he was saying. "All of them?"

He nodded. "The rest of the drinks have been pulled and are being tested, but the ones Fabian and Kalen had, also had traces of it."

"Are they okay?"

"They won't be affected by such a substance."

"Because they're fae?"

A muscle twitched in his jaw. "Because you're pregnant."

I drew in a shallow breath, but it went nowhere.

"The flower, when consumed in large quantities, can cause expectant mothers to miscarry," he continued, his voice strangely flat. "Luce believes it affected you more because you're mostly human, causing the vomiting and the seizure." He inhaled deeply. "And she believes that is also why you survived. Someone fully human wouldn't have. You'll be weak for a while. You may have more seizures, but she believes that you will recover fully."

It connected in the back of my mind that he must've told Luce about the Summer Kiss, but that didn't matter at the moment. His features blurred as tears filled my eyes. My brain wasn't working right. A part of me knew that this wasn't how I'd wanted Caden to find out. How I'd planned on any conversation about the baby going, but I had to know. Even though I was terrified, I had to know.

"Is the…am I still pregnant?" I whispered.

His eyes closed briefly. "The poison caused you to have contractions, which created a tear and then the bleeding. Luce was able to get the poison out of your system quickly."

I could feel myself trembling as I tried to brace for the inevitable.

"Once she had you stabilized, she was then able to check on the…on the baby." His throat worked on a swallow. "Luce didn't find any tissue in your bleeding. She did an ultrasound—sonography—to check for a heartbeat." He took a shuddering breath, his eyes meeting mine. "According to Luce, the baby is incredibly strong-willed and determined to be born."

I blinked once and then twice. "W-what?"

"You didn't lose the baby. At least, not now," he explained. "She said it's a high-risk pregnancy and that you need to be monitored, but she's cautiously optimistic."

"I… I'm…." Stunned, I couldn't find words as disbelief rose. "I'm still pregnant?"

Caden nodded.

Tears welled so fast that I smacked my hands over my face. Relief and happiness turned out to be way more powerful than the crushing dread and fear. I couldn't believe it. This baby has survived Aric and a poisoning. Strong-willed was an understatement.

"Are those tears of happiness?" Caden asked. "Or disappointment?"

I yanked my hands away from my face. "What?"

"I think it's a valid question," he said. "Because I don't know if you're happy or sad to know that you're still pregnant."

"I'm happy," I told him, shocked. "Why would you even ask that?"

"Why?" A harsh, short laugh left him. "How would I know what you're thinking? You've known this whole time that you were pregnant. Eleven weeks, actually. Luce was able to confirm definitively, by the way."

I gave a little shake of my head. "I'm happy. I want this baby—"

"You do?"

"Yes," I said without hesitation. "I was planning to tell you. That's what I wanted to talk to you about later." The cloudy feeling in my head had completely disappeared. "I didn't tell you, because—"

"Because you were trying to save the world. Yeah, I know. Luce told me." The tension brackets increased around his mouth and then he rose, turned away.

"Caden—"

"I didn't know," he said, voice rough. "I thought I was hearing things when you asked about the baby." His voice cracked on that word, and I felt it in my heart. "I learned that I was going to be a father at the same time I learned that someone out there knew and tried to kill not only you but also my child."

"I was trying to do the right thing," I told him. "I was doing the right thing—"

"I stood there, trying to process that someone had almost killed you and my child," he cut me off. "And in the midst of watching you nearly die and being unable to do a damn thing, I realized that the only reason Kalen knew to tell you not to drink any more of that soda was because he knew that you were pregnant."

"I'm sorry. He wasn't supposed to know. He overheard me telling Tink—"

"I know." He faced me. "He knew. So did Tanner. So did Faye. Are there any more who are sworn to be loyal to me that knew you were carrying my child?"

"No. They weren't supposed to know. I told Tink because I had to tell someone—"

"You should've told *me*, Brighton."

"I wanted to. I did. But I thought that if you knew, it would be harder for us to do the right thing—"

"Doing the right thing never should've included you keeping the fact that you were pregnant with my child from me." His eyes weren't cool then. They burned with anger. "I get what you were trying to do. Your desire to protect my Court and others is something that I love about you, but this is different."

"How is it different?" I tried to sit up but found it was harder than expected. Caden snatched a pillow from the counter and shoved it behind my back. "Thank you."

"That is our child, Brighton. Not just yours. Ours." After ensuring that I was sitting up easily, he stepped back from the bed. "And *our* child should matter more than everything else. That's why it's different."

"I agree, Caden, that's why I needed you to choose a Queen because I didn't want our child to grow up in a world that was being overrun by Winter fae," I reasoned, trying to keep my voice calm.

"I chose you as my Queen."

"But I didn't know that!" The heart monitor beeped loudly, earning a dangerous look from Caden. I forced myself to calm down. "I didn't know, and I planned to tell you tonight—"

"You mean last night. You've been out for almost twelve hours."

"Oh," I whispered.

He shoved a hand through his hair again. "This isn't the time for this conversation. You need to take it easy—"

"I am taking it easy, and there is no other time we should be having this conversation. I'm sorry, Caden. You have to believe that. I wanted to tell you. If you don't believe me, you can ask Tink. You can even ask Tanner. I wanted—"

"Then why didn't you tell me the moment you realized we could be together?" he asked.

"I was just overcome. I knew I should have, but my head was all over the place," I admitted. "I thought we had time."

"You thought wrong," he said, and my gaze flew to his. "If I had known, I could've stopped what happened."

"How?" I asked. "How could you have stopped this? If someone wants me dead, whether or not I'm pregnant won't change that. You said this flower or whatever would've most likely killed me if I hadn't been given the Summer Kiss."

"If I had known, I would've made sure you weren't given something that could've killed our child."

"How? Are you going to taste everything I eat and drink?"

"Fuck, yes!" he shouted. "I would taste everything that wasn't prepared by my hands."

"And if I wasn't pregnant, you would've been like YOLO then? Let me drink whatever?"

His eyes narrowed. "It would've taken a lot more than that to kill you. And no, that doesn't mean I wasn't or wouldn't be worried about someone targeting you, but at least I know that you wouldn't be easy to kill. Our child is a whole different story."

I dragged my hand over my face, realizing then that he was a hundred percent serious about tasting my food and drink. "I…I don't know what to say other than I understand why you're upset. I do. And I hope you understand why I didn't say anything. But I'm sorry, Caden. I don't know what to say to make this better."

Jaw working, he looked away. "Neither do I."

My chest squeezed. "What…what does that mean?"

"I don't know. I really don't," he said, and my chest clenched. "If I hadn't told you that you being with me wouldn't be a risk, when were you going to tell me?"

"I planned on telling you as soon as you were married—"

"So, you were going to wait until I did what? Moved on from you? Picked a fae?" He took a step toward the bed. "Did you really believe that I would just choose to be with someone else when I knew that you love me? That I would've just walked away?"

"Before I knew that I could be with you, that's what I'd hoped you would do," I admitted. "I wouldn't have liked it. I would've hated it—loathed every second of it—but it was the right—"

"You can believe all you want that it was the right thing to do. Maybe on a superficial level, it was, but our child changes that. Keeping that knowledge from me was never the right thing. Not when you love me. Not when you know I love you." He turned, his body stiff. "And the worst part of this is the fact that you really believed I would move on. That I could just happily go and marry someone else."

"I didn't think you'd do that happily."

"But you told Tanner to do whatever was necessary to make sure I married a fae," he shot back, and I stiffened. "Yes, he told me how the woman I love conspired with others to make sure I ended up with someone else while she was carrying my child."

It felt like my heart had stopped. "I didn't conspire. It wasn't like that. I couldn't risk the whole world. Not when our child would have to grow up in it." My hand went to my stomach. "What I was trying to do doesn't change that I love you, Caden."

"But you didn't love me enough to fight for me, did you? You didn't love me enough to trust that things would be okay." His jaw hardened. "And you sure as fuck didn't respect me enough to tell me about our child."

"Caden—" I started, but the door opened then, revealing Luce. "Can you give us a moment?"

"I don't think so." Luce was rocking one hell of a no-nonsense tone and expression. "I've been monitoring Brighton's heart rate and blood pressure remotely, and I apologize, my King. I know you two have a lot to discuss, but we need to keep her heart rate and pressure stable."

"I'm fine."

"This is not keeping her stable," Luce continued as if I hadn't spoken. "And so soon after everything, this could threaten the pregnancy."

"You're right." Caden folded his arms. "When do you think it will be safe to move her?"

"I think tomorrow will be fine, as long as her stats remain stable, and she's kept as…" She glanced over at me. "Stress-free as possible."

"She will be," barked Caden, and I raised my brows. "I don't want her here for one second longer than necessary."

"Understood."

Caden turned to me. "When we leave tomorrow, you'll be coming home with me."

"To your apartment?"

"No. To a place very few are aware of," he said. "And do not argue with me about this and cause yourself unnecessary stress. Your house is not suitable."

Too much was happening, and strangely, my brain focused on that statement. "Why is it not suitable?"

"Because too many people know where to find you, and I cannot possibly begin to secure the house," he replied, turning back to Luce. "Notify me the moment you leave here."

She nodded.

There was no way he was leaving. "Where are you going?"

Caden didn't answer. He simply turned around and left the room, closing the door behind him without answering my question.

Without so much as looking at me.

Chapter 15

"He hates me."

"No, he doesn't." Tink patted my arm. He'd followed Luce in, advising that he was on the approved visitation list.

In other words, he was allowed to see me.

I had a feeling that Caden had prohibited everyone else from getting close to me, which was understandable. But Tanner and Faye? Kalen? Ren and Ivy? Fabian? They were the only ones I trusted, but apparently, Caden was taking no chances.

While that should give me some relief because it meant that he still cared, I had a sinking feeling that he was more worried about the baby.

After all, according to him, I wasn't all that easy to kill. Or whatever.

"You don't understand, Tink." I sighed as Luce came over to check my blood pressure. "He feels betrayed, and I can't blame him. Not really."

"Neither can I," he agreed. "But I think he just needs time. He knows you were trying to do the right thing."

I nodded.

"He was dealt one hell of a shock, learning he was a baby daddy while you were vomiting up your guts and seizing," Tink pointed out as bluntly as possible. "I imagine most expect to learn that kind of news in any other way than how the King learned it."

"I know. It's just…" I could still hear him saying that I hadn't loved him enough. That wasn't true. It was the exact opposite. I loved him enough to not be the source of his downfall, and I loved our child enough to do everything to bring him or her up in a world that was stable.

Well, as stable as it could be.

"Is everything still okay?" I asked as Luce placed the cuff on the counter.

"All of your stats look good." Luce came back to the bed. "I'll check the hormone levels in the blood I just took, and then I'll take some more blood tomorrow. If you were to start to miscarry, we'd see those hormone numbers going down."

My stomach dipped. "Do you think there's still a chance that I could lose the baby?"

"The pregnancy is considered threatened, so yes, there is a chance. But you're different, Brighton. You're not entirely human." Her pale eyes narrowed on me. "Which would've been something useful to know when I first examined you."

"Hey." Tink lifted his hands. "She didn't even tell me." He slid me a look. "Hussy."

I sighed once more. "I'm sorry. I didn't think it was something I was supposed to share, and in my defense, a whole lot of shit has been happening. I obviously haven't been making the best decisions."

"That's an understatement," Tink muttered under his breath as he leaned back in the chair.

I ignored that.

"Learning that you were given the Summer Kiss explains why you've been healing so well from your previous injuries," Luce went on. "Since you were given it before conception, it probably aided with that too. That's got to have something to do with the child being so resilient, but I can't be sure. I've never met a human who's been given the Summer Kiss." Her brow puckered. "But you stopped bleeding last night, so that's great news. You haven't been experiencing any more cramping or nausea, right?"

I nodded. "I feel normal-ish. My stomach is a little sore, and I feel like I just got over the flu or something."

She nodded. "That's normal. It appears your body is...well, repairing the damage. And to be honest, that is not something that would normally happen. Not even for a female fae who'd been given this poison."

Unease blossomed, but I tried to shut that down. Luce was giving me good news. Just because this was nothing short of a miracle didn't mean I'd lose the child.

"Luckily, we were able to get it out of your system as soon as possible. A few more minutes, I don't think even the Summer Kiss would've changed the outcome," she said, and that was hard to process. "I'm optimistic, but a lot is going to depend on what happens in the next couple of days to weeks."

"What can I do to make sure the baby is okay?"

Luce took a moment and then softened her voice. "In most of these circumstances, there is nothing you can do to change the outcome. It's often out of your hands. If you were to lose this child, it would not be your fault."

"I know, but there's got to be something I can do, right?"

"There are things that can help. One of them is to remain as stress-free as possible, and I know that is going to be hard, but keeping stress levels low is what you need to do," she advised, and I almost laughed, because I had no idea how I would do that. "I do suggest bed rest for the next week just to be safe."

Bed rest? "What about our appointment?"

"I think we can delay it a week since I've done a lot of the tests that I would've been doing, but I will be checking in on you—tracking your hormone levels." She folded her arms. "I would refrain from any physical activity until you feel completely one hundred percent—no longer sore or tired. That could be a week or slightly longer. No physical activities also includes sex."

I didn't think that would be an issue.

"You're going to need to keep your hands and body parts to yourself," Tink advised.

"Thanks for the clarification," I said. "I can do that. Bed rest and no physical activity. I'll do whatever I can to keep the baby healthy."

"That's good to hear," she said. "It's good that you'll be staying with Caden in a secure location."

"Because once the fae who tried to kill me realizes they failed, they'll come at me again?" Anger flashed through me, so potent and hot that Luce frowned at the color that highlighted my cheeks. "I can't believe someone tried that. I mean, I can, but what in the hell did they think they'd gain from killing me? That Caden would somehow revert back to his evil self and open the doorway? That's not how that works."

A huge part of me couldn't believe how easy I'd made it for them. I almost always drank soda when I was here. Any number of fae could've paid attention to that. I really needed to change up my routine.

"Perhaps they thought that by killing you, it would simply distract and weaken him. Which it would," Luce advised. "It could have nothing to do with their attempts to free their Queen, but more so to level a blow that our King would find difficult to recover from. Choosing a poison that affects pregnancy so adversely was extremely lucky for them—and most unfortunate for you."

I tried not to be offended by her word choice. "Do we have any idea who could've done it? Were the other bottles contaminated? Any other drinks?"

"So far, only about a dozen tested positive," she said.

"Are any of the fae here at risk?"

"We've notified those who are pregnant, and it doesn't appear that any have been put at risk," she answered.

"That's good news," I whispered, hands curling into the thin blanket.

"Caden has been holding an inquisition, questioning all the fae who had access to the drinks that were in the cooler," Tink said. "Which is pretty much every fae here."

It almost seemed like an impossible task, but Caden could compel the truth. Something that I doubted he wanted to do to every member of his Court without due cause. He was smart enough to know that he'd create more enemies using glamour to find the one who was responsible, but now he had a reason.

I just hoped it didn't hurt his relationship with his Court.

But I wanted whoever was responsible dead. Actually, I wanted to be the one to kill them myself. That would probably violate the whole bed rest thing, but I also thought it could be fairly therapeutic.

"You know, I've been thinking," Tink said. "And I know that usually means I'm about to say something completely irrelevant, but I promise that's not the case right now."

My brows rose. "What have you been thinking about?"

"Why do we think it's someone who didn't know you were pregnant?" Tink asked as he glanced between the two of us. "Because there are a lot of ways they could have tried to kill you—well, poison is definitely a quieter way, but there are other poisons they could have used. Right, Luce?"

"Right," she replied, drawing out the word.

"All I'm saying is that it seems way too coincidental that the poison that was chosen, was the one that has that kind of effect on a pregnancy."

A trickle of unease skirted through me. "But there are only a handful of people who know I'm pregnant. None of them would've done something like this."

"I don't think they would've, but that doesn't mean they didn't say something," Tink reasoned. "That everyone kept their mouth shut."

"You're suggesting that one of us jeopardized her safety?" Luce demanded. "I can tell you that those who know never would've done that."

"I'm not suggesting that anyone did it thinking it would jeopardize her safety," Tink responded. "Look, everyone talks. Even the fae. You may be special, Luce, and you're a fortress of secrets, but there ain't a single race of beings out there that isn't infected with the need to gossip."

"I get what you're saying, but those who know would never be so careless with such information."

"Maybe not." Tink sat back. "Perhaps they weren't so careless at all."

My gaze sharpened on him, but I didn't say anything until Luce finished up and left the room. "What are you really thinking? And don't say nothing. You were being purposely vague. Maybe Luce didn't see that, but I did."

Tink glanced at the door. "Okay. I was being a little vague, but Lite Bright, something doesn't seem right about this."

"A lot of things don't seem right at the moment."

"Yeah, but I just think it's strange that out of all the poisons—and there are many that have been brought over from the Otherworld—that would've killed you with just one taste, *that* one was used." His gaze slid back to me. "Sure, you were given a large dose that would've taken you out if you were completely human, but why take that risk when there are far more effective ones? Think *Game of Thrones* level of quick and messy death. It's almost like killing you wasn't the priority."

"If I wasn't the priority, then—" That was something I didn't want to even think. Because it would mean that the baby was the target, and that meant Tink was right. "Who would you think would've talked?"

"I don't know. I want to say none of them, but…"

"But you just said everyone gossips." There was a great sense of dread. "And you said maybe they didn't speak carelessly. I'm thinking you meant someone shared the news with intent."

"But I do agree that none of those who knew would've done anything to harm you. Kalen stopped you from drinking. Tanner wouldn't do something like that. He's too dignified. And what reason would Faye have?"

"And Luce?"

"She's had plenty of opportunities to end you or the baby."

True. She could've poisoned the prenatal pills, and no one would have known. "Then who could it have been?"

"Do we know that no one else was in the courtyard? No. We don't.

Someone else could've been out there," he said. "Whatever fae is working with the Winter Court could've followed you, or it could be someone else."

"Then that would mean we have not one but two fae we need to locate."

Tink nodded. "And that Caden is definitely going to kill."

"Caden?" I coughed out a humorless laugh. "I'm going to kill the sons of bitches."

Chapter 16

After Luce had returned later with a light dinner, she wanted me to get up and move around a little, which consisted of me walking around the small room.

Then came the part I usually dreaded whenever I went to the doctor. She weighed me, and for once, seeing that I'd gained a few pounds even though I'd been a volcano of vomit the night before made me breathe a sigh of relief. She took some more blood, and after my twentieth or so lap around the room, I returned to the bed, surprised by how much that had worn me out.

"Like I said, you're going to be weaker than usual," she told me, slipping the vial of blood into a small bag. "But I have a feeling you'll regain your strength quicker than even I expect."

"The Summer Kiss, huh?" I leaned back against the mountain of pillows.

"It's a kiss of life." Luce placed the bag on the counter and then crossed her arms. Her gaze fell to the small table. I'd engaged the blade earlier, just in case. It was only a few inches in length, but it was long and sharp enough to do its job. "I wish you would've told me about that, and yes, I know I already said that, but I feel the need to restate it. I could've told you then that you had nothing to worry about when it came to our King choosing you—that *I* had nothing to worry about."

"I'm sorry. I didn't know that changed things. Caden never told me," I explained. "And I get why he didn't. He was trying not to overwhelm me after everything, but I wish he'd told me."

"And I'm sure he wished you'd told him about the child," she replied, and I flinched. "I meant no offense by that. What I mean is that it seems like you and Caden could've benefited from a very in-depth conversation."

I laughed dryly. "No doubt."

"But you have both been processing a lot," she said, picking up the bag.

"Have you seen Caden?" He hadn't been back.

"I believe he's still carrying out the questioning," she answered.

I wondered who was standing guard outside because I doubted Caden was relying on a locked door. But who had Caden deemed trustworthy enough? I picked at the blanket. "Who's playing babysitter?"

She arched a brow. "Kalen."

A slight smile tugged at my lips. "I owe him a lot. If he hadn't…"

Luce inclined her chin. "He would make a fine Knight for our King."

As far as I knew, Caden hadn't chosen any of his Knights yet. I had a feeling Aric's betrayal all those years ago played a role in that. "He would. I'm glad to see that Caden trusts him." I watched Luce slip the vial into her pocket, thinking about what Tink had said. I actually hadn't really stopped thinking about it. "Can I ask you something?"

She nodded. "Of course."

"Do you really think the choice of poison had nothing to do with my pregnancy? That it's possible that no one who knows spoke?"

"I've thought about this. It's an herb that's widely available—actually grown in our greenhouse as it has amazing healing properties. Some of the other poisons that Tink mentioned are simply not easily accessible. That could be the reason." She smoothed the lapel of her coat. "But if Tink is right, that one of those who knows did speak, who would they have told that would've done something like this? Would it then be a coincidence that the person unknowingly told the fae who has been working with the Winter Court, and if not, then are we dealing with two fae who have done the unforgivable?"

I nibbled on my lower lip, mulling it over. I couldn't shake the feeling that I was missing something. "Maybe this has nothing to do with the other fae. I mean, I'm sure there are tons of fae who would probably act upon the knowledge that I was pregnant."

"You don't seem to have a high opinion of the fae," she replied, "if you think there are so many who would wish to harm an unborn child. If you're to be our Queen, I hope that changes."

Chastised, I realized that what I'd said hadn't come out right. "I didn't mean that I think there's a ton of fae who would gladly harm a child, but I bet there are many who would do anything to protect their

Court, right? Isn't that what Kalen said about Benji's family? That they wouldn't even keep their own child alive if it was a risk to the Court?"

Luce's brows puckered. "Yes. Many fae are willing to protect their Court," she said slowly.

"And how many fae would see me as a risk to the Court? Even before the pregnancy. After all, Tatiana came to me before I knew I was pregnant," I reasoned. "Without them knowing I'd been given the Summer Kiss, wouldn't they see this child as a threat to their future? It's why I hadn't told Caden that I was pregnant. It's why you agreed to remain silent, as did the others."

"I see what you're saying." She sighed wearily. "It's just that I have a hard time believing that those who knew would've said anything. That knowledge in the wrong hands doesn't only mean someone viewing you as a threat, but it could also cause panic."

"Then…then that person may have told someone they trusted. Someone who may have…" Someone who may not have been sent into a panic. Who would've already known that Caden was in love with me. Suspicion dawned, and I was grateful that I wasn't hooked up to the heart monitor.

"What?" Luce asked.

I didn't want to say anything in case I was wrong. "Can you do me a favor? Can you get Tanner for me?"

"Why do you want to see him?"

"I just thought of something he said to me, and I'm not sure if I heard him right," I lied. "Please? Tanner cannot possibly be banned from seeing me."

"The King decreed that no one without his express approval—"

"Or I can just go find Tanner myself. I doubt you're going to chain me to my bed. So, do you think Caden would be more upset with me roaming around, or you getting Tanner for me?"

Her eyes narrowed. "That sounds like blackmail."

"More like presenting you with options," I suggested.

One side of her lips curved up. "Uh-huh. I doubt you'll have any problems assuming the role of our Queen." She turned away. "I'll go find Tanner now."

"Thank you," I said, unsure if her comment about the whole Queen thing was a compliment or not.

But I didn't have the brain space to really deal with that. If my suspicions were on point, then I might know who poisoned the drinks.

When a soft knock came about fifteen minutes later, I knew Luce had done what I asked. Tanner stepped in, quietly closing the door behind him.

"Luce said you needed to speak with me?" he asked.

I nodded. "Thank you for coming, even though I have a feeling that Caden has told everyone to stay away from me."

A faint smile appeared. "He has, but Luce said that she sensed it was important." Walking forward, he sat in the chair. He looked rough, as if he hadn't slept well. Whether or not my suspicion was correct, he had to have a lot on his mind. "Luce told us that the child is well, which I'm grateful to hear. But how are you feeling?"

"I'm okay. Just a little tired. Thank you for asking."

The shadows under his eyes looked like bruises as he nodded. "I don't mean to be rude, but I'm confident that Kalen didn't even want to allow me into the room. I imagine the only reason I was allowed is because the King is with Faye and her family."

Benji.

Jesus, I'd practically forgotten about him. "He hasn't gotten better, has he?"

Tanner shook his head sadly. "He is…he is lost to us."

Sadness found its way into my already crowded heart. "They'll…" What had Caden said? Peace. "They'll give him peace now?"

He nodded. "Yes. Our King is there in case they have need of him."

I glanced at the door, wanting to go and find where they were. I wanted to be there for Caden, even if he didn't have to be the one to end Benji's young life. That suddenly seemed as important as why I'd asked for Tanner.

"I wouldn't want to further displease the King," Tanner said. "What did you want to see me about?"

"Understood." I drew in a shallow breath, fighting the urge to run off and find Caden. While I'd threatened to do that earlier, even I wasn't that stupid when there was someone out there actively trying to harm the baby and me. "I want to ask you something, and I hope you'll be honest. It's an uncomfortable question."

Tanner nodded for me to continue.

"Did you tell anyone that I was pregnant?" I asked, watching him closely. A muscle twitched near his right eye. "And I'm not suggesting that I think you told someone thinking they'd do what they did, but I know I told you to do whatever was necessary to make sure Caden chose a fae as his Queen, and I don't think you would've told just anyone because of the panic or risk it could cause. I know you would do anything to protect your Court, and maybe that included telling someone that I was pregnant. Maybe so they'd pursue Caden, knowing that Caden would eventually find out that I was pregnant."

Tanner stared at me in silence for several heartbeats. "You think I spoke to Tatiana?"

I nodded. That's exactly what I suspected—that he'd told Tatiana, maybe even her brother. "It would make sense. Tatiana and Sterling already knew what was happening in terms of the engagement. They would have a reason to view the child as a real threat. I don't want to believe it," I quickly added as Tanner's eyes widened. "I honestly think that Tatiana came to me in the beginning out of concern and not to get me to leave Caden. So, I'm not saying this out of jealousy or anything like that. Caden loves me." Even if he wasn't quite sure about that now. That thought hurt, but my suspicion wasn't coming from making the other woman who wasn't even really the other woman the villain. "It just makes sense."

Tanner leaned forward. "Tatiana would never do such a thing. Neither would her brother. I know you don't know them well, and I can even understand why you'd think it was them, but those misdeeds cannot be placed on them."

"Are you sure? How well do you know them?" I asked.

"I don't know either extremely well." Lifting a hand, he dragged it over his head, clasping the back of his neck. "But I know they had nothing to do with this tragedy."

Tragedy? As if what had happened was due to an unexpected car accident. "You mean attempted murder?"

His silvery skin paled as he tipped back, recoiling from what I'd said. A moment passed. "You're right. It was attempted murder. I…" He dropped his hand to the arm of the chair. "Caden gave you the Summer Kiss. He did this years ago?"

Caught off guard by the change of topic, it took me a moment. "Yes. When I was injured by Aric and the other fae. It was why I didn't die then."

"You are his *mortuus*," he said, his voice thickening as his gaze roamed over my face. "You hold a piece of his soul. That makes you a far more worthy choice than any fae that could be presented to him. The entire Court, once they are aware, will not only support his choice but will celebrate such a union. It is rare for one to find their *mortuus*."

"That's what Caden told me." Emotion clogged my throat, and I couldn't think about how things were now. "I didn't know what it meant until yesterday. He hadn't wanted to overwhelm me. If I knew, I never would've tried to hide my pregnancy from him, and I wouldn't have asked you to do that or to help make sure he chose someone else."

"I know." A small, sad smile appeared as his eyes glistened. "I wish he had told you. I wish I had paid attention enough to realize what you meant to him. Looking back, it was obvious. I should have known. I found my *mortuus* once, but I lost her."

"I'm sorry," I told him.

"It wasn't Tatiana or her brother." A tear slid unchecked down his cheek. "It was me."

Chapter 17

"I can barely live with myself now," Tanner said. "I can't let someone else take the blame for my actions. Not when this reckoning was always coming."

Blood pounded in my ears as I stared at Tanner in disbelief.

"When I saw him with you, I thought you'd changed your mind. That he'd convinced you to stay with him," he explained, staring at his open hands. "And I believed that after everything I'd done, the dirt I'd sunk my hands into, that it was all for nothing. That our King was going to forsake our entire Court."

I couldn't think.

"I didn't know if you'd already told him about the baby. I thought you hadn't, because if you had, I couldn't imagine that he'd allow you into the room with that poor youngling," he continued. "I thought that if I could at least end the pregnancy, it would cut one of the threads that bound him to you, and you to him. After all, it would not be the worst sin I have committed to protect the Court."

I couldn't move.

"In the beginning, I thought you were just a passing fancy and then a distraction. I knew he cared for you. Deeply enough that even if I hadn't known you were his *mortuus*, I saw that he would not easily choose another." His voice rasped, barely audible. "Aric lied to you, Brighton. There was no Summer fae willing to work with the Winter Court to release that monster. There was only me."

I couldn't breathe.

"I knew I could get a message to him through Neal, and I did. I met with him twice, and there was a moment when I considered killing him. I'd brought a sheathed dagger with me. I could've done it. The Ancient was so arrogant. I had a window of opportunity." He continued staring at his hands. "But I didn't take it. Not the first time when I told him that…that you were important to our King, and not the second when he told me that he planned to use you to force Caden to open the gateway. I didn't know then that was possible. I thought…"

The shock of what he'd admitted snapped me out of my stupor. "You…*you're* the reason Aric came for me? You knew that he had me alive? That he was keeping me there, torturing—?"

"I thought he would kill you. I didn't know he'd keep you alive," he said without looking up.

"You thought…he would kill me. As if that makes a difference, makes it better," I whispered, disbelieving what I was hearing.

This was Tanner.

Prim and proper Tanner, who wore polo shirts and khaki pants. Who I could easily imagine playing golf on the weekends. Tanner, who was nice and always calm, who I knew had harbored a crush for my mother and had been genuinely upset over her murder.

Murder carried out by the Ancient he'd later all but handed me over to.

And now he'd tried to kill my child.

"How could you?" I demanded, hands shaking. The betrayal cut so deeply that it was all I could feel. It hurt, because never in a million years would I have expected that he'd do something like this. It *hurt*.

"It wasn't personal."

"Are you serious?" I cried. "How could this get any more personal?"

"I know that sounds absurd. I like you, and you know I liked your mother—"

"How could you do this? I trusted you. My mom trusted you." A rising tide of anger chipped away at the pain of his betrayal. "Caden trusted you."

"I know." He lifted his head then. Tears tracked down his face, and seeing them made me even more furious. What right did he have to be upset? He'd tried to kill our child. He was responsible for my seemingly never-ending weeks in hell. "I thought I was doing the right thing." He sat back, arms limp at his sides. "Caden thought he was doing the right thing by not telling you everything. You thought you were doing the right thing by pushing him away and not telling him about the baby. And I thought I was—"

"What you did is not even remotely the same," I snapped. "We were trying to protect one another. You—"

"And I was trying to protect the entire Court and the world!" His shoulders shook. "That's what I was trying to do."

I stared at him, trembling. The rage building inside of me diminished everything else—the betrayal, the disbelief, and the pain. I'd told Tink that I would kill whoever had been responsible. I wasn't being overdramatic then, and that was before I knew that the person responsible for nearly ending my child's life was also responsible for the horror I'd suffered at Aric's hands. Out of the corner of my eye, I saw the cuff and blade on the table.

Murderous fury was a cyclone inside of me. I liked Tanner. I trusted him. My mom had trusted him, and maybe later, the pain of his betrayal would haunt me, but the bitter burn of vengeance consumed me now. I moved without thinking, twisting at the waist as I kicked the blanket off. I reached for the cuff, fully intending to slam the blade deep into his throat. I would sever his head from his shoulders, ensuring his death.

Tanner was quick, like all fae were, no matter if they fed or not.

He shot from his chair, knocking it over as he swiped up the cuff with a linen napkin that had been left beside it.

Shit.

Sliding off the bed, I grabbed the lamp just as the door burst open. I yanked the lamp from where it was plugged in and swung it at Tanner as Kalen burst into the room.

"What the hell is going on?" Kalen demanded as Tanner jumped back, blocking the blow with his other arm. The ceramic base shattered, cutting into his flesh. "Brighton!"

"It's him!" I shouted, refusing to take my eyes off Tanner. "He poisoned me. He handed me over to Aric!"

"What?" Disbelief filled Kalen's voice.

"It's true." Tanner backed up, his gaze briefly darting to where Kalen stood inside the room. "She speaks the truth."

"What?" Kalen repeated, denial still evident in his tone.

"I was trying to protect the Court." Tanner kept backing up.

"I don't care what you were trying to do!" I screamed. "We trusted you!"

"Tanner." Horror had replaced the shock in Kalen's voice. "Our King will kill you."

"No, he won't," I said, hands balling into fists. "Because I'm going to kill him first." I took a step forward.

"That won't be necessary." Tanner's back hit the wall as his tear-stricken pale gaze met mine. "Neal has left the city. I know you have no reason to believe me, but I have nothing to gain by lying. Neal is gone." The thin linen wasn't giving much protection against the iron. Wisps of smoke drifted from the cloth and the fae's skin. "Aric didn't tell me you were the King's *mortuus*, but he would've told Neal. He may be gone, but he knows you're the King's greatest weakness. And he would've told others. They'll come for you, thinking they can use you to control the King. Do what I failed to do. Protect the King and the future of my Court. Never let your guard down."

It happened so fast.

Tanner jerked his hand back, then plunged it toward his chest. Kalen was at my side, pushing me behind him as he shouted. Tanner's entire body jolted, and his eyes flared wide with pain. It took me a second to realize that the hand that had slammed into his chest had been the one holding the cuff blade.

I stumbled back in shock, knocking into the bed. "What…?"

"I'm sorry." Tanner's voice came out as a whisper. His eyes closed, and then he just…sucked into himself, folding from the top of his salt and pepper hair to the polished loafers on his feet. He crumpled like paper. There was a crack, a sound like a muffled gunshot, then a flash of intense light.

Then…nothing.

All that was left where Tanner once stood was the iron blade, remaining where it had fallen.

Chapter 18

I sat on the bed while Kalen called…well, I don't know who he called. In situations like these, he normally would've called Tanner, and I doubted he'd call Faye when she was dealing with her cousin.

But he spoke to someone while I sat there, holding the iron cuff and staring at the spot where Tanner had been standing.

I was still angry, but I was also…I just couldn't believe that Tanner had sent himself back to the Otherworld. Whatever Caden or I would've done to him would've paled in comparison to what would happen to him in a realm ruled by the Winter Queen. We would've killed him. End of story. But a fae stabbed by iron didn't die. It basically sent them home, and being sent to the Otherworld was a fate worse than death.

Not that he didn't deserve it, but I…

I just couldn't believe any of this.

"Brighton."

Blinking, I realized that Kalen had been speaking to me. "I'm sorry?"

"It's all right. I said…" He dragged a hand through his hair, trailing off as he stared at the same spot as I did. "I can't believe this. I wouldn't have believed any of this if I hadn't seen it with my own eyes."

"I thought that maybe he'd told Tatiana and perhaps her brother. So that they'd know what was happening and she could pursue Caden, you know?" I explained hoarsely, running my fingers over the cuff. "I had no idea."

"I don't know what to even say." Kalen turned away from the spot. "I really don't."

"Neither do I."

It was only a few minutes later that Caden filled the doorway. I looked up, my heart seizing at the sight of him. The urge to race over to him hit me hard. I was starting to stand when I realized what I was doing and stopped myself. Was he still mad at me? Well, obviously, he had to be. One didn't get over all that he learned in a matter of hours. I wasn't sure if he would want me to go to him, to touch him.

And God, that was another sting on an already raw, rapidly spreading wound.

Caden had halted, but then he was striding forward, coming to where I sat. I half expected him to stop there or to put space between us.

That's not what he did.

He knelt, gently taking my face in his hands. The contact was a jolt to the system as his gaze searched mine. "Are you okay?"

I started to answer, but his touch threw me for a loop, and all my hesitation slipped away.

Dropping the cuff onto the bed, I all but launched myself at Caden. If he were unprepared, he didn't show it. He caught me in his arms and straightened, holding me tightly. He didn't push me away. I buried my face in his chest, inhaling deeply. That didn't mean that everything was peachy and perfect between us, but I needed him—needed to feel him, to smell him, to be held by him—and he was here.

That meant everything.

"Brighton?" he murmured, smoothing a hand through my hair and down my back as I felt his head turn. "Is she okay?"

"Physically, yes," came Kalen's answer.

"I'm fine." My voice was muffled and probably barely coherent, but I didn't lift my head. "I'm just…it was Tanner, Caden. It was *him*."

Tension strummed through every part of his body as he said to Kalen, "Tell me what you know."

Kalen did exactly that, but he didn't know everything. I did. Forcing myself to put it together, I lifted my head and reluctantly stepped back. I told Caden everything Tanner had told me, and he went from tense to downright rigid when I got to the part about Aric.

I was pacing by that point, one arm curled over my stomach. "He kept saying that he thought he was doing the right thing—"

"He wasn't," growled Caden.

"I know." I stopped, meeting his gaze. "I was going to kill him. I trusted him. My mom trusted him. *You* trusted him. But I was going to kill him." Tearing my gaze from Caden's hard one, I started walking again. "That's when he grabbed the blade with a napkin and told me that Neal had left the city, but that he had to know that I was your weakness, and that Neal would've told others. He then told me—" I cleared my throat. "He told me that I needed to do what he'd failed to do. Protect the Court by never letting my guard down. And then he…"

"He sent himself back to the Otherworld," Kalen picked up where I left off. "What will be done to him there will… It will make whatever we could do to him here look like nothing."

A muscle worked along Caden's jaw. "That knowledge doesn't ease me. I want to watch the life seep out of his eyes."

Kalen didn't object to that.

Neither did I.

"Can you please sit?" Caden asked, and I stopped. "You should be resting, and nothing about any of this is restful." He turned to Kalen. "Can you get Luce? I want Brighton checked."

"Of course." Kalen bowed and then turned to leave.

I sat because he was right. I felt okay, but none of this was exactly stress-free.

"Are you sure you're okay?" Caden asked.

"I feel all right. He didn't try to hurt me." I pressed my lips together. "At least not this time. Are you okay?"

Caden stared at me. "You don't need to worry if I'm okay."

"But I do," I told him. "He said you were with Faye, handling Benji, and I know you trusted Tanner. Everybody trusted him."

"I'm worried about you and the baby right now—"

"And I'm worried about you," I cut in. "Those things aren't mutually exclusive."

His head tilted and, for a moment, I wondered if he was going to say anything. "I trusted Tanner as much as I trusted anyone. I never would have expected him to be behind this."

"I still can't believe it." I picked up the cuff, turning it over in my hands. "I should be relieved that at least we know who was responsible, but I can't feel that. I don't understand how he thought this was the right thing."

"Fear."

I looked up at Caden.

"Fear is what made him think it was right." He approached slowly, sitting beside me. "Some of the fae here have limited their contact with the outside world so much that the Winter fae and their Queen have become like…what do you call it? The thing that scares children?"

"Bogeymen?"

"Yes. That." He turned his head to me. "It's not that I don't think they're not a threat. They are, but fear and panic are far more dangerous than any creature out there. It's the only reason I can think of that would've caused him to take this path. His fear of the Court weakening was far greater than his fear of what I would do to him." His gaze dropped to the cuff. "Maybe some would say that I should make myself into something greater to fear, but my father didn't rule that way. Neither will I."

"I'm glad to hear that." I stopped turning the cuff. "Making people fear you only works for so long. We humans have a long, sordid history of doing that and failing, and…" I peeked up at him. "And that's not you. I mean, you're badass and can be very scary at times, but you're also kind. I never would have…"

"What?"

I lifted my gaze to his. "I wouldn't have fallen in love with you if you were the type to believe that fear is a tool to be used to rule people." I turned my attention back to the cuff, quickly changing the subject. "I can't imagine how people are going to react."

"This is going to hit everyone hard. Tanner was well-respected. He was cared for. Loved. Trusted," he said, exhaling roughly. "I could lie. I could swear Kalen to silence. But lies…they never work out as one intends, even when they're told with the best of intentions."

"No." My shoulders sank. "They don't. He…he said that he thought he was doing the right thing, just like we thought we were doing the right thing."

"He's wrong. What he did is nothing like our situation, Brighton. Not at all."

"I know. It's not the same, but I get the sentiment. You thought it was best to give me time before you told me everything. I thought it was best to push you away and keep the pregnancy a secret so everyone was safe. Neither of us was right. It's still not the same. I know that." I leaned over, placing the cuff on the end table. "But I…I keep seeing his face. He knew what he'd done was wrong. I think he even knew when he told Aric I was important to you, but he kept doing it anyway. And I know a lot has happened. God. Things won't stop happening, but I…" I looked up at him as something occurred to me—something important and powerful. "I don't want to keep messing up and making the wrong choices. I love you, Caden. I want this baby. I want us to be together. I don't know if I'll make a good Queen. Honestly, I'll probably suck at it, but I don't care. I want to be *your* Queen. I know you're mad at me—"

"I'm not mad at you, Brighton."

"Really? You sure you don't want to rethink that answer?"

His eyes met mine once more. "I don't need to think about it. I'm not mad. Even when I'm furious with something you've done, I'm never angry at you."

That sounded like it would be good, if a bit confusing, but I had a feeling that whatever he was going to say next might be worse.

"I'm disappointed," he said, and my shoulders drooped. I was right. That was worse. "I—"

Whatever he was about to say was cut off by Luce's arrival. My blood pressure was a little high, which wasn't exactly surprising. And then others arrived, one after another. Faye. Tink. Fabian. Ren and Ivy. Some fae I recognized but didn't know their names. Others I wasn't sure I'd seen before.

There was a lot of disbelief. Not a single person or fae who came through the door could believe or understand why Tanner had done what he did. There were long moments of shocked silence, there were tears, and then Caden reassured everyone that life at Hotel Good Fae would continue, and that things would be rough, but that it would be okay. And as I sat there, listening to how calm he was, how sure he sounded, I didn't doubt for one second that things would eventually be okay once enough time had passed to move past the shock of Tanner's betrayal and the grief of his loss that was still to come, no matter what he'd done.

I didn't think I realized until then that Caden had truly been born to be a leader. I think he even eased Ren's and Ivy's concern, which was truly saying something. They left to share the news with Miles.

The whole time, Caden remained at my side. I kept expecting him to leave. I imagined that he needed to make a statement to all the fae at one time, but he didn't go.

There wasn't much for me to do as I sat there, other than to replay what'd happened with Tanner over and over and also wonder what it would take for Caden to no longer be disappointed.

If that was even possible.

I had to believe that it was. Like Hotel Good Fae, it would take time. There would be grief. There would be anger, but we had to get past this.

We had to.

Eventually, only Fabian and Tink remained in the room with us.

Tink was standing in the corner, leaning against the wall. He'd been quiet through most of this, and I worried about him. He really liked Tanner, and I knew this had to be hitting him hard.

"There is something I can do," Fabian said after he and Caden discussed what needed to be done and whether what Tanner had said about Neal could be believed. Like me, I didn't think there was a reason to doubt what Tanner had claimed. Neal wasn't a problem. For now, at least. "I know you'll need to speak with the Court, but Tink and I can hold things down here while you make sure Brighton and my future niece or nephew actually get some stress-free rest."

I opened my mouth.

"We got this." Tink pushed off the wall, joining Fabian. "Consider these early godfather duties."

I closed my mouth as Caden frowned at the whole godfather thing. I fully expected him to thank them for the offer but pass. He was King, after all.

"Thank you. I appreciate it," Caden said.

Slowly, I turned toward him. "But aren't you needed? Don't you have to talk to them?"

"I'm needed here more," he said.

Too afraid to hope that was a positive sign, all I could do was nod. Tink came to my side, then bent and kissed my cheek. "Please get some rest."

"I will," I promised, catching his arm as he pulled away. "Are you okay?"

He gave me a small, sad smile. "I will be."

"It's a lot."

"It is." He slipped free, and then he left with Fabian.

The door closed behind them, and then I was alone with Caden, sitting close but not touching. I was exhausted, but I knew I wouldn't be sleeping anytime soon. There was too much going on in my head and—

"Tanner was wrong," Caden stated, pulling me out of my thoughts.

"I think there are a lot of things he was wrong about."

"Yes, but there was something he was very wrong about." He looked over at me then. "You're not my weakness."

My lips parted on a sharp inhale.

His gaze searched mine. "I could sense that you expected me to leave."

"I…I did. I imagined that they'd want to see you. You're really good at calming others."

"They will want to see me, and they will. But like I said, I'm needed here. I know you're tired. I can sense that too, but there's something I need to finish telling you."

Heart rate picking up, I nodded.

"I *was* disappointed, Brighton. I tried to clarify that, but we got interrupted. We keep getting interrupted," he said. "It seems like that's a trend for us."

"Yes," I whispered. "It is."

He lowered his chin, leaning in so that our faces were only a few inches apart. "I was disappointed and overwhelmed. Of all the ways I'd thought to find out I was going to be a father, this wasn't one of them. It was a lot to process, but what you said earlier? About not wanting to keep making the wrong choices? I agree. What Tanner did is nothing like us, but we both thought we were doing the right thing. I should've told you. You should've told me. We both messed up."

I felt like I couldn't breathe again, but this time for an entirely different reason. "We did."

"I think we're going to mess up again, sunshine," he said, and my breath caught at the use of my nickname. "It's bound to happen, especially since we're going to be raising a child. I imagine we're going to mess up a lot with that, too, but you know what that doesn't change, right?"

I nodded. "That…that we love each other?"

"Right." He took my face in his hands. "You hold a part of my soul, Brighton. You are my everything. Nothing will change that. Ever."

A strangled sound left me as I grasped the front of his shirt. "I love you."

We moved at the same time, and the moment our lips touched, it was like taking the first deep breath of summer air. The kiss was sweet and somehow more powerful than any we'd shared before. Maybe because it was the first kiss we'd shared with nothing hidden between us. Perhaps because it felt like a beginning.

Ending the kiss, he rested his forehead against mine as he slid a hand down my arm, to the curve of my hip and then to my lower stomach. "We are going to have a baby."

I smiled widely, blinking back tears—happy ones as I placed my hand over his. "We are."

"I haven't even thought about having a child, sunshine. But from the moment I learned that you were pregnant, even with everything going on, I knew in that moment that I wanted to be a father."

"I know the feeling." I squeezed his hand. "It was a shock, but I knew immediately that I wanted this child."

"You'll be a great mother."

"You think so?"

He pulled back so he could see my face. "I know so. Why would you doubt that?"

"I…I haven't had any more hallucinations or…breaks in reality. But that doesn't mean I won't. And I know you think it will be different for me, but I can't help but worry. I want to give this child what I didn't have. I want to be a mother who is always there, and what if…what if I'm not?"

He touched my cheek again. "We have no idea what tomorrow holds, but I can promise you that you're not alone. If you have more moments or not, I'm here. You have me. Our child will have both of us, no matter what, and we've got enough love already for this child that it will be enough. We will give him or her everything they could ever need." He kissed my forehead. "Besides, I have a feeling this kid is going to be strong. They'll be able to handle anything."

I shuddered. "Luce thinks that the child is already strong-willed and determined to live."

Caden folded his arms around me, gathering me close. "I don't doubt that for one second, not when it's you who's carrying this child. I don't know anyone, human or fae, more strong-willed and determined to live than you."

I lifted my head, kissing him again, and for the first time in my life, I felt no fear, no anger, and no worry.

Both of us had gone through our own hell to get here. We deserved it. Our child deserved it. All I felt was love.

I was whole.

Epilogue

Caden

Lounging on the plush grass of the enclosed courtyard outside of Hotel Good Fae, I watched my baby girl toddle after Tink. The brownie was, well, brownie-sized at the moment, his translucent wings nearly invisible in the bright, warm sunlight as he zipped up and then dipped down, staying just out of reach of Scorcha's chubby little fingers. She laughed and shrieked, attempting to jump in hopes of catching Tink, who taunted her by sticking out his tongue and tugging on a half-undone pigtail. With her blond hair and her mother's eyes, she was a bouncing beam of sunlight.

Scorcha.

My damn heart felt like a fist had taken hold of it and squeezed. Naming our daughter after my sister had been all Brighton's idea, one that had surprised me, but I'd wholeheartedly supported it the moment I got over the shock. The thoughtfulness behind the gesture still choked me up and didn't stop amazing me.

I shifted my gaze to the woman behind my baby girl. Every time I saw her, it happened. Every damn time. There was a hitch in my throat, and a sense of wholeness that never failed to render me utterly dumbstruck.

Brighton's hair was loosely braided, and several golden strands had slipped free, resting against her cheek and the slope of her neck as she caught Scorcha as she stumbled back in her hundredth attempt to catch Tink. Laughing at whatever Tink said to her, Brighton made sure that Scorcha was as stable as possible on her feet and then let go.

Brighton had been worried about what kind of mother she'd be, and I'd been right when I'd told her that I had no doubt she'd be absolutely wonderful. She knew exactly when to catch our daughter and when to let her go.

My gaze swept over her hungrily. Since the temps were expected to rise, she'd donned a gauzy, deep blue dress this morning. One with those silly, little straps I wanted to follow with my fingers, my tongue, and then my teeth. They drove me crazy, especially when they slipped off her shoulders—like now. A bolt of pure, complete, and absolute lust pounded through me. The corner of my lips tipped up as I watched the breeze lift and ruffle the panels of the dress, playing peekaboo with her legs. It reminded me of this morning when I woke, starving for her, and saw the curve of one exposed thigh. Her flesh had looked oh so lonely, peeking out from between the sheets, and I'd been more than happy to reintroduce the lovely expanse of skin to my hand and then my lips. I'd reached the junction of her thighs by the time she woke.

She was the best breakfast I'd ever eaten.

Hell. I could practically taste her on the tip of my tongue right now.

I shifted on the ground, giving myself a little extra room as I counted down the hours to Scorcha's afternoon nap. I was very, *very* hungry again.

Seeming to sense my damn near obsessive perusal, Brighton looked over at me. Our gazes connected as I ran the tip of my tongue over my upper lip. Pink flushed her cheeks as she shook her head at me, but I scented the sharp rise of arousal. It reminded me of roses drenched in vanilla, and it was addicting.

At least once a day I found myself wondering how in any world I had gotten so damn lucky. And there were still times when I couldn't shake the feeling that I wasn't worthy of her, our daughter, and the life we were building together, the future that was waiting for us. My time under the spell of the Winter Queen still followed me into my sleep and invaded the most hidden corners of my mind, but Brighton always found me in those moments. Whether at night, where she chased the nightmares away with sweet kisses, or when I fell into sullen silences and she was there to pull me from the grasp of the darkness. Just like I was there when the nightmare of Aric found her. I always reminded her that she was safe. I'd been right about the breaks in reality. She never had another one, but even if she had, we'd be okay.

We'd be more than okay.

Scorcha let out a squeal of triumph when she caught Tink's leg. I winced in sympathy. My baby girl had one hell of a grip. Just the other day, she'd grabbed my nose for whatever reason, and I'd thought she was going to yank it right off my face. And considering that with each passing day, her fae strength grew, it seemed plausible.

Tink only laughed and shouted, "You win! You win!"

Letting go of his leg, she clapped happily. "Again! Again!"

Swooping down, Tink kissed the crown of blond hair and then darted out of her reach. "You won't catch me again."

"Nuh-uh!" Scorcha did her funny little jerky knee run after Tink that was stopped by a loud, lioness yawn.

"I think she's going to end up sleeping through the afternoon once it's her naptime." Brighton tucked a strand of hair back from her face. "I may end up right with her."

Not if I had anything to do with that. I planned to make good use of our alone time.

The brownie glanced over at me as his wings beat furiously. "You're welcome."

I chuckled. "I owe you one."

Tink zipped up, narrowly avoiding Scorcha's grasp as Brighton's gaze met mine again. I read the unspoken message and nodded in agreement. We really would owe Tink for today. Since he and my brother had taken over the management of Hotel Good Fae, both were busy, and I didn't think anyone was more surprised than Tink by his dedication to continuing the success of the safe harbor for the fae.

"This is great practice, though," said Tink. "Since I plan on being the Mary Poppins of brownies."

"That reminds me. Have Ren and Ivy decided on a name yet?" Brighton asked.

"No," he answered. "They're still arguing between two names, and neither will listen to any of my suggestions."

"Did you suggest they name their son after you?" she asked.

"I did, but you want to know a secret?" Tink hovered far above Scorcha's head. "I gave them a whole list of names, and one of them was my actual name. They have no idea."

Brighton's mouth dropped open.

Shaking my head, I wondered if I should ruin Tink's day by telling Brighton what his actual name was. But as Brighton attempted to guess what it was, and her eyes narrowed in fond annoyance, I decided that piece of information could be shared at another time.

Glancing over my shoulder at the hotel, it was almost hard to believe just how well Hotel Good Fae was running these days. Things had been a mess after Tanner's betrayal, with half of the Court considering leaving. If it hadn't been for Tink and Fabian, I'd have grave concerns about the future of the sanctuary.

Recently, Ren had suggested that we may be experiencing a welcomed lull in the war against the Winter fae, but the truth was, the war for mankind hadn't really started.

The hotel was invaluable to the survival of the Summer Court. Not just because there were so many expecting females now, who were about to usher in the next generation, or the fact that nearly every room was filled. But because the threat of the Winter fae was still very much a concern, one that would not fade anytime soon.

There were still more Winter fae than Summer. If anything, their attacks had become more violent, commonplace, and senseless. With Aric's death and the disappearance of Neal, they lacked any true leadership, which was far more dangerous. Numerous Winter fae were doing their best to prove that they were more than capable of stepping up, and that led to even more deaths. Then there was the Devil's Breath, capable of turning any fae into a monster that needed to be dealt with. Just last week, a youngling had turned and had to be put down. Neal's disappearance only slowed the supply of the toxic drink. He was still out there, as was the Devil's Breath, but finally, the Order was working alongside the fae to discover the source of the supply. There were still Ancients, who I was sure, at this very moment, were plotting how to free Queen Morgana.

And then there was Queen Morgana herself.

While trapped in the Otherworld, she wasn't exactly the most pressing concern, but she was still alive, and I knew she was still attempting to find a way to open the gateway between the Otherworld and this one. Eventually, she would find a way, and that was when the real war would begin, one that would rapidly spread throughout the human world, involving them whether they liked it or not.

But that war wouldn't start today.

Focusing on the here and now, I exhaled slowly, heavily. Content despite what we may one day face, I refused to borrow from tomorrow's problems. No one could live like that.

Not even a King.

So, I watched what was most important to me. Right here, a handful of feet away, was my entire world.

Well, minus the brownie.

Although, his babysitting skills were incomparable.

But Scorcha would one day grow older, no longer just our little princess but the Princess of the Summer Court, and she would become as fierce and brave as her mother. She would be a fighter. The hand that now clutched her mother's would one day be just as confident holding an iron dagger, clutched in a gloved fist. That, I would make sure of.

And Brighton was…she was and always would be my *mortuus*—the most beautiful, courageous, strong, clever and kind woman I'd ever known. How much she meant to me could never have been seen as a weakness, and it never would be again. I wouldn't allow it. If anyone ever tried to use her or our daughter to control or manipulate me, it would be the very last thing they ever did. And it wasn't just me who would ensure that. I pitied the imbecile who thought Brighton an easy target. She'd always had claws, but with the birth of Scorcha, those claws had sharpened into deadly points. A smile tugged at my lips as Scorcha almost caught Tink once more. Brighton could take care of herself and then some, but if she needed backup, she had me.

She always had me.

Hours later, once Scorcha had fallen asleep and we were finally alone, I stripped Brighton bare and showed her just how beautiful I thought those faded scars were. I worshiped them with my lips and then my tongue, and always with my soul. I kissed her on the mouth and then lower, driving her to the peak of release over and over until my name was a prayer on her lips. Then, and only then, did I roll her onto her side and slide into her hot, tight depths.

"Fuck," I groaned, dropping my cheek to hers. I held myself still as long as I could, until the urge to move became almost painful. "I need you."

She knew exactly what that meant. "You have me."

I did.

Shuddering, I gripped her by the hip and lifted her onto her knees. For a moment, I was a little lost in the graceful slope of her back and the rounded, plump ass. She was beautiful. Always. I curled my arms around her shoulders, holding her in place as I took what she gave me.

Love.

Acceptance.

Understanding.

Strength.

There was no more slow buildup. No more time to play. I moved against her hard, slamming into her, driven by her soft moans filling the room and how she didn't just take each thrust but met them, riding me just as fiercely as I took her. She felt too damn good. My blood pounded, and I lost all semblance of control the moment I felt her clench and spasm around my dick. It was like losing my mind as I thrust into her, over and over until release found me. It was like lightning streaking down my spine, obliterating my senses. Hell if I knew how we'd ended up on our sides, her in front of me, my front to her back.

"I love you," she said, letting her head fall against my chest.

I smiled against her flushed skin and then kissed her shoulder. "You are my sun. My strength. My redemption. My heart. My everything. My Queen. I will always love you."

* * * *

Also from 1001 Dark Nights and Jennifer L. Armentrout, discover From Blood and Ash and Dream of You.

Sign up for the 1001 Dark Nights Newsletter
and be entered to win a Tiffany Key necklace.

There's a contest every month!

Go to www.1001DarkNights.com to subscribe.

As a bonus, all subscribers can download
FIVE FREE exclusive books!

Discover 1001 Dark Nights Collection Seven

For more information, visit www.1001DarkNights.com.

THE BISHOP by Skye Warren
A Tanglewood Novella

TAKEN WITH YOU by Carrie Ann Ryan
A Fractured Connections Novella

DRAGON LOST by Donna Grant
A Dark Kings Novella

SEXY LOVE by Carly Phillips
A Sexy Series Novella

PROVOKE by Rachel Van Dyken
A Seaside Pictures Novella

RAFE by Sawyer Bennett
An Arizona Vengeance Novella

THE NAUGHTY PRINCESS by Claire Contreras
A Sexy Royals Novella

THE GRAVEYARD SHIFT by Darynda Jones
A Charley Davidson Novella

CHARMED by Lexi Blake
A Masters and Mercenaries Novella

SACRIFICE OF DARKNESS by Alexandra Ivy
A Guardians of Eternity Novella

THE QUEEN by Jen Armentrout
A Wicked Novella

BEGIN AGAIN by Jennifer Probst
A Stay Novella

VIXEN by Rebecca Zanetti
A Dark Protectors/Rebels Novella

SLASH by Laurelin Paige
A Slay Series Novella

THE DEAD HEAT OF SUMMER by Heather Graham
A Krewe of Hunters Novella

WILD FIRE by Kristen Ashley
A Chaos Novella

MORE THAN PROTECT YOU by Shayla Black
A More Than Words Novella

LOVE SONG by Kylie Scott
A Stage Dive Novella

CHERISH ME by J. Kenner
A Stark Ever After Novella

SHINE WITH ME by Kristen Proby
A With Me in Seattle Novella

And new from Blue Box Press:

TEASE ME by J. Kenner
A Stark International Novel

FROM BLOOD AND ASH by Jennifer L. Armentrout
A Blood and Ash Novel

QUEEN MOVE by Kennedy Ryan

THE HOUSE OF LONG AGO by Steve Berry and MJ Rose
A Cassiopeia Vitt Adventure

THE BUTTERFLY ROOM by Lucinda Riley

Discover More Jennifer L. Armentrout

From Blood and Ash

Captivating and action-packed, From Blood and Ash is a sexy, addictive, and unexpected fantasy perfect for fans of Sarah J. Maas and Laura Thalassa.

A Maiden…

Chosen from birth to usher in a new era, Poppy's life has never been her own. The life of the Maiden is solitary. Never to be touched. Never to be looked upon. Never to be spoken to. Never to experience pleasure. Waiting for the day of her Ascension, she would rather be with the guards, fighting back the evil that took her family, than preparing to be found worthy by the gods. But the choice has never been hers.

A Duty…

The entire kingdom's future rests on Poppy's shoulders, something she's not even quite sure she wants for herself. Because a Maiden has a heart. And a soul. And longing. And when Hawke, a golden-eyed guard honor bound to ensure her Ascension, enters her life, destiny and duty become tangled with desire and need. He incites her anger, makes her question everything she believes in, and tempts her with the forbidden.

A Kingdom…

Forsaken by the gods and feared by mortals, a fallen kingdom is rising once more, determined to take back what they believe is theirs through violence and vengeance. And as the shadow of those cursed draws closer, the line between what is forbidden and what is right becomes blurred. Poppy is not only on the verge of losing her heart and being found unworthy by the gods, but also her life when every blood-soaked thread that holds her world together begins to unravel.

* * * *

Dream of You: A Wait For You Novella

Abby Erickson isn't looking for a one-night stand, a relationship, or anything that involves any one-on-one time, but when she witnesses a shocking crime, she's thrust into the hands of the sexiest man she's ever seen - Colton Anders. His job is to protect her, but with every look, every touch, and every simmering kiss, she's in danger of not only losing her life but her heart also.

From Blood and Ash

A Blood and Ash Novel
By Jennifer L. Armentrout

Captivating and action-packed, From Blood and Ash is a sexy, addictive, and unexpected fantasy perfect for fans of Sarah J. Maas and Laura Thalassa.

A Maiden…

Chosen from birth to usher in a new era, Poppy's life has never been her own. The life of the Maiden is solitary. Never to be touched. Never to be looked upon. Never to be spoken to. Never to experience pleasure. Waiting for the day of her Ascension, she would rather be with the guards, fighting back the evil that took her family, than preparing to be found worthy by the gods. But the choice has never been hers.

A Duty…

The entire kingdom's future rests on Poppy's shoulders, something she's not even quite sure she wants for herself. Because a Maiden has a heart. And a soul. And longing. And when Hawke, a golden-eyed guard honor bound to ensure her Ascension, enters her life, destiny and duty become tangled with desire and need. He incites her anger, makes her question everything she believes in, and tempts her with the forbidden.

A Kingdom…

Forsaken by the gods and feared by mortals, a fallen kingdom is rising once more, determined to take back what they believe is theirs through violence and vengeance. And as the shadow of those cursed draws closer, the line between what is forbidden and what is right becomes blurred. Poppy is not only on the verge of losing her heart and being found unworthy by the gods, but also her life when every blood-soaked thread that holds her world together begins to unravel.

* * * *

"They found Finley this eve, just outside the Blood Forest, dead."

I looked up from my cards and across the crimson-painted surface to the three men sitting at the table. I'd chosen this spot for a reason. I'd…felt nothing from them as I drifted between the crowded tables earlier.

No pain, physical or emotional.

Normally, I didn't prod to see if someone was in pain. Doing so without reason felt incredibly invasive, but in crowds, it was difficult to control just how much I allowed myself to feel. There was always someone whose pain cut so deeply, was so raw, that their anguish became a palpable entity I didn't even have to open my senses to feel—that I couldn't ignore and walk away from. They projected their agony onto the world around them.

I was forbidden to do anything but ignore. To never speak of the gift bestowed upon me by the gods and to never, ever go beyond sensing to actually doing something about it.

Not that I always did what I was supposed to do.

Obviously.

But these men were fine when I reached out with my senses to avoid those in great pain, which was surprising, given what they did for a living. They were guards from the Rise—the mountainous wall constructed from the limestone and iron mined from the Elysium Peaks. Ever since the War of Two Kings ended four centuries ago, the Rise had enclosed all of Masadonia, and every city in the Kingdom of Solis was protected by a Rise. Smaller versions surrounded villages and training posts, the farming communities, and other sparsely populated towns.

What the guards saw on a regular basis, what they had to do, often left them in anguish, rather it be from injuries or from what went deeper than torn skin and bruised bones.

Tonight, they weren't just absent of anguish, but also their armor and uniforms. Instead, they donned loose shirts and buckskin breeches. Still, I knew, even off duty, they were watchful for signs of the dreaded mist and the horror that came with it, and for those who worked against the future of the kingdom. They were still armed to the teeth.

As was I.

Hidden beneath the folds of the cloak and the thin gown I wore underneath, the cool hilt of a dagger that never quite warmed to my skin was sheathed against my thigh. Gifted to me on my sixteenth birthday, it wasn't the only weapon I'd acquired or the deadliest, but it was my favorite. The handle was fashioned from the bones of a long-extinct wolven—a creature that had been neither man nor beast but both—and the blade made of bloodstone honed to fatal sharpness.

I may yet again be in the process of doing something incredibly reckless, inappropriate, and wholly forbidden, but I wasn't foolish enough to enter a place like the Red Pearl without protection, the skill to employ it, and the wherewithal to take that weapon and skill and use them without hesitation.

"Dead?" the other guard said, a younger one with brown hair and a soft face. I thought his name might be Airrick, and he couldn't be much older than my eighteen years. "He wasn't just dead. Finley was drained of blood, his flesh chewed up like wild dogs had a go at him, and then torn to pieces."

My cards blurred as tiny balls of ice formed in the pit of my stomach. Wild dogs didn't do that. Not to mention, there weren't any wild dogs near the Blood Forest, the only place in the world where the trees bled, staining the bark and the leaves a deep crimson. There were rumors of other animals, overly large rodents and scavengers that preyed upon the corpses of those who lingered too long in the forest.

"And you know what that means," Airrick went on. "They must be near. An attack will—"

"Not sure this is the right conversation to be having," an older guard cut in. I knew of him. Phillips Rathi. He'd been on the Rise for years, which was nearly unheard of. Guards didn't have long lifespans. He nodded in my direction. "You're in the presence of a lady."

A lady?

Only the Ascended were called Ladies, but I also wasn't someone anyone, especially those in this building, would expect to be inside the Red Pearl. If I was discovered, I would be in…well, more trouble than I'd ever been in before and would face severe reprimand.

The kind of punishment that Dorian Teerman, the Duke of Masadonia, would just love to deliver. And which, of course, his close confidante, Lord Brandole Mazeen, would love to be in attendance for.

Anxiety surfaced as I looked at the dark-skinned guard. There was no way Phillips could know who I was. The top half of my face was covered by the white domino mask I'd found discarded in the Queen's Gardens ages ago, and I wore a plain robin's egg blue cloak I'd, uh, *borrowed* from Britta, one of the many castle servants who I'd overheard speaking about the Red Pearl. Hopefully, Britta wouldn't discover her missing overcoat before I returned it in the morn.

Even without the mask, though, I could count on one hand how many people in Masadonia had seen my face, and none of them would be here tonight.

As the Maiden, the Chosen, a veil usually covered my face and hair at all times, all except for my lips and jaw.

I doubted Phillips could recognize me solely on those features, and if he had, none of them would still be sitting here. I would be in the process of being dragged back, albeit gently, to my guardians, the Duke and Duchess of Masadonia.

There was no reason to panic.

Forcing the muscles along my shoulders and neck to ease, I smiled. "I'm no Lady. You're more than welcome to talk about whatever you wish."

"Be that as it may, a little less morbid topic would be welcomed," Phillips replied, sending a pointed look in the direction of the other two guards.

Airrick lifted his gaze to mine. "My apologies."

"Apologies not needed but accepted."

The third guard ducked his chin, studiously staring at his cards as he repeated the same. His cheeks had pinkened, something I found rather adorable. The guards who worked the Rise went through vicious training, becoming skilled in all manner of weaponry and hand-to-hand combat. None who survived their first venture outside the Rise came back without shedding blood and seeing death.

And yet, this man blushed.

I cleared my throat, wanting to ask more about who Finley was, whether he was a guard from the Rise or a Huntsman, a division of the army that ferried communication between the cities and escorted travelers and goods. They spent half the year outside the protection of the Rise. It was by far one of the most dangerous of all occupations, so they never traveled alone. Some never returned.

Unfortunately, a few who did, didn't come back the same. They returned with rampantly spreading death snapping at their heels.

Cursed.

Sensing that Phillips would silence any further conversation, I didn't voice any of the questions dancing on the tip of my tongue. If others had been with him and had been wounded by what most likely had killed Finley, I would find out one way or another.

I just hoped it wasn't through screams of terror.

The people of Masadonia had no real idea exactly how many

returned from outside the Rise cursed. They only saw a handful here and there, and not the reality. If they did, panic and fear were sure to ignite a populace who truly had no concept of the horror outside the Rise.

Not like my brother Ian and I did.

Which was why when the topic at the table switched to more mundane things, I struggled to will the ice coating my insides to thaw. Countless lives were given and taken by the endeavor to keep those inside the Rise safe, but it was failing—had been failing—not just here, but throughout the Kingdom of Solis.

Death….

Death *always* found a way in.

Stop, I ordered myself as the general sense of unease threatened to swell. Tonight wasn't about all the things I was aware of that I probably shouldn't be. Tonight was about living, about…not being up all night, unable to sleep, alone and feeling like…like I had no control, no…no idea of who I was other than *what* I was.

Another poor hand was dealt, and I'd played enough cards with Ian to know there was no recovering from the ones I held. When I announced that I was out, the guards nodded as I rose, each bidding me a good evening.

Moving between the tables, I took the flute of champagne offered by a server with a gloved hand and tried to recapture the feelings of excitement that had buzzed through my veins as I'd hurried through the streets earlier that evening.

I minded my business as I scanned the room, keeping my senses to myself. Even outside of those who managed to project their anguish into the air around them, I didn't need to touch someone to know if they were hurting. I just needed to see someone and focus. What they looked like didn't change if they were experiencing some sort of pain, and their appearance didn't change when I concentrated on them. I simply *felt* their anguish.

Physical pain was almost always hot, but the kind that couldn't be seen?

It was almost always cold.

Bawdy shouts and whistles snapped me out of my own mind. A woman in red sat on the edge of the table next to the one I'd left. She wore a gown made of scraps of red satin and gauze that barely covered her thighs. One of the men grabbed a fistful of the diaphanous little skirt.

Smacking his hand away with a saucy grin, she lay back, her body forming a sensual curve. Her thick, blonde curls spilled across forgotten coins and chips. "Who wants to win me tonight?" Her voice was deep and smoky as she slid her hands along the waist of the frilly corset. "I can assure you boys, I will last longer than any pot of gold will."

"And what if it's a tie?" one of the men asked, the fine cut of his coat suggesting that he was a well-to-do merchant or businessman of some sort.

"Then it will be a far more entertaining night for me," she said, drawing one hand down her stomach, slipping even lower to between her—

Cheeks heating, I quickly looked away as I took a sip of the bubbly champagne. My gaze found its way to the dazzling glow of a rose-gold chandelier. The Red Pearl must be doing well, and the owners well connected. Electricity was expensive and heavily controlled by the Royal Court. It made me wonder who some of their clientele was for the luxury to be available.

Under the chandelier, another card game was in progress. There were women there too, their hair twisted in elaborate updos adorned with crystals, and their clothing far less daring than the women who worked here. Their gowns were vibrant shades of purple and yellow and pastel hues of blue and lilac.

I was only allowed to wear white, whether I was in my room or in public, which wasn't often. So, I was fascinated with how the different colors complemented the wearer's skin or hair. I imagined I looked like a ghost most days, roaming the halls of Castle Teerman in white.

These women also wore domino masks that covered half their faces, protecting their identities. I wondered who some of them were. Daring wives left alone one too many times? Young women who hadn't married or were perhaps widowed? Servants or women who worked in the city, out for the evening? Were Ladies and Lords in Wait among the masked females at the table and among the crowd? Did they come here for the same reasons I did?

Boredom? Curiosity?

Loneliness?

If so, then we were more alike than I realized, even though they were second daughters and sons, given to the Royal Court upon their thirteenth birthday during the annual Rite. And I…I was Penellaphe of Castle Teerman, Kin of the Balfours, and the Queen's favorite.

I was *the* Maiden.

About Jennifer L. Armentrout

1 New York Times and International Bestselling author Jennifer lives in Martinsburg, West Virginia. All the rumors you've heard about her state aren't true. When she's not hard at work writing. she spends her time reading, watching really bad zombie movies, pretending to write, and hanging out with her husband and her Jack Russell Loki.

Her dreams of becoming an author started in algebra class, where she spent most of her time writing short stories…which explains her dismal grades in math. Jennifer writes young adult paranormal, science fiction, fantasy, and contemporary romance. She is published with Tor Teen, Entangled Teen and Brazen, Disney/Hyperion and Harlequin Teen. Her book *Wicked* has been optioned by Passionflix and slated to begin filming in late 2018. Her young adult romantic suspense novel *DON'T LOOK BACK* was a 2014 nominated Best in Young Adult Fiction by YALSA and her novel *THE PROBLEM WITH FOREVER* is a 2017 RITA Award winning novel.

She also writes Adult and New Adult contemporary and paranormal romance under the name J. Lynn. She is published by Entangled Brazen and HarperCollins.

Discover 1001 Dark Nights

For more information, visit www.1001DarkNights.com.

COLLECTION ONE
FOREVER WICKED by Shayla Black
CRIMSON TWILIGHT by Heather Graham
CAPTURED IN SURRENDER by Liliana Hart
SILENT BITE: A SCANGUARDS WEDDING by Tina Folsom
DUNGEON GAMES by Lexi Blake
AZAGOTH by Larissa Ione
NEED YOU NOW by Lisa Renee Jones
SHOW ME, BABY by Cherise Sinclair
ROPED IN by Lorelei James
TEMPTED BY MIDNIGHT by Lara Adrian
THE FLAME by Christopher Rice
CARESS OF DARKNESS by Julie Kenner

COLLECTION TWO
WICKED WOLF by Carrie Ann Ryan
WHEN IRISH EYES ARE HAUNTING by Heather Graham
EASY WITH YOU by Kristen Proby
MASTER OF FREEDOM by Cherise Sinclair
CARESS OF PLEASURE by Julie Kenner
ADORED by Lexi Blake
HADES by Larissa Ione
RAVAGED by Elisabeth Naughton
DREAM OF YOU by Jennifer L. Armentrout
STRIPPED DOWN by Lorelei James
RAGE/KILLIAN by Alexandra Ivy/Laura Wright
DRAGON KING by Donna Grant
PURE WICKED by Shayla Black
HARD AS STEEL by Laura Kaye
STROKE OF MIDNIGHT by Lara Adrian
ALL HALLOWS EVE by Heather Graham
KISS THE FLAME by Christopher Rice
DARING HER LOVE by Melissa Foster
TEASED by Rebecca Zanetti
THE PROMISE OF SURRENDER by Liliana Hart

COLLECTION THREE
HIDDEN INK by Carrie Ann Ryan
BLOOD ON THE BAYOU by Heather Graham
SEARCHING FOR MINE by Jennifer Probst
DANCE OF DESIRE by Christopher Rice
ROUGH RHYTHM by Tessa Bailey
DEVOTED by Lexi Blake
Z by Larissa Ione
FALLING UNDER YOU by Laurelin Paige
EASY FOR KEEPS by Kristen Proby
UNCHAINED by Elisabeth Naughton
HARD TO SERVE by Laura Kaye
DRAGON FEVER by Donna Grant
KAYDEN/SIMON by Alexandra Ivy/Laura Wright
STRUNG UP by Lorelei James
MIDNIGHT UNTAMED by Lara Adrian
TRICKED by Rebecca Zanetti
DIRTY WICKED by Shayla Black
THE ONLY ONE by Lauren Blakely
SWEET SURRENDER by Liliana Hart

COLLECTION FOUR
ROCK CHICK REAWAKENING by Kristen Ashley
ADORING INK by Carrie Ann Ryan
SWEET RIVALRY by K. Bromberg
SHADE'S LADY by Joanna Wylde
RAZR by Larissa Ione
ARRANGED by Lexi Blake
TANGLED by Rebecca Zanetti
HOLD ME by J. Kenner
SOMEHOW, SOME WAY by Jennifer Probst
TOO CLOSE TO CALL by Tessa Bailey
HUNTED by Elisabeth Naughton
EYES ON YOU by Laura Kaye
BLADE by Alexandra Ivy/Laura Wright
DRAGON BURN by Donna Grant
TRIPPED OUT by Lorelei James
STUD FINDER by Lauren Blakely
MIDNIGHT UNLEASHED by Lara Adrian
HALLOW BE THE HAUNT by Heather Graham

DIRTY FILTHY FIX by Laurelin Paige
THE BED MATE by Kendall Ryan
NIGHT GAMES by CD Reiss
NO RESERVATIONS by Kristen Proby
DAWN OF SURRENDER by Liliana Hart

COLLECTION FIVE
BLAZE ERUPTING by Rebecca Zanetti
ROUGH RIDE by Kristen Ashley
HAWKYN by Larissa Ione
RIDE DIRTY by Laura Kaye
ROME'S CHANCE by Joanna Wylde
THE MARRIAGE ARRANGEMENT by Jennifer Probst
SURRENDER by Elisabeth Naughton
INKED NIGHTS by Carrie Ann Ryan
ENVY by Rachel Van Dyken
PROTECTED by Lexi Blake
THE PRINCE by Jennifer L. Armentrout
PLEASE ME by J. Kenner
WOUND TIGHT by Lorelei James
STRONG by Kylie Scott
DRAGON NIGHT by Donna Grant
TEMPTING BROOKE by Kristen Proby
HAUNTED BE THE HOLIDAYS by Heather Graham
CONTROL by K. Bromberg
HUNKY HEARTBREAKER by Kendall Ryan
THE DARKEST CAPTIVE by Gena Showalter

COLLECTION SIX
DRAGON CLAIMED by Donna Grant
ASHES TO INK by Carrie Ann Ryan
ENSNARED by Elisabeth Naughton
EVERMORE by Corinne Michaels
VENGEANCE by Rebecca Zanetti
ELI'S TRIUMPH by Joanna Wylde
CIPHER by Larissa Ione
RESCUING MACIE by Susan Stoker
ENCHANTED by Lexi Blake
TAKE THE BRIDE by Carly Phillips
INDULGE ME by J. Kenner

THE KING by Jennifer L. Armentrout
QUIET MAN by Kristen Ashley
ABANDON by Rachel Van Dyken
THE OPEN DOOR by Laurelin Paige
CLOSER by Kylie Scott
SOMETHING JUST LIKE THIS by Jennifer Probst
BLOOD NIGHT by Heather Graham
TWIST OF FATE by Jill Shalvis
MORE THAN PLEASURE YOU by Shayla Black
WONDER WITH ME by Kristen Proby
THE DARKEST ASSASSIN by Gena Showalter

Discover Blue Box Press

TAME ME by J. Kenner
TEMPT ME by J. Kenner
DAMIEN by J. Kenner
TEASE ME by J. Kenner
REAPER by Larissa Ione
THE SURRENDER GATE by Christopher Rice
SERVICING THE TARGET by Cherise Sinclair
THE LAKE OF LEARNING by Steve Berry and MJ Rose
THE MUSEUM OF MYSTERIES by Steve Berry and MJ Rose

On Behalf of 1001 Dark Nights,

Liz Berry, M.J. Rose, and Jillian Stein would like to thank ~

Steve Berry
Doug Scofield
Benjamin Stein
Kim Guidroz
Social Butterfly PR
Asha Hossain
Chris Graham
Chelle Olson
Kasi Alexander
Jessica Johns
Dylan Stockton
Richard Blake
and Simon Lipskar

Made in the USA
Middletown, DE
19 February 2021